Book One

Knyght

Magic is what you create

Nightvision
Twilight Shadows

A novel of the Mother's Realm

C. H. Knyght

Nightvision Twilight Shadows - C. H. Knyght

© 2017 C. H.

www.chknyght.com

All Rights Reserved. This book or any portion thereof

may not be reproduced or used in any manner whatsoever

without the express written permission of the publisher

except for the use of brief quotations in a book review.

This is a work of fiction. Names, characters, places, and incidents either are the products of the author's imagination or are used fictitiously. Any resemblance to actual persons, living or dead, businesses, companies, events, or locales is entirely coincidental.

First Edition, 2017

Printed in the United States of America

10 9 8 7 6 5 4 3 2 1

Createspace Publishing

ISBN-13: 978-1542328401

ISBN-10: 1542328403

Cover art and design by INKmagine and Create Studio

Edited by C. Halverson, Michelle Dunbar, and Cayleigh Stickler

Formatting by Lacey Sutton

For my Dad, who read my first books to me, and started me on the journey to find the magic of imagination and creativity.

Acknowledgements

So many thanks to my family and friends who nudged, encouraged—and downright pushed—me to keep at my writing. Nightvision has been a long time coming, but it is now a dream realized and a foundation placed for more adventures. Deepest gratitude to my editors Michelle Dunbar and Cayleigh Stickler, they took my rough jumble of words and made them flow.

Chapter One

Dante crept through the brush. The scars on his hip and thigh stretched taut as he stalked the wounded animal. He couldn't see it yet, but he smelled the blood, heard the pained wheezing.

Swollen clouds carried the weight of impending rain. He ignored the threatening summer storm and slinked closer to the creature. A bit of rain wasn't going to hurt him any. Mysti might, but rain wouldn't. Mysti's wrath wasn't to be scorned; it was expected and familiar, the cost of escaping his entourage.

He'd suffer it when he got home. Right now, he needed to focus on the hunt.

There it was: a white blob huddled in the ferns. Dante crept closer—one paw in front of the other, pressing silently on the cool moss.

Whiffs of old terror wafted around the creature like a lingering memory. Not because of him. This was not his doing; he'd only just sensed it. The Heart's Pulse had shown him the creature's magic as it showed him everything on his land. Such was his birthright.

He'd delayed his return home to put it out of its misery.

The animal was alone, vulnerable. Its innate magic guttered like a dying flame. It was weak, dying a slow, drawn-out death. Dante would make it a swift end. Its magic would return to the Mother to be remade.

Powerful muscles bunched and coiled beneath his fur, and Dante leapt. The creature fell back with a startled shriek as Dante caged it between his legs. He swooped in for the kill then hesitated, fangs poised over a feathered throat.

An owl.

A white owl.

Confusion stayed his attack. White owls did not nest in Ookamimori. They lived in the forests of Hanehishou with the Owlderah shifters, just as the majority of the wild wolves settled here. Like was drawn to like. So why was it here?

Saliva dripped from Dante's teeth and splattered onto dirty, blood-stained feathers. The owl shrieked. Its golden eyes widened in alarm, and talons raked futilely at the thick fur on Dante's belly. The will to live had ignited some fight in the owl.

Despite the weak flickering, the owl's magic was too strong to be a mere animal's, though not strong enough to be an elemental's. Elementals didn't bleed either. Not in the natural sense.

That left only one option. A sick dread settled in his stomach. He really wanted to be wrong.

Magic blurred the owl's body.

Oh, Mother bless it! A shifter. Dante sprang away. He'd attacked another shifter.

Dante stayed back and watched warily as magic coalesced into a new form.

Who would emerge from the transformation?

Mother bless, his council would give him hell for this. Him, a prince, attacking a shifter from another family was going to get him a duel at Communion if the shifter demanded one.

What was a wounded Owlderah doing this deep in Ookamimori's wild forest? They were well away from the trade roads. Relations between his family and the Owlderah were cordial, in that there was little to no contact with them. They were content to be quiet neighbors. The merchant guilds did business together happily enough. As far as he was aware anyway, but that didn't explain who was in front of him now. Or why. There was nothing out here; it was wild. Only his range wolves passed through on their patrol circuits.

The owl's human form settled as the brilliant glow of magic withdrew inward to quiescence. A petite woman scrambled into a guarded crouch, nursing her arm. Blood oozed from a gash tearing her flesh from shoulder to elbow. Dried blood stained her nightshirt. The wound looked painfully inflamed. How had she gotten all the way out here with a serious injury like that?

Dante kept a cautious distance. She was injured and on the small side, but that did not mean she didn't pose a threat. Mysti routinely kicked his ass, after all. And just because he couldn't see a knife, didn't mean she didn't carry one.

Thunder rumbled a warning of the looming storm.

Matted silver hair, matching her feathers, fell over her dirt-smudged face. She glared at him. "Go away, Wolf. I refuse to become your meal." She gasped in pain as she tried, and failed, to stand.

He should help her, but, he didn't know what was going on. He'd already attacked her once. If she knew who he was, it could start a feud between their families. He should've stayed home.

Retreating a few paces, Dante gave her some breathing space. He could leave and pretend this incident never happened; however, she was alone and injured. Ookamimori was a couple hours away at a steady lope, and the Owlderah lands lay several days in the opposite direction. Where was she trying to go?

Dante lurked in the shadows to see what the woman would do.

She grabbed an oak sapling to pull herself up. The unsteady movement dragged the loose nightshirt off her shoulder and exposed the hollow of her collarbone. The elaborate crest tattooed on her pale skin told Dante far more than he wanted to know. His stomach plummeted. Oh, bless it all. He was screwed.

This tiny woman was not just an Owlderah shifter, not just one of the hundreds of common people—she was a royal. The ink staining her skin marked her as the Crown Princess of Owlderah.

A princess. In his forest. Wounded and alone of all things. Where the hell were her chevaliers?

Dante melted deeper into the forest under her fierce stare. He lurked in the shadows to watch. After a minute, her clenched fists relaxed, and she slumped.

The princess certainly didn't look like she was on a diplomatic mission. She was dressed for bed: barefoot, wearing only a nightshirt. She carried no traveling supplies of any sort. She was too far from Hanehishou for a casual flight.

The Heart's Pulse thrummed with knowledge beneath his paws as Ookamimori told him that there was no one else in range—no entourage, no chevaliers. No decent bodyguard allowed their charge to roam alone, his own notwithstanding. He had a habit of escaping and left them little choice, a habit he regretted today. So many other things he could've done. Should've done.

For now, following her seemed wisest. She didn't know he was a shifter. He'd like to keep it that way.

Dante stayed low as she looked around. Apparently, she decided he was gone, and she set off toward the roaring river not too far away. Slinking through the brush, he tracked her. Occasionally, she seemed to hear him and stared at his position pointedly.

When she reached the river, the petite woman turned downstream toward the city.

The river rushed with a flooded fury that threatened the top of its banks. The silver-haired girl stopped and braced a hand on a slender birch as she swayed. Her breath came in wheezing gasps. Thunder boomed, shaking the air. The dark clouds finally dropped their horrific burden, and they were both drenched within seconds. Even his thick, double-layers of fur could not protect him against a downpour such as this. He was soaked. The princess's poorly-chosen clothes offered no protection, and the thin cloth plastered transparently against her skin. Dante flushed. Propriety made him look away.

A yelp pulled his attention back to her. She'd fallen to her hands and knees. Fresh blood seeped from her wound and trickled down her elbow to her wrist. She knelt perilously close to the riverbank's muddy edge.

The urge to help her was overwhelming. He paced in the cover of the brush. If he went to her now, he'd startle the girl, possibly causing her to fall into the river.

She laboriously got up, but numerous summer rains had weakened the mossy banks, and the rain-drenched earth gave way from beneath her feet. She screamed and tumbled into the frothing waters. Almost instantly, the foaming river dragged her ten feet, then twenty more, downstream. In mere seconds, she was lost to the river.

Dante raced down the riverbank. The princess surfaced and grabbed a tree fallen across the river. He cursed as the heavy rain weighed him down and blurred his vision. Mud sucked at his paws as he ran. She scrabbled at the tree. There was no way he would reach her in time. He ran past her, aiming further downstream.

The current dragged her underwater, beneath the tree and away. He lunged into the shallows, scrambling to find purchase on the mucky bottom and braced as the princess rushed toward him. Frigid mountain water numbed his paws and stole the breath from his lungs. The river pulled her into the center of the raging waters. He was going to miss.

Dante plunged deeper. His fangs snapped empty air. Another frantic lunge and he caught her thin nightshirt with his teeth. With a painful jerk of his jaws, the river dragged him with her. He dug his paws into the riverbed, slowing the inexorable pull. If he slipped, he wouldn't be able to touch the bottom, and they would both be lost. She looped an arm around his neck, and her fingers fisted his fur with adrenaline-born strength. She found some footing and added her meager strength to the effort of fighting the river.

It wasn't enough. The water's buoyancy lifted his paws from the riverbed.

The deep, churning waters pulled them into merciless depths. Dante flailed against the current, but his strength was no match against the river. If he took dyre form, he could reach the bottom and fight the torrent; however, he'd lose the princess. Her tenacious grip around his neck would fail if he shifted. Dante clenched his fangs tighter into her shirt with fierce resolve and prayed the fabric would hold.

They tumbled together in a mass of tangled limbs. Snorting water from his nose as he broke the surface, Dante tried to find the nearest riverbank. To survive, they needed to reach the shore before the river drowned them and beached their corpses. Even the sky was trying to drown them. The downpour of rain blurred the distance to shore. He couldn't see which direction to swim in.

His nostrils flooded as they bobbed downstream. Her hold on his fur yanked painfully with every abrupt change in direction. The river swallowed them, submerged them, and jerked them around until Dante's teeth ached. His lungs screamed for air. A certainty set into his soul; they were going to drown. The river cared nothing for royal bloodlines. It was a pure flowing force.

The princess lost her grip in his fur. Abruptly, the fabric of her shirt snapped tight. Her full weight fell into his teeth, and Dante felt the thin fabric shred against his gums. Threads stretched and snapped. The river swirled them around and around in dizzying circles. Her nightshirt tore. The woman was gone, lost in the current.

His lungs burned.

Which way was up? He couldn't tell anymore.

Dante shifted forms to lose the waterlogged weight of his fur. Bobbing to the surface, he choked as gritty water spilled into his mouth. He flailed. Went under. Fought back up.

A strange face parted the churning waters in front of him. Liquid, transparent features grinned at him, with glass-like needles for teeth. An undine, a water elemental. Lithe, inhuman fingers rose out of the raging water and waggled in greeting. Dante knew of them. Keer's endless fount of knowledge spouted in his ear made sure of that, but he'd never seen one. It was nice to meet one before he died; however, he could think of better things to do before he died if he had another minute to think about it.

The undine whirled him through the water in a parody of dancing.

Dante slammed into something hard. A boulder? A tree? He didn't know, but it hurt. Hard-won air exploded from his lungs, and water replaced it. He gagged for air, but there was none to be had. Water flowed out of his lungs and back in as his body forcefully tried to survive. He was not an aquatic shifter, he could not grow gills. Every automatic gasp only killed him faster. His lungs hitched in rhythm, fell still.

Shadows tunneled the edges of his vision as he sank. The river dragged him ever down. He didn't have the strength to fight anymore.

Dante let the water encompass him and he drifted. He could feel the magic draining out of him. Soon, his soul would rejoin the Mother's lifeforce until he was reborn.

A chill pressed against his back. Something wrapped around his chest and lifted him to the river's surface. Dante floated, held in place against the current by the undine. He stared up at the gray sky. He felt... untethered as though there was nothing anchoring him to his body.

Lightning flashed with violent forks. Was it still raining? Water poured over his face, but he couldn't tell if it was rain or river water. His lungs no longer moved in his chest. The lack of breath should hurt. It didn't. His sight turned monochrome, colors fading away like his lifeforce.

Fluid fingers hovered over his face and undulated hypnotically. Water rose unnaturally in his throat, as if he had swallowed a thread and the undine was pulling it out in one long strand. His body no longer had the care to gag or the strength to cough.

Liquid eyes peered into his face, blocking his view of the stormy sky.

A cold fist pounded his chest. Dante gasped and coughed. Breathed. Air burned gloriously into his lungs. The cold arms held him steady as he lay in the river. Darkness receded from his vision.

The river's torrent tugged at his arms and legs, but he didn't budge. The undine held him still. The water parted around them without dragging at him.

Dante raised his head and saw that he was floating in the middle of the river. Three figures bobbed toward him, against the flow of the current. One of them was the princess. Two more of the elementals towed her limp body upstream.

As the three drew near, his water elemental moved, ferrying him across the river. It cut through the water as though it were mist. The undine let go of him as they reached the calmer shallows.

Dante assumed his dyre form, the hybrid shape, a merge of human and wolf, gave him the height and strength to stand in the river. Silt squished between his clawed toes. The other undines brought the woman to him. Vaguely female-shaped, the elementals rose out of the water, up to their translucent hips, and presented the princess for him to carry. He cradled her to his chest.

The undines watched until they seemed sure he had her secure. Then, they melted, dissipating back into the water as if they'd never formed.

Bleary, golden eyes peered up at him with fatigued confusion. "Who?"

Dante winced. Now was so not the time. He avoided her question with one of his own. "Think you can hang onto my back while I climb?"

Even with his dyre form's height, the riverbank loomed over his head: high, mucky, and steep. He prayed to the Mother he had what it took to climb it. Elementals were fickle creatures and could not be counted upon to save them twice.

Her lips were blue as she nodded. Dante helped her climb on his back. She clung to him like a child riding piggyback, her heels hooked over his thighs.

Dreading his task, Dante whimpered. Mother bless, he should have stayed home today.

He climbed. Slimy cold mud squelched beneath his feet as he began his ascent. Dante sank his fingers into the riverbank for a handhold. Rain beat down on them, warm compared to the river. Teeth chattered in his ear as the woman shivered.

Halfway up, he started to slide. The mud refused to hold their combined weight. Making a fist, Dante punched into the muck. His arm sank in up to the elbow. Anchored, he clung to the earth. After a second's pause to slow his racing pulse and regain his balance, Dante climbed again.

It was slow going. They gained only inches with each precarious step. Almost at the top, he started to fall backward, pulled off-balance by the woman's weight. He scrambled for a new hold. Moss crumbled in his fingers, but they stopped falling. It took a moment for him to figure out why.

Dante looked around. Reaching over both their heads, the princess clung to a jutting tree root. Despite her size and injuries, she was strong. She held the limb steadily while he dug his claws into the bank for purchase and pulled them up.

His muscles burned with exertion as he climbed over the top of the bank. They crawled away from the edge. Dante collapsed in a tangled heap of limbs with the woman.

It was still raining. Thunder rumbled through the storm clouds, a slow growl that vibrated the very air.

The fight with the river had seemed to take an eternity; however, in reality, it had been just a few long minutes.

Slowly, his numbed mind registered that they had to find shelter. His teeth chattered as he tried to muster the strength to move. He reached out to the Heart with a mental touch, and the answering pulse showed him of a nearby cave system. Dante crawled out from under the woman's limp weight. He was going to have to carry her. There was no way the princess could walk any farther even if he roused her. Not that his condition was much better. Hyperthermia was nothing to scoff at, even in the dead of summer.

Rain plastered his hair to his face. Dante scooped up the woman. Staggering even with her slight weight. Dimly, he noticed that she wasn't shivering, even though her skin was cool to the touch. He knew this was bad, but he couldn't think why. Violent shivers rocked through him, and his steps wobbled as though he were a child learning to walk. The only clear thought was the need to reach the caves and get warm and, even better, dry.

Every branch was determined to trip him. After a senseless and dreary trudge, Dante looked up only when the rain stopped falling on his head. A stony roof covered them. The caves. Ookamimori had guided his feet to shelter. Dante sagged to the dry stone, ignoring the debris of branches and old leaves that crunched under his knees. He had neither the energy nor a flint to light a fire.

The princess lay limp and utterly pale in his lap. Her heartbeat thumped softly in his ears. The bleeding on her arm had stopped for now. It was an ugly wound, deep and ragged. Dante scanned her for other injuries. She was barefoot. The tender flesh of her feet bled from several punctures and slices. Yanking strips of fabric from his shirt, he wrapped her feet carefully. A small protection, but it was the best he could do under the circumstances.

He was tired. It was hard to focus. Warmth. They needed warmth. Fire was not an option. Lying down, Dante curled around her. Body heat, it was all he had to offer.

He woke up shivering. The cave floor was hard and unsympathetic against his bruises. He felt as though he'd been pummeled by rocks. Oh, wait, he had. One, anyway. Unless it had been a tree. He didn't know; he'd only felt the bruises form.

The dim gray light of dawn brightened the cave mouth. The storm had blown over in the night, and the forest was hushed and sleepy. Water dripped from the leaves with soft plops as the earliest of birds greeted the morning.

Dante groaned. He ached everywhere. Pulled muscles screamed over the bruises as he stretched.

Then his thoughts cleared, and he remembered why he hurt. The river. The princess.

She lay curled in a tight ball on the cave floor. She hadn't stirred at all. Concerned, Dante examined her. The princess wasn't as pale as snow anymore, quite the opposite actually. He frowned and pressed the back of his hand to a rosy cheek. Hot. Too hot. She burned with a tremendous fever. She needed a healer.

The princess didn't even stir at his touch. He'd have to carry her.

It was going to be a long walk.

The journey was harder than he'd imagined. Small as she may be, tiny even, she was a deadweight that grew heavier with every stride. To his chagrin, Dante found that he had to rest often. He was fit and in decent condition—he had to be to survive his training—but Ookamimori was not as close when using only two legs. Four covered the distance with an ease that his rarely-used dyre form could not. It was slow going weaving through the brush and dodging branches that were normally too high to bother him. The added inches of his dyre form threw off his normal grace.

He didn't dare summon his chevaliers. They'd panic. The whole city would take immediate notice of them racing to his rescue, and he had no way to explain the princess or how he'd met her with violence. Never mind what they might've been doing alone in a cave together. The nobles would have absolute fits over that. A foisted marriage was not on his agenda. No, better to keep her presence quiet until he knew what she was doing half-naked and alone in the middle of his forest. Sneaking her in was his best option—for him and her.

Once in the city of Ookamimori, Dante skulked down dark alleys and through the brushy edges of the parks to avoid as much of the population as conceivable. He stopped and leaned against the wall of a grimy alley.

The midday heat was suffocating, and he couldn't catch his breath. His arms had long since gone numb. He couldn't put the princess down if he wanted to; his muscles had seized like rusted iron.

Nothing for it. He had to keep going.

With a groan, Dante stumbled deeper into the narrow alley. He still had the city to cross.

The solid thud of landing feet roused him from a daze. He blinked blearily at the shadowed figure that had dropped out of the air in front of him. His pricked ears alerted him to the rustle of someone else behind him. Really? Right now? He couldn't even see straight. Even the thought of a confrontation sapped the last dregs of energy from his soul.

The figure in front of him spoke, "Well, don't you look like you've been having fun? Why didn't you invite us to play? We could have made it funner." A lithe, dark-haired man crossed his arms and settled against the alley's wall effectively blocking the way.

Dante sagged against the opposite wall with a huff of relief. "Derrick, why would I want you tagging along? You always get into trouble."

"Idiot." Dante lurched as another voice breathed right in his ear. "And what, pray tell, do you think you're in, if not trouble?" Derrick's younger twin, Raiven, peered at the princess from beneath his familiar hood. Without bothering to ask, he lifted her from Dante's arms.

Derrick caught Dante as he nearly fell over, suddenly off-balance and floaty feeling without the deadweight of the princess.

"Um, a situation in need of aid?" Dante joked, attempting to hide his utter exhaustion. It didn't work; the thieves knew him too well. After all, they had practically grown up together. Dante blurred back to human form, forsaking the dyre's too-heavy strength. Derrick kept a steady hand on Dante's shoulder.

"Trouble, indeed," Raiven said. "Your chevaliers have been scouring the city for you—again. That sharp-tongued one, Mysti, is about ready to commit murder. We've been trying to find you and give you the heads-up, but she was obviously right to worry this time."

Dante didn't normally disappear overnight, or if he did, it was right alongside these two. Then, at least they knew exactly what kind of trouble he was getting into.

"Right, thanks for that," Dante said. The brick wall made a nice pillow. Maybe he could just sleep here for a while?

"Who's the lady? Are you holding out on us?" Derrick asked. "And why do you look like you died and turned into a shade?"

Dante snickered. "Nice imagery, Derrick. I am not that bad off. I found her in the forest while I was hunting. She's an Owlderah royal."

"What!" Derrick yelped and dramatically flapped his hands in the air while Raiven inhaled sharply, the equivalent of a shriek from the normally stoic wolf. The thieves peered at the princess with renewed interest.

"I don't know what she was doing out there. She fell into the river—hasn't woken since we got out." His lungs seized in a fit of coughing. Curling around his stomach, Dante coughed until his throat ached, and phlegm filled his mouth.

Derrick pounded a fist on his back. "Hey, breathe already."

It helped. Coughing up one last glob, Dante straightened and wiped his face with a shaking hand. "I'm fine, but she's got a nasty wound and a fever. We have to get her to the palace so the healers can look at her."

He sagged into Derrick's support as they moved to leave the alleyway, too tired to tweak the ebon ponytail hanging down his friend's back. These men may be two of the best thieves in the city—in fact, they were both second-in-command of the thieves' guild—but they were his pack brothers too. He trusted the twins with his life and the welfare of Ookamimori, and with the secrecy of this stray princess. If his chevaliers ever found out about his connections with the thieves and the fact that he was a trained thief, Mysti would murder him, prince or not.

The petite princess looked tinier now that he wasn't carrying her. A frizzed braid spilled over Raiven's arm as her head slumped into the hollow of his shoulder. "She's kinda light, isn't she? I mean, she's skinny and needs to eat a few extra meals, but Leigha isn't any bigger and she weighs a lot more."

Derrick and Dante winced. "Don't let Leigha hear you say that," Dante said.

"Maybe it's because she's a bird. They are lightweight, right? Hollow bones and all that?" Derrick asked. "Hold up a second. We can't walk the open streets with her looking like a beaten streetwalker. A patrol will be summoned before we get two blocks."

Derrick pushed Dante off his shoulder, leaving him to sway into the wall. Pulling off his cloak, Derrick draped it around the princess. It covered the bloodstained nightshirt and the ugly wound. He tucked in the edges so the woven fabric wouldn't slip and expose her. "She's a total mess." He pulled a rag out of his pocket and glanced at Dante. "So are you, by the way. At least we can play you off as drunk if we're stopped," Derrick said, wiping grime and fever sweat from the princess's flushed cheeks. "This girl's been through something."

Looking down at himself, Dante could only agree. He was filthy, his shirt was shredded, and mud-caked strings of hair hung in his face like dreadlocks.

"That's better. At least she doesn't look like we've mugged her now." Pulling Dante's arm back over his shoulder, Derrick led the way onto the busy streets.

They garnered only a few concerned glances and a warm, matronly smile from a Grand'Mere, who cuddled two sleeping cubs in the crooks of her arms. "Heat a bit much for all of us today, eh?" she asked as they passed.

"Hmhm," Raven murmured noncommittally.

Dante mustered a polite nod of respect. The wrinkles around her eyes spoke of warm smiles. He bet she made the best sweet cakes. Lucky pups.

It was a good thing that mismatched eye colors, like his, weren't uncommon or he'd be caught. Imagine, the prince caught running around the streets of Ookamimori looking like he'd been in a fight and lost. Oh, the horrors. His noble council would keel over and die of mortification. Hmm, that was a thought. Maybe he should stage something and knock off a few of the worst annoyances via heart attack. Dante smiled blearily at his daydreams as Derrick dragged him down the street.

Unimpeded by a patrol, they reached the castle grounds quickly. Dante planted his feet before they reached the main gates. "We should go the back way. I'm not waltzing up to the front door like this. I'd have called my chevaliers if I wanted to make a spectacle. The fewer people who know, the better." Dante waved a hand at the forbidding hedge walls.

"Ah, no, tell me you don't want to go through there!" Derrick whined even as he turned around. They followed the hedge to a side entrance.

"I can't walk through the front gates with an injured princess carried by two thieves, now can I," Dante croaked. His throat hurt, and he was desperately thirsty. "It's not like I'm going to get lost. I know the way."

He tugged on the wrought iron gate. The hedge clung to it with leafy tendrils, reluctant to relinquish its guard. He hadn't used this entrance in a while.

In the massive garden maze, there were no locks on the gates. The labyrinth of shrubbery was legend. Everyone knew that to traverse beyond the first row of hedges was to be swallowed by the maze and get lost to the untamed garden. Only the royals knew its paths. Ookamimori guided their feet always.

"Yes, you do; however, I do not. How are we supposed to get back out, huh?" Despite his protests, Derrick added his strength to Dante's and they pulled the gate free of the branches.

Dante talked to ensure he stayed awake. "Please, you're better than that. The Thief Lord's best afraid of a little maze? Surely, you can find some way off the castle grounds without getting caught." Gathering his waning reserves of energy, he concentrated on putting one foot in front of the other. Something inside of Dante relaxed as he entered the maze. This was his safe place. He was home. The Heart pulsed beneath his feet in welcome.

Raiven snorted. "Little, he says." He boosted the princess higher onto his shoulder as he stepped through the deep hedge.

Derrick took up the derision. "Little? Ha! Your maze hogs over half of the castle grounds."

Dante focused on the familiar banter to distract from the pressure building in his head. He shrugged and wobbled with careless movement. "The maze is little," he insisted. "If it went all the way around the castle, then you could call it big." A violent sneeze exploded, nearly sending him to the ground with the force of it.

Derrick scruffed the back of his shirt. "Hey. No passing out. You're the only one who knows where we are inside this Mother blessed giant bush."

Dante nodded. His head felt like it was going to wobble off his shoulders. "I'm trying."

Ever-present shadows kept the grass cool and damp enough to squeak underfoot. He led them through the twisting, twining rows of bushes. It was not a neat maze. His mother had liked it that way, or so he'd been told.

"Keer should be in the library. If we get there, he can help me while you two take your sticky fingers away from my castle. I just had to sneak back a half a drawer worth of silverware stamped with the Canidea crest. My crest." He cast a narrow look over his shoulder and was met with unrepentant grins. "I found the silverware in the basement at the guild. Did you know that a prince gets some strange looks when he's caught fiddling with silverware? I think they thought I was trying to set the dining tables or something." Dante blathered on, trying to stay awake and semi-coherent. It was getting harder; he was so tired. "The poor serving girl practically fainted before trying to chase me away."

The maze didn't normally take this long to traverse, or so it seemed, at least it was cooler in the shade. A chill crawled up his spine. Maybe too cool. He couldn't decide if he was hot or cold.

Relief and the promise of an approaching pillow spurred him on when a gap in the hedge opened up—the exit. Almost home.

"I will take her from here," Dante said.

The lawn between him and the library steps looked vast and blisteringly hot. Heat waves lifted from the steaming grass, or was that his vision wavering? He wasn't sure.

Raiven transferred the princess into Dante's hold, lifting her dangling arm onto her chest so it didn't flop around, and he gave it a gentle pat. He fixed concerned amber eyes on Dante. "You look like a puddle of sewage. Take a bath and get some sleep."

Derrick sniggered.

Rolling his eyes, Dante stepped out of the cool, protective embrace of the hedges into abrasive heat. "Your overwhelming concern is touching. Really, I have never felt so loved. I'll be sure to keep that in mind next time we spar. Now, shoo, before a guard comes along."

"Let her keep the cloak," Derrick quipped over his shoulder as he followed his twin out of sight around a corner.

Dante trusted them to be fine and not cause trouble today of all days, even though they reveled in it.

He was reaching his limits, though. If the twins hadn't found him, he probably would've passed out on the streets. He waddled across the wide lawn, his legs bowing with exhaustion. The weathered statues guarding the marble steps seemed to mock him with stone-cold eyes as he stared at the last test of his strength.

"Keer, if you aren't here today of all days, I am rescinding your book privileges," Dante muttered. Laboriously, he climbed the sunbaked steps and nudged one of the massive doors, grateful for the ease it swung on its oiled hinges. He made a mental note to give the caretaker a bonus.

Compared to outside, the library was dim. All he could see were silhouettes of the bookshelves. Keer's usual table was beneath the window. Despite heaps of books, his retainer was not there.

"Keer!" he barked.

Mother, please, let him be here.

"Dante?" a muffled voice deep within the ranks of shelves asked.

Dante's foot caught on the edge of the rug. He stumbled, almost dropping the princess as he tried to keep on his feet. "Keer, I need your help."

"Yes, you certainly do. You do know that Mysti is on a rampage, right?" Keer's head popped out from around the shelves. Green eyes widened as he sighted Dante. "Sire! Are you alright? What happened? Who is that?" Questions flooded out of Keer faster than Dante could answer.

Dante wavered as his eyesight blurred and grayed around the edges.

"I'll answer your questions in a minute, but could you take her first?"

"Oh, right, of course. I am coming," Keer said, and he hurried across the room. He took the girl and laid her on a divan. Dante wondered why he hadn't thought of doing that.

"She needs a healer." Dante said as he stood in the center of the room, lost. He'd made it here, now what? Oh, right. That bit was important. "Keer, she's an Owlderah royal."

Keer's head snapped around so fast Dante rubbed his own neck in sympathy. "Truly?"

"She has the tattoo." Like he would make something like that up. "I'm going to sit down."

Keer hadn't heard him. He was too busy staring at the princess, his mouth gaping. He was going to catch a fly if he wasn't careful.

Dante leaned against a pillar and let his knees buckle. The smooth marble supported him as he slid down. Exhaustion pulled at his eyelids. A nap right here on the floor sounded good. At this point, he'd accept the cave again if it meant he could sleep.

Hands patted his face. "What's wrong?" Keer knelt in front of him. His thumbs pried Dante's eyelids open. "Are you hurt?" A worried crease furrowed Keer's brow.

Dante sneezed.

Keer didn't have time to block the spray, and he turned slightly green. "Gross, Dante. Really?" He scrubbed his snot-splattered face with a sleeve.

"Sorry. I think I have caught a cold along with a princess."

Keer lifted him off the floor proving a strength belied by his slim form. "You can't sleep here."

"Why not? It's better than the cave," Dante whined. The space in his skull behind his nose throbbed, and he sniffed wetly trying to relieve the building pressure.

"You slept in a cave?"

"Mm-hmm much better than the river's bed, don't you think?"

Keer lowered him onto another divan. His lips were pressed white. "Rest here while I call the healers. I think the princess isn't the only one with a fever." Concern strained his voice.

Dante wondered if he was missing something important, but he couldn't focus. The divan was a welcome cushion to his aching muscles. He curled up, trying to get warm.

"Hush, sire, everything will be fine. I'll handle it."

"Thanks, Keer." Dante allowed sleep to claim him, knowing Keer could, and would, handle everything with skillful aplomb.

Chapter Two

Time passed in a haze of fevered heat with vile medicines poured down his throat every few hours. The gentle warmth of healing magic spread throughout his body and eased the bruises. It was familiar magic. Healer Gracia's magic. There was no better healer. If she was here, everything would be fine; otherwise, he was dying. He felt like that was an option.

A few days had passed when Dante finally woke with any true sense of awareness. Even without forcing his sticky eyes open, Dante knew he was snug in his four-poster bed. The smell was right. The slight squish of his mattress was perfect. Home.

Peering out from his cocoon of blankets, he saw his First, Mysti, curled in a chair at his bedside. Distress creased her face even in sleep. Had he truly been that ill? If so, she was going to kill him for making her worry. Maybe he should pretend to be sick until he regained enough strength to outrun her fury. Mysti did not handle stress kindly.

A beaker of something medicinal sat on the bedside table. It looked goopy, like chunky, gray applesauce. Nasty. He was not voluntarily drinking that. Ignoring the concoction, Dante grasped for the glass of water beside it with clumsy fingers. The cool water was bliss as it slid down his scratchy throat. He drained the rest in one breathless gulp. The small victory of returning the glass safely to the table gave him the courage to try for the bathroom.

Moonlight lit the way as he tiptoed from rug to rug. It was harder to move than it should be. His joints felt overstretched, and his head felt stuffed with straw. Still, he made it without mishap and, more importantly, without waking Mysti.

The cool ceramic tiles of the bathroom on his naked toes shocked him awake and cleared the last of the fever's haze from his system. Dante sucked water out of the faucet until his stomach sloshed.

He stumbled back to his bed and curled up in the still-warm nest of blankets. He rolled over. The moonlight cast an unholy glow in Mysti's narrowed eyes, who stared at him unblinking. He couldn't help it; he squeaked. He did manage not to burrow under the covers in a childish effort to escape her wrath.

"You." That single word echoed with the darkest fury and rage, and yet, hiding underneath it, he heard the worry that inspired it. Mysti was his First Chevalier. She was supposed to protect him and had done her best since he came of age at eleven. She had made her vows, accepting the tattoo that linked them until death.

He had not made it easy for her. He hadn't appreciated her attempts to keep him away from the city streets and his friends. The city was his freedom, and it had taken a long time for him to accept Mysti as a friend and not his jailor. Her partner, Alexion, had helped considerably, even before he became Dante's Third. His easy nature bridged the gap between Dante and Mysti's tense formality and coaxed them to an understanding. Between them, Alexion, Mysti and Raphael, came up with an agreement filled with conditions and left it at that, pretending to be content. Through the circumstances of his last outing, he had unintentionally broken some important rules.

"I am sorry." An apology was all he had to offer. Extenuating reasons were obvious.

Her rich brown eyes softened. "I know. The healers are watching the Princess of Owlderah closely. Her fever was dangerously high. They believe she was on the edge of collapse even before the dunk in the river. The healer said she was near starvation, probably went at least two weeks without proper nutrition. The wound was newer, perhaps a few days old, but it was infected. It was good that you came across her when you did. She never would have made it alone."

That was the closest Mysti would come to saying she forgave him. It didn't mean she wasn't going to beat him to a punishing pulp in the training ring later, but he had been forgiven.

"Sleep, my prince. There is time enough for you to rest. All that can be done is being done." Worried anger banked to a sisterly warmth.

"Thank you," Dante said, no longer fighting to keep his eyes open.

"Wait!" Mysti said. Dante heard her clothes rustle as she sat up. "You have to drink this or Healer Gracia will have my hide."

Dante opened his eyes to slits. She was holding that vile beaker. He opened his mouth to refuse, and the nameless gloopy liquid poured down his throat. He had to swallow it or choke.

"Bleh!" He scraped the top of his tongue with his teeth, trying to remove the residue. Mysti shrugged unrepentantly when he glared at her. Dante pointedly rolled his back to her in betrayed disgust. She owed him for that. Just wait and see what happened the next time she got sick; he'd find the nastiest herbal concoction he could, this exact one probably.

The morning dawned in a splendid array of color, from purple to red and finally a cloudless blue; a false promise for a beautiful day. There would likely be a thunderstorm by afternoon as was the wont of summer weather.

Dante felt no particular urge to move until the aroma of sausage wafted through the doorway, along with the hushed voices of all four of his chevaliers followed by Keer. Fresh, warm bread probably surrounded the spicy sausages in a layer of fresh-baked heaven, the cook's breakfast specialty. Those were worth crawling out of the deepest grave for; a cozy bed was no match whatsoever.

Randomly grabbing clothes from the wardrobe, Dante hurried to get dressed. They'd eat all the rolls, including the crumbs, if he didn't claim some.

He crept into the lounge on the balls of his toes, and Stipes was the only one to notice him tiptoe in the room. His Fourth smirked but didn't give him away.

Dante chose his target. He was getting a roll, even if he had to steal it.

Alexion sprawled over the full length of the couch with his head pillowed on Mysti's lap. His cheeks bulged as he shoved the last bite into his mouth and grabbed another. Cheese oozed out of the roll's crusty edges.

Dante drooled and crept closer.

Alexion aimed the food at his mouth. Taking his chance, Dante leaned over the back of the couch and snatched the sausage roll. He stuffed half of it into his mouth before Alexion could react.

"Hey!" Alexion yelled. "I thought you were supposed to be bedridden, not running around stealing other people's food."

"You should have been paying more attention. How you can protect me if you can be caught so unawares?" Dante sniped back before gleefully shoving the other half of the roll into his mouth.

"Yeah, yeah. Just wait until I have to save your butt, then you'll wish you hadn't stolen my food. I'll be weak from hunger and unable to defend you properly," Alexion said, frowning as Dante deliberately licked the buttery crumbs from his fingers.

Dante settled on the floor, leaning against the couch. In his own chambers, he could act as he pleased and his nobles couldn't judge him for it. He often teased his chevaliers and sat on the floor at their feet.

Raphael wandered away and returned with a goblet in hand. "Sire, the healers insisted that you were to drink this."

"Not another one!" Dante moaned. "I drank one last night. Isn't this an overdose or something?"

"Sire, I believe that they have prescribed several over the next moon or two," Raphael said.

Disgruntled, Dante took it. He stared down into the goblet and sloshed the liquid back and forth. This one was orange instead of gray. He wasn't sure that made it any better. Tilting his head back, he hoped the medicine would go straight down and he wouldn't have to taste it. No such luck. This one was agonizingly sweet. Dante gagged, and Alexion burst out laughing.

"Shut it, Alexion, or I'm going to make you drink the next one," Dante snarled. "This stuff's nasty." If this mockery continued, they'd all be getting a dose.

Alexion sobered. "Sorry, sire."

Mysti snorted, but no one called him on the obvious lie.

Dante moved on, "How is the princess? Has she been able to explain anything?"

Keer balanced his mug of steaming tea on his knee. "The wound on her arm was infected. Healer Gracia believes it will heal with full function as long as they can keep it clean now. She has not awoken with any coherence. Healer Gracia said that her body was pushed to the brink and the river took the last drop from her reserves. The fever nearly killed her. If you hadn't brought her home, it would have. Dante, why was she out there? What happened?"

Heat crept up his ears. That was quite the subject, wasn't it? Better to prepare Keer, though, so he could cover him if it got to the nobles. "She was in owl form and bleeding. I thought she was an animal. I attacked her, followed her, and then pulled her out of the river." Really, there wasn't that much to tell. The princess's story was still hers. He couldn't explain anything useful because he didn't know anything useful.

Dante pressed on before a scolding broke out. "Anything desperately needing my attention?"

"Your Lady Aunt has been asking after you," Raphael said. If he'd been anyone else, or any less restrained, his eyes would have rolled. Even he found Lady Petria slightly aggravating.

"What does she want now?" Dante asked.

An old wave of sadness washed over him. His aunt had been the closest thing he'd had to a mother once upon a time, before her husband's fatal illness broke her. It was hard to see her fallen so far. Ever since her husband had passed away, she had been almost childlike, spoiled, and desperate for attention. Dante understood why she was the way she was, but it didn't make her emotional outbursts any easier to handle. Thank the Mother, Lady Petria was good at raising her son, even if she was overprotective of Korren and never let him go anywhere.

"She swears that you forgot her birthday last week."

"I gave her emeralds for her birthday. What does she think she wants now?"

"Spidarian silk, delivered personally by your hands."

"Right, of course." Dante sighed. What she really wanted was for him to visit her. It had been a while since he'd spent more than half an hour at the dinner table with her. "I'll go to the market later and find some." He rushed the next sentence out before Mysti's hand moved to connect with the back of his head. "With an escort. I promise I won't slip away on this trip if I can help it."

"If he can help it, he says," Alexion muttered under his breath.

Dante hid a smirk behind his cup. They really did know him too well. "How is Korren? Is she cooping him up again?" Being ill and out of touch with his duties left him scrambling to make sure his world had held steady in his absence.

Stipes joined the conversation. "Doing well. He's been asking after you, though. You've been sick for two days and gone for a day and a half before that. He missed you." Dante knew Korren reminded Stipes of his five little brothers. The chevalier held a lot of fond patience for the little prince.

Keer slid into assistant mode. "Ookamimori is as quiet as any city of its size, nothing requiring your immediate attention. Your nobles would demand it, of course, but they have nothing truly pressing to present, no matter what they say. I've managed to keep Princess Owlderah's presence under wraps for now."

Dante accepted that and finished eating; it was time to resume his duty. Pushing up from the floor, Dante shooed them out of his room so he could clean up without them hovering. He could get dressed just fine by himself, even if bending over to lace his boots made blood roar in his ears.

The princess's rooms were his first stop. An astringent smell led him through the halls to the suite where the healers attended to the woman he'd carried home. One of the attending healers approached him fussily. "You should still be in bed, sire."

He waved off the concern. "I'm fine. How is she?"

"We've done all we can. The rest is up to her. Though the fever has lightened, she does not seem to be getting any better. It is as though she has lost hope. Something has broken her spirit. We can feel it, but she will not come forth out of the darkness that embraces her. We fear death magic may have been used on her."

"What?" Oh, Mother bless, why? It couldn't be true. It was an unfathomable action. "Who would dare practice the forbidden? The Mother will reject them for the trespass," Dante snarled.

He crossed his arms to keep from striking out or shivering at the thought of the Mother's rejection. Even as a bedtime story, death magic was forbidden, and for a good reason—the cost of its use upon a soul was terrible. That soul would never return to the Mother. They would be forced to suffer eternal darkness as a Shade. That was the price of slaughtering another to boost one's power. The hairs on the back of his neck rose and quivered at the thought.

The healer was grim. "I have no idea, sire; however, we found burns on her skin that relate to what little is known about death magic, but there doesn't seem to be any taint to her magic or soul. We believe the spells have done their work and have gone." The healer wrung his hands together. "It is her own pain that causes her to sleep. A failsafe of life to retreat within until the emotional wound heals."

"She hasn't woken at all?" Dante demanded sharply.

"No, sire. She has murmured a lot in her fever, but nothing sensible, nothing to give us clues to her distress and help. Even with magic, there is only so much we can do."

As they spoke, Dante studied the princess. She lay limp and sickly pale as if the river had drowned her inner fire. He leaned down and brushed sweaty strings of hair from her fever-flushed face.

He searched for words and finally remembered something his aunt had once said in one of her brief moments of clarity.

"You are a princess of the Royal Owlderah. You are the heir to your throne, the strength of your people. Whatever darkness has befallen them, you must be their light. You are on a mission, and you must complete it. It is your duty and bond as the Crown Princess. Know that when you wake, my aid will be yours."

Lady Petria had given him a similar speech when he'd faltered under the sudden weight of his father's crown upon his brow. He hoped the princess could hear him in whatever darkness held her captive.

Dante turned to the healer. "Give her what strength you can. I want to know immediately when she wakes."

"Of course, sire. It shall be done." He bobbed his head in respect.

Dante's pace down the hall was morose, weighted with lead. He'd have to approach the council of nobles about the princess soon. Even though he had little to tell them and was sure this would be all his fault somehow, as if he were the one who dumped a princess in the middle of the woods. He just didn't know what to do. He had nothing to go on. A runner could be sent to the Owlderah, but what if the princess had a purpose for being alone. She needed to wake up. Explanations would make his life so much easier.

A booming voice rattled Dante out of his thoughts. It sounded like Lord Kiba. What was he yelling about now? Didn't the man have his own place to manage?

A tense ache spread into his temples at the thought of confronting Lord Kiba; however, Dante refused to let him stomp around the castle yelling at people.

Dante followed the ruckus.

"Look at this bloody disaster!"

There was only cowed silence.

Had Lord Kiba moved into the castle while he was ill? What gave him the right to act this way under Dante's roof? Mother bless, he would murder him. Dante rounded the corner. Lord Kiba's imposing back was to him as the man loomed over two young servants. Tears tracked down the face of the youngest. Shattered pottery and dirt littered the marble floor at the boys' feet.

"What would the prince think of you dumping this filth all over his home?" Lord Kiba sneered. The fabric of his coat pulled taut over his burly shoulders as he crossed his arms.

A silent sob shook the boy. The older boy stepped protectively in front of the younger with a trembling but defiant tilt of his chin. The colors on their uniforms marked them as trainees. Their trainer should have been the one standing up for them.

Dante steeled his nerves and made his presence known. "The prince thinks it was an accident made while they are learning the arduous ropes of their new job. It is only a pottery jar and some dirt. Easily enough swept away and replaced," he said to Lord Kiba's back. He cursed his own height. His head only came to Lord Kiba's chin as the man turned around. Dante tried not to hunch his shoulders defensively.

"I don't see how a simple accident requires your attention, Lord Kiba." Dante left off the 'in my castle', not yours that desperately wanted to tumble off his tongue. The man was, unfortunately, on his council and opposed his decisions often enough without him adding in a pissing contest.

"Well, if you had been present the last few days perhaps my attention would not be needed to keep everything in order."

Dante ground his teeth until his jaw ached. Movement out of the corner of his eye caught his attention. The trainees did not need to deal with this. "You two, go and find your trainer and something to clean this up." Dante looked down at where white roses lay trampled into the dirt by Lord Kiba's boots. "And"—the boys paused mid-step in their escape—"let's put up some of the sunrise yellow roses instead? My mother's favorite." Relief brightened the boys' eyes as they bowed and scurried down the hall as fast as they could without actually sprinting.

"I had things that demanded my attention, Lord Kiba, and I've been ill. I trust everything has been handled appropriately during my bedridden absence?"

It would probably take him a full moon to regain the trust of his council, as much as he ever held it. He had to work for every inch of respect. He had held the crown for four years, and the Mother had yet to issue her final Test. Until she did, Dante would not have her blessing and gifted elemental. Until he did, the council would hold some doubt about his right and ability to rule. Lord Kiba was the worst of his dissenters.

Rarely ever disagreeing with him directly, but he made sly comments and occasionally gave him verbal pats on the head, like Dante were a little puppy begging for attention.

Behind his back, Dante's fist tightened until his tendons creaked over knucklebone from the strain.

Lord Kiba's smile flashed fangs in a blatant scoff, quickly hidden behind lying lips. "Of course, sire. Everything has been well taken care of."

Dante swallowed the growl boiling in his ribcage. He needed this man's veneer of good graces. Lord Kiba held too much sway over his nobles for him to call him on the disrespect. He stared at the air over Lord Kiba's shoulder, refusing to meet his eyes. If he met his smug, yellow stare, Dante thought he'd lunge for the noble's throat.

Don't piss him off, don't piss him off. Let him lord it over you today, and your life will be easier tomorrow. Dante counted each of his breaths in an attempt to control his temper. He didn't even know what to say to the man.

Thankfully, Lord Kiba saw his victory and took it.

"If you will excuse me, Prince Dante, I have duties to attend to." Lord Kiba sketched a low bow.

Dante nodded. "Of course."

The infuriating man spun neatly on his heel and turned his back with an air of dismissal. Dante was glad the servant boys had not been there to witness the interaction. It was a wonder anyone respected him when he had nobles like Kiba to contend with.

Chapter Three

Dante went to the one place Mysti wouldn't yell at him for going and where no one would find him. The nobles could live without his presence amongst the court for another day.

The weight of unknown portent chased him into the maze.

The sun only shone on the tall corridors of plants when it was at its peak. Wild hedges entwined with vines and supported by old gnarly trees towered over him. Despite the familiar peace of the maze, he felt on edge. Princess Owlderah had brought a mystery with her, a shadow. Death magic, truly? He shivered. Mother bless, he hoped not.

Vibrant leaves chattered softly in the warm, summer breeze. He shifted and trotted onward on four paws. In the depths of the maze, Dante stopped at a stone serpent coiled beneath the leaves. The small statue marked a hole in the hedge. He sucked in his breath and squeezed through the branches. Twigs snagged at his fur as he crawled through the hole. A grove nestled comfortably on the other side of the concealing hedges with a centuries-old oak, twisted with age, shading the water fountain in the center.

Colorful clover sprawled between the knobby roots of the tree. Dante dropped his head on his paws. His eyelids slid to half-mast. Even after being confined to bed for days and neglecting his duties, he was exhausted.

It was no wonder his father had held little interest in his childhood. He'd probably sensed that his son was ill-suited to the crown; it was so hard to keep up the appearance that he knew what he was doing.

Dante drifted into a daze as the morning shadows grew shorter.

Something rustled in the bushes, disturbing his peace. Dante twitched his ears to catch the curious sound.

A ball of fuzz sprang wildly from the foliage. He had only seconds to brace himself. The mass of energy crashed into Dante, and he tried to pin the wriggling pup beneath his paws.

The pup squiggled away and yapped, "Found you!"

Dante shifted to human form and dashed after the wolf pup, catching up with him. "Ha! I got you!"

He shoved all worries aside in favor of his nephew and heir-apparent. Dante staggered under the abrupt weight of a six-year-old boy as Korren shifted form in his arms. His puppy-blue eyes gleamed with mischief.

Dante dropped a kiss on Korren's blond hair.

"You're all better!" the boy squealed.

"Yes, I am." Dante tossed Korren in the air and caught him. The infectious giggles made him laugh.

"I've been waiting ages for you to wake," Korren complained. "Did you really rescue a princess like Mama said? Is she nice?"

"Yes, I did, and I don't know. She has been sleeping the whole time."

"Why is she sleeping? Is it like the story where the bad guy put the princess under a curse, and now you have to break the spell?"

Dante settled on the ground, pulling his cousin into his lap. "Not quite. She's sick, like I was."

"Is she pretty?"

He gave the boy a startled look. "Aren't you a bit young to care about whether a girl is pretty or not?"

"Yes, but you're old, so if she's pretty you can give her the kiss of true love and break the curse and wake her up," Korren said. "Mama's told me lots of stories and how a prince is always supposed to do it."

Dante sat there slightly stunned by the onslaught of his heir's intelligence and total innocence.

"Well?" Korren asked.

"Well, what?"

"Is she pretty?"

The imperious demand forced him to picture the girl's ash-tinged hair, offset with her brilliant golden eyes. "Yes, she is."

"So, are you gonna kiss her?" Korren asked.

"I don't think that would work. There's not a curse on her right now. She's just sick."

"Oh. I hope she gets better soon."

"Me too."

"Did you have to kill some dark creature to rescue her?" A hopeful note snuck back into Korren's sad voice.

Dante smiled at his desire for a heroic story. "No, but we were rescued by some elementals."

Korren's eyes widened, and he practically vibrated with excitement.

"The undines saved us from drowning, and then I pulled her from a dark, scary river and carried her to an enchanted cave." Dante dared to embellish a touch on the adventure.

After he had finished, Korren beamed, his puppy fangs shiny and sharp. "And now you will kiss, get married, and live happily ever after," Korren said, bobbing his head with the absolute certainty only a child could summon.

His little cousin had quite an obsession with kissing all of a sudden.

Dante laughed. "We'll have to wait and see about that."

An orange, spotted butterfly floated into view on the breeze, completely capturing the six-year old's short attention span. The brightly colored insect poised on a violet. Its wings fluttered to keep its balance. Korren's heels dug into Dante's thighs as he launched from his lap to catch the butterfly.

He missed. The butterfly took flight and escaped the descending fingers. Korren shifted, yapping in excitement. He tumbled after the fluttering insect on clumsy legs, head craned to track it through the air.

Dante snickered as Korren plowed face-first into the hedge, too busy staring at the butterfly to watch where he was running. Korren shook it off and dove beneath the branches. He wiggled through the bushes and disappeared into the maze after his prey.

Closing his eyes, Dante tilted his face to the warm sunlight. He wasn't worried about him getting lost. Korren was the only person he'd let roam the maze alone. His bloodline would guide his little paws. Even at his age, Korren's pulse matched the Heart's. Royal blood ran strong and pure through his cousin's veins.

A serene statue graced the center of the fountain and stone-hewn pups cuddled into her legs. Dante's chest tightened as it always did when he dared imagine that the wolf was his mother, and the pups snuggled against her was he and his lost brother. It wasn't, of course. This fountain had been lost to the depths of the maze generations ago. However, what would it have felt like? Warm and safe was his belief.

The idea had comforted him many times over the years when he had hidden away from the empty glances and subservient words as the nobles talked over his head with his father.

Losing his life-mate, his queen, had broken Dante's father. Losing his firstborn, Dante's elder twin, at the same time had shattered him. Nothing remained for his second son, the one-too-many that had killed his wife. Carrying twins had weakened her too much for the strain of birthing even one child. Dante had had to be cut from her cooling womb.

Well, that line of thought wasn't helping Dante's mood any. Dante folded his legs underneath him. Centering his thoughts, he slid into meditation. Magic infused the world around him, welcoming his spirit with a gentle pulse. Here, it was only him and the Heart of Ookamimori, the pool of magic upon which his city was built. Ookamimori held no expectations of him, just acceptance. This was what gave the royals their strength, the city itself. Against this silent power, the buzzing questions and worries seemed inconsequential. As long as Ookamimori welcomed him, he had not failed, the Mother had not disowned him, and he was still eligible. Dante drifted in that knowledge as the Heart's magic flowed around him like blood through veins.

When he opened his eyes to the daylight, the throb of stress in his temples had eased, and he could roll his shoulders without his muscles creaking with the strain. Confused questions and worry still buzzed in his thoughts in an endless loop, but until the princess woke, nothing could fill in the missing knowledge.

Days of fever had left him wrung out and restless. There was one thing he could think of that would silence the questions in his head, work out the knots in his muscles, and repair a relationship all in one go. It was time to face the music.

"Korren!" he yelled, pitching his voice to carry. "I'm going to the training rings."

A dirty-blond head popped out from beneath a bush. "Can I come?"

"Yes, you can come" He chuckled at the leaves sticking out of Korren's hair like an extra pair of ears.

"Ride," the boy demanded imperiously.

Dante rolled his eyes but lifted Korren to his shoulders. Alexion had taught him that command, and he used it often.

Instead of returning to the library entrance, he wove his way deeper into the heart of the maze. After a little way, he stepped sideways through a narrow gap in the hedge wall. This one was not marked, meaning it was one of his own, personally created, gaps. The Kobrona artisans who had designed the maze for his family had marked their passages with a statue.

With small fingers fisted in his hair like reins and a bridal, Dante made his stride even and smooth. He knew from experience that if he stumbled he would lose the clutched hairs.

Dante sucked in his breath to squeeze through the last gap. The leafy wall ended on a sprawling field. Guard barracks marched neatly around a square. Ignoring the huge center arena, Dante aimed behind the barracks where smaller training rings hid beneath the oak trees.

Smug satisfaction curled his mouth at finding his chevaliers exactly where he'd thought they'd be, even without using the link. They clustered in and around the sandy ring. He nodded at the off-duty guards who gawked at his training chevaliers.

Korren bolted as soon as his feet touched the ground and bee-lined for Stipes.

"I feel so loved, outclassed by my own bodyguard," Dante mumbled as Stipes scooped Korren into his bulging arms. A fond warmth filled his heart. It was an expected abandonment. If Stipes was not on duty or training, the chevalier could often be found entertaining the castle children. He grinned as Korren waved from his new perch.

A furious duel whirled in the arena. His chevaliers were among the best fighters, and it showed in the speed of their fight. Alex wielded two short swords in a mastery of steel against Raphael's lightning-fast rapier. The colliding metal screamed. Alex ducked and twisted under Raphael's backslash. Sunlight gleamed over the swords, making the runes shine and sparkle across the blood-forged weapons. The two were going all out, using their soul-wields rather than the training blades. If not summoned for training, the blades only saw the light of day during ceremonies and the rare occasion that someone was idiotic enough to attack a royal. The soul-wields were forged in magic and the blood of their wielder. Each was a weapon unmatched. And hideously expensive. Only a Master Forger could create a soul-wield.

"Raphael will win today," Stipes said. He seemed completely oblivious to Korren, who watched the duel with his elbows propped on Stipes's head.

Dante rubbed his own scalp in sympathy; the kid had the sharpest elbows. "Such loyalty to your cousin, Raphael," he teased.

Stipes shrugged. "Alexion ate too many sausage rolls for breakfast. He's getting stomach cramps."

"Good observation." Stipes was right. Alexion was moving slower than normal. He wasn't dodging fast enough, and Raphael's sword nicked his clothes to shreds.

It always came to a close finish between these two. Raphael had the longer reach while Alexion could use his dual blades as two separate entities, so any handicap tipped the balance.

Blade rasped across blade as Raphael repelled an attempt from Alexion. His gauntleted arm blocked the second sword sweeping in from above and forced Alexion to flip backward to dodge a kick. He landed off-balance and found Raphael's sword poised at his throat.

"You called it," Dante said to Stipes.

Korren bounced on Stipes's shoulders. "Your turn now, Dante?"

He pretended to think about it. "I don't know," he said, drawing out the last syllable.

"Please, please, please!" Korren begged. He grabbed fistfuls of Stipes's hair to keep his balance as he wiggled imploringly, heedless of the chevalier's silent, enduring pain. If Korren had been in pup form, his tail would be wagging as fast as it could go.

"Well, alright, but only if Mysti agrees. Will you go ask her for me?" Dante pointed in Mysti's direction. She leaned against a nearby tree next to her mirror-image who was dressed in range-wolf leathers. Rayne, Mysti's twin, was back from her circuit.

"'Kay!" Korren squirmed off Stipes's back and scampered over to the two women.

"Scaredy cat," Alexion said, draped over the fence.

Dante put a hand on his chest, playing wounded. "Alexion, that is just cruel. I did not just send my one and only heir, a mere child, to face the wrath of Mysti for me."

The three of them watched Korren wiggling in excitement in front of Mysti and her amused twin. His high-pitched voice could be heard clearly, "But, Mysti, he's all better now. He's not been tired all morning! He rescued the princess and gave me a piggyback ride; he can take you on no problem!"

Dante groaned and hung his head as Alex sniggered. "I think your plan to get in the ring worked splendidly."

"I am so dead," Dante moaned. That hadn't quite gone to plan. He had hoped Korren would convince her he was fine, but the little brat had provoked her instead.

Alexion planted his boot on a weathered board and hopped out of the ring. "Mysti will take you on just to put a hole in your swollen head," he said. Frowning, he peered at his palm. "Damn, I got a splinter from your old-ass fence."

"The Mother's karma," Dante sneered. "That's what you get for scoffing at my incoming trauma."

Korren dug Dante's grave a little deeper. "He's the strongest prince ever! Even the river couldn't beat him!"

"Yep, hole, fat head." Alexion picked the wood slivers out of his hand.

"I am the royal prince. Such praise is my due. Perhaps you should do the same and sing my praises in the bazaar." Dante stuck his nose in the air. He might as well earn his beating.

Drinking from the well nearby, Raphael choked on his water. When he could speak again, he said, "That was horrid, sire. Please, never do that again. Mysti and I taught you better manners than that." He wiped his chin with a disgusted grimace.

Playing it up, Dante struck a haughty, offended pose, making his chevaliers and the lurking onlookers laugh.

Korren hurtled back and latched onto Dante's legs. "Mysti says you can fight, but she is your opponent so she can make sure you don't get overtired." Korren grinned up at him innocently. "Isn't that smart of her since she's your First and she's supposed to take care of you, right?"

"Of course. Thank you, Korren." Overtired his ass; Mysti just wanted to beat him up herself.

"Stay away from me. I don't want to be splattered with your blood." Alexion took an exaggerated step back and crabbed sideways as though Dante were contagious.

Dante sneered and pushed past him to enter the ring. Mysti brought in two wooden swords, handing him one as he met her in the center of the sand. At least she wasn't using a shield. He was proficient with short swords, but Mysti far outclassed him, even without the use of her shield, unless he chose to fight dirty and reveal his nightlife, which wasn't happening.

Mysti smiled at him. He cringed. It was not a nice smile. Magic roiled around her in an angry aura. Widening his stance as dust puffed around his boots, Dante braced for her advance. Mysti struck like a feral demon. Her blade swung in a downward arc. He parried, focused only on the fight. The strange edginess of his nerves burned out by adrenaline.

Her fist snaked forward and sank into his stomach.

"Ow." He coughed and wheezed. "Cheap shot." She was playing rough and dirty herself. Twisting to the side, he slashed at her exposed side. Mysti danced out of his range, forcing him to overextend. The flat of her sword thwapped against his ribs. Pain came with an instant welt. She was really pissed and going all out despite his recent illness, or perhaps because of it. Mysti had been forced to wait to ream him out. Her temper normally burnt out in a flash fire, but this time it had built up and was ready to explode.

The leather-wrapped hilt twisted in his sweaty hands as he blocked a hard cut to the same side. He kicked her knee. Mysti stumbled and cursed under her breath as her wavy hair fell out of its pins. He took advantage of her distraction and punched her shoulder. She fell.

Jeers came from outside the ring as Dante jumped to dodge a swipe at his ankles. Sweat beaded along his lip. He licked the damp salt away as he waited for Mysti to regain her feet. She came up with a furious cry and lunged. He blocked a torrent of blows. Mysti yelled wordlessly at him with each strike. Somehow, it was worse than her cussing him out; the barrage of noise throbbed in his ears. Sweat dripped down his forehead and into his eyes. The edges of his vision blurred.

He hated wielding a short sword. Hers slipped straight through his guard, stabbing him in the chest. His soul-wield, a katana, was considerably longer and thinner, giving him extra reach and speed.

A fumbled, simple parry left him wide open.

"Got you," she snarled, slapping her solid oak sword into his elbow. Dante's muscles lost their strength as his nerves shrieked, and the sword slipped from his senseless fingers.

"Surrender?" Mysti asked, quirking an eyebrow. She stood balanced on the balls of her feet, poised for a continued dance.

His hand spasmed from abused muscles. Ignoring the dizziness, Dante stooped and picked up the sword with his left. The weighted tip drew a furrow in the dirt as he lifted it. "I never disappoint a lady." In all honesty, taking a breather sounded like an idea he could live with, but better to let Mysti get it out of her system now.

His stance shifted and strengthened as he twirled the sword around in his left hand to aim the tip at her. "Do you?" he asked.

Lips curled in a fanged snarl, Mysti paced forward, a hunting prowl.

Dante braced for the charge. She circled. He didn't turn with her, only waited, and tilted his head to keep her in his blurring peripheral.

When she moved, it was another physical explosion of his First's temper. "You moron, idiotic, imbecilic prince!" she yelled, each word forcefully punctuated by a jarring blow of her sword. "Disappearing into the forest for days, bringing trouble in on your heels, and gallivanting around like you haven't been bedridden for days!"

He might deserve that. He knew he did.

Dante wished he'd stayed in bed instead of gallivanting.

His pulse rushed in his ears as he struggled to keep up with his First's furious attack. It felt as though his blood was boiling in his veins. He'd thought to beat out the weakness of the fever and Mysti's anger all in one battle; instead, it seemed he'd fueled them both. Dante faltered and missed a vital block. The last thing he saw was Mysti's wooden sword descending toward his face.

Worried faces shaded his bleary eyes from the sun's fire. "Sire, are you all right?" Stipes asked. Korren's teary, blue eyes begged for a positive answer from where he crouched, tucked under Stipes's chin. Only Stipes's arms kept Korren from falling on Dante's face.

"Of course, he's not all right. He passed out in a training spar because he's an imbecile," Raphael said scathingly. He bent over, his long hair brushing against Dante's cheek.

Dante wanted to reach up and pull it for being a jerk.

Tears welled up to the brim of Korren's eyes. Raphael turned his head, and Dante went crossed-eyed as Raphael's hair tickled his nose. Dante's fingers inched up and curled around the irritating follicles.

Alexion shoved Raphael out of the huddle, and the hair slid harmlessly out of Dante's fingers. "Budge over, Raphael, and watch where you leave your golden carpet of hair. You just about suffocated our prince with it."

"Everyone, move. Give him some space to breathe. Alexion, help him up," Mysti ordered, chasing the others away with a glare.

Dante opened his mouth to question the look. She aimed a darker glare his way. "And you, sire, pardon me, but why the hell didn't you tell me you were feeling faint. I almost cracked your skull open." Worry lines creased her face.

Alexion sat him up with an arm under his shoulders. Mysti pushed a ladle of water at him. "Drink before you dry up and wither away."

"I didn't faint," he protested.

"You did. You probably brought your fever back by running around in this heat."

Dante grumbled under his breath and shook Alexion off. "Stop gawking and let me up. I'm fine."

Alexion put out a hand and hauled Dante to his feet. He wavered like an hour-old fawn learning to balance. A smaller hand braced his back. Turning his head to look, Dante found Mysti's sister supporting him. "Hi, Rayne."

Rayne's hair was redder than her sister's. It was almost copper, belying her much calmer temper. Mysti should have been the redhead, and then they'd have some forewarning for the her short-fused temper.

"Sire," she said. Her lips twitched, but she was kind enough not to laugh at him.

He grinned. "Going to be home long? You've just returned from border patrol, haven't you?" he asked, hoping to change the subject from his health or lack thereof.

"Yes, sire, I hope to be here until after Ryver's mate completes his vows and she hers," Rayne said. The youngest of the triplets, Ryver had found her life-mate. It was all Mysti was talking about right now, when she wasn't pissed at him. Rayne's eyes flicked to something in front of Dante.

Mysti loomed beside them. Furious spots still flushed her cheeks. "You need to be more careful." His First truly did not handle worry very well.

A small whimper stopped another tirade. They collectively looked around. A page girl shifted nervously at the edge of the hot sands. Her fingers twisted into her tunic as she waited under their gaze. "Sorry," she squeaked, looking everywhere except at Mysti.

"Go on, child," Stipes encouraged from the sidelines.

"Right." The page girl sucked in a big breath and blurted, "Healer Gracia requests your presence, Prince Dante, milord. She said to tell you that the patient is awake and asks to speak with you at your earliest convenience." She gasped for breath, almost twisting holes into her tunic now. "Um, Healer Gracia said you'd best hurry before she falls asleep again, milord, and that if you know what's good for you, you will take a nap afterward, because she's sure you've been running around, like"—she stared at her feet— "um, like a child, milord." The page girl flinched as though she expected him to rip her to shreds for repeating the outspoken healer.

"See, Healer Gracia agrees with me. You are a childish idiot." Mysti gleefully pounced on the description.

Dante stitched together some dignity and straightened away from the supporting hands of Alexion and Rayne. "You'll have to yell at me later, Mysti."

"Oh, I think I'm good, until you do something stupid again. I'm sure it won't be long."

Dante ignored the jab and kept walking. Did she really think he was that bad? If his own First thought he was incompetent.... He tried his best; he really did. Sometimes he just didn't know what to do. He couldn't run around asking for help all the time like a lost pup. He was the prince. It was his job to know what to do and how to do it. Dante locked the thoughts away in the lurking darkness with all his other doubts.

Time for some answers from Princess Owlderah.

Chapter Four

Raphael and Stipes followed him, of course. They would not leave him alone with a stranger, injured princess or not. They stopped in the outer suite as Healer Gracia beckoned him into the princess's room. "Make this fast. She is still quite weak."

"Of course." He knew better than to challenge Healer Gracia. She presided over his mother's birthing chambers and his every sickbed since. Dante wrinkled his nose from the powerful scent of medicinal herbs permeating the suite.

Trying to project a capable strength—wasn't that a laugh after today—he stepped into the inner bedroom. The silver-haired girl sat propped up on pillows. Warm sunlight radiated through the gauzy curtains, giving her skin a false glow of health.

He began with full formality. "Princess Owlderah. I am glad you are awake at last. I am Prince, Dante Rayve'en Canidea. Welcome, find shelter in my lands and among my people." Clasping his hands behind his back, he forced his posture taller. He was short enough without slumping in front of the princess.

"Thank you. I ask sanctuary as Crown Princess, Nakai Cattrianna Owlderah."

"Granted." Oh, Mother bless, what was happening?

"I fear my reasons for asking sanctuary are going to sound insane. The Kobrona…." She wavered in undisguised terror. Sucking in a deep breath, she looked down at clasped fingers. "The Kobrona have taken over my home, Hanehishou. Anyone who opposed them was sacrificed in death magic rituals. Queen Jeziah, my mother, is bound by the magic and enslaved at their Lord's feet. Before I escaped, they spoke of their next target." Her voice dwindled to a frightened whisper. "Prince Dante, they have chosen Ookamimori as their next conquest."

Dante saw pain, fear, and a deep-wounded sorrow in her golden eyes. She had lost so much in so little time. "I am sorry for what you have endured."

It was utterly lame and was so miniscule of a platitude, but what else was there to say? Mere words could never heal that kind of wound.

"Be assured that we will do everything in our power to aid you and your people. Thank you for this warning."

He had no idea what to do with her warning. War? Was that what faced him? "You have given me a chance to save my people. Please, rest and heal. My healers will take good care of you."

Princess Owlderah drooped into the pillows. "I'm sorry," she said, even as her eyelids fluttered shut.

"You brought us an invaluable warning. Thank you, Princess Owlderah," he repeated. She probably didn't even hear him, already wiped out from the conversation and asleep.

Dante walked away in a stunned haze. War, dear blessed Mother. War was nearly unheard of amongst the family. The occasional skirmish maybe to settle a dispute, but full-out war? No.

Healer Gracia bustled into the room as soon as Dante opened the door. She paused on her way. "Make sure you get more rest, my prince," she said, patting him on the cheek with her wrinkled fingers. "Still looking a bit peaked, dear. You are taking your potions?"

"Yes, ma'am," Dante managed automatically. He scurried out of the room to avoid her concerned frown. He had bigger issues than a bygone cold to deal with, and he was not about to tell her he'd fainted only a few minutes ago.

Raphael and Stipes stood silently at his shoulder, allowing him his thoughts.

Death magic. War.

What was he supposed to do with that? His skin crawled.

The Kobrona were using death magic.

Blood magic was one thing. Properly used, the magic came from a willing sacrifice of blood, one that could be fully recovered. Life energy, magic, refilled with rest and food. If used by one with a dark soul, blood magic could be used for evil deeds, of course; however, when used with conscience, it was merely another tool. Healers used it daily. Forgers used it in their work, as did countless other crafters.

Death magic, though? Death magic was the slaughter of another's spirit. Nothing could make death magic a force to be used. Any could sacrifice another's life and channel the power. None would do so. It stained one's soul beyond reparation and damned them to nothingness as a shade, to wander through the in-between, never to join the Mother to be reborn.

Despite the muggy heat, Dante shivered, cold to his bone marrow.

Death magic was supposed to be a legend, a nightmarish one not even told in bedtime tales or by the bards in taverns. It was the darkest sort of power, scorned by the Mother and banned by the families in unanimous agreement.

His hands trembled as he scrubbed at his face, trying to force his thoughts into order. Dante believed the princess; fear like that could not be faked. Also, his healers had seen evidence of death magic tainting her.

The same page girl perched on a divan outside the rooms, a scroll in her lap, apparently there to run errands for the healers. Well, she was about to get something to do for him instead.

Dante schooled his face to absolute calm, so she did not think he was upset with her. "Little one," he called.

"I'm not little!" Her eyes flew up from her reading with affronted fury. She dropped the scroll and clapped her hands over her mouth, staring at Dante in horror.

Nonplussed, Dante couldn't decide whether to laugh or cry. "It's all right, page. I don't like being called little either."

"Sire?" Raphael's disapproval was clearly pronounced in that single syllable.

Stipes thumped Raphael's shoulder. "Be nice. She's just a kid, new to castle duty," he hissed under his breath.

Ignoring his bickering chevaliers, Dante mustered a shaky smile and crouched on his haunches. "It's fine," he restated. He pretended not to hear Raphael's aggrieved huff. His stuffy, noble principles would survive a kid's lack of respect. She hadn't done anything wrong. "Page, I need you to run for me."

The girl nodded behind her clamped hands.

"I need you to find Captain Lask of the range-wolves and Captain Brice of the patrollers. When you find them, tell them I need them in the castle library."

His court of nobles would need to know too, but he refused to face them without some sort of plan in place or they would rip him to shreds as if it was his fault the Kobrona had gone insane.

"Also, find me Krane Timbrias."

"The Storyteller down in the bazaar?" she asked, her voice lilting at the end with excitement. "Yes." Once his father's right-hand man and Keer's father, Dante needed the old man's insight. His nobles would not refute Krane's advice.

"I know right where he is." The slight girl waited to see if there were more instructions before she gave a respectful bob and bolted down the hallway. The soft leather of her shoes made no sound on the marble as she settled into the ground-eating lope that made the runners who they were.

Dante smiled a little more genuinely. With a stride like that, the girl would outstrip her peers in the runner's guild. The youngest hopefuls trained as pages, running errands throughout the city. At ten years of age, the initiated began their training for real.

His smile froze in a rigorous mask.

If war truly came, the girl would likely not reach the age of ten. Ookamimori was not a fortress, and he commanded no army. They were defenseless.

Dante ducked into one of the servants' passages. He didn't want to be seen while in such turmoil.

There had never been a reason to retain a full army. Why should they? The forest and mines provided more than enough economy. No great quarrels occurred between them and the neighboring families. The Mother designed each family's land with subtle borders—the ley lines—with the cities' Heart at the center of each. To the royals anchored to the Heart, it felt utterly wrong to go outside their lands, much less to take over another Heart. Dante wasn't even sure that was possible. Krane had once told him and Keer of a royal who'd never been able to attend the Communion beneath the Mother's branches because he was so strongly tied to the Heart of his city that just stepping over the borders almost killed him. So, fighting over land just never happened. Grand Elementals were the only real threats, and an army was not required for that rare occurrence.

Crystal sconces on the wall cast blue pools of light that broke up the tunnel of darkness. Dante led the way through the passages. It was like an enclosed version of the hedge maze, but he knew it as well.

Before Dante could push open the entrance, Raphael dropped a hand on his shoulder. "What is going on, sire? Why are you summoning the captains?"

"I will tell you all shortly. I'm not ready to speak of it yet." Not that he ever would be. Sucking in a lungful of gloomy air, he stepped away from his chevalier. The look on Raphael and Stipes's faces forced him to say something. "Just, it's bad, and I don't really know what to do. No idea." Dante barked a hard laugh at his own pathetic helplessness.

Raphael's hand came back with a different weight to it and squeezed Dante's shoulder. "Whatever it is, we will deal with it together, Dante. Keer and his father will figure it out."

"Perhaps," Dante said and pushed the door to the library.

Panic rose as acidic bile burned his throat. Dante forced it down. Finally rubbing the tattoo on his wrist, Dante sent a summons to his other chevaliers. A tiny thread of magic went into the inked runes that allowed them to track him. He should have called them already, but he couldn't seem to get his thoughts into order. Horror and confusion were on a continuous loop.

He was the prince. He would be strong enough. He had to be. There was no other choice.

Keer, as usual, sat under the window and was scrawling a missive. Ink stained his fingers, and he had a smear on his ear and down his face. The man had an office, but he only used it when he was kicked out of the library for the night and went there instead of going to sleep.

"Dante?" Keer asked. He lifted his head from his work and flashed a distracted smile. "Is it lunchtime already? I'm almost done with this, and then we can go." He bent back to his work, still talking. "The morning went too fast, I swear. I barely got anything done." Keer signed the parchment with a flourish. "Right, I told you I was almost done." His long fingers rolled the parchment into a tube and tied it with a ribbon. He dripped green wax over the ribbon knot before pressing the Canidea seal into the wax as it hardened.

Keer scooted his chair back to stand. "You're awfully quiet. What's wrong now?"

Dante waved away his concern. "I will tell you in a minute with the others."

Raphael caught Keer's eye and shook his head before Keer went into interrogation mode. Dante was absurdly grateful for the intervention.

The library was blessedly quiet. No rumors would start when there was no one around to hear them.

Death magic; it tolled in his skull like a death knoll, over and over again. It wouldn't stop.

Boots clomped, and laughter rang down the hall as his chevaliers arrived. Rayne had accompanied them.

Should he send her away? Mysti would only tell her sister later. She might as well hear it now. She was a range wolf and would follow orders. He stared blindly out the large windows. Storm clouds were stacking up in the east. How apropos.

"You summoned us, sire?" Levity brightened Alexion's baritone.

"Yes." The single word clipped out hard. "We are waiting for a few more people to arrive." Everything he said sounded so harsh, cold; however, if he relaxed even an increment he'd have a breakdown in the middle of the library. He was only nineteen summers. How by the blessed Mother was he supposed to fix this? Four years wearing the crown and the Mother still hadn't graced him with acknowledgement.

Dante heard them still and come to silent attention. He rarely demanded deference from them, but they knew him well enough to know when it was required.

Several agonizing minutes of waiting went by before another set of footsteps shuffled in. "My boy, what has you summoning me at this hour, and by such a busy little page girl? Why, she wouldn't even let me finish my story. The little pages usually spare a few minutes to sit and rest for the duration of a tale," Krane scolded gently as he joined them.

"She's not little, so I've been rather emphatically told. I'm afraid her errands for me were rather urgent. I apologize for the interruption of your tale." Dante stayed at the window.

"Ach." The older man shrugged. "Keeps the pups in suspense until next time. What's this about then?"

Keer caught his father's arm and whispered into his ear.

"Huh, in suspense ourselves then, aye?" Krane hitched his robes and sat on a divan. "Well, we will have to be patient and wait, won't we?"

Dante itched at the burn scars that rippled the skin over his hip. They ached today as they always did when a storm was building. Captain Brice and Captain Lask arrived within minutes of one another. With all his people gathered, he moved to one of the solitary bookshelves, another of the servants' passages.

"Captain Brice, Captain Lask, thank you for coming so quickly. There are matters we need to discuss." He led the group into the hollow walls. During normal council hours, they would use the regular halls, but he wanted to keep the rumors to a minimum so they could get a plan in place before panic set in. They slipped into the map room behind closed doors.

"Alexion, secure the doors. I don't want barged in on."

Dante waited until they settled and took his seat at the end of the huge, oval table. Frowns scored the faces of his people. Dante focused on the world map embossed into the surface of the table, the Mother tree dominating the center. He didn't want to see their faces fill with fear. "As some of you know, I rescued the Owlderah Crown Princess a few days ago and granted her sanctuary. She was wounded and alone, feverish. Today, she informed me that the Owlderah citadel has fallen. Her people are held captive by the Kobrona family. Princess Owlderah has told me that they do not plan to stop there. The Kobrona are targeting our people next."

"What?" Keer asked. In other circumstances, it would be hilarious to see that look on his face. Dante didn't get one up on him often.

"But, why?" Captain Brice asked. "What do we have that they want? Alternatively, the Owlderah? What do they have? Why are the Kobrona doing this?"

Dante raked his fingers through his hair. "I don't know. I don't believe that Princess Owlderah knows either." He hesitated, wondering if they'd even believe him. "One thing the healers found, and the princess confirmed herself, is that the Kobrona are using death magic." Even the air stilled as all breathing stopped in horror. His heartbeat pounded in his ears. There, he'd said it.

Krane braced his arms on the table. "My boy, are you quite sure?"

Dante said, "She is."

"Can we trust the word of a girl?" Captain Brice asked. "Even if she's a princess?"

"She is no younger than I, and I believe her. There is no faking a fear like that, and Healer Gracia found traces of the death magic taint upon her. Princess Owlderah said Queen Jeziah has been enslaved under its influence. Through her, Lord Kobrona undoubtedly controls the entire family."

"Death magic hasn't been heard of for centuries!" Captain Brice's bulk slumped back in his chair with a defiant thud.

"And yet the evidence lies in bed mere rooms away from us." Dante dared them to question him again. He knew how insane this sounded, but it was true, and they had to do something—anything.

"Captain Lask?" Rayne spoke up. She fidgeted under their sudden focus. "Aren't the eastern border patrols late in returning this month?" Her face was pale and pinched with worry. She shared a glance with Mysti.

The beads in Captain Lask's hair rattled as he shook his head. "Only by a few days. Nothing to cause any concern. I was going to send a recruit to fetch them tomorrow."

Dante jumped on that. "If it is as it seems, then the Kobrona have already begun. Send two range teams out. Tell them to be on high alert. It is likely the Kobrona have sent out their own teams to eliminate anyone who walks the borders. We currently have the advantage of time, thanks to Princess Nakai. They do not know that Princess Nakai made it here and gave warning. We must prepare. It is only a fortnight's travel from the Owlderah fortress."

"That is not a lot of time, sire. However, snakes do not travel as the owls or we do. I believe it will take them longer. Plus, a full army takes a long time to move." Keer had his fingers steepled in front of his mouth as he spoke.

"So, about a month perhaps?" Mysti said.

Captain Lask nodded. "Sounds right."

"How are we to defend against death magic?" Raphael snapped across the table.

Dante stifled a growl. He didn't know. The last war took place two hundred years ago. He knew how to fight a duel; yet, he knew little about warfare. He was the prince, but he did not know how to protect his people. Death magic was supposed to be a legend.

In the silence of horrified confusion, Keer's quill tapped incessantly. Dante gritted his teeth against the sound and let his friend think. The impending thunderstorm weighted the room with oppressive heat, and it felt as though he couldn't get enough air.

"Why aren't we discussing this with the court?" Raphael asked. "We cannot do anything without their approval. Lord Kiba, at least, should be here." He planted his hand on the table as he leaned forward to make his point—that they were stupid for even discussing this without the nobles. Never mind that Dante did not, in fact, need to ask them permission for anything.

Rayne and Mysti gasped in unison. Even Captain Lask grunted at Raphael's audacity.

Dante's innards froze. A sense of betrayal shattered into stabbing, icy shards that bled away the last of his strength. Not Raphael too? Mother bless, was he so unfit for his birthright that his First and his Second doubted him? He knew Raphael was sometimes disappointed in him because he didn't measure up to his father's high example, but did he fail so utterly? Did he truly believe that Lord Kiba, and the sniveling dogs that ate out of his hand, were a better option than he was?

"Why should we?" Keer dared ask Raphael the question Dante couldn't bring himself to.

"Because we have no king!" Raphael paled as his words hit the air, but pressed on. "Because Prince Dante has not been blessed by the Mother, even after four years of bearing the crown." He dropped back into his chair as everyone stared at him.

"So... you feel he is unfit to lead? That Lord Kiba and the court can commune with the Heart of Ookamimori better than Prince Dante?" Stipes leapt to Dante's defense, against his cousin. That was going to make waves in their tentative truce.

"No." Raphael swore. "Sire, no, that's not what I intended to say. I only meant that, perhaps, someone with more experience would be of a benefit right now."

Dante covered his face with a shaking hand, blocking out the light glaring off the glossy table. The headache that had been steadily building spiked with painful intensity. Raphael had pushed for more from him since the day he had transferred from the king's chevaliers to Dante's, as tradition dictated. It was an honor to be the heir's shield and guide, an already-experienced chevalier given to support the heir and the First chevalier. It was an unwanted honor. Raphael had wanted to remain in the service of the king. Dante thought that Raphael had never completely forgiven him for that; nevertheless, Raphael pushed Dante to be the best he could be. Sometimes he pushed too hard and overstepped, but this....

Enough.

"Enough," he said it aloud against the stilted silence. "The Mother has not yet gifted me her blessing, but neither has she reputed me. Until she does, I will do by best for Ookamimori." Dante lifted his head, glaring at Raphael and daring him to challenge his authority again.

"Right now, my best plan is to hash out all possible solutions to our approaching enemy before inciting a squabbling panic amidst the nobles. I brought each of you here because I trust you to help me lay out a workable plan. Is that something you can do, or do I need to cut down our numbers and sequester myself and leave you out of it entirely?" Dante aimed the question at the whole table, but he stared at Raphael. Raphael looked away and tilted his head to expose his throat submissively.

"Anyone else want to present doubts about my general incompetence and unworthiness to carry the Canidea bloodline?"

Raphael shrank deeper into his seat. Nobody else spoke.

"I know my father was a better king than I can ever hope to be. My court tells me so every single day." Dante mentally locked it all down, the stress, the betrayal, and the overwhelming jumble of fear. "Today is not about issues with me. Today, right now, is about giving everything we have to ensure my people's survival against a war that was inconceivable an hour ago. If you believe that I am incapable of leading and cannot bow to my orders, then leave. I will expect your resignation tomorrow."

"This is foolishness," Captain Lask said. "The Heart still speaks with you, sire, does it not?"

Dante nodded sharply.

"Then I say, foolishness. You are our prince. I have heard of the blessing taking decades before the Mother bestows them upon her children. The nobles of the court"—Captain Lask drew it out like a dirty word— "are selfish and pampered, minus Lord Kiba, of course. He's just an ass."

Raphael was white with rage, but he wouldn't dare chew out the man for his disrespect. The captain was a noble of the highest breeding, above even his own. That was part of Raphael's strength and his weakness—his knowledge and observance of the noble hierarchy. It interfered with his relationships. Especially with Stipes, as his half of the family was low-born. Somewhere a rift, a feud, had been born between the noble side and the common side, and Stipes bore the brunt of Raphael's attitude over it. Dante hadn't settled on a solution for it yet. There was one, but its resolution was years away, when Korren came of age.

"Is evacuation a viable option?" Mysti asked. abruptly, bringing them back on topic.

Dante flinched when he met her eyes. She vibrated in her seat with a fury unlike any he'd witnessed, even after this morning. Alexion had a hand clamped on her shoulder and was whispering into her ear. Dante hoped her fury was aimed at Raphael. He deserved it after that outburst. If his Second had said his piece in front of the court, Dante would have spent months rebalancing the scales he struggled to maintain. If Dante had a bonded elemental at his side, none of them would doubt his reign. The Mother would not be rushed, assuming he was not merely a placeholder for the throne until she chose someone worthier, like Korren when he came of age.

Krane picked up the theme of subject change. "Not everyone will leave, and we do not want a panic. However, the Jacklyn and the Mother's forest are our best chance for refuge. The other families are too far and in the wrong direction."

"So, if we prepare two caravans to leave with everyone that will go, what about those who remain?" Captain Brice asked.

"You and I, old friend," Captain Lask said. "We must distract the Kobrona. My range-wolves can slow them down in the forest. Hit and run tactics. Maybe even cut off their supply train. If your men can do the same within the city, we can buy some time for the other families to step in and provide reinforcements. They will not allow this sacrilege to continue."

Stipes joined in. "What about the Lupinic family? They are the closest. Could they take some of our people or help hold back the Kobrona?"

"The pass is too small for a large group to make it through, and they are reclusive. No one sees them outside of the Communion."

Keer cut off Alexion's ramble. "The Communion is on the equinox. All the families will attend. Kobrona cannot stand against the combined force of the families. If we can hold out until then…."

The Communion. A meeting of the families where all disputes were settled and enforced by the royals and the Mother's priestesses. Every three years, the families gathered beneath the Mother's branches. It was a few short months away. It could be their salvation. Dante's thoughts raced. With his runners, the other families would be alerted to the threat and prepared. The Mother's high priestesses would not allow death magic to be worked upon the sacred lands. Kobrona's war would be lost.

"With Lask's aid, I believe we could hold out that long, sire. However, you, Lady Petria, and the little prince should evacuate with the caravans. Everything is lost if they capture you. Through you, they will have all Ookamimori," Captain Brice said.

Krane grunted an immediate agreement. "If they are using death magic to enslave the Owlderah Queen, they will almost certainly attempt the same here. You must make your escape plans, sire. Do it for us, or we will fall."

They wanted Dante to abandon them then. No. He refused to let them die while he ran away. Dante kept this resolution to himself as they started piecing together the semblance of a plan.

He had one more resource to tap for advice, and perhaps he could provide his patrollers and range wolves with a little bit of backup.

Chapter Five

Nakai

A haze of distress and sticky heat confused her mind. Nakai flopped fitfully. Her legs tangled in the cloying bed sheets. Moaning in pained fury, she kicked futilely at the blankets. They twisted tighter and trapped her arms in an uncomfortable embrace. She lay still, defeated. Someone made hushed orders that she couldn't quite understand. She looked around. A white blur bent over her. Nakai flinched before it focused into the face of an old woman wearing a healer's headdress.

"Oh, poor dearie, all tangled up." Gentle hands tugged at the constricting blankets. Nakai gasped. Weary heat dragged her back into the darkness of sleep as the healer leaned over her. "There now, dearie. You rest up."

Nakai didn't struggle against sleep. Here, she was safe. No nightmares, no reality. Both of which frightened her, though she could not think why.

A hand traced softly over her skin, leaving a clean, bright sensation in its wake. Healing magic. She followed the strands of magic until her eyes opened. Blinking sleepily, Nakai saw unfamiliar bed-curtains drawn about the bed, light crystals glowing through a crack. The color was wrong, too greenish a hue. Those were not the crystals of Hanehishou. She was not at home. Confusion stole over her jumbled thoughts until sleep drew her back to its spell.

The clinking of glass woke her this time. Nakai rubbed her eyes and planted a hand on the mattress, struggling to sit up. She didn't get far. The pillow caught Nakai as her arms shook and gave out. "Ow," she moaned.

Pain ached from her shoulder to her elbow, reminding her of the wound given to her by Kobrona's guards. Kobrona! Terror fused her muscles with energy and dulled the pain. Nakai scrambled to sit upright, trembling on her knees. Looking around for some sign of Kobrona guards or an escape route, Nakai saw only a bright, sunny room with large windows opened wide to let in the fresh summer air. Fabric rustled, and Nakai turned too fast, making her head spin.

"Oh my." It was a healer, her uniform similar to those at home, red scarf draped over her hair and all. "Little Dearie, everything is just fine. You are safe here. Our Prince Dante will protect you. He is a youngling, like you, but he is honorable. He will help you with your troubles if you but ask. Now, there will be time for that later. We will bring him in as soon as you are well enough. Here, let us get you settled."

Bewildered, Nakai allowed the elderly healer to guide her back to the fluffed pillows. She stretched out her legs, and the woman pulled the blankets up with a neat snap.

The healer brushed her tattooed fingers over Nakai's forehead, and a warm sparkling sensation spread through Nakai's skin. "Ah, your fever has cleared away completely now. Good. You still have a bit of a cold though, dearie." She picked up a glass from the side table. "Here, drink this. It will help with the pain from your wound. I'm afraid it was infected and too much for me to heal entirely. Even with magic, the body can only do so much. This will help you heal faster and give you some nutrients to put some fat on those bones. You need to eat more. You are much too skinny."

Nakai swallowed a bitter response—it hadn't been her choice not to eat—before it burdened the kind healer. She took the glass filled with a brownish, herbal-smelling liquid. "I will try to. Thank you for your care, Lady Healer," Nakai whispered. She obediently tipped the liquid into her mouth. Shuddering at the taste, Nakai gulped it down as fast as she could. It wasn't magically going to go away if she drank it slowly.

"Oh posh, none of that lady stuff. The healer waggled a gnarled finger under Nakai's nose. "You may call me, Gracia."

"Gracia, thank you."

A deep cough rattled her lungs. Nakai sniffled and brought her arm up to rub snot from her nose like a small child too exhausted to be ashamed.

"Oh my! Here, use this for your nose. Your sleeve is not a good handkerchief." Gracia brought her a square of soft fabric.

Nakai took it, blushing. "I'm sorry." Blowing her nose increased the pressure in her head. Curling onto her side, Nakai pulled the comforting blanket up nearly over her head and burrowed in the pillow. The pounding in her head eased with the cushioning and support, and she slept.

She awoke a few times for brief moments to receive more potions. Each one of the medicines had a varied, horrible flavor or texture. Many of them seemed to make her tired, shoving her forcefully back into sleep. The sunbeams shone through the curtains when Gracia finally propped her up on her pillows. She placed a tray of soup, fresh bread, and diced fruit over her lap.

"Ah, truly awake at last, dearie. Here, eat this and I will send a page after our prince. He has been asking after you. He caught a fever as well and has only just got out of bed himself. He will be glad to speak to you."

Abruptly reminded of the horrors that had brought her to the Canidea Family, Nakai peered into her soup bowl with a squelchy stomach. How could she eat while Ashliene starved in the tower?

Healer Gracia seemed to understand. "You must eat to regain your strength. As a princess, I am sure you have many important things needing to be done, and you can't do them on an empty stomach."

Nakai nodded, gathering up her spoon and ignoring the rebellious roil of her stomach, took a slurp from the broth-filled spoon. Small bits of chicken floated with the flavors of onions and herbs. It was good, better than anything she had eaten in a long time. The warm bread pulled apart with a crunch of the flaky crust. Butter dripped into her soup as she used the bread to soak up more of the broth. A moan of appreciation escaped her, despite her guilt.

Gracia nodded with a pleased smile. "Good. You will feel much better."

Indeed, her stomach growled for more. Nakai savored every bite. Only years of court manners kept her from tearing into it like a beast. It had been weeks since she'd had more than stale bread and gruel. Whatever Kobrona wanted them for, he didn't need them well-fed.

One of Gracia's apprentices handed over a potion. "One more, please."

Nakai sighed and reached for the glass. As she lifted it toward her mouth, she heard a male voice in the sitting room Gracia had entered. A young man with shaggy black hair stepped into the room. He exuded a lethal grace.

"Princess Owlderah, I am glad you are awake at last. I am the Prince, Dante Rayve'en Canidea. Welcome. Find shelter in my lands and among my people."

Nakai pulled on all of her training as a royal and responded formally. "Thank you. I ask sanctuary as Crown Princess, Nakai Cattrianna Owlderah."

"Granted."

Relief flooded through her veins. Help. She finally had help. Bolstering her strength, Nakai fought to stay upright and spoke, the darkness spilling out of her lips like venom out of a wound. She saw the weight of her words fall on Prince Dante shoulders. He swayed as he left, carrying the burden Kobrona laid upon them all.

It was a guilty relief to burrow back into the pillows and sleep, leaving another to deal with the terrible doings. Kobrona had ripped everything away from her, and with her duty as princess done, she could mourn as a young woman who'd lost her entire world in a storm of blood.

Silent tears scalded her cheeks as she waited for the prince to leave and for the door to close, leaving her alone. Only then did she sob. A pillow pressed to her face muffled the sound of her grief.

Her father was slain brutally, and his death used to turn her mother into a doll keyed to Lord Kobrona's every command. Her baby sister, Ashe, she'd abandoned in the tower, chained to the cold stony walls and surrounded by evil serpents. Nakai had failed to free her when she'd made her escape.

Nakai wailed into the fabric as the emotions she'd locked away to complete her mission finally broke free. She swept her thumb across the four grayed tattoos on her wrist, desperate for a response from the chevalier connection, even though she knew none would come. They were dead. The precious lifeblood of her chevaliers painted the cobblestone streets of Hanehishou. Never again would Asumi's confident words spur her onward when her mother disregarded the common people's troubles for the nobles' petty squabbles, or Osskair's heavy presence lend strength to her back when she was weary and overwhelmed. Never again would her First Chevalier, Talaya, give her a motherly hug and stare down any who defied her; and the deepest blow of all, her Fourth, Shota, her constant silent shadow, always there when she needed him, offering that gentle smile.

Nakai cried until she couldn't breathe. Until the storm clouds blotted out the sun and the sky cried with her.

Chapter Six

The swelling storm clouds were like a hot, sweltering blanket. The bazaar overflowed with people. Some in human form, others running their errands as wolves. There were even a few in dyre form, a merge of wolf and human. They carried great loads of goods that the other forms could not have managed.

As planned, Dante's clothes were just plain enough that no one would recognize him as their prince. He did not wish to be swarmed. Merchants would shove their wares under his face for approval. Girls, shyly approaching, would offer flowers, and women would tug their blouses low. Men would glare jealously while the boys would beg to be allowed into his guard. Walking among his people freely, required subterfuge. Blending in as a commoner was a precious gift, one given to him by the thieves' guild years before. It let him feel the emotions of his city without the subservient masks portrayed to the prince.

A pack of kids played tag nearby. They shifted from humans to pups and back again as they raced to dodge the 'it' one. The pups yipped and giggled in excitement as they fled. A brown pup shifted in midair. She landed on two feet instead of four and sprinted for a low-hanging tree. She scrambled up just in time to avoid the touch of the tagger's wet nose. The girl crouched safely in the tree and giggled as the tagger dashed after easier targets. The other kids shrieked in playful fear and scattered.

Dante watched their careless freedom wistfully.

Indulgent mothers laughed at the game and turned back to their shopping. One father scooped up his boy as he raced past and proclaimed it was time to go home to multiple moans of disappointment.

Kobrona wanted to destroy this peace. Why? It was pointless destruction. There was nothing for him to gain from it that Dante could see, only senseless slaughter.

Dante touched the tattoos on his wrist to ensure the bond was open. He had people to talk to, people he was not introducing to his chevaliers anytime soon, but he didn't want Mysti to worry. Not today. Not with the impending threat.

Hard hands grabbed his arms on either side and hauled him backward into the bushes. Dante twisted and struggled, but he didn't try to summon his chevaliers. He could handle this himself. The two men held him tight.

A third person, a woman, leaned in close enough that her breath ghosted over his lips. Dante kicked out, half-heartedly trying for a shattered kneecap, but she danced away as soundless as a wraith. She sneered her disdain for his failed attempt. The lithe woman led the way through the park into the darkest alleys.

Trapped between his captors, weariness kept him compliant. If he hadn't so desperately needed to talk to Calume, he would not have braved the streets at all. The trio kidnapping him dragged him to a nondescript house that sat between several other nondescript houses. Nothing stood out about the building. It was built of plain brick. Ivy framed the worn door as it did on nearly every other house on the block. Dante wondered if he was going to regret not putting up more of a fight as they dragged him inside. Probably.

The two men holding his biceps released him in the dim hallway. The door swung shut on his heels, and heavy bars dropped into place, closing off all possibility of escape.

"Crap, Dante, you really did get sick. You always fight us when we tag you. Not even one proper escape attempt. Pathetic." The woman crowded closer and poked at his stomach with a sharp fingernail. "You, all right?"

Dante shrugged. "I was coming here anyway. Did not really see the point of fighting. Besides, Mysti kicked my butt a few hours ago. I don't need any more bruises." He didn't feel the need to admit to passing out too. The twins would never let him live it down.

She frowned and placed a bare wrist against his forehead. "You ain't fevered."

He knew he should have fought harder. Now, Leigha was going to fuss as bad as his chevaliers. He did not enjoy being smothered by mother hens. Dante caught her fingers and kissed them lightly. "I'm fine, Leigha. Just tired. I did have a nasty fever, but I am fine now. Your sweet, cooling touch shall ensure it will not return."

The kidnapper on his left rolled his eyes. "Oh, shut up, Dante," Derrick said and dug an elbow into Dante's bruised ribs.

Dante winced. Mysti had landed some solid hits. Dante retaliated with a foot hooked around Derrick's ankle. A satisfying thud declared his revenge as Derrick hit the floor. The remaining member of the kidnapping trio had taken refuge in the shadowy rafters.

"You don't really believe you are safe up there, Raiven?" Dante asked, tilting his head back to watch, not focusing on the shadows but waiting for them to move.

"I'm quite safe." Raiven's voice held quiet laughter.

Dante pulled two of his small blades and flicked them into the concealing shadows. One struck wood with a reverberating thud. The other blade made no audible landing. Dante listened carefully. The near silent slicing of air was his only warning. He turned his head to the side as the small blade whispered past. He was not stupid enough to try to catch a blade he could barely see. He valued his fingers, thank you very much. Pulling the throwing knife from the door, he sheathed it.

"You're right, Derrick, there's nothin' wrong with him," Leigha said, rolling her eyes.

"Would you be so kind as to return the other blade as well, Raiven?" Dante asked. The throwing blade slammed into the floor at his feet. "Thank you."

His mission to set his friends at ease completed, Dante waved them off. "I need to see him." They nodded and let him walk away.

Dante trudged the squeaky stairs to the second floor. The Thief Lord's door was closed. Dante rapped and opened it when assent came as a calm rumble through the door. Once more, his only warning was the whisper of air splitting. This time though, he caught them. He knew from experience that they were training blades. The wooden replicas would not fillet his fingers if he fumbled them.

"Calume!"

"Oh, Dante, it's you. Sorry, I thought it was Jothan. I have been training him lately." The grizzled man sitting comfortably behind the heavy desk had a mischievous glint on his otherwise stern face.

"Of course. Quite all right. Practice makes perfect, after all." Dante did not believe his mentor's pitiful excuse whatsoever. The wooden blades, while not sharp, were heavy, and thrown by his mentor could leave painful knots on the skull of his target. Calume enjoyed tormenting his students, new or old, but especially the old.

"Ah, you have retained some of my imparted wisdom. I'm so proud!"

"This Jothan must be quite the prodigy if you are testing him with five blades already." Dante displayed the smooth, oak weapons in his hands. The five weapons, instead of being pointed and streamlined like knives, were rounded and knobbish, perfect for giving unfortunate students bruises.

A twitching lip gave him away. "Well, he catches three sometimes."

"I see," Dante said, nodding. "Yet you winged five at the door. Is the poor boy in for a harsh lesson, or did you know one of your top apprentices approached by the knock on the door?"

Calume snorted with disgust. "Sit down before the floor collapses from the weight of your princely fat head. Of course, I knew it was you. I sent the trio to fetch you, didn't I? And actually, yes, Jothan is good. For a beginner, Jothan is doing splendidly.

"Keep him away from Derrick then. He'll make him a smart-aleck. Raiven will take the wind out the kid's sails though if he gets uppity."

Calume laughed. "Yes, but the problem there is getting the kid to Raiven while avoiding Derrick. I swear those two are handcuffed together. Must be the twin thing." Dante tossed the training blades on the desk.

Calume got up and moved to a cupboard. "Brandy?"

The question was a formality. Usually, Dante disliked the fiery stuff. "Please."

"What?" Calume's eyes narrowed.

Dante knew Calume's mind was already calculating potential issues. He would never guess this one. "I could use it. It's been a bit of a day."

Calume quirked an eyebrow but obligingly poured two shots. He said nothing, only handed over a glass of amber liquid, and retook his seat behind his desk. Dante was glad he did not pry, allowing him time to gather his depressed thoughts.

He took a fortifying swallow and grimaced at the warm burn. He really did hate this stuff. Still, it dulled the turmoil in his head. "I believe our lands are going to fall under Kobrona rule within a month. Two, tops."

The whole terrible story poured out as his mentor listened intently. Dante clutched the glass in his hand. "I don't know what to do, Calume. It seems so unreal, but I have Princess Owlderah starved and wounded in my castle as we speak. She is absolutely certain of what she has witnessed." Leaning forward, Dante gently set the glass on Calume's desk before he threw it against the wall. "Have you heard of anything abnormal from your sister guilds?"

Calume aged before his eyes as the weight of Dante's news furrowed his brow and formed new wrinkles. Dante wondered if he'd added yet another gray hair to his mentor's head. The thief lord answered him wearily, "No, I'm afraid I haven't. It's been relatively quiet on all fronts. Although, if he is binding them with death magic, perhaps they haven't been able to get anyone out with a message. The Kobrona have one of the largest cities. If they are all bound or following their insane prince, then we are vastly outnumbered. You said that Queen Owlderah is bound. That means Prince Kobrona owns her people's obedience for fear of her safety." Rubbing his temples, Calume said, "I just don't understand why he's leaving the royals alive. If he wants the land, he'd be better off killing the royal bloodline. It takes time for the Mother to choose a royal lineage. There's just no purpose to any of it."

Dante sagged. If his closest mentor was befuddled and unsure, how the hell was he supposed to know what to do?

"You can do this, Dante." Calume read him too accurately. "I trained you well. You need to stay clear and calm. You are a leader. A good one. You can save your people."

"Do you really think so?" Dante begged softly. Here with Calume, he could let the mask of capable prince fall. His father had not succeeded to the throne until he was thirty-seven. Dante was only nineteen. Without his friends and Calume's support, he would have failed before all of this. He still might.

"Call in Leigha, Derrick, and Raiven. We must make our own plans to accompany the ones already laid," Calume ordered. Dante did so, stepping to the door and shouting down the hall, and they settled down for his second war council of the day.

Chapter Seven

Dante flailed out of sleep and away from the image of his fiery death. Mother bless, he hated that one. More so because it was a memory. His scars itched. Dante rubbed the tight skin around his eye. The memory of flames still flickered at the edge of his vision.

It had been two deceptively peaceful weeks since Princess Nakai had given her dire warning.

The princess had offered precious little new information when she awoke again, so Dante had sent his runners to warn the other families. One messenger had returned with laughter ringing in his ears. The Eagalia hadn't believed him. Even Dante's court doubted the news. They refused to listen or prepare. Lord Kiba stayed quiet, not adding to the derision. Dante wished he understood how that man's mind worked. Undermining Dante constantly and then keeping his mouth shut when it was something serious, when Dante almost wanted the man to step up and say he wasn't good enough to handle it. Dante wasn't good enough; he knew that. He still had to try, though. It was his duty.

Dante gave up sleep for the remainder of the night.

The new moon shadowed his window. The only light in the sky was that of the thousands of twinkling stars. The awful, early hour did not matter. Dante shoved the sweat-dampened, Spidarian silk sheets away. His hands shook as he dressed. He tried to slow his racing breath, but the Heart was distressed. He'd never felt it pulse beneath his feet like this before.

The urge to move drove him toward the door, but he stopped, still feeling naked and vulnerable. Dante went back and lifted his soul-forged sword from the wall mount. He could summon it anytime, but right now he needed the weight of steel along his spine. Dante secured the heavy katana and ensured his sheath held his daggers.

Nightmares of fire and terror throughout the recent nights ruined any sense of rest, and his nerves were frayed. He hid it as best he could behind a cool, determined mask. It wasn't really working. Mysti was going to start nagging if he didn't pull it together.

His feet carried him toward the princess's suite instead of the kitchens as he'd intended. He didn't wish to wake her. He just needed to see her. Didn't that make him sound like a creep? He slunk into her room anyway.

Healer Gracia slept on the couch. Dante smiled fondly and crept past her. She always stayed with her patients. She did much the same for him since he was a babe, always there to comfort him and take away his hurts.

Dante ghosted into the bedroom on a thief's feet. He didn't go further than the threshold. With a touch of magic, he drew on the wolf and enhanced his hearing. He'd listen to her heartbeat and then go, assured of her life. Nothing more.

Light flared from a crystal.

Dante jumped, like a guilty peeper. The princess was awake. She sat cross-legged on the bed. A crystal cradled in her hand, and she stuck her thumb in her mouth to suck off the blood required to awaken it.

Her golden eyes pinned him with regal confidence. "Prince Dante," she said, greeting him as though a man strolling into her bedroom in the dead of night was a common and droll occurrence.

Dante coughed, exposed under her pinning gaze. "Ah, please forgive me for disturbing you. I merely wished to ascertain your health." Busted, he was completely busted. She had every right to scream his house down and demand his head. Mother bless it, this looked bad. It was bad.

He only hoped this didn't get around. He didn't know who would be worse about it: Derrick, who would tease him mercilessly; or Mysti, who would straight-up murder him.

The princess stayed absurdly calm. "I am feeling much better. Your healers are quite skilled. Although, the brews are not particularly desirable." She kindly did not point out that it was beyond the middle of the night.

"I agree most sincerely with you there. They have been forcing them down my throat quite regularly these days too," Dante said. Why wasn't she having hysterics? Lady Petria would if she caught him in her room, and she was his aunt.

She twisted the fabric of her blankets around her fingers. "That is my fault. You became ill trying to save me. I am sorry." A harsh cough rasped out of her throat and she folded over, wheezing. Dante almost went out to wake Healer Gracia, when she sat back up and stopped him. "Please, no, I am all right. Don't wake her. She has been busy. I'm so sorry."

"You have no reason to be. You didn't ask me to jump in a freezing river. You aren't bringing an army here. You warned us." He looked away, ashamed, and said, "Though there is little we can do to oppose them. Our city is not built to defend."

"What will you do then?" Princess Owlderah asked. Her concern sharpened the question until it stabbed.

Dante flinched. "I tried to convince my nobles that they should evacuate to one of our allies or claim refuge beneath the Mother's branches. They would be out of his reach for a time, at least; perhaps long enough for the other families to take control of the Kobrona." Dante couldn't meet her eyes.

"Did they not wish to leave you? Their loyalty is to be applauded."

Dante's shame deepened. "Quite the opposite, I'm afraid. They refused to entertain the idea and laughed themselves out of the castle." A bitter laugh of his own escaped him.

"But why? Do they not believe you? I am strong enough to give testament if they are too blind to trust in their prince."

"I have worn the crown since I was fifteen. The Mother has yet to give me her blessing. Some of the nobles believe I am unworthy of my bloodline."

His father's blessing, an earth elemental, had held impressive stature, all lichened wood and mottled stone, a merging of living and foundation earth. A perfect fit for the Canidea King. Dante's father had gained the Mother's blessing and direct guidance mere months into his reign. The elemental had died with him in the fire elemental's attack upon Ookamimori.

"That gives them no right to ridicule you!" Princess Owlderah's scorn echoed in every syllable.

The abrupt absence of rumbling snores from the outer room caused him to glance at the doorway. Healer Gracia would scold him to an inch of his life if she caught him in here. He would hide under the bed if he had to.

A flicker of magic and glowing crimson eyes rushed out of the darkness. Startled, Dante fell backward to the floor, avoiding the slash of a blade at his throat. Without his ability to see magic, he would have died right there. Rolling with the momentum brought him back to his feet with two daggers firmly in hand from his boots. The masked assassin bore down on him with a wet stiletto gleaming in one hand, and a sword in the other. Dante redirected the sword with his right blade, twisting sideways to slip away from the stiletto aimed at his stomach. The assassin overextended. Dante plunged his dagger into vital kidneys. It was a vicious wound. A fatal wound. He kept coming. The musky scent of spice and blood wafted in his wake. A Kobrona shifter.

Distantly, Dante admired the stamina of the shifter and wondered why he wasn't dead yet. Ducking low, Dante lashed out at the assassin's stomach. His blades caught only cloth. The assassin was obviously faster than he was.

He growled and retreated into the open floor of the princess's room. The assassin's eyes gleamed a violent shade of purple in the crystal's blue light.

Princess Owlderah crouched on the bed poised with a wide, serrated knife. Where in the Mother's branches had she gotten that?

Dante sidestepped to keep the assassin's attention on him. He kicked the shifter's knee. Bone cracked. The assassin stumbled and hissed, the first sound he had made. With a slash of the dagger, Dante feinted the assassin into one final turn, offering the shifter's unprotected back to Princess Owlderah. She struck without hesitation. Her knife sank deep between his shoulder blades, crunching into bone. Air stilled. The assassin slid off the knife to the thick rug, a limp corpse where only seconds ago had been one of the Mother's children.

Dante heaved in deep breaths to slow his racing pulse, and tried not to gag. "We must rouse the others. There will be more than one. Kobrona has begun his attack with assassins rather than an army. You will have to leave with us to be safe. I had hoped to give you the option of traveling with the nobles if I convinced them to leave."

"I will come with you. Give me a moment to dress." Princess Owlderah gave the body a trembling sneer. The forced composure didn't last. She clamped a hand over her mouth as she skittered around the corpse to the wardrobe.

Dante stepped into the outer room to give her privacy. His hands shook as he tried to sheathe his daggers in his boots and nearly stabbed his leg.

The room was still and quiet. Healer Gracia! What had the assassin done to her? Dante locked down the fact that he'd killed a living, breathing person. Ended a shifter's life. He had to take care of his own before he wasted concern on the person who'd attacked him.

Healer Gracia lay exactly as she had when he'd snuck through earlier, only the slackness in the wrinkles of her face was wrong. The smell of blood filled his nostrils. It was strong. Too strong. He knew that but still felt for a pulse. Gracia's skin was warm, but life no longer thrummed through her veins. Blood oozed from a wound at the base of her skull. The assassin had thrust a blade through her spine into her brain. An instant, silent kill. Thank the Mother for that at least. Grief burned his eyes, but tears didn't fall.

The healer that had nursed him since birth was gone, stolen by a thin spike of metal and a royal gone insane. He pulled the crocheted blanket over her face. "May the pack run swiftly to greet you as we howl our goodbyes. Let the moon shine brightly as you hunt, and the Mother's branches cradle you close," he whispered. The magic of her strong spirit would spill out and merge into the wild magic, as they all rejoined the Mother when they died. Knowing this didn't quench his guilt. He had been right there, and he had failed her. Just as he failed to save his father.

He had never killed before, not a person anyway. Calume raised a thief, not a killer. Dante had a sinking feeling it would be a long time before he forgot the feeling of his blades slicing through flesh. The princess struck the killing blow, but his would have killed the serpent shifter eventually, only it would have taken longer and been painful.

Fingers brushed his arm. Dante lurched and reached for his blades. "We should go," Princess Owlderah said. "Healer Gracia was kind to me, and I mourn her return to the Mother."

He didn't doubt the sincerity of the tears sparkling unfallen in her eyes. "Yes, the Mother will welcome her home." Dante swallowed heavily and led the way out.

There was a tentative escape plan in place, and this was the reason they'd made it.

Dante pushed alarmed magic into the bracelet of tattooed runes until they glowed. He willed all of them to awaken through the connection. Four sparks of magic answered. His chevaliers were alerted, but he had to get to Keer.

The empty corridors were deathly silent. It was, after all, the dead of night. Even the bakers would not have risen yet to begin their loaves.

Dante did not pause to knock at Keer's door. He pushed in carefully and scanned for shadows that moved. All seemed peaceful. Not even bothering to check the bedroom, Dante went to the office. As expected, Keer slumped over his desk; his cheek smooshed on his papers. For a long, terrifying moment, Dante wondered if Keer lay too still. If he'd find another puncture in the skull of a loved one.

Keer snuffled.

Dante jabbed his cheek. "Keer, wake up. Wake up!" Mother bless, his best friend could sleep like a block of granite. Dante grabbed a half-filled pitcher and upended it over his friend's head, heedless of the paperwork. It could be rewritten.

Keer bolted upright. "Whah?"

"We have to leave. Now. Assassins are in the castle. Actually, I do not think they are trying to kill us, but they are here now and not for peaceful reasons."

"Assassins? What? How do you know? Did you fight them? Are you alright?" Keer's hands flailed around furiously.

Dante huffed and slapped a hand over his pack brother's mouth to stop the flood of questions. "A thousand times yes, before you ask again. He's dead and I'm fine. Get ready to go, and hurry. We have to bring Korren and my aunt with us too. Meet the others at the barracks and tell them what's going on."

"Understood." Keer shoved his chair back with a painful screech. Trotting into the bedroom, Keer called over his shoulder, "Go! I'm just grabbing some things."

"Be careful," Dante begged. Spinning around he prayed to the Mother that he would lose no one else tonight.

Every familiar shadow seemed to leer with a new threat. Dante had never felt fear within his home before. He struggled to keep his fingers relaxed around the hilt of his dagger. Princess Owlderah kept up. He should have sent her with Keer. She would've been safer with his chevaliers, but he was glad for the fierce presence beside him.

They were forced to abandon the supposed safety of the servants' passages within the walls to reach Lady Petria's rooms as none of them connected directly to any of the rooms. Easing out from behind a concealing tapestry, Dante felt a crawling in his nose as dust filtered down from the heavy fabric. He clamped a hand over his nose to stifle the explosive sneeze. Holding the tapestry open for the princess with his free hand, he peered down the hall. The sneeze almost escaped him as he startled. A shadow bent at the lock on Lady Petria's door.

Thank the blessed Mother that his Lady Aunt was neurotic and kept her doors locked even within the castle.

The urge to sneeze died.

Easing up behind the assassin, Dante squelched down the sick in his stomach. This man was here to harm his family. He plunged the dagger down. Skull bone crunched as the dagger slid into the soft brain it failed to protect. The assassin let out his final breath, a choked gurgle, as he dropped.

Bile burned the back of Dante's throat. That was the third life taken tonight, two of the deaths committed by his hand. The servants would have a terrible morning of cleaning ahead of them. If they didn't keel over of heart attacks from finding corpses in every wing of the castle.

Dante shakily wiped the dagger clean on the assassin's clothes. He couldn't leave him in the hall. He had to lead Korren and Lady Petria through here. His aunt was certain to have hysterics and draw every assassin remaining in the castle to them. Grabbing the shifter under the shoulders, he pointed with his chin at the passage they'd just emerged from. Princess Nakai obligingly held the tapestry aside as he dragged the body inside. Blood streaked the floor. He didn't have time to do more. Hiding the body would have to be enough.

Dante pulled his own lock picks out of a pouch. He unlocked the door with an experienced twist of his picks and tiptoed over the toys scattered across the floor. Six-year-olds were not neat creatures. Waking Korren first would be easier. Lady Petria didn't like to go hysterical in front of her son. Princess Owlderah disappeared into the closet.

Snuffling snores lead him to the bed and a mound of blankets with no visible sign of a child. Staring at the mountain of pillows and blankets, Dante wondered if it was safe to reach into the heap. Last time he'd dug Korren out to play, he had found five snails, two frogs, and a turtle tucked in with the boy. The snails and frogs had slimed the sheets, the turtle bit him. His hand had carried turtle-mouth bruises for a week.

Not that he had a choice. There were worse things than bruises. Dante blocked out the mental horror of a hole oozing with the lifeblood of a friend that was sure to haunt his nightmares.

Plunging his arm into the blankets, Dante wondered not for the first time how Korren slept under such suffocating covers in the middle of summer. A chubby leg was the first thing he found. Dante pulled the boy free.

Korren grumbled sleepily, white-blond lashes firmly shut against his cheeks.

A door shushed open across the rugs. "What do you think you are doing with my son?"

Dante's blood chilled at the sharp words. Carefully tucking Korren into his shoulder, Dante turned to face his aunt. "I'm taking him and you away to safety. I don't know if you've bothered to listen to me recently, but Prince Kobrona has sent assassins to subdue us before his arrival." That was his strongest theory anyway. "We have to leave. Now. He wants the royals of the families enslaved to him, and we have to get out of his reach. At least until the royal council can pass judgment on him." Dante begged the Mother that she would listen, that she was in one of her calmer, more reasonable moods.

Her fine features took on a nasty twist.

Maybe he should've dragged the body in here. There was proof.

Hurrying to speak before her uncertain temper unleashed, he pleaded with her. "Please, Lady Aunt, listen to me. I've already killed two of them.

I'm not even sure why I am not dead right now, because I should be, except I think they are trying to capture us."

Princess Owlderah stepped out of the closet holding clothes for Korren. "He's not lying. Kobrona did this to my family. I barely escaped from our prison."

"Where did you find this little chit?"

Definitely not in a reasonable mood.

Before Dante could intervene, Lady Petria looked Princess Nakai up and down. "How much did he pay you for this little charade?" The princess's mouth gaped. Dante winced. Not a great introduction to his family.

Lady Petria had become exceedingly protective of Korren since his uncle's death, to the point of practically caging him. Korren was all she lived for, and she was afraid of being left alone again. Heart torn by death. It seemed none of the Canidea took death and loss in a sane fashion. Losing a life-mate did that to a person. Wolves rarely took a new partner after losing the first, if they survived it at all.

"Please, Aunt Petria," he pleaded. "Lady Aunt, we have no time for this. I am asking you, please. Get dressed. We must leave in secrecy."

"No! I will scream this castle down to the foundation if you try to take my son."

He had said the wrong thing, giving her a weapon. Korren's hot breaths panted into his neck. They were running out of time.

"It isn't safe, Aunt!"

Lady Petria's eyes narrowed, and she sucked in a deep breath.

He lunged forward to stop her, but Princess Owlderah was faster. A weighted knife hilt slammed into Lady Petria's temple, and she went limp. Dante caught her with his free arm.

It pained him to see her like this. He had many memories of her when she had been strong, proud, and unbroken. She had once been one of the few people inside the castle he would listen to, unlike his generally distant father.

"Please, Princess, would you get her something to change into?" He propped Lady Petria against his shoulder and waited the stretching minutes until the princess reappeared.

"Do you have any idea how many useless clothes she has?" the princess muttered when she returned with a shirt stuffed fat with clothing. She crammed an outfit for Korren in along with his shoes. Tying the sleeves together, she slung it over her back giving her petite body the slouch of a hunchback.

"Not in the slightest."

"Here, give me the boy." She tugged Korren from Dante's arms and tucked him onto her hip, draping a blanket around him. "You cannot carry them both. I can handle it." Taking her at her word, Dante nodded his thanks and hoisted his aunt over his shoulder. He hoped she wouldn't wake while he was carrying her like this. She would beat him over the head for the indignity.

Dante lead them toward the dining hall. From there, it was a short gap across the lawn to the maze. The dining hall, usually clustered by nobles and servants, was eerily silent. Chairs and small tables created far too many hiding places for assassins to lurk, and Dante inhaled through his nose, trying to smell the musky scent the serpents carried with them. Stale bread and a multitude of unnamable foods permeated the dining hall from years of use, but nothing fresh, nothing foreign. Still it was a relief when he stepped onto the dew-dampened grass outside. The maze of hedge roses was only a few dozen paces away. His sanctuary. He defied any assassin to find them in there, and on the other side, his chevaliers awaited. The moonless night did nothing to brighten the lawn, but he strode confidently out. There were no shadows deep enough to hide anything in the broad expanse of grass.

Lady Petria moaned and stirred. So much for his hope that she wouldn't awaken until they were at the barracks. Dante stopped to let her down. He hoped he could talk some sense into his aunt before she freaked again.

A glimmer of magic and sinuous shadow wound about his ankles as he bent down to set Lady Petria on her feet. He stumbled into the princess, knocking her over. A shadow separated from the ground and Ookamimori shrieked a warning. Too late. The sinuous shape swarmed up his legs. He'd been careless.

It wrapped around his waist, pinning Lady Petria's legs against his stomach. She groaned, squirming on his shoulder as the pressure increased.

"Prince Canidea?" Nakai whispered harshly from the ground.

"Constrictor." He gasped as the serpent wound even higher, a solid length of pure muscle that held his arms down with bruising force. Dripping fangs gaped in his face as the snake hissed. Dante's arms ached under the combined weight of his aunt and the serpent, but he couldn't move without falling over. The snake was long enough to wrap around him multiple times, and there was still more of it in the grass. And it was strong; Mother bless, it was strong. It roiled in one sinuous movement, coiling tighter.

Lady Petria shrieked in his ear. "What is that? Put me down, you heathen!"

Dante slammed onto his knees as she flailed and writhed. It was all he could do to keep from falling onto his face. "Lady Aunt, please." He didn't know what he was trying to ask her to do. They were stuck.

Princess Owlderah gasped behind him, a horrified sound. "No. Get off."

Dante strained to see. There were two constrictors. The second snake wound bodily around Princess Owlderah and Korren. Korren whined.

That captured Lady Petria's attention. She stopped flailing. "Korren!" she cried.

A vicious growl vibrated from her chest. "Get away from my son."

Something jerked at his belt. Dante heard his knife slide free of its sheath.

He caught the constrictor's gaze, staring into its black orbs. It was so close to his face he could count the tiny individual scales that lined its nostrils. He bared his teeth and growled, desperate to keep the snake's attention on him and not his aunt. If the constrictors held them until their reenforcements arrived, then it was over. They had to get away.

Lady Petria moved. The constrictor screamed in a way Dante had never dreamed possible from a serpent. Muscle loosened, falling to the ground in a ropey tangle about his knees. Lady Petria was gone before the snake's disemboweled body hit the ground writhing.

Dante fought to his feet. He fumbled numb fingers around the hilt of his katana. Almost casually, he lopped off the constrictor's head. Disembowelment was a slow and painful way to die. The snake deserved it, but it was not getting another chance to attack.

He turned to help Princess Owlderah. Lady Petria was already there. She hacked and slashed at every part of the second constrictor she could reach. The snake stubbornly held onto its captives and took every blow.

Dante dithered; he didn't know where to strike. There wasn't an opening where he wouldn't hurt the princess and Korren. He didn't need to help. Lady Petria sank the knife in nearly to the hilt and, grabbing it with both hands, dragged it down the serpent's helpless body. Cool blood sprayed as she ravaged something vital.

Dante sheathed his sword and grabbed the cold-blooded corpse, dragging the heavy coils off the princess and Korren. The smooth scales slid out of his hands. He shifted to dyre form and sank his claws into its flesh, allowing him to keep ahold of it and drag it clear.

He lifted Princess Owlderah to her feet. She made sure to keep the blanket tucked over Korren's face, shielding him from the bloody mess.

Lady Petria knelt on the damp ground. Her eyes were glazed and empty.

"Aunt Petria?"

She shivered from head to toe. Shock. Wrapping a coaxing arm around her, he shuffled her toward the maze. "Come on. We have to get away."

She sobbed, but walked with his guidance. They walked the maze in muffled silence as Lady Petria swallowed her cries and Princess Nakai soothed Korren back to sleep. The scent of sleeping roses infused the air. It was strong enough to mask the smell of any serpents hunting them. Which kept Dante on edge, even in the supposed safety of his maze. He kept a constant grip on the hilt of his katana, even as he guided Lady Petria with a supportive arm. It was like taking a quiet stroll, calm and uninterrupted. He could almost pretend that everything was all right.

The weapons vault stood in the center of the barracks where it could be easily accessed by anyone at the fighting rings or on the run out of bed. The barracks to the left were reserved for any of the range-wolves at home, and those on the right for the patrollers.

Loud voices argued from within the vault.

The arguing stopped when he opened the heavy door and ushered Lady Petria inside the vault. He waited for Princess Owlderah to slip in before closing the door.

Relieved voices overwhelmed him.

"Where have you been?"

"Where are you hurt? All the blood!"

"What's going on, sire?"

The questions swarmed over him as fast as his chevaliers could utter them. Dante's held-up hand silenced them. Mysti pushed through the others. He talked while she prodded at him, looking for wounds under the blood spray. "Kobrona has made his opening move. He sent assassins, or perhaps a better word would be kidnappers. They weren't trying to kill us or I'd be dead. I believe if they catch us, they've won without any need for an army. Immediate triumph if they control me and Korren."

"Then we do as we planned and leave." Raphael stood at the back of the cluster. His shoulders were ramrod straight with tension.

Lady Petria whined, an injured sound, as she stared at her blood-splattered hands. Dante hurried to head her off before it became a full-blown wail. "Here, let's get you cleaned up, Aunt Petria." He grabbed a semi-clean rag out of the bucket of cloths in the corner; it hadn't been used for oiling the leathers yet, so it would do. "Does anyone have any water?" Mysti dug a canteen out of the prepared travel packs and handed it over.

"Do we have time for this?" she asked, not unsympathetically, as she picked up another rag and dabbed the blood off Lady Petria's fingers.

"We make time or she will scream the walls down. She's in shock or she would have already," he said, while washing as many tear stains as blood stains from his aunt's face.

"Aunt Petria, it is time for you to find your strength again. Be that woman I used to look up to. She is still in there, lost in her grief." Dante cupped her face, drying her cheeks with his thumbs. "You must stand up for your son; he needs you. Tonight, you killed for him. Now, you must run for him."

In her eyes, a glimmer of self birthed into awareness. Lady Petria looked at the blanket-covered lump the princess still cradled close. "Korren." Dante felt his aunt gather herself under his hands. "I need clothes." She didn't quite whimper, and Dante counted that as the best he'd get.

Princess Owlderah stepped up. "I have some of hers, not that they are useful for travel, but they are clean. If someone could take the boy?"

Stipes scooped Korren out of her arms. Ever the experienced childminder.

The princess unslung the bulging shirt. "I brought clothes for the boy, too."

With a nudge from Mysti, Lady Petria accepted the clothes and crept behind the racks of staves and spears to change out of sight. The staves were used for training and the spears for the castle guards to stand around and look intimidating with.

Dante wondered if he'd had more guards if Healer Gracia would still be alive, or if he'd have more bodies for the servants to stumble across in the morning. Probably the latter.

"Finish kitting up." Raphael ordered, even as he pulled one of the standard carry-all harness off the pegs. He shoved extra supplies in, on top of the basics that were kept in the pouches.

"Stipes, can you wake up Korren and get him dressed? If we are running as wolves, he needs to be awake," Mysti said.

Dante turned to his chevaliers. "We will move as wolves through the city. I am stopping somewhere before we leave. A few people will be joining us on our journey. You may not like them, but I expect you to deal with it on your own time. They have been friends of mine since I was nine, and I trust them as much as I trust you."

"Are they the ones you disappear with?" Alexion asked.

"Yes, most of the time. They have been a part of my family for a long time too. I will not accept any arguments against them." Dante gave his overprotective chevaliers a stern look and held his breath for an explosion. He would protect his family, both sides of it, from each other. None came. Mysti visibly bit her lip, and Raphael arched an eyebrow in curious disdain. His thief brothers would not start any trouble; however, they would do their best to finish it. Dante was desperate to limit the conflict.

"So… we aren't going to like your friends?" Alex piped in with a snigger. "I'm sure we are all big kids now, sire, we can play nice."

Dante forced a stiff smile. Would they still feel the same by morning? He doubted it.

Pained resignation filled his heart as he watched his people pick up their travel packs, designed with straps for either form shift to carry. He was leaving his people to unimaginable horrors. His nobles had refused to listen when he warned them, but the commoners had not gotten that chance. They had no idea what approached. Without the nobles backing the journey, no caravans had left Ookamimori. A few families had slipped away, but most who heard the rumors didn't have the funds, ability, or will to travel alone.

"Princess Nakai, have your wounds healed enough for you to fly?" Raphael asked while he helped Stipes adjust the straps on his pack.

The owl shifter flexed her shoulders, stretching her arms out and back, and winced at the pull on the stitched skin. "No. I won't even make it off the ground in this state. Healer Gracia"—she winced and cast a sorrowful look at Dante— "had planned several exercise sessions to strengthen the muscles."

Mysti frowned. "Do you think you could hold onto one of our harnesses in your shift form? Owls are relatively light, aren't they? If you can hold on, we should be able to take turns carrying you and Korren."

"I can do that. I won't be able to carry a pack, though," Princess Owlderah answered. Her shoulders hunched as she cradled her wounded arm to her chest.

Mysti shook her head. "We are prepared, and the packs are evenly distributed. There is no need for you to carry one as well."

The princess nodded. She selected a solid dagger and sheath to attach to her hip. Before he thought to urge her to pick something more, Dante noticed the soul-wield rune tattooed on her palm. She had no need to carry another weapon when she had that. He wondered what weapon would come to her call.

Hiding his scrutiny before it became rude staring, Dante bent to buckle Raphael into the harness. Had one of his forgers smithed her weapon? It was likely. The forgers of Ookamimori were the best.

Lady Petria emerged in fresh clothes. She wiped fresh tracks of tears from her cheeks. "I'm ready."

Dante wasn't sure how travel worthy a long skirt like that was going to be. At the first patch of brush, it would be shredded to rags. At least her boots appeared adequate.

"I've got Korren dressed, but he sleeps like the dead," Stipes said.

Dante cringed at the description. It struck much too close to home tonight. Enough people were already dead.

Lady Petria held out her arms, sniffling. "Hand him here. I will get him." Like a heavy ragdoll, Korren transferred arms again without stirring. Holding her son close, Lady Petria whispered in his ear and gently tickled the nape of his neck.

He moaned and grumbled, but his puppy-blue eyes opened. "Mama?" he slurred sleepily.

Dante tried not to pace. They couldn't rush Korren or they'd have a wailing child on their hands, an immediate beacon to their hiding place. They'd been hiding here for a while, and he was starting to feel vulnerable, hunted. What a terrible feeling. He would be happy to never feel it again after tonight.

"Baby, I need you to wake up. We are going to play a game with Dante. That sounds fun, right? But, you need to wake up, or he's going to play without us." Lady Petria kept up the soft tones and brush of her fingers.

Rubbing his eyes with a chubby fist, Korren looked around. "A game, Mama?"

Dante's heart clenched at his confused innocence. He jumped in to help convince him. "A game! Even your mother is going to play." Dante leaned in conspiratorially. "It is like hide and seek and tag all at the same time." He pulled this out of thin air and was running with the idea for all it was worth. A game that was surprisingly accurate if somewhat deadlier than any game had a right to be. "Want to play?"

"All right." Korren yawned and wiggled in his mother's arms to look around at everyone. His gaze landed on Princess Owlderah. "Are you the pretty princess Dante rescued?"

Instant heat burned in Dante's ears. He knew they'd turned bright red. He hoped the shadows in the armory were enough to hide them. With Alexion snickering at his shoulder, he doubted it. Dante palmed his face, hiding behind his fingers. "Mother bless it."

Princess Owlderah smiled, her face softened. "Well, Prince Dante rescued me, yes."

"Did he kiss you yet?" Korren asked. "He's supposed to. He's the prince."

Vivid pink spots bloomed across her cheeks.

Dante scrambled to salvage some dignity for them both. "Right! Korren, enough questions or we won't have time to play the game. We need to go before our hunters find us."

That reminder shut down the amused smiles on the surrounding faces. Princess Owlderah paled faster than she'd blushed. Korren was sleepy enough that he failed to catch the somber atmosphere before they covered it with the business of harnessing up. He bounced excitedly on his mother's hip, waiting for the game to start. One by one, they shifted and took their places by the door.

Mysti was the last to shift as she snuffed out the single glow crystal in the weapons vault. Korren's blond fur shone silver in the moonlight as he sat under his mother's feet. He would run with them until he was too tired to keep up. When that happened, they would carry him.

Chapter Eight

Dante took point to his chevaliers' obvious annoyance. The market was shut for the night, shutters drawn closed and carts pulled away to be returned filled with fresh goods again tomorrow. No pups played tag in the streets at this hour. Korren bounced around excitedly enough for all of them. Keeping him restrained within the safety of their center proved quite a task. The night seemed peaceful. A mere illusion, Dante knew, but it felt nearly the same as any of his night forays, even with his escort. If only he could return to his bed and wake up to happy sunshine

Taking every shortcut he knew, Dante led them into the cobbled streets of the city. He felt exposed. Would the assassins be stalking the city? It was doubtful. He and his family were their target, and they were supposed in the castle.

He focused much of his attention inward and back out through the Land connection. Life magic bloomed in his sight, strong in his blind, blue eye, weaker in his other. The magic overlaid the physical view, adding a bright glow. He would see anyone snooping around the streets. No matter the depth of the shadows they hid in.

The numerous parks were silent except for the soft burbling of water filling the hot springs, and the river tributaries filling the cold swimming holes. Few wandered outside at this early hour unless it was the full moon. His city slept at peace for now, except for them and the assassins hunting them.

Gravel scuffed under their boots as he led them down the alley. "Wait here a few minutes." Before they mustered a protest, he ducked around the corner, striding to an average-looking house amidst a row of average-looking houses. Bypassing the front door, which was sure to be locked and barred, Dante dropped into the window well and pulled a hidden latch under the sill to pop the window. Sliding into the basement, he didn't linger. He powered up the steep stairs with the strength of four legs instead of two.

Leigha's room was first. The crazy female had insisted on coming. She said that the twins needed someone to keep them out of trouble. She was more likely to cause it, invalidating her excuse, but Dante was glad to have another member of his personal pack at his back. Her odd obsession with things that could mix together and go boom could make up for it.

After clearing the door of traps, for no one entered Leigha's room without risk, Dante purposefully placed a heavy paw on the loudest, squeakiest floorboard. The atmosphere changed into a dangerous silence as the lumpy form buried under the blankets stopped snoring. Dante whined anxiously. "Hurry up!"

The blankets wiggled. A slender hand poked out. A crystal flared to life at her touch. "Dante? What is it? Something wrong?" Leigha's tousled, brown head poked out of the lumps.

Explaining might be a good idea. This was happening much earlier than planned. Dante shifted so he could speak, easier to get it across with words than wolf-speak in the dark. "It's time to go. Snakes hunt in the palace tonight. I don't know quite what their plan was, but they are here, so we are leaving."

Leigha rolled out of bed, tossing the blankets aside and reaching for her pants.

Dante rolled his eyes. No sense of modesty, that one. He left her to dress and went to Derrick and Raiven's room. The halves of their room were distinctly lined by the state of each side: clutter and clothes on Derrick's, and swept, tidy floors on Raiven's. Dante wondered if Raiven knew he snored. He doubted it. Derrick slept so much it was a wonder he was ever awake, much less awake enough to catch Raiven snoring. Derrick would never let his twin hear the end of it. Raiven did not do loud. He was the reserved, silent one, except snoring was not quiet or reserved.

Once again, Dante stepped on a squeaky floorboard, this time with a booted heel. Every room had at least one. It was the safest way to wake dagger-happy thieves. Even throwing things at them wasn't safe. They tended to throw it right back, then roll over and go back to sleep.

"Bugger off," Raiven snapped, flinging a book toward the door.

Stepping sideways, Dante avoided the haphazard projectile. Even the squeaky floorboards didn't always stop the dangers. "Raiven, get up. Leigha is getting dressed, and I need your help with Derrick." Dante searched the room for something to rouse the other twin as Raiven's lean form stretched and yawned.

"Is it time? So soon?"

Raiven was always quick on the uptake. "Yes, Kobrona has sent his men in. They are all over the palace. I killed two. Help me with Derrick. Mother bless. Why do half my friends sleep like bloody rocks?" Not finding a convenient source of water, Dante grabbed Derrick's heel and hauled him off the bed. Derrick's slumbering body landed with a thump.

"That won't work. You should know that. Here, let me." Raiven tugged his shirt over his head and crossed the room, stepping with unconscious practice over the dirty clothes and discarded things.

"It was worth a try. I don't see any water sitting around. That's what I used on Keer."

"Really? I bet he loved that. He's as bad as Derrick. This, however"—Raiven popped a finger in his mouth and pulled it out with a slurpy pop—"works much better." He grinned maliciously, crouched over his brother, and stuck his slobbered finger into his twin's ear.

"Euch!" Derrick flopped over and scrambled upright. He scrubbed at his ear. "Raiven, you bloody bugger, what was that for?"

Grabbing a selection of clothes off the floor, Raiven dumped them into his brother's lap. "It's time. Get dressed."

"I'll meet you at the door. Wait for me. I don't want Raphael trying to truss you on sight. He'd leave you in the streets for the patrollers to pick up if given the choice," Dante said as he slipped out of the room.

Heading upstairs, Dante carefully avoided the squeaky boards. The rest of the guild did not need to be woken for this. He tapped softly on Calume's door. His mentor needed to know that it had begun. He dearly wished Calume was joining them, but the thief lord had declared that the city would need him. Dante knew Calume would harass the Kobrona throughout the city. Raiding their supplies and picking off strays. The Guild Master was nothing if not resourceful and inventive.

Footsteps padded up to the door. Through the Pulse, Dante felt his mentor's life presence.

The door cracked open. "Who is it? Dante! What are you doing here so late?"

"We are leaving. Kobrona sent an assassin team, or something. They didn't seem to be trying to kill us. Maybe incapacitate us until Kobrona can get here. We fought them off."

"So quickly? He must have sent them behind the princess or perhaps ahead of her. He has been planning this takeover for a while, it seems. He is not randomly attacking families. He has an agenda, and he must either bring it to a conclusion or incapacitate the families before the royal council convenes at Communion. The only way to overrule the council is to remove the royals," Calume rasped sleepily. He waved Dante inside. Dante waited as Calume went to the chest at the foot of his bed and drew out a small, leather bundle. The leather was inked with intricate designs and swirls. His mentor picked up Dante's hand and turned it palm up, setting the bundle in it.

"These have served me well over the years. I know you have a good set, but these are the best. They won't fail you," Calume said.

Unrolling the leather, Dante's breath hitched. They were a master's lockpicks. Tiny runes roughened the feel of the slender metal tools. Blood-magicked. Only a master's tools would get such treatment. They had to have cost a bloody fortune, nearly as much as a soul-wield. They would not break, and few locks would withstand them.

"But…"

Calume shook his head. "I won't hear anything else. You are like my son, and you are my prince. I cannot join you on your journey, but I can give you tools and people I trust to help you."

Dante tried to swallow past the knot in his throat. "I, um, thank you."

They both knew Dante wasn't just thanking him for the lockpicks. Calume had picked him off the streets when he had first wandered out to explore the city after being shooed by his busy father. Dante had gotten lost. Calume brought him to the guild, showing him a few of the showier tricks while filling his growling stomach. He'd returned Dante to the castle and told him that he shouldn't wander alone. Dante had used his connection with the Heart to retrace his steps to the guild house, again alone, and met the twins, quickly making friends.

With his father's attention on his city and not his son, Dante was free to join his newfound packmates whenever he could escape his tutors. Keer was dragged out with him, and they learned the ways of the streets together. When his father had died, he had practically moved into the guild. Mysti and Raphael had been frantic the time he'd vanished for three full days. Calume filled a part of the hole his father left behind.

Dante tucked the leather bundle into the pouch on his thigh and made sure it was buckled. He grabbed Calume in a hard hug. "Be careful. I want to come home to find all of my pack still here. I will make sure Kobrona is stopped somehow. I won't leave you all to suffer his wrath for nothing."

"I know you won't. We'll be just fine," Calume said, pushing him back. "You are a fine Alpha. Your father would be proud of you. Go. Be safe. Join us at the Communion. The runners will warn the other royals, and they will be on guard."

"Right. The other royals will help us stop him. Even death magic cannot hold against magic of the full royal council and the priestesses of the Mother. Not at the Mother Tree." Kobrona would have to be there. Dante knew the call of the Mother. It hadn't started yet, but it would soon, when the time for Communion approached. All the royals felt it, the intense summons that drew them to gather at her roots.

Dante gave one last clasp to Calume's arm and offered a farewell smile before slipping out the door. It was time to go.

Meeting the others in the basement, they exited from the same bolt hole he had entered. This left the main entrance still protectively barred.

He led them into the starlit street where the rest of his pack waited. Raphael paced the mouth of the alleyway. His chevaliers were just eyeing his thieves when a faint scrabbling alerted them to an uninvited presence. A protective circle of both thieves and chevaliers sprang up around him and Lady Petria, who stood over Korren.

A gangly, dirt-colored wolf stumbled into sight, tripping over his large paws and landing on his nose at their feet.

Leigha growled. "Jothan! What do you think you're doing?"

The overgrown pup shifted and sat up on his knees, rubbing his nose. "I'm coming too!"

"No, you are not!" Leigha snarled, bristling up. An older sister scolding a bratty sibling.

Derrick waved his hands angrily. "Calume would kill us. We cannot take another youngling. Prince Korren will slow us down as it is, and we have to keep him safe."

Mysti turned on Derrick. "How is it you are so familiar with our mission?"

Raiven stepped slightly in front of his twin brother, obvious in his intent to protect him from the glares of the chevaliers. Mysti put a hand on her sword. Her lips curled, baring her fangs.

"Enough!" Dante stood in the middle of them all. "We do not have time for this. I told you I had friends, family, joining us. They know our mission because they have helped me plan it as much as you have. I know well who and what they are. I trust them with everything, and now I am trusting you with them. I will tell you what you want to know later, and you will be given a chance to yell; however, dawn is not that far away. We need to be well away from the city before the castle guards find the bodies. Our people can't know where we are going or Lord Kobrona will torture it out of them." Dante growled, feeling the short hairs on the back of his neck rising in anger. There were more important things to fret over.

"The kid will have to come," Alexion said, nudging Mysti's shoulder and calming the sparked temper. "He obviously knows too much about our plans, so it's not safe to leave him here."

"If he can't keep up we will leave him behind." Derrick said.

Jothan whined and groveled before the irate adults. "I'll keep up. I swear!"

"We could knock him out and just leave him," Leigha said. "Then he won't slow us down. He's untrained, there's not much he could do to actually help us."

"We can't leave him lying in the street with those things hunting us, and we don't have time to drag him inside without waking people up and causing a commotion," Raiven said from inside his concealing hood. "Commotion at this hour would draw the assassins right to us."

"Jothan, if you don't keep pace, you will be left behind," Dante said. "Calume would understand it being a part of your stupidity for barging into this. It will not be a pleasant journey." Dante felt rather like wringing the teenager's scrawny neck. He did not want the responsibility of keeping his mentor's newest protégé alive. The sorrow and disappointment from Calume, if he failed, would break him. The teenager nodded meekly. "Enough then. Let's go."

Chapter Nine

Thick moss and pine needles padded the forest floor for their paws. Derrick, Raiven, and Leigha took point, while Mysti and Raphael covered their back trail.

Korren kept up admirably until the sun began to peek cautiously over the horizon. When the pup faltered, Stipes picked him up with gentle jaws. Jothan was panting, but even the inkling of complaint earned him hard glares. If he started to falter, a nip to the flank spurred him on.

The dawn brightened the shadows with rosy rays of light breaking through the gloom. It couldn't reach the darkness of Dante's despair. He had not wanted it to come to this. He had been hoping it was all a horrible mistake.

Beneath his feet, the Heart's Pulse carried the fear of his people to him as they found the bodies in the castle. Their reflected panic was a bitter taste on the back of his tongue.

Dante kept putting one foot in front of the other. He didn't know what else to do. One paw in front of the other in a ground-devouring lope, taking him away from danger, away from his home, his people.

A constant litany of prayers for forgiveness ran through his mind. He could only pray to the Mother that the deranged serpent at the head of this attack wouldn't harm his people because of his absence. If he wasn't there, Lord Kobrona had no need for them, right?

The sun had not yet reached its zenith when Alexion trotted close. "We have to stop soon. It will be a long journey. We should not push ourselves too hard in the beginning, or we risk failing in the end."

"That, plus, Lady Petria and the kids are tired already," Raphael added, having caught up to say the same. Dante knew they were right, he was tired too, the adrenaline rush having worn off an hour ago.

Derrick dropped back to join them. "There is a clearing ahead with berries to supplement our supplies if we want to risk the time to pick them." He cast a wary glance over Dante's back at the two chevaliers who glared in return.

"We should have enough of a head start, even if they can track us." Dante barked to get the whole pack's attention. "We will stop in the clearing ahead."

Here, the river was wide and shallow, calm, unlike the furious stretch where the princess had fallen in. Korren dashed for the burbling water with newfound energy. Colorful striped stones underwater caught his attention, and he shifted, happily gathering them in his shirt. When his shirt could hold no more, he dumped the bright stones carelessly on the shore and went back for more. Jothan joined him after a moment of indecision and stole a glance back at the adults. Shaking his head, Dante decided that the pups' idea of fun, playing in the frigid water, was beyond him. His recent brush with the angrier version of the river was enough to reinforce that idea.

"Korren, you may choose two rocks to bring. No more!" Lady Petria said when Korren began stuffing stones into all of his pockets.

"Aw. But, Mother!" Korren pleaded.

"Two!" A stern look ended the protests and Korren pouted, but he decided to go back in for more rocks to choose.

A red stone bobbed to the surface as Dante kept a watchful eye on his cousin. Korren poked at it but didn't reach out to pick it up. Jothan saw it and bravely waded over to pick up the rock between two fingers. A large drop of water clung to it, stubbornly wiggling about in the air. Dante snickered at the pups' awed and freaked-out faces. It was a tadpole undine, a baby elemental sharing its stash of rocks. Even on the darkest days, there was a spot of light. The tadpole dropped back into the river, and more rocks bobbed to the surface, lifted by the curious elementals.

As the adults gathered the food together and added handfuls of the fresh blackberries to the offerings, Mysti's patience ran out. "Now, sire, would you properly introduce us to your friends here?" Mysti said.

"Fine. My chevaliers, Mysti, Alexion, Raphael, and Stipes, meet Raiven, Derrick, Leigha, and the tagalong Jothan. Lady Petria is my aunt, and Korren my heir. You all know Keer. The last is Princess Nakai Owlderah. Let's eat!" He reached for a handful of berries.

Glares from his chevaliers stopped him.

Dante groaned. "What? Yes, they are from the thieves' guild. Top of the ranks, actually." He put his food down. There was no getting around this quietly. "So am I, and Keer too. Yes, that's where I run off to most of the time. They have been my best friends since I was nine. They have invaluable skills that will aid us on the journey. They are obviously not dirty or filthy, as the rumors portray. We have had a strict system of twisted honor pounded into our heads since we joined the guild, so we do not steal from just anyone. No, I didn't tell you about them before, mainly because of the explosion you are going to inflict on me in about five, four, three, two, and…" Dante trailed off as Raphael's lungs drew a bellow of air.

"What?!" Raphael yelled.

Dante nodded with an 'I told you so' air. He sidled a glance at Mysti. She looked furious. Oh boy. She drew in a breath to start her rant. Dante wanted to plug his ears; however, his noble-born, Raphael, stormed over anything Mysti might have said.

"How dare you consort with lowly thieves! You are the Alpha-Prince! It is not your place, and far below you! What would your father think?"

Dante flinched. He had been fully prepared to take a scolding from Mysti and anger from the rest, but this—this was going too far. "Raphael." He did not yell or even snap. His tone was an even purr that had Raphael shutting up and stumbling back several steps. "It is not your place to choose who I associate with. I could befriend the sickliest beggar or the bloodiest assassin, and it would still not be your place to tell me otherwise. Most certainly, it is not your place to yell at me as though I were an unruly child. When my father silently blamed me for the death of my mother and my twin, nearly all the palace inhabitants ignored me, following his example. I was tended to and kept alive, but I was otherwise invisible. Thief Lord Calume found me alone in the city and took me in. It is him you can thank for my raising. If he had not taken me in hand, I would now be a hateful, cold little brat with no care for my people. You were not even in my life when I met them. So, don't make me choose."

"They are thieves!" Raphael choked.

"They showed me how to accept my responsibilities and grow up! They showed me how to be a member of a family. They taught me that life isn't always about giving orders, no matter how ridiculous, but sharing the burden between friends and making life easier all around." Dante drew in a sharp breath and let it out slowly, turning away from the shocked eyes upon him. He had not meant to explode like that, but the thieves were a solid part of his family, and his father was a sore spot.

"Dante." Mysti coaxed him to turn around, her own fury banked and well-hidden. "We will accept your friends. It may take time for some of us. Personally, I had some not-so-elegant friends before I joined the range-wolves and then your guard. I have no problem with their occupation.

Even if the idea of my Alpha being trained as a thief will take some getting over." She spread her hands wide and tilted her head to bare her throat.

Dante relaxed slightly. It seemed even Mysti knew when her temper was best stored away. She turned on Raphael and grabbed his ear, hauling him off the ground and into the trees. On the other hand, perhaps she was redirecting it. Angry mutters and the occasional thwack reached them from the arguing duo.

"Nice one, Dante!" Derrick quipped. "Ow!" Derrick rubbed his head where Raiven and Leigha had both smacked him. "Hey, do you think they will talk to us now instead of about us? Ow!"

Dante rolled his eyes and plopped down. He reached again for food. He might as well eat while everyone was busy getting over themselves. "Princess Nakai, please forgive our display and eat. We have a long journey ahead. The sandwiches should be eaten today, for they will not last. Lady Aunt, some berries perhaps?"

The two noblewomen took over divvying dinner to the pack. An awkward silence was filled with polite small talk. Mysti stalked back to the group, a cowed Raphael at her heels, nursing a split lip. Tension clouded them like a thunderstorm.

Korren was oblivious to it all. He crouched on the bank, a messy sandwich clutched in one hand while he sorted through his collection of shiny rocks. A sploosh announced his every dismissal as he winged them back into the river where the elemental tadpoles played with them. "No, no. No. Hmm, no. Ooh. No. Ah-ha!" Korren triumphantly scrambled to his feet holding up a red-striped stone for all to see. "Look at this one, Mama. I want this one for sure!"

His childish enthusiasm forced them all to smile. Jothan scarfed his food and rejoined Korren in the rock hunt. By the time the rest of the pack was done eating, Korren and Jothan had each gathered their chosen rocks. Lady Petria caught Korren's eye and held up two fingers. He grinned sheepishly, and an extra rock fell out of the fist behind his back.

Dante urged them all back onto the trail. It would be many days before they reached the mountains, and it was anyone's guess beyond.

As they moved back onto the deer trail and his pack fell into line, the hairs on the back of his neck rose. Dante stared through the trees. Visibly, there was nothing. No shadows that didn't belong. Dante closed his eyes and reached for the Heart. Ookamimori welcomed his touch with a warm buzz of magic. He asked his question, glad when the answer came back negative of any shifter magic. There was no one following them yet, neither his range-wolves nor the serpentine hunters. They were alone.

Ferns grew rampant over the forest floor. The game trail cut a narrow path through the green. Soon, the pack spread out in their respective places, and the ground vanished beneath their steady lope. Even the summer heat was pleasant under the trees' shade.

When the sunset's rays burned the sky red and purple, Raiven and Derrick split off to hunt with Alexion and Raphael. In the plentiful forest, it was not long before triumphant howls summoned the rest of the pack.

They ate the meat raw. Smoke would mark their position so close to the city. Either to his guard or the Kobrona. Besides, it was delicious. He and Alexion did skin the large doe first, though. Deer fur was a great irritation when stuck in one's teeth or coating the insides of one's throat. Nakai picked at the corpse with her curved beak. She glared fiercely at any who came too close to her chunk.

Sated, they left the bloody remains for the smaller denizens of the forest. They would not return to eat it.

"We should keep an eye out for a place to sleep," Mysti said.

Dante agreed. They had long since passed the cave he had slept in with the princess, but that cave system ran all over, breaking to the surface at random.

Dante focused on the Heart and allowed Ookamimori to guide him. "There is a suitable cave not far from here."

As soon as they reached it, Korren flopped down in the dirt, snoring within seconds. Jothan at least attempted to hide his weariness by just sitting there watching the others.

"There will be no waking him now," Lady Petria murmured. "Not for a few hours at least." She shifted, arranging her skirt as she sat on the dirt beside her son.

Leigha shifted and plopped her bag on the floor, sighing as the weight left her shoulders. "He's done well for a cub."

"He is the Crown Prince," Lady Petria said. "Korren brings honor to his station."

Stipes dug around in his pack and drew out an odd bundle.

Dante eyed it curiously. "What, precisely, is that?"

"Hmm? Oh this? Why, sire, it is your potions, brewed by the healers. I made sure to stockpile them. There are a few here for the princess as well."

Identical looks of horror and disgust were directed at the vials currently filled with a mud-like substance.

Dante crossed his arms defiantly. "I'm not taking them."

"But, sire, you would not want to get sick again, would you? I'm sure Healer Gracia would love to find you back in her care after this is over just because you didn't take these."

He hadn't told them yet. Grief silenced all protest. He reached out and meekly accepted the corked beaker of medicine. Stipes handed it over with a confused frown.

The sweet stench from the opened potions did nothing to dissuade their shared disgust. Together, they grasped the deathly-looking bottles and upended them.

A repulsed shiver rattled Dante from head to toe.

"Oh, that was just nasty," Nakai gasped.

"I really don't know how they do it. Making each one worse than the last." Dante resisted the urge to gag. "I swear, Stipes, any more of those in your pack, you may just as well pour them out because I am not touching another if it tastes like that. I don't care how good it is for me."

He studiously ignored the fact that his chevalier's response was an unconfident 'hmm' and turned away to the watching, snickering group. "I swear the next time one of you so much as sniffles around me you will be getting one of those poured down your throat. I'm sure Princess Nakai would be willing to pour while I hold you down."

"Quite," she said.

He couldn't pretend any longer. "Healer Gracia is dead. The Kobrona murdered her in her sleep," he blurted. Oh, Mother bless, there had to have been a better way to say it. He didn't need to bludgeon them with it.

Mysti gasped, her sword-roughened hands flying to cover her mouth. Tears already sparkled in her eyes. Raphael slumped, his head ducked low to hide his face as his noble-born composure faltered. They had known her as their healer nearly as long as Dante. Her death was a terrible loss to their pack. Stunned silence broke as Lady Petria sobbed into Korren's hair.

Dante left them to their grief. His own sorrow was a cold numbness that filled his chest with ice. He couldn't share their tears. He had to be strong for them.

He turned his attention to Princess Nakai, who stood off to the side. "How are your stitches holding up?"

"Um…" Nakai lifted her arm and twisted her head around and downward with a strange flexibility to peer at the back side of her arm. "They seem to be holding fine." Her expression showed chagrin. "Though, I fear it may be a few more days until I can attempt to fly."

"Lady, that's just weird," a sleepy Jothan said.

"What?"

"I think he meant the way you can twist your head that far. It is a bit unusual, actually," Keer explained, clearing his throat to speak. His voice was tight, but he contained his emotions.

"Oh, all owls can do that, even in human form." Nakai settled gracefully on her knees. Slender fingers moved up to comb through her hair and divide it into three even strands. A silvery braid grew quickly. "What are we doing exactly? Where are we going?"

The question surprised him. In all the bustle of planning and the meetings, and then fleeing for their lives, he had forgotten that she had never been informed of their decision.

Lady Petria joined them, wiping her eyes with her skirt. Dante passed over a cloth for her nose. "Yes, please tell us precisely what we are doing? I would like to know what's going on." Lady Petria grimaced as she sat in the dirt. Korren snuffled at the sudden movement. He stretched and rolled over, sprawling across his mother's lap with gangly legs.

Dante quirked a brief smile at the cuteness and reached out to stroke his soft puppy ear. "Our plan is to protect Korren," he said, and proceeded to fill in the last two members of their pack.

The mugginess of the summer night made his shirt cling uncomfortably. Dante tugged it loose.

His aunt lay sleeping against the cave wall. Her dark gray fur contrasted with her cub's blond fluff where she curled protectively around him. She had taken the news with a soft wail of weak misery and had broken down into scared sobs. In all honesty, she had held up better than Dante had thought she would. It saddened him to see her pushed over the edge so easily. The strength with which she ran with them the day before had given him hope that she had found herself again. Perhaps the rest of the journey would help her regain her former grace.

There was no chance to recuperate as Raphael decided to channel his emotions into conflict.

"Dante, now seems to be a later point in time. You said you would tell us why we are cavorting with thieves," Raphael said, his words clipped and hard, leaving no room for argument despite the split lip Mysti had left him with earlier.

Dante heaved a deep breath. Sleeping would be nice, but he owed them an explanation. "Right, fine. I will tell you why we are traveling with the other half of my family." He was not going to let his chevaliers forget that he considered them all his pack.

The scars on his thigh ached, a dull burn from the steady travel. He stretched the limb out straight on the ground, hoping to avoid the cramps of overworked muscles.

Keer pointedly sat down beside him, gesturing for Derrick, Raiven, and Leigha to settle next to him. Relief filled Dante at the show of support.

He loved his chevaliers, and they were doing their best to protect him; they always did their best to protect him. When Mysti had taken her vows to protect him, he was eleven, and she had tried to mother him to death. Raphael joined them a few months later, taking on a role more like a superior, older brother. They had both tried hard to break through Dante's defensive walls. Mysti had learned the hard way that Dante would not accept someone trying to be his mother. Mysti had chosen a role in his life similar to Raphael, like an older, overprotective sibling. He seemed to have many siblings. Alexion and Stipes collaborated with the senior two as they joined their efforts to tame him.

The princess politely retreated to the cavemouth and tucked her head under her wing, giving them an illusion of privacy. Dante appreciated it. He'd hoped to never have this conversation, much less in front of a stranger. What she must think of him and the division he'd caused in the midst of his pack.

His chevaliers sat down, completing the circle. Stipes willingly took the spot beside Leigha.

"Let me introduce you properly. Guys"—he nodded toward Raiven, Derrick, and Leigha— "you know of them. Meet Mysti, Alexion, Raphael, and Stipes."

His street sibs waved meekly, having been waiting for this day for a while now. Dante prayed his chevaliers would at least try to be tolerant. Happy acceptance was probably more than he could ask for.

Anxiety made him ill. Dante gestured toward the others. "This is Raiven, Derrick, Leigha, and the tagalong is Jothan." Raiven nodded politely, eyes hooded. Derrick smiled sharply, the tips of his fangs flashing. Leigha wiggled her fingers cheerily. Jothan just swayed sleepily.

"I was found wandering in the streets by the Thief Lord when I was nine. He cleaned me up, fed me, and was the first adult to sit down in a long time and talk to me. Raiven and Derrick already lived at the guild and became my friends. I kept finding my way back. Keer, too, when I dragged him out of the library."

Raphael turned his glower onto Keer at that. Keer met his gaze coolly. Resisting the urge to roll his eyes, Dante continued. "The Thief Lord Calume trained us along with his own younglings."

"Why did you go there so often?" Mysti asked.

"You know. I reminded my father too much of my mother. He loved me dearly, yes, but between remembering her and being plain busy as king, I didn't see him a lot. I didn't have you yet either. I was lonely."

Dante eyed Jothan, wondering if the boy was sleeping with his eyes wide open. He was swaying in place, head sinking low and then bobbing back up with each spike in the conversation.

Mysti frowned with remembrance. "I am sorry I wasn't there for you. But, thieves, Dante?"

"They took care of me when few others would stretch beyond their general duties to the prince. You were not with me yet. Keer's father spent more time keeping mine on track as Keer does for me. Neither of us saw them much." Dante brought a knee up and wrapped his arms around it. "The thieves kept me from wandering around and getting into trouble. My city is large. Many would not recognize their prince or care if they did, being scoundrels of the worst kind. Calume kept me out of the darkest areas of the city. He made sure I could handle myself by the time I did walk them. Raiven and Derrick have always had my back when you were not there to cover it and sometimes even when you were. Leigha slinks around in the shadows causing mayhem where ever she treads."

Jothan lost his battle to the draw of sleep. He fell into Leigha's lap, snoring softly. His shaggy bangs flopped over his face. Leigha jumped, startled at the sudden lap-invader. Derrick and Alexion snickered. Amusement was a sudden bridge to cross the gap of enmity.

Leigha glared at them both, but did not disturb the teenager. Her hands fluttered before she gave in and stroked the hair out of the kid's eyes. Moving her legs to settle him more comfortably, she gave them a look daring them to say anything about her mothering.

It didn't work. Alexion swooned onto Mysti's lap. "Be my pillow tonight!"

Dante hid a grin behind his knee. Alex to his rescue, distracting his life-mate from her anger, as usual.

Derrick only rubbed in the ribbing, flopping over Raiven's knees, sniggering. "Ha, sing me a lullaby." Dante watched Leigha digging at the wall of the cave at her back. He was sure that she planned a messy revenge.

Dante tried hard not to draw any attention to his mirth while Mysti and Raiven shared grieved looks at the antics of the idiots flopping on them. They simultaneously shoved the idiots off.

"Oof." Alexion grunted. "Mysti that was mean."

"No, this is mean." Leigha hefted a large, wet clump of moss and chucked it at Alexion's defenseless head. Derrick laughed harder. "Here's one for you too. So, shut it." Bringing out her other hand from behind her back, she threw another clump of cave moss at Derrick. By now, everyone was laughing. Even Raphael had a reluctant smile curving his lips. Dante leaned on Keer's shoulder, taking a deep breath to calm his mirth. Alexion sat up, brushing dirt furiously out of his hair.

Derrick lay face down, the moss still plopped on the back of his head. "You've killed me, Leigha. I will now proceed to haunt you forever."

"Fine, whatever. Can we sleep now, or are we to be grilled some more by your overprotective chevaliers, Dante?" Leigha asked, raking her fingers through her short, curly hair. And there was tension again as everyone remembered that they weren't exactly friends, only forced allies with a common factor.

"We should rest. We have a long journey ahead of us," Stipes said. As usual, he had not spoken much. Dante knew he would wait until he had figured everything out, then say his piece if he felt it was necessary.

"Mysti, Raphael, anything else you want to know tonight?" Dante asked, just to be sure. He really did want them all to get along. They were his pack.

"No, Stipes is right. We need to sleep," Mysti said.

Raphael looked emotionally constipated, but shook his head. Dante accepted this and shifted, not bothering to get up or off Keer's shoulder. Despite the summer heat, the cave was cool with the nighttime air. Fur was warmer than clothes.

The rest joined them in fur, aside from Jothan who slept soundly on Leigha.

Chapter Ten

Jothan groaned and grumbled when Leigha nudged him awake. She whacked him on the back of the head. "You made us bring you. You don't get to whine about anything."

They ate quick handfuls of nuts and fruit, drinking water from the small creek branching from the river. Keer sulked moodily without his usual cup of tea but soldiered on.

With a child's usual morning buzz, Korren bounced around, ready for more of the adventure. "Let's go!"

Dante shook his head in bemused wonderment. "I want some of that energy."

Even with a wolf's fur as padding, cave floors were not a comfortable resting place. Running from assassins did not do much for a peaceful sleep either. Everyone was tetchy.

Dante pretended not to notice the stern looks Raphael leveled at the thieves. He could not build a bridge in a day. Alexion and Stipes seemed fine with it, but they remained aloof, waiting for their partners to come to terms with it.

While the packs were strapped on the harnesses and divvied, Princess Nakai took a moment to stretch her wings. Watching her as she hopped and fluttered ungracefully, Dante admired her perseverance and endurance. The injured wing was obviously stiffer than the other, throwing off her balance. She labored at the exercises until they were ready to go. One final fluttering hop brought her onto Raphael's back. She fastened sharp claws around the leather straps. Stipes bore the other harness, and Korren, in human form, rode piggyback, clutching the leather straps.

Stipes took the lead, beginning a steady lope that they should be able to hold for most of the day. Dante fell into line ahead of his aunt. Raiven and Derrick flanked him, much to Raphael's sneering displeasure. Dante trusted them to keep him on the trail and he closed his eyes, reaching within for his connection to the Mother's energy, to the Heart. Immersed this deeply in the life magic, he could feel the signatures of all the animals and people within a wide radius. He could not yet feel the entirety of his lands or even all the way back to Ookamimori. He searched through the signatures for anything following them, but for the moment, he found only the forest's natural inhabitants. A shifter's life energy read differently, no matter what form they wore. They were still safe.

Withdrawing from the main connection, Dante opened his eyes, retaining enough of the magic to see faint lines of the earth's energy through his blind eye. He did not always pull on his magic to see the surrounding life. It was draining and mostly unnecessary. Being blind in one eye did not slow him down at all. It was something both Calume and his chevaliers had worked hard to teach him during training. He only used the magic sight when he was on unfamiliar territory. Such as now.

Dante grimaced at the morning dew soaking the fur of his belly as they followed a thin deer trail. The trail meandered northeast toward the foothills of the Crystalline Mountains. At the steady pace they were traveling, it would take several days to reach the pass over the mountains into the frigid lands of the Lupinic. The maps Keer carried showed that the Lupine's icy city was somewhere near the middle of the northlands, meaning at least a few more days' journey beyond the pass.

Lady Petria held her peace until the sun passed its peak. "I am tired. I demand we stop and rest. Some proper food would be nice too. Dante knows there are not any of those creatures around. I want to stop."

Dante slowed his pace, and the others grouped around as he spoke. "We should rest. Korren and Jothan are getting weary, and food would be appreciated," he suggested. Weariness weakened his legs as well, though he would not admit it. The cold had passed but he was not used to constant exertion.

"All right, we have some jerky in the packs, though we should try to conserve it for the northlands. We do not know what kind of hunting is to be had beyond the mountains," Mysti said as she waited patiently for Alexion to pull the pack off her shoulders before shifting.

"We'll eat only a little of it. We can hunt small game as we go and stop again later," Dante said, plopping down in the shade of a gnarled tree.

His pack settled down to rest around him in an obvious split, his chevaliers on one side and his thieves on the other. He knocked his head back against the tree and winced as his hair snagged on the rough bark of the willow. Dante did it again, solely because it distracted his body from the aching muscles. Magic bloomed in the tree at the repeated action.

"Whoa." He scrambled away from it. The magic kept swelling around it as though awakening from a deep sleep. The entire root system glowed with it. Seeing the typically gentle and quiescent magic flaring so vibrantly weighted Dante's breaths with apprehension. There was a power here.

"What? What is it, Dante? What do you see?" Alex asked.

"Can't you feel it?" Princess Owlderah asked, kneeling to place her palm against the earth. "It is like cold and heat at the same time."

Dante tilted his head, agreeing with her description. He couldn't feel it, but the cool greens and warm yellows of the magic matched. The flow of magic running like lifeblood through the trees brightened until Dante closed his eyes against it.

"Children," a breeze whispered around them. "Hush, hush. You and yours disturb my peaceful forest, little king."

Looking around for the source of the voice, Dante almost opened his mouth to protest any claims on the forest beside his own; however, a woman's form stepped from the tree.

"You bring a darkness upon us, little king." She moved from the concealing embrace of the branches, and Dante's breath caught in his throat, glad he hadn't spoken. Elementals cared not for a shifter's claim to ownership. She was a dryad, lady of the forest, a queen amongst even the greater elementals. A crown of branches grew out of the dryad's head, her skin the gray-green of the willow's bark. "Darkness follows you," she repeated. Her voice whispered and crackled like dry leaves. "The blood dripping from its feet feed my children."

Fear shivered the hairs on the back of his neck. Dante didn't know if the dryad's words or the dryad herself were the cause of it. Her soulless gaze shone with magic, the same kind of power that had killed his father. Willow branches swayed with her, deeply rooted in her fibrous flesh.

The willow queen glided across the clearing and leaned down until her nose nearly touched his. Not a breath touched his lips from hers as she contemplated him. "You have led them here." It wasn't a question.

How? He hadn't sensed anyone following them. "I led them away from my people," he said. And that, while putting himself in further danger, was a relief, a lessening of the burden he'd abandoned his people to. "How far away are they?" Far enough that they were outside of his range without tapping into the wild magic of the ley lines.

The dryad loomed over him. "The darkness will come with the moon's dawn. You will stop it so that my children may cleanse its stain upon my forest."

Her continual claim of ownership grated on Dante's already stung nerves. Ookamimori was his to protect. Not that he was doing such a great job of it. Her long, spindly fingers curled around his throat.

Mysti brandished her sword at the queen dryad. "Get away from our prince," she snarled. Balanced on the balls of her feet, she was poised to lunge to his rescue, with Raphael at her back. Alexion and Stipes inched to the other side of the clearing, hands ready on their weapons.

The crowned head tilted to stare at his chevaliers. Dante saw the silent judgment pass in the soulless flicker of her eyes. Willow branches whipped through the air, coiled around their throats and wrists, and tightened until their skin purpled. Dozens of dryads emerged from their trees. Roots erupted out of the ground at their beckoning and reached for the rest of his pack, tangling around them until no one could move. Korren wailed as he was pinned to the ground inches away from his mother. The tips of his short fingers strained to curl into the edge of her skirts.

Dante refused to flinch as the dryad queen's blank eyes swung back to him. He reached for the Heart. "Let them go," he demanded. The reassuring magic of Ookamimori filled his channels until his skin felt too tight to contain it all. Even a greater elemental could not stand again the focused power of an ancient Heart and its royal. Even if it charred his channels closed, he would save them.

"You can have the serpents' blood after we shed it; however, you will not have my people." He flung a hand out toward his captured family. "You will release them. Now." Magic laced every word as Dante struggled to control it. It hurt. Mother bless, it hurt. Without a bonded elemental to help channel the magic it was like trying to contain an inferno. The dryad queen hovered over him.

"They are mine," he growled.

Heartbeats pounded in his ears as they stood poised over the precipice of the dryad queen's choice. Power thrummed between them; hers rooted in the earth, deep and strong; his dancing and burning wild. Different entities of magic. Gritting his teeth until ivory creaked, Dante held his ground.

The dryad's crowned head dipped forward until her leaves brushed over his cheek as she bowed. "Prince Canidea of Ookamimori."

The ground beneath his boots vibrated as the roots snaring his pack retracted into the ground and the lesser dryads faded back into the shadows of the trees. Dante and his pack fell to their knees as the roots dropped them. Mysti gagged for air as she rubbed the bruises ringing her throat.

"Korren!" Lady Petria gathered her son into her arms, clutching him to her chest. Korren hiccupped through his tears.

"We await the tainted blood," the dryad queen said. The elemental stepped back into the fronds of the willow. The slender branches draped around her like heavy robes until the elemental leaned back into the trunk and sank beneath the wood.

Dante slumped, boneless, as he let the heavy magic drain back to

Ookamimori.

Alex caught him. "Sire."

"I am all right." He gasped as a blinding headache struck. "I think."

Reaching out, Alex wiped something wet from Dante's face. "No, I don't think you are," he said, showing that his fingers were stained crimson with blood.

Licking his lips, Dante tasted the bitter ooze of copper. Alex answered his unasked question. "Your nose is bleeding. What did you do?"

Dante wasn't sure how to feel about the unusual amazement in Alexion's voice. He'd upheld his birthright, and it had left him trembling and weak. "I called Ookamimori. I'm fine now. Go check on your partner." He pushed at the arm supporting his shoulders.

"I can see her from here," Alex said. "She is fine, just catching her breath. Mysti can handle herself."

Dante gave up on shooing his chevalier away. "Everyone else all right?" He didn't have the energy to turn and look. His skin itched as though sunburned from the inside out.

"Korren is still scared to death. Your thieves appear to be fine, and Keer is marching over here with that pinched look on his face."

"Sire!"

Oh, Mother bless it. He was too tired to get scolded right now.

"What the bloody hell was that?" Keer yelled. Dante refused to open his eyes. "You called Ookamimori, didn't you? What an imbecilic thing to do. Are you trying to turn your brain into mush? Because if you'd slipped that's what would have happened, royal or no."

A sharp finger prodded his chest, forcing him to open his eyes. "Ow," Dante protested.

Keer jabbed him with his javelin finger again. "Completely brainless and idiotic." Keer's green eyes blazed. "That was a greater elemental."

"Why is everyone yelling at me lately?" Dante grumbled. "I did what I had to do." He had the headache to prove it. Did even his pack mates think he was so useless that he couldn't protect them? A deeper ache settled into his chest. "I'm fine. We are all safe. For now. The dryad said that the serpents were coming." It worked to redirect Keer as a new worry flared into his eyes, and it halted Mysti who'd been approaching to add her own scolding.

"But, you haven't sensed them on Ookamimori's soil?"

Dante forced a shrug. "Out of my range, maybe. We are safe for now. Why don't you all rest and eat. I will meditate and see if I can search them out. The dryads wish us to take care of the serpents here and will not bother us anymore."

Keer stabbed him again. "Rest and eat first, and use this already." He waved a handkerchief.

The fabric stained quickly as Dante held it to his nose. "This isn't covered in your snot, is it?" he asked. "You'd better not have given me a rag covered in your boogers." He raised his voice to carry around the glen. Korren's teary giggle was his reward. "If I just wiped boogers on my face, Keer, I'm gonna get you."

Derrick and Jothan sniggered, as easily amused as the six-year-old. The atmosphere significantly lightened. Terror and tears dropped to unease and tremulous smiles. Their hands white-knuckled with tension, flexed and relaxed, though not falling away from the hilts of their weapons.

Rolling his eyes, Keer pushed him to lean forward into his knees. "Keep your head down until the few brains you have stop pouring out of your nose." Lowering his tone to a worried hush, he asked, "Are we truly safe here? From them?"

"If we take care of the assassins, yes, I believe so." Dante sat up, willing the headache away. "I need to meditate, see if I can find them." Keer's face pinched back into a frown. "No, I'm not taking a nap first. Look, the blood has stopped. I'm fine. If the death magic is hiding them and not their distance, they could be upon us at any minute. I have to try."

He pointed his chin at his aunt who was kneeling on the ground and sobbing into Korren's hair while Stipes stood a wary sentry over them. "They come first. If we are being hunted, we need to stop it now."

As his pack started on various tasks of making camp, Dante leaned against a tree and sank into a light trance. Ookamimori answered him eagerly, and he winced at the touch of magic on his scorched channels. Instead of gathering the Heart's power close, he flung it out into awareness and it was as though the shadows lifted around him and he could see. Life was magic and it infused everything. His pack and the dryads flared brilliantly with it. Farther away, he felt the magic of the forest creatures, and further still, the blinding conglomeration of his people in the city. He searched. There. Not so much the magic, but the absence of it—a dark blot in his forest. Estimating the distance in this state of spiritual awareness was difficult, but Dante judged they had until between sunset and moonrise.

As he resurfaced into bodily awareness, something heavy weighed on his shoulders. One of his pack had tucked a rough woolen blanket around him. Despite the summer heat, Dante pulled it tighter, shivering. Cold invaded his bones. He was tired.

"Eat, now," Raphael said. He pushed a bowl into Dante's hands and glared until he fumbled the food to his mouth. "There is a ridiculous amount of edible plants within a radius of here. Plenty of animal tracks as well. Presumably, when they aren't waylaying weary travelers and stringing them up in their roots, the dryads provide a haven to the forest creatures."

Raphael looked around and a frown wrinkled his face. Dante followed his gaze to where his thieves huddled and sighed. "No, Raphael."

Raphael twitched guiltily.

"You are a noble. Act like it. No more accusations. As a member of the thieves' guild, anything you say about them you say about me. Every royal chooses a guild to support. They are mine. Respect that if nothing else." Dante set aside the empty dish. "Go away." He could not deal with nitpicking chevaliers on top of everything else. It was ugly, but he did not care. Pulling the blanket over his head, Dante curled into his knees. He needed a minute alone. A minute to breathe.

Someone prodded him.

"Mother bless! Can't you leave me alone for a blessed minute?" Dante yelled.

Tears welled in Korren's puppy-blue eyes. Dante hadn't thought it was possible to feel worse. His stomach sank, and he reached out. "Korren."

His heir's face screwed up for a wail.

"Shh. I'm sorry. I'm not mad at you." Dante tucked Korren under his chin where he quivered and gulped for air. Lady Petria glared, ready to storm over in a fit of motherly fury. Dante begged her mercy over Korren's head. Visibly reluctant, she stayed back. Dante cuddled Korren until his sniffles drifted into soft snores. Lady Petria rescued him as his arms went numb from the dead weight. Something fell out of Korren's hand as she picked him up.

"Wait." Dante plucked the red stone out of the grass and tucked it into Korren's pocket. "He likes that thing."

Dante pulled himself together with a sense of disgust. "We don't have more than a few hours." His pack came to attention. "I believe there are about five of them." Dante dropped an apologetic hand on Raphael's shoulder. "It's hard to judge their speed of travel, but we will see them by moonrise."

Raphael elbowed him, and Dante knew his Second had forgiven him. They didn't always agree, but they were always pack.

Dante nodded. They would be ready.

Pain lanced through his shoulder, and he stumbled from the force of it.

"Sire!" Only Raphael grabbing his arm stopped him from falling as his knees gave out and everything went fuzzy.

Dante rubbed his eyes. "What was that?" His voice slurred at the end. He felt rubbery all of the sudden and it had nothing to do with the magic he'd channeled earlier. It felt as though something was sucking the strength out of him.

"What happened?" Mysti asked.

Dante probed his shoulder and moaned as his fingers pushed a sharp something deeper into his flesh.

Hands batted his out of the way. "Let me see." Mysti leaned in close enough that her hair tickled his nose. "It's some kind of dart."

Dante sagged into Raphael. "Dizzy," he mumbled, and wasn't he all kinds of pathetic today.

A ping of metal striking metal made them jump. "Whoa," Alexion said. "We are under attack. It hit my armor."

"Spread out. Cover Lady Petria and the children," Mysti barked. "Raphael, take care of Prince Dante. I've got the princess."

Dante tried to muster a protest, but his tongue felt engorged. The clearing spun around him as Raphael dragged him over to the trees and pushed him between the large roots. His chevalier brandished his rapier as he stood over Dante.

"I've got two over here," Derrick yelled.

Dante willed his limbs to move, but they were numb, paralyzed. He lay helplessly cradled by the roots and wheezed for air. Whatever toxin he'd been shot with worked fast.

The wood he leaned against moved. Twisting and crawling over his chest, pinning his arms and legs. Dante tried to yell at Raphael's back. His Second stood at his toes, watching the rest of the clearing for the attackers, oblivious to Dante's desperation.

Gritty damp roots squirmed over his chin and down into the hair at his nape. A scream reverberated in his skull. Nothing responded to his commands: not a toe, not a finger, not his lungs. He was going to suffocate, wrapped up by a tree, inches from Raphael. His heart thumped painfully in his chest.

The dryad queen leaned out of the tree. "Hush, my princeling. I mean you no harm. A snake's kiss is a deadly thing."

The dryad picked a root and held it over his face. "Drink." She snapped it in half and sap beaded out of the splintered wood. A root pried his mouth open, and a cool ooze rolled down his throat. His lungs loosened, and his heartbeat steadied.

"Bring me my blood, princeling. My children are thirsty." The blanket of roots pulled away, leaving him cold. As the dryad freed him from her embrace, the clashing of furious metal rang through the clearing. Dante summoned his sword before staggering to his feet.

Blood stained the moss around Raphael as he battled to shield Dante's resting place. Enough of that. Raphael held the shifter's blade trapped against his as they struggled. Taking the opening, Dante lunged out of his radius of protection and slit open the shifter's belly as though he was gutting a deer. Long organs bulged out of the opened skin.

"Sire?"

"I'm fine. The dryad queen neutralized the toxin."

Mysti and Alexion cut down the last assassin as Dante and Raphael watched. Leigha stood over another assassin who tried to slither away. She ruthlessly cut off its scaled head.

"Are any of them left alive?" Raiven asked. "We could get answers."

Dante cocked his head toward Leigha.

"Oops." She shrugged. "It tried to bite me. I don't care for hickies."

"So much for answers," Derrick said.

"Oh, stuff it. You killed yours."

Dante grimaced and flicked blood from the oiled metal of his sword.

A rumble started under their feet. Raphael put his back to Dante's. The trees surrounding the glen shivered and the leaves chattered together like teeth. Moss writhed and bubbled as something twisted beneath it. Roots rose out of the ground again. Dante was really starting to wish they would stay where they were supposed to—in the dirt.

"Mother, protect us," his aunt moaned, clutching Korren tighter.

Dante gave his chevaliers a meaningful glance, and Mysti and Alexion joined Stipes in a defensive cluster around Lady Petria.

"Sire," Keer said.

"I know."

They were trapped. The trees seemed closer than ever with no room for escape between. Princess Nakai hissed as several roots snaked out of the ground at her ankles. They did not follow when she danced away. Instead, they coiled around the assassin's body.

Raphael muttered under his breath. "What I wouldn't give for an axe right now."

"Just wait," Dante cautioned.

"Dante's right. They aren't after us," Raiven said.

The web of exposed roots divided five ways and enveloped the assassins in cocoons. The web convulsed and constricted. Skeletons cracked. Dante blanched and leaned into Raphael's back for comfort. There was nothing comparable to the sound of bones breaking. Leigha caught Jothan as his eyes rolled back in his head.

"Mother bless." Alexion audibly swallowed as wet crunching noises came from the cocoons.

Dante prayed that his stomach held.

Wood creaked and groaned as the roots retreated. "The darkness has been cleansed and my children nourished." The dryad queen rose in place of the roots.

"Then your kindness in saving my life has been repaid." Dante bowed, one royal to another. "If we may continue our journey now? We ask your leave."

"I detain you no further. Your journey will be guarded for as far as my children's roots reach."

Dante inclined his head a final time. Careful not to rush. This was a greater elemental, he wanted no room left for offense. He waved the others to move, and the packs were quickly gathered and slung over their shoulders. No one wanted to linger long enough to be properly harnessed.

"Ready," Mysti said.

"Lead them out." Dante stayed, facing the dryad as his pack streamed out between the trees. As Raphael trotted through the gap, Dante whirled around, shifting as he moved, and hit the moss on all four paws.

They ran until Lady Petria collapsed in her tracks. She hadn't complained, but she clearly could not physically go any further. Young, slender poplar trees cluttered the forest. None more than a few years old, certainly nothing with enough age to have gained an attached elemental. He'd had enough of dryads for the day.

Jothan was asleep before the packs hit the dirt.

"Food?" Derrick asked.

"Tired. Eat later," Alexion said.

Princess Nakai launched from Mysti's back and settled on a low branch while the pack formed a pile of fur beneath her.

Despite his deep exhaustion, sleep did not come quietly. Dante dozed in fits, and he twitched awake at every creak of the trees.

Chapter Eleven

They continued a similar pattern of travel for three days. Korren did his best to run with them as often as he could. Riding one of them as a boy became his next choice. Dante was proud of his cousin. The young boy, though tired and scared, complained little; at least compared to what he'd heard from other six-year-olds in the city. Korren seemed to draw some comfort from the red-striped rocks he had chosen from the stream. Whenever the pack stopped and shifted, he would continuously rub the river-smooth stones in his fingers.

During one of their rest periods, Raiven knelt before the crown prince. "I think you dropped these, little one." Opening his hand, Raiven revealed the two shiny stones. His ever-present hood shielded his eyes, but a soft smile curled his lips.

"Oh!" Korren yanked his pockets inside out. Only leaves and dirt fell out. "Those are mine!" Raiven extended his hand with the rocks. "Oh, thank you, Raiven, sir!"

Dante watched as Raiven nodded. "You are welcome," the thief said. "Here, perhaps I have something that will keep them safer than your pockets." Raiven waved for Derrick to toss his pack to him. The leather bag landed at his feet with a thud and a few clinks from within. Raiven's nimble fingers unbuckled the opening and reached in, digging around for several moments. Korren watched wide-eyed, clutching his precious rocks to his chest. Raiven produced a small pouch. He dumped its questionable contents into the pack. Boring two holes into the soft leather pouch with a knife, Raiven threaded it with a cord. "Here, keep this around your neck. They won't fall out that way."

Dante grinned as Korren took the pouch with a happy squeak. "Thank you!" Before Raiven knew what hit him, Korren leapt forward, grabbing his neck in an enthusiastic hug. Lady Petria grimaced at the interaction but waited with forced politeness until Korren released the thief before pulling Korren away. Tugging her son close, she gave Raiven a wary look. Raiven did not react to her distrust. It was a typical reaction to the thieves' guild from the nobility.

Later when they stopped to rest, Mysti grabbed Dante's collar and dragged him off to the side.

"Ack!" he choked out. "Mysti, let go."

She did, but not until she deemed them far enough away. "I wanted to talk to you."

Dante rolled his eyes, rubbing his abused throat. "And you couldn't just ask me to walk with you?"

"I've been thinking about your friends," she said, ignoring his question. Mysti locked her hands behind her back and stood at attention.

Ah. Here it comes. Dante braced himself for a scolding. Honestly, he was surprised it had taken her this long to get around to it; though, he supposed they'd been rather distracted.

"I can see why you count them as family. I have watched them the last few days. Despite their livelihood, they are good people. They work together as a family, protecting each other—and you. Even though they have not said anything directly, they have been standing up for you. Keer too. They treat you both as part of their family. It has been that way for a long time, hasn't it?"

Dante nodded, still expecting her to yell at him.

She didn't. "I am glad they were there for you before I was. I am not thrilled with where they are from, but I trust your judgment."

"Really?" The words that spilled out her mouth were not what he'd expected

Her brown eyes narrowed. "Yes, really."

Dante didn't question her blessing, lest she take offense and hit him. "Um, thanks, I guess." He relaxed. "I am glad you are giving them a chance."

Mysti socked him in the shoulder.

"Ow!"

Snickering, she walked away. "That's for doubting me."

With Mysti's approval given, Alexion and Stipes warmed up to the thieves; Raphael was not so easily swayed. He'd forgiven Dante for having them as friends. He hadn't forgiven them for befriending Dante.

Princess Nakai's wing had healed enough for short flights. When they hit the trail again, she flew in circles around them, carefully working out the stiffness from inactivity. Dante was her perch today while Raphael took a turn carrying Korren. She was far lighter than Korren and had long since perfected landing on the harness without throwing the running wolves off-balance. Dante kept a steady lope as she landed on his back. Her wicked talons gripped the leather harness tightly.

"You flew longer this time." Communicating as a wolf or owl was vastly different than just opening one's mouth. A twitch of fur or feather could say more than the longest sentence.

"Yes."

They mused in their own heads for a time.

Princess Nakai interrupted the silence. "I wish I could fly home before we reach the mountains."

"Why? There isn't anything worth getting caught by the Kobrona for, is there?"

When she answered, her voice was a tight rasp. "My sister."

"What?" Dante almost stopped in his tracks, but managed to keep his feet moving rather than throwing his passenger off.

"Never mind. It is not an option. I know. If we are caught, there will be no one to save her or anyone else. Not to mention it is over a day's run out of the way."

Dante wanted to offer some comfort, but what was there to say? "If she is as strong as you, she'll be fine."

"Perhaps." She cried a soft mournful whoo. "I left her alone in the tower."

"The tower?"

But the princess had gone silent, composing herself.

Keer moved closer and answered for her. "A solitary building with a set of rooms at the top. It is about five-hundred feet high and completely separate from the other buildings."

"A prison tower?" Dante asked.

Keer nodded. "There is no way up without flying. Correct?" he looked to the princess.

"Yes," she agreed.

"I know she is strong, but that is part of what worries me so. She is ten years old and not afraid when she should be. I fear she will cause trouble that will make them hurt her or use her in death magic"

"You should steal the princess!"

Dante and Keer came to a bounding halt and stared at Jothan incredulously.

"You, Raiven, Derrick, and Leigha are at least four-star thieves, right? So, stealing a princess shouldn't be too hard, and it's not like the Kobrona will think anyone can actually do it."

"That is the dumbest idea I've ever heard!" Keer snapped. "I mean, honestly, first you'd have to get past the Kobrona, then get to the Tower, find a way to fly, convince the princess you are going to help her, and get all the way back out without getting caught!" Keer's tail flipped in agitation.

The pack gathered around as Dante grinned toothily at his friend. "You think we should do it?"

"What! No! Well… but, it's dangerous, and you are our prince. It's a stupid idea," Keer muttered.

"And you think we should do it." Dante grinned inwardly. Keer was a pushover for sob stories.

The idea excited him. They could do it. As Jothan had pointed out, they were the top members of the guild.

"Do what?" Leigha asked.

"Steal a princess!" Jothan said.

"Absolutely not," Raphael snapped. "The idea is absurd."

Mysti did not look thrilled either. "Who is this princess you wish to steal?"

"My little sister, Ashe," Nakai hooted softly.

"Oh." Mysti was silent for a moment. "I see." The thick pine trees muffled the rest of the forest sounds, giving their conversation a conspiratorial air.

Stipes shifted his hulking weight. "Sire, what will they do with her?"

"She will not acquiesce quietly to their orders. We still don't know exactly what Kobrona is after," Princess Nakai said. "She is stubborn and willful. She won't listen."

"Then we should get her out," Stipes said firmly. The look on his face was that of a well-practiced big brother surging forth to protect one of his own.

Alexion cocked his head, ears flopping forward. "Can you?"

Dante looked to Raiven and Keer. "What you do think? Could we do it?"

"I don't know the terrain or the layout of the city," Raiven said. "However, we are good at what we do."

Lady Petria screeched into the conversation. "You would risk the family royals in an endeavor that is doomed to fail?!"

Dante glared. "What if it was Korren held prisoner and alone? How would you feel then?"

Her lips twisted petulantly. He held her under a firm stare. Finally, she subsided. "Fine, do what you want, but you will leave Korren and me out of your shenanigans. The only reason we are traveling is to stay away from the serpents."

His head hurt. Her mood swings were driving him crazy. The journey forced her to stay stronger than at home, but her moods could still turn nasty, like now. "Of course, Lady Aunt. We will not risk your safety." Dante pivoted in place, the soft grass and moss tickling his paws. "Well, we should turn farther east if we are going to try it."

Raphael snorted. "It sounds risky to me. We are fleeing to protect you and Prince Korren, sire. Not become a rescue service."

Stipes shook his shaggy head. "She is a little girl, Raphael."

Leigha snarled. "You, Raphael, I thought you were honorable and noble."

Growling, Raphael turned away. "I am here to protect our Alpha-Prince; the rest of you seem happy enough to throw him at danger."

"Enough. I want votes. Now. Left group, we go to save the little one. Right, we continue onward." Dante deliberately padded to the left side of their small trail and sat down.

The owl shifter on his back spread her wings to keep her balance. Her long talons combed his thick fur as she adjusted her grip to accommodate his movements. He could order them all to follow him and do it either way; however, he wanted an agreement.

All of his thieves joined him. They knew they could accomplish the mission. Lady Petria defiantly stalked to the right side of the trail, dragging Korren with her. Alexion glanced at Mysti and sidled to Dante's side of the trail. Curling his lips to reveal his fangs, Raphael stood at Lady Petria's side, challenging Dante with a glare. Keer did not take long to decide; he too, knew they could do it. Mysti and Stipes were all who stood in the middle.

Stipes seemed torn between loyalty to his partner and his feelings on the matter. "It's a little girl, Raphael." He chose the left. Raphael snorted disdainfully. Stipes scolded him. "He is our prince, if not yet our king."

"Mysti?" Dante prodded. He twitched his ears forward hopefully. The votes were already stacked for him, but Mysti was First Chevalier, her choice carried a heavy weight.

"We go, but only those who can be of use. The rest of us will wait in the foothills for you. If it looks like you failed, we will continue taking Korren and Lady Petria to safety." Mysti sealed the decision.

Princess Nakai directed them away from the main river. Mountainous foothills made their progress exhausting and slow. They spent more time climbing up and down than going straight.

The pace obviously frustrated Princess Nakai, though she didn't gripe or even frown. It was in the slump of her shoulders. In the impatient beat of her wings. She flew as often as she could, stopping to rest for a few moments before taking off again. In the dim gloom of the thick trees, her white form was a ghostly blur.

Dante thought that if she had the strength, she'd leave them behind and rescue her sister through sheer determination. He wondered what had made her flee alone in the first place.

Rest breaks came a little more often as the pack felt the effects of the days of travel. Young Jothan struggled to keep pace, and even Korren's enthusiasm had dwindled. Still, most of them plugged along gamely.

Most of them.

Lady Petria stopped abruptly. "I cannot go any farther today."

This declaration was not new coming from her. Dante whined, letting out his frustration for a brief moment. "Lady Aunt, we have discussed this twice today already. We need to keep moving."

"Why? You haven't sensed anyone behind us, and I am tired. Korren is about to fall off Raphael's back he's so weary. Dante glanced to where Raphael followed. Korren slumped over Raphael's neck. His fistfuls of Raphael's fur were probably the only thing keeping him on.

"Again?" Raphael asked when he noticed Lady Petria's standstill.

"Yes, but I think she may have a point. I cannot sense anyone within a couple of days of us, and we are all too tired to keep moving like this. Especially if we are going to rescue a princess."

The reminder of their disagreement brought a sour slump to Raphael's tail, but he didn't make any comments against their mission. "You may be right. We need more than a few hours rest. None of us are used to traveling like this."

Dante barked sharply to bring back the front runners who hadn't seen them stop. Nakai was the first to return, swooping and shifting as she landed. The princess stretched and rolled her shoulders with a wince. "Are we stopping again?"

"It seems like a good idea. The trees will provide a decent shelter, unless you saw something up ahead?" Dante said.

She shook her head. "It is more of the same. We are getting close to the borders of my lands. Hanehishou, the city, is only another day farther."

It suddenly occurred to Dante that this slight woman had already made this journey, alone and wounded. Amazing.

The pack gathered around. "We will stop here for the night."

"The sun is not even three-quarters of the way through its time!"

Keer didn't seem to be trying to dissuade them. He flopped on his belly and dropped his head on his paws.

"And we are running ourselves to total exhaustion," Lady Petria complained.

Mysti agreed. "It seems a wise choice as long as you don't sense any enemies, sire."

Dante jolted upright, fleeing the flames of his nightmares. His abrupt movement dumped Mysti's head off his stomach.

"Hm, what? Dante?" she asked. It was a testament to her exhaustion that she wasn't kneeling over him with her sword drawn to defend him. Alexion stirred from where he was wrapped around his partner. They had all chosen to nap in human form. It brought an impression of comfort and familiarity for a while. It didn't stop them from sleeping in a large puppy pile. Even Lady Petria slept curled up beside Raphael and Stipes with Korren sprawled under her arm.

"Shh, it's nothing, just a bug biting me."

"Hm'kay," Mysti mumbled, squirming to snuggle closer to Alexion.

Dante tried to pull his legs up, but something pinned him in place. Gathering the energy to pay attention, he looked for the source of the problem. Derrick's legs laid over both his and Raiven's. He slumped back with a grumpy moan. With the way Derrick slept, Dante wouldn't be going anywhere for a while. Keer's arm flopped into his face. He didn't bite it, though he dearly wanted to. Instead, Dante shoved it away, then remembering sleeping with his pack brother in the past, pulled it back, tucking the limb beneath his own head as a pillow. It would keep Keer from hitting him again. The bookworm was a sound sleeper, but it didn't stop him from flopping around like a dying fish. It was Keer's own fault if his arm went numb. He wouldn't have pinned it down if Keer could keep his sleeping body parts to himself.

The next time he woke, Dante found Raphael and Mysti awake and poking through the travel packs. Derrick had curled into a ball, freeing Dante's legs. He was careful not to step on anyone in his escape. Leigha lay with Jothan. She counted it as her personal duty to protect Calume's youngest protégé. Not that any of them wanted to let their mentor down by allowing something to happen to the teenager.

Having navigated the tangle of snoozing bodies, Dante stretched, all the joints of his spine popping. A fluffy mattress, pine needles were not. "We should hunt again."

Mysti jumped and glared at him for startling her. He offered an unapologetic shrug.

"Yes," Raphael agreed. "We still have a good bit of dry food, but we still need to save it. Something fresh besides meat would be nice. Maybe we could find some more berries. We haven't found any for a couple of days."

Dante tilted his head to listen to the forest. "What about fish? I think I can hear a stream. Do we have any line in the packs?"

Raphael brightened with a smile. "Fish would be good. I saw some line in this pack." The chevalier reached sideways and dragged one of the packs across the ground to his feet. Digging around in the outer pockets, Raphael quickly uncovered the fishing line. "We have two. Shall we try our luck?"

"Yes, let's. If the fish are biting, we can surprise the others when they awaken." Dante accepted one of the lines. A dead branch quickly turned into a pole with the line coiled around the end. Following the trickling sounds, the two men found a quiet stream just large enough to carry fat trout. They followed it, looking for a likely spot.

"Here, this looks good." Raphael crouched where the bank curved out over the water, casting a cool shadow.

"We need bait." Dante looked around and spotted a rotting log. He strode to it and kicked it over with his heel. Worms and slugs squirmed in the moist dirt. Dante grabbed for the worms first, handing the slimy creatures to Raphael as he caught them. One slipped through his fingers and down a hole, leaving dirt and slime behind. Only the fattest slugs were selected for bait duty. Raphael grimaced as he held a handful of squiggly, slippery creatures. Dante could not help but snigger.

"Find me something to put them in, you ninny," Raphael snapped. Still laughing, Dante looked around for a container. A curved section of bark had broken off the rotten log.

Scooping it up, he held it out. "Here, this should work."

Raphael dumped the wriggling ball of worms and slugs into the bark. An extra sticky slug clung to his thumb. Raphael tried pushing it off with a finger, but the slug just slid around his nail. He pinched the slug, pulling it off, and holding it up for inspection. "You, my friend, are going on the hook first."

Dante propped up the bait container with smaller chunks of bark to keep it from tipping. Selecting a long nightcrawler, he pierced it with the fishhook and dropped it into the water. Raphael relaxed cross-legged a few feet away. Silence reigned for several peaceful moments with the only sound of the burbling water and chirping chickadees.

"Sire," Raphael began. "Dante."

"Hmm?" Dante glanced over at his Second Chevalier.

"I plead forgiveness for my actions recently. It has been unbecoming of my station and you."

"Raphael..." Dante didn't know what to say. Raphael was right, after all. He'd been rude and obnoxious.

Raphael held up a hand. "No, please, sire. I have been unpleasant and unforgiving. I am sorry that I have not tried to be better." He hesitated. "I don't really have a defense for myself, only that I wished the best for you and did not see that in your chosen friends. I know you had a lonely childhood despite your father's best efforts. I am glad they found you." Raphael picked at the flaky bark on his makeshift fishing pile. "I think rescuing the little princess is a noble idea. I only worry for your safety, as is my chosen duty. I don't want you to go. Lord Kobrona is there practicing death magic and hunting for royals. You want to waltz right up to him and stick out your tongue and run away with the prize."

Finding out what was bothering his eldest brother figure so badly was a relief. "We can do it, Raphael. We can save her and get away clean. You can trust Raiven and Derrick; they will always have my back. Leigha's a little crazy with her explosive powders, but she's good at what she does."

"They have proven that merely by following you out here," Raphael replied, "but I still worry."

"I guess you are allowed." Dante grinned, he was about to say something else when his line gave a hard tug in his hand. "Bite!" He jerked the line to set the hook. The fish fought hard, even splashing out of the water once, twisting on the line. Rolling the branch, Dante reeled in the fish until he could flip it onto the bank. It landed and flopped furiously. Seeing that they didn't have an extra line to string it on, Dante drew the long knife from his boot and cut off its head. "Well, I get to eat trout tonight at least," he crowed, throwing a triumphant grin at Raphael, who was totally ignoring him in favor of reeling in his own fish. Together, they caught fourteen fat trout.

The sun sank into the horizon with a brilliant display of pinks and purples by the time they returned to camp. A few glow crystals chased the shadows away with blue light.

"Derrick, get a fire going, would you? We are having fish for supper tonight!" Dante triumphantly displayed the mess of six fish he carried on his line.

Raphael held up his eight trout. "I caught more."

It was an evening of relaxation and laughter as they all talked together. Dante found himself almost regretting introducing the two halves of his family as they exchanged humiliating stories about him. Lady Petria even got in on it with tales about his younger escapades from before the rest had known him. He discarded that thought, though, watching his family truly together for the first time.

Chapter Twelve

In mid-pace, his connection with the Heart snapped. The Pulse stopped beating beneath his feet. Dante staggered. His sight went dim. The magic was gone.

What was happening?

He buried the fear of being blinded and glanced discretely around to see if anyone had noticed his discomfort. Emptiness echoed when he reached for the connection. Straining harder, he caught a brief glimmering sense of his home before his strength ran out. Dante stopped in his tracks. Korren yanked handfuls of his fur painfully to stay seated.

"Dante, why'd we stop?" Korren asked in his squeaky child's voice. His heels thumped impatiently on Dante's ribs.

Before he could answer, Princess Nakai flew in exuberant circles. "We've reached my lands. Hanehishou is less than a day's journey."

"How do you know, princess?" Alexion asked, plopping down and scratching his ear.

"I can feel it, of course. I am a royal. We always know where the borders are."

Dante tried to hide how lost he felt. He should've known that. They weren't on his land any more; of course, he couldn't feel Ookamimori's Pulse. The sudden disconnection was logical, if not appreciated. If Dante wanted to reach the Heart, he would have to tap into the ley lines. Ookamimori could no longer feed him the magic required to sustain his sight. He hadn't realized how dependent on it he was. He could use his own magic to see, but it would not be as vivid or far reaching, and would dwindle rapidly under the strain. He was truly half-blind until he returned home. The last time he had crossed the borders, he'd still been able to see, and his father had been alive.

Oh, Mother bless it all. Despair fueled his urge to wrap his hands around Kobrona's scaly throat. He wanted to go home.

"How can you feel it so strongly, Princess Nakai? You are not the regent. Queen Jeziah is," Keer asked.

Nakai hooted in agreement, rustling her feathers to smooth them from her flight. "I've always had a strong connection to Hanehishou's Heart." Something like shame or sorrow shadowed her face. "The Heart seems to like me better, and since Kobrona caught Queen Jeziah, the connection has grown stronger."

Derrick, always uncaring of his word's impact or rudeness asked, "How old are you, anyway?"

The princess twitched at the forwardness of the question. "Not that it is any of your business, but I am nineteen. How old are you?"

"I'm twenty-one, so is Raiven, obviously, and Dante is nineteen, if you care to know." Derrick slanted a sly grin at him. Dante rolled his eyes in response to Derrick's obvious plotting. The man had been trying to set him up for years. Keer wore a contemplating expression. Growling at his friends, Dante stalked over the pine-needle carpet. "Ignore them, princess. They are meddling where they do not need to. We have your sister to save. If we make good time, we can do it tonight."

Derrick yipped and came to walk at his side. "Aw, you know we just want to find someone worthy of you."

Dante's lips curled into a snarl as he remembered the last girl he had courted. "So, you are going to set me up like that noble, Lord Riskus, did with his daughter, and then try to scare her off?"

"You didn't like her!" Derrick protested. "And any woman who is to take the throne beside you has to be able to take a few pranks."

"A few? You harassed her for weeks. Then you made a mud pit, dragged her out of bed in the middle of the night, and dumped her in it. You threatened her life if she pursued me. I had to station five of Captain Lask's patrol wolves with her for months before she could sleep again. I didn't like her, no, but that was no way to treat a lady. I was prepared to shoo her away after a proper amount of courting time. Even the stuffier nobles didn't expect me to marry the first lady I courted." Dante nipped at Raiven's ear, for he'd been in on the disaster too. "The poor girl is traumatized even now. She can barely look at me across a ballroom. Much less talk to me. I didn't want to marry her, but she was alright to talk to; better than the nobles trying to twist me into doing their bidding."

Raiven grunted, pawing his abused ear. "It was Derrick's idea!"

"You planned the bloody thing!" Dante rammed him with his shoulder, sending Raiven stumbling a few steps sideways. Derrick stayed a safe distance away, snickering at his twin.

"Wait, are you talking about Lady Layla?" Raphael asked from a few steps behind.

"Yes." Keer answered for Dante, since his teeth were clamped onto Raiven's tail.

Raphael snorted. "So, that's why she was so timid after the first couple of days. I apologize, sire, I believed you had spooked the girl yourself, leaving her alone in the labyrinth or something."

Suddenly, Dante realized he had a way to turn the tables on his thief friends. They had told a bunch of embarrassing stories of him. Well, he knew of several pranks he had been blamed for that were completely the fault of the twins. "Hey, Raphael, do you remember when you pinched me about twenty times a day for a week because you thought I'd told that girl with a crush on you that you had a fetish for being pinched?"

Raphael snarled, fangs flashing. "I still have a bruise from the last time she caught me."

"Well, I had nothing to do with it—like I told you. Derrick listens to the maids gossiping, heard about her crush, and made it all up." He didn't bother trying to hide his triumphantly evil grin. It was true, after all. Never mind that he'd told Derrick to eavesdrop on the maids.

"Oh, really." Raphael leveled a dangerous glare at the suddenly skittish thief.

"Uh, look at that, I'm gonna go run away, like way over there." Derrick darted off.

Raphael leapt after him. "I am going to kill you for that. She pinches me all the time! It bloody hurts!"

Hmm, what else should he tell? Oh, yes that would do. "Alexion, that time your soap turned your skin purple for, like, three days? Yeah, Raiven made that and switched it out himself." Rumbling contentedly, Dante dropped back to walk with Stipes and Mysti as Alexion leaped at Raiven, bowling him into the dirt.

"Having fun causing conflicts, sire?" Mysti asked.

"They have no problem getting me into trouble, so yes. It is their turn to feel the pain." If his wolf's throat had been capable of the noise, Dante would have cackled. He used the momentary amusement to force his paws to continue trotting forward and away from the comforting touch of Ookamimori.

Chapter Thirteen

The deeper they went into the Owlderah lands, the larger the foothills grew with deep valleys between them. It became so that it was impossible to see what lay before them until they reached the peak of a hill. Hanehishou remained unseen until they crested the final hill. It sprawled out in the valley directly below. The city with multiple towers encompassed the entire valley and climbed the hills beyond. Thick pine trees hid the pack's presence as they surveyed the beautiful land. The houses and other buildings were only slightly more numerous than the towers casting them into shadow.

Shifting forms, Dante pointed at the tower standing imperiously high above the others. "Is that where your sister is being held?"

"Yes," the princess said, balancing on the pine boughs above him.

"Where is the serpent army camp?" Raiven asked.

Princess Nakai stayed silent for a long moment, surveying her home. "I don't see them. It looks like he has sent them onward already, most likely to Ookamimori."

An angry growl erupted out of his chest. Dante dug deep furrows into the loamy earth with his claws. He had left his people to face Kobrona alone. He was a failure.

A comforting hand landed on his shoulder as Raiven knelt beside him. "We should wait until nightfall to enter the city. Do you have any idea of the patrol schedule?"

"Only the one for my people, if Kobrona hasn't changed it. He hadn't when I left. He has sentries on some of the towers and ground patrols, but I don't know the schedule. I could see them from my window. That's how I knew where to fly, but they changed places every shift. I don't know where they are now."

Shrugging his shoulders free of the travel pack, Alexion sat at the base of a tree. "How did you get away?"

"I don't know." Nakai rubbed her wrist as though wiping away the weight of chains. "He bound me to my human form, the same as my mother and sister, with death magic. A person died for each of us to be bound." Her breath hitched. "The… the runes were written on our skin in blood. It hurt like nothing I've ever felt before. My skin burned. I could feel the magic sinking into my body like poison."

They were held silent by the horror of her tale.

Nakai stared dully over their heads toward her home. "I fought it for days. Something in the binding magic broke. I don't know what I did to get free. It was just gone. I remember the guards being lax. It was nearly the end of their shift, and they were dozing. My memories after the death magic are blurry. It hurt so much." Her soft voice stuttered in remembrance of the pain. "After it broke, nothing could stop me from shifting out of the chains. I tried to get Ashe free, but the magic bound her form still." Dante saw her fingers curl and dig into her arm like talons as she continued. "I left her there..."

A lump rose in Dante's throat. He couldn't think of anything to say. No words of comfort to soften her guilt and pain. Damn Kobrona to the shades for inflicting this darkness upon them.

Nakai, sitting alone in the tree, wrapped her arms around herself in an empty embrace. "The tower has always been used for the most dangerous of prisoners, ones awaiting judgment during Communion: murderers, rapists. Ashe..." She swallowed hard. "Kobrona kept mother at his side, along with the other royals he captured. Ashliene is alone in that horrible prison because I left her there." Self-recrimination cried from every line of her body. Blood welled beneath the fingernails she dug into her skin.

Mysti stood to her full height, just able to catch Nakai's foot braced on a branch. Mysti gave it a light shake to get the princess's attention. "You did not fail her. You got her help. You warned us. We will rescue your sister." Nakai jumped at Mysti's firm tone, sending pine branches dipping and swaying.

"Now, take a deep breath, and help us plan a way to save her. How far out do your patrols fly? Will we be undercover here, or do we need to move deeper into the forest?"

Nakai's golden eyes were wide and damp. "We... we should hide out here as long as we don't create any light. The patrol flights stay over the city, and the greater elementals don't normally wander around close." She was obviously thinking of the dryad queen. No one wanted to have another confrontation.

Princess Nakai resettled on the branch so she was talking to them instead of over their heads. "Kobrona kept most of his soldiers around the castle." She pointed to the left of the city where a four-story castle competed with the surrounding towers for height. "He kept three soldiers in the tower with us and a patrol of five at the base."

"Wasn't he worried that your people would attack and free you?" Derrick asked from where he sat propped up against the pack he had been carrying.

"No. He let them try. The guards caught them in a perimeter spell that paralyzed them. They didn't have time to reset it before I escaped." Nakai curled into a ball, still perched in the tree. "Kobrona...sacrificed them in the central courtyard as an example to the others. Three of them were my chevaliers. It was"—she swallowed heavily— "it was not a clean death. I cannot feel my Fourth, Shota, anymore. I believe he died trying to get me free from the tower. The death magic muted so much I'm not even sure when his rune went gray." Her fingers were white-knuckled around her wrist.

Dante rubbed his tattoos, touching his chevaliers' links to ensure he could still feel them, even though they stood right in front of him. Imagining the loss of his chevaliers brought a painful lump to Dante's throat. Despite everything he put his chevaliers through, they stayed with him. Mysti, more of an older sister, was still the closest thing he had to a mother. Raphael made an awesome big brother, when he wasn't being a snob. Alexion and Stipes fit right in beside them. Losing them to Kobrona in a public death magic ritual would be unbearable. Dante wanted to hug the woman and offer her comfort for a pain he could imagine all too well. Since Nakai sat well out of his reach, he settled for planning her baby sister's rescue and let her grieve in peace.

"Those not entering the city should continue onward to the mountain pass," Raiven said. "That ensures Lady Petria and the children's safety. If we are caught, they can still reach the Lupinic lands and wait there until the Communion." Dante nodded in agreement.

"I'm going with you," Alexion commanded. "I can guard your back while you do your sneaky thief things."

"I second that," Mysti said. "The rest of us will stay with Lady Petria. Alexion won't slow you down or get in the way."

"Keer, Leigha?" Derrick asked, cocking an eyebrow.

Leigha finally joined the conversation. "Jothan and I will go toward the pass. Jothan is not trained for a mission of this caliber. You boys can handle it without my help. I do have a few small boomers that might come in handy though."

Keer sighed. "I will go with Lady Petria. A smaller team is better. Less noticeable."

Nakai dropped out of the tree. "You aren't leaving me here. I'm not running away again." She clenched her fists.

"Of course not." Dante gave her a startled glance. "You are showing us the way and convincing your little sister that we are rescuing her. Why would we leave you behind?"

"I am a girl, and I've already failed her once." The reply was immediate.

"Um…" Dante verbally stumbled, reaching for appropriate words. "Who cares if you are a woman? You can still show us the way and carry weapons; I assume you can use them?" Nakai nodded. "Then why wouldn't you come?"

She didn't answer.

"Exactly." Dante turned back to the twins. "Now, Raiven, do you have a grappling hook? We'll need it to climb the Tower." He pretended not to see his chevaliers' confusion. He was so not getting interrogated about a thief's life right now.

"We both have one," Derrick answered for them both.

"Good. I do too, so if we lose one, we'll have a backup." Digging into his pack, Dante pulled out a slender roll of leather with a strap that wrapped over his chest. The weight of the lock picks Calume had given him and a few other tools rested comfortably against his sternum for easy access. A Spidarian-weave rope attached to a hook built into the strap of the pack with a clip that went over it. The rope was the finest money could buy. The Spidarian family wove the strongest of threads and the softest of silks, all forms of it were as light as air, rope woven from it would never break, or fray, unless cut by a blade forged of magic.

Raiven and Derrick gathered what they needed. Everything was ready long before nightfall. Eating came next. Lady Petria was being helpful and passed out granola and jerky. Dante accepted a canteen from Stipes. He swallowed the lukewarm water in gulps that ran down his chin and soaked into his shirt.

"Dante, manners. Just because we are in the woods, that does not mean you can eat like a pig." Lady Petria waited until he lowered the canteen to thwack him.

"Ow!" Dante rubbed his smarting ear.

"Serves you right." Lady Petria sniffed and knelt gracefully beside Korren, wrapping her arms around him and pulling him close. She spread a handkerchief over her lap and urged Korren into eating as she nibbled the jerky herself.

"Princess Nakai, can you tell us the layout of the city and anything else you think will help?" Raiven asked.

They passed the time until dusk shrouded the hills.

Relief warmed Dante as he watched his aunt and cousin disappear into the gloom of the forest under the protection of his chevaliers.

Keer waited for Leigha who tossed a pouch to Derrick. "Here, these are some of my smaller boomers. A small spark of magic will set them off. The red ones are just smoke. The white ones are a bit more damaging. They will blow a lock if you don't have time to pick it. They are bright, though, so only use them if your position is compromised—and do not look at them. It takes a full two minutes to see again. I know; done it a few times."

Dante eyed the pouch in Derrick's hand. Raiven beat him to it. "I will carry that, thank you." He grabbed the pouch from his twin's hand and hooked it to his belt. "Thank you, Leigha. I hope we don't have to use them."

"Awe, but they are so much fun!" Leigha snickered. "See you later!" She tossed a wave over her shoulder and dragged Jothan by the hood on his shirt to join Keer.

"Mother, keep them safe," Dante prayed from the depths of his soul. "Let us rejoin them quickly. Don't let anyone die for me."

Chapter Fourteen

Nakai

Nakai closed her eyes and relished in the fragile strength of her newly healed wings and the freedom of the air. A soft breeze caught her wings, extending her silent glide. Focusing on the ground below, she watched the four Canidea wolves flowing as shades through the moon's sullen light. Without the strength of her owl sight, Nakai doubted she would be able to see them. The wolves kept an easy pace with her flight.

The blue crystal lights of her city blanketed the valley like a sea of stars. Homesickness welled in her chest at the sight. Through the Pulse of Hanehishou, she could feel the temper of her lands, the fear of her people, and the blight Kobrona left behind with his death magic. The Heart sang to her, but it was faint and the magic felt oily.

The wolves followed her, running to the side of the stony mountain path, which wound around the first of the houses and the old lookout towers. The towers were only two stories high, the bottom level containing a small kitchen and beds, and the upper floor being for the actual lookout. The squat towers encircled the city. Most were rotten and crumbling. There hadn't been a use for them in centuries.

Why the wolves dared accompany her into the depths of the enemy encampment eluded her; however, for the sake of her sister, she would not refuse this chance. If this prince and his men believed they could steal Ashliene away from Kobrona's scaly coils, who was she to tell them no? If this harebrained scheme worked, she would be forever indebted.

Reaching the city proper, Nakai shifted to land in one smooth motion. Huffs of surprise came from the four wolves behind her as they stopped. She hid a smile. "It is safer to journey as humans. Only the royals fly with white wings, and we have few wolves living here right now."

It killed her that her own city could not be trusted. For the first time in her life, Nakai felt uncomfortable on the streets of Hanehishou. Her people loved her and she often wandered amongst the people, welcomed and loved. Now, in the midnight hours with Kobrona's curfew in effect, fear clung to the air she breathed. She could almost taste it.

"Do you think Kobrona is in the city, or did he join his army?" one of the twin thieves asked after following her to human form.

Nakai thought it might be Derrick, but even after the long journey, she could not be sure. These men were sacrificing their safety for her, and she couldn't' even call them by name. Shame curdled in her stomach. She answered, resolving to do better. "I have no idea. We would have to go by the castle to find out. That would create much more risk of being seen."

It was child's play to slink through the shadows. At a main street intersection, Nakai crept back against the wall to peer around the corner. Kobrona's guards clustered around a fire bowl for warmth. Hatred surged in her breast at the sight of their golden armor. Images of those soldiers trampling through her city and in her home, causing destruction in their wake, made her tremble. Ominous pikes stabbed into the stones beside each soldier. A checkpoint. Her people would have to pass through it every day to reach the markets from their homes, a constant reminder of their capture.

Whispering to the wolves at her back she said, "There is a group of guards in the courtyard. We'll have to go around. This way." Nakai cut across the cobbled street and darted down an alley. One day you will pay for your desecration of my home, she vowed silently. The alley led to a meandering street, running along it with certainty; Nakai chose another murky alley. Cobbled streets twisted and curved through her city with no reason. There was no proper planning. The streets were confusing for anyone who wasn't born to them, and to some who were.

Blue crystalline streetlamps cast everything in an eerie glow. She had always loved the color. The depths of blue in these crystals were warmer than the crystals grown in Ookamimori. Each city had their geographical variety of crystal, creating colors unique to it. At the Communion, each family displayed and sold their colors, but amongst all of them, she loved Hanehishou's brilliant blue.

Nakai caught the wolves' unspoken question. "Kobrona established a curfew: everyone home by moonrise. That is why we have only seen the guards. I think he may have stopped the patrol flights too. We should have heard or seen one by now."

"It's more logical for him to keep his serpents on duty than shifters who hold no loyalty to him," Alexion murmured.

Nodding agreement, Nakai guided them farther in a winding arc, well around the guards blocking the main intersection. Her city was unnaturally quiet as they skirted the edge of a courtyard.

The cobbled streets changed from rough brownstones to smooth gray ones as the center of the city grew closer. A thick wall surrounded the tower, and Nakai's heart sank upon seeing the wrought iron gates wrapped in chains. Despair ate at her heart as she faced the approaching wolves. "I don't know how to get in now. We never chained it, even when a prisoner was up there."

Alexion looked as lost as Nakai. "What do we do now?"

"You got us here. It's our turn now," a thief, Derrick again, said.

The prince nodded. "Let us take it from here. Your sister will need your full attention."

Curious, despite her trepidation, Nakai watched as he pulled a strange little bundle out and knelt before the three chains constricting the iron bars. She glared at the monstrous locks, wishing they'd turn into slag and melt away, but they remained solid and imposing. Prince Dante selected two metal twigs out of his bundle. He slid them into a lock and cocked his head in intense, radiating focus as he slowly twitched and twisted the sticks. As the chains clanged against the bars with a dangerous rattle, Nakai peered over his messy hair at the glow of the guards' watch fire for any sign of movement. The bloody light of the fire threw the guards' nightmarish shadows against the wall.

"Please hurry," she whispered. The prince didn't acknowledge her. He bent over his task with utter concentration.

The twins pulled long braids of rope out of their packs and some kind of fishhook as big as her head. Nakai rubbed the goosebumps pimpling her skin as she tried to keep an eye on everything at once. The louder twin held the hook and twisted the end until the metal split into three, turning it until they sat in place back-to-back, forming a triad. A grappling hook. How strange. A strange prince with even stranger friends, and they were going to save her sister. Nakai tilted her head back to stare at the tower's pinnacle, searching for any sign of life within those cold, stone walls. Almost there, Ashe, just a little longer. Not even a crystal light shone from the window, and a suffocating fear clutched her lungs. What if they'd moved her? Taken Ashe with them? No, she couldn't think that. Ashe had to be there.

Alexion stood to the side. "Is there anything I can do to help?"

"No." He was shot down before the last syllable faded. Nakai winced for him as he was abandoned to his nerves and the sense of uselessness she shared.

Prince Dante sighed. "Derrick, stuff it. Alexion is only trying to help, and he is still capable of kicking your ass."

A hysterical snicker escaped Nakai when Raiven smacked the back of his brother's head, and she clapped a hand over her mouth, unsure whether the next sound would be a laugh or a sob. She whipped around to stare at the flickering shadows of the guards, hoping she hadn't been heard. Such a bloody mess, and they were standing there bickering in the middle of a captured city, with enemy soldiers only yards away.

They didn't pause in their work as they snipped at each other, their hands constantly working with a seriousness belied by their mouths.

The prince hummed, a triumphant noise, and Nakai saw the first lock give up and fall into his hand. The coils of chain loosened, and Raiven left his brother to help Prince Dante lift it soundlessly from the gate. Together, they knelt to deal with the last two locks.

Just a little longer, Ashe. I'm almost there.

Memory told her that Ashe would be shivering against the stones that refused to warm even in the heat of summer. The cold-blooded guards had given them only a small blanket to huddle beneath. How could she have left Ashe to suffer alone? Nakai blinked rapidly to clear the wet blur in her eyes.

Derrick stood ready with a rope, dulled metal hook attached and swinging like a pendulum. "Got it yet?"

Raiven's lock clicked open. The prince cussed under his breath, and Nakai felt her cheeks pinking from the vulgarities that would've gotten her mouth scrubbed had she dared to repeat them.

Raiven leaned over his shoulder. "What is it?"

"Bloody tumblers keep dropping. The only thing worse than a seven-pin lock is an ill-kept seven-pin lock," Dante muttered around a mouthful of picks. "It's rusty and stiff. I can't seem to hold them."

Raiven stood up, stretching. "You're slipping, Dante, if you let that old thing beat you."

Nakai stiffened in affront for the prince risking everything for her; however, before she could open her mouth in his defense, Prince Dante twisted all the picks at once and the lock popped free.

Dante tugged it off the chain and tossed it at the thief. "We're in."

His smug smirk calmed Nakai. They'd only been teasing. It seemed so odd to her, their casual comradery. Her beloved chevaliers wouldn't have been so informal despite their great loyalty and love for her. Not even Shota. She closed her eyes against the sting of tears. Opening them, she saw the sly grin of the prince and he winked at her.

"Alexion, help me get the chain off."

They abandoned two of the massive chains in the bushes across the street. After they were all inside, Raiven and Derrick lifted the last chain carefully back in place so a careless inspection would assume the gate still bound.

"How is your wing strength?"

Nakai jumped as the prince breathed into her ear. "Um," she stammered. "I can do what needs to be done."

"If you can fly the hooks up, it will be quieter than us throwing them."

"Of course," Nakai whispered, glad to do more than just stand and hope the guards stayed by their fire.

After she shifted, the prince courteously offered his arm and Raiven held out the rope. Nakai grasped the rope and hook in her sharp talons. Prince Dante threw his arm up, giving her enough momentum for a silent lift. A draft caught her wings, and Nakai swooped higher. It was a simple matter to land on the railing and let the grappling hook slide gently through her talons to the balcony floor without making a clank. With a blur of magic, Nakai reclaimed her human form and threaded the hook through the railing posts.

Bracing her hands on the railing, she leaned over and watched as the quiet, hooded thief started climbing. The rope swayed precariously until the other twin grabbed it and stabilized the end. The glow from the fire bowl lighting the far side of the courtyard drew her attention, but fear kept her feet anchored. She refused to risk the rescue of her sister on the possible scuff of her foot for being curious and snoopy.

The thief monkeyed effortlessly over the railing before she could move to offer him a hand. The grappling hook scratched the stone as Dante climbed. Radiating protective concern, the thief looked ready to lunge back over should the prince fall. Evidence that the thieves were as protective as his chevaliers. Only, perhaps, a bit subtler, standing behind to support him instead of in the front as a shield.

It reminded her of her loyal chevaliers. That imposing shield wall had held her together during the trials of being the crown princess while also upholding many of the queen's duties. They had shielded her when she needed a minute, just a minute, to gather her strength to carry on. Mother bless. She needed them right now. The gray tattoos on her skin remained dull and silent as she rubbed a thumb across them in a silent, hopeless summons. Her support was gone, and the world outside that wall was cold and bloody. They never would have let her do something like this—climbing the prison tower in the middle of the night. Loss choked Nakai's breath while Raiven hauled Prince Dante over the railing. Shaking the sorrow away, Nakai hardened her heart. Now was not the time to lose composure.

Prince Dante poked the grapple with his foot. "I think we should leave it in place. Easier to get down fast if we need too."

Raiven nodded and pulled another hook out to twist open. She waited uselessly as the prince unwound a rope from around his chest. They had definitely come prepared for a lot of climbing. A good thing, she supposed.

Nakai clasped a hand over her mouth as Prince Dante passed off the rope to Raiven and slipped around the tower. The guards were on that side. He stayed over there for a few long, horrible minutes. What was he doing? She waited in quiet terror for an uproar. When nothing happened, Raiven snuck around the tower too. Nakai leaned against the wall and hugged herself, anxiously waiting for them to return. If those two screwed this up because they were eavesdropping on the gossiping guards, she would never forgive them

Raiven returned and held up the second rope in silent entreaty. Nakai propped her butt onto the railing before shifting to accept the second hook and rope in her talons. Poised on the railing, Nakai dropped over the edge to start the flight.

A few beats of her wings and she soared to the top level of the tower. She could see beyond the wall and across the city. The familiar buildings almost seemed to huddle together like frightened mice. It was, of course, completely illogical, but the shadowy fog rolling into the streets roiled with coils and hints of scales. Adrenaline pounded in her ears. Her wings beat faster. Time grew shorter.

Repeating the setting of the hook, Nakai resolutely did not look at her beloved city. It was tainted. She saw the shadow of death in the fog. Until Kobrona was gone—forever—Hanehishou could not be free.

Once both young men joined her on the second balcony, Nakai gestured to the only door. It stood cracked open to let fresh air inside. The narrow slits in the wall were not enough to refresh the rooms. Nakai stayed behind as they leaned against the doorframe listening. The two looked at each other and held a silent debate with their eyes. Prince Dante drew a dagger and moved deeper into the room of guards; Raiven faithfully flanked him.

Grimacing, Nakai tiptoed over the legs of the guard sleeping against the wall. It was disgusting how secure the soldiers felt on her lands, and there was nothing she could do about it. For now, at least. Someday they would pay for this. The guard on the floor snored easily, with no disturbance even as she thought about stomping on his throat. In the light of the single dim crystal, Nakai watched as the prince and thief held a silent communication. The glint of a dagger told her it was about the sleeping guards. A wounded, angry part of her heart wanted their throats slit so their lifeblood poured out to cover the stain of her own people's blood on the stones. Prince Dante made the decision with a shake of his head and moved for the jail door.

He reached for the doorknob. Nakai slapped his hand out of the air. A blood rune gleamed small and dark against the pale oak of the door. It could have passed for a tiny knot in the wood grain. But she had seen Lord Kobrona write it, as he'd written on her flesh, using the blood of the dead as ink.

Nakai reached inside her jerkin and pull out a slender steel blade. She sliced her finger and squeezed it until blood dripped onto the rune. Summoning a burst of magic, Nakai canceled the rune's power. Mustering her courage and unwilling to let the men beside her risk it, Nakai twisted the knob. The metal felt cool and natural under her touch. She sighed. The death magic was gone. She turned the knob. It rattled but didn't open. Locked.

The thief knelt and fiddled at the lock with two jagged picks. He pushed the door open with a gentle touch. It creaked. They held their breath. Nakai prayed to the Mother.

A snore rumbled out of one guard's nose and the other two didn't even stir, sleeping with the surety of being untouchable. Pushing Raiven out of the way, Nakai stepped into the dark cell, calling on her owl to allow her to see through the gloom. Something huddled against the wall. A whimpered cry escaped her. "Ashe!"

"Quiet," Prince Dante growled in her ear.

She didn't even spare him an apologetic glance as she reached for her sister. A thin whine stopped her, inches away. Ashe pushed away from her, bony, bare toes frantically scrabbling for purchase on the cold stone. Nakai bruised her knees falling to Ashe's side. "Hey, hey, hey," she soothed. She gathered Ashe in her arms, catching her before the chains clanged. "Ashe, it's me. Shh. I've got you. I'm here."

Prince Dante joined them on the floor. A nip of his fangs pricked his finger. A smear of blood and a crystal lit the room. Ashe stilled at the light.

Nakai turned to him with pleading eyes. "Please, please tell me you can get them off her."

Small fists bunched her shirt as Ashe went from trying to get away to trying to crawl into Nakai's skin. Nakai pulled her closer until it was hard to breathe from the pressure. They'd collared Ashe because of her own escape, Nakai was sure. The prince cradled Ashe's fragile ankle with the utmost of care, and a grateful lump lodged in her throat at the gentleness.

Chains clinked as he pulled her foot to rest in his lap. He turned the manacle to find the keyhole. The leather roll of picks made another appearance.

Nakai cradled Ashe as Dante bent over the lock. A soft click heralded the opening of the manacle. Ashe yanked her foot free and curled into a bony ball in Nakai's arms with a whimper.

"Shh. I've got you." The protruding knobs of her sister's spine dug painfully into her flesh, but Nakai refused to lighten her hold on Ashe. They needed the contact to know that they were together again.

"I need to reach the other one." Prince Dante gestured at the iron collar hanging around Ashe's neck, a literal anchor. Nakai coaxed Ashe to sit up straighter. A wet spot dampened her shirt under Ashe's face. Nakai wanted to sob with her. "Hold this please. I can't see." He thrust the glow crystal at her. It required a ridiculous amount of will to loosen her hold enough to take it. She held the light as the prince's mismatched eyes glared in determined focus at the collar.

"There's magic in the collar," he muttered around the picks in his mouth.

Her fingers clutched the crystal tighter. "How do you know?"

His hands kept on steadily working. "I can see it," he said, as though seeing magic were a normal skill. Was that his bloodline gift?

"Is there a rune on it? Maybe you should wait." She reached for his hands to pull him away, frightened.

He moved away. "No time. I've almost..." He twisted the last pick into place. "Got it." The collar split open. "Ow," he hissed, and shook his hand. "It just zapped me. Static shock or something. I'm all right," he said.

"Let me see."

He shook his head and gently pulled the collar away from Ashe. "I'm fine. We need to go."

Nakai didn't believe him. Pain etched deep lines around his mouth. It was clear he wasn't fine. As he slid his picks reverently back into the pouch, she saw a bruise darkening his palm. Fear sparked along her nerves.

"Can she fly?" He interrupted her thoughts. "The faster we get down, the better." Ashe frantically shook her head against Nakai's shoulder. "All right. We'll figure it out." He cast a questioning look at her.

"My wings won't hold her weight."

"Alright. I can carry her down piggyback. Think you can do that, little one?" he asked Ashliene directly, soothingly. Ashliene gave a minute nod. Nakai's heart swelled with pride at her sister's courage. She coaxed Ashliene off her lap and climbed to her feet. It was no strain to carry her sister on her hip as she would a toddler. This fact broke her heart. A few weeks ago, Ashliene was a strong, healthy ten-year-old. Now, she weighed like a feather and felt like a knobby skeleton.

Nakai carried Ashliene outside, stepping lightly over the guards. Raiven waited until they were all out and followed at Dante's heels. Nakai was puzzled when the prince closed the outer door and messed around with the lock again. What was he doing? They needed to leave.

The thief seemed to understand and found it amusing. "That should slow them down a bit."

Prince Dante sneered. "They are incompetent enough sleeping on the job, but every advantage, right?"

Nakai realized that he'd relocked the door. The guards were stuck until somebody came to let them out. The ever-hooded thief was halfway down the rope before she noticed he had climbed over the rail.

"Prince Dante will carry you down since you can't fly yet. It will be alright, I promise. We are getting out of here." As she spoke, the prince crouched down in front of her, his back presented to carry her sister. Nakai tugged gently at Ashe's clinging arms. "Shh, it's alright. I am not going anywhere. I promise. I will see you at the bottom."

Ashe reluctantly pulled away and wrapped her bony arms around Prince Dante's neck and her long stick-like legs around his waist. The prince rose steadily, his arms looped under Ashliene's butt to make sure she was not sliding. Raiven was already on the lower balcony and holding the tension in the rope. Nakai held onto Prince Dante's arm with one hand and supported her sister with the other as he swung a leg over the stone railing. Her heart pounded in her ears. If he slipped, she was not strong enough to catch them. If they fell…they would not survive. Their bodies would crush against unyielding stone.

She gripped his arm before he could go all the way over. "Do not drop her," Nakai ordered with all the years of royal command training she had endured.

He met her gaze. "I won't."

Prince Dante took a firm grip on the rope and began his descent in a strange inchworm fashion with the rope looped around his foot. Nakai leaned over the railing, watching fearfully, bile churning in her stomach. Ashliene clung to the prince, face buried into his neck. If only she could fly properly. She would carry Ashe herself; however, even in human form she could feel the strain along her shoulders and down her arm. Flying she could do; flying while carrying someone else would destroy her muscles. Being grounded was a nightmare. The skies were her home. Her safety.

Few threats could reach the sky.

Nearly halfway to the second balcony, Ashliene's grip slipped. Nakai heard her scream stifled in the prince's back. Ashe clung to Prince Dante only by her small hands clutching around his neck. Nakai clenched her hands over the railing, uncaring of the fingernails that splintered against the stone. Mother, please, no! The prince snaked an arm to his back and caught Ashe's thigh and hoisted her up. Nakai had eyes only for her sister. Ashe hooked her toes in his pants pocket to clamber up his back. He had her. He still had her.

Nakai held her breath to keep from hyperventilating until Prince Dante's feet hit the balcony. As soon as he was down, she yanked the grappling hook from between the rails and coiled the rope around her hand and elbow. Using the last few feet of the rope, Nakai secured the coil and knotted it so it wouldn't tangle. The smooth metal of the hook left thin smears of oil over her fingers. She tried to remember how they had opened the hook. A wide circle of grooved metal over the bottom of the prongs loosened as she twisted it. Nakai grinned with the relief and triumph of being able to do something. The three-pronged hook folded back together as one as she unscrewed the circle, and Nakai tucked it into her belt. It was small enough to shift with her now. Flapping her wings, knowing the sound could not possibly reach the guards below, Nakai hopped and took to the air. The soft breeze filled Nakai's wings and slowed her descent until she folded them in to drop faster. She didn't want to be here anymore.

A shout made her head swivel at an odd angle to see down to the courtyard. The three men on the ground were fighting. Prince Dante was on the last rope with her sister still clinging to his back. They had to get rid of the guards before the commotion drew more of them. Nakai tucked her wings closer and swooped dangerously fast to land on the balcony. It took but a moment to shift and another to call her soul-wield by touching the rune on her palm. The ebony bow shimmered with magic as it appeared from the containment glyph. A second summoning brought her quiver, which had a strong blood-bound magic tying it to her bow and her, an unusual accessory. The quiver bristled with arrows, at her chevaliers' insistence. They had constantly nagged her to keep everything sharp and full, ready for use at a moment's notice, even if she only used it for hunting. Now, it might save Ashe.

Nakai pulled the strap of the quiver over her shoulder and head so the familiar weight settled against her back. She nocked an arrow and leaned over the railing to peer at the ground, looking for a target. A guard ran up behind Alexion while he fought off another. Nakai trailed the guard with her arrow before releasing the string with a snap. The arrow whistled a quiet warning as it flew; the guard didn't heed it. The hunting arrow pierced the light metal of the helmet and the thick bone of the guard's skull. The shifter dropped in his tracks.

What she saw next made her blood freeze in her veins.

A guard aimed a crossbow at her sister. Ashe clung helplessly to Prince Dante. They had nowhere to go. The prince had seen the danger and was trying to slip down the rope. Nakai brought an arrow up, pulling the taut string back to her ear even as the guard fired. Ashliene screamed.

Mother bless, she was falling. Nakai released her arrow. It slammed home in the guard's throat. Blood gurgled from his mouth.

Nakai looked for her sister and wanted to puke. Ashliene hung upside down from Dante's grip on her ankle. The only thing keeping them up was the rope twisted around his arm, biting into his flesh. His shoulder looked wrong—unnaturally long—and had a crossbow bolt protruded from his back. Ashliene wasn't moving. Her arms dangled as she hung like a rag doll. Nakai watched in frozen horror as the prince tried to pull them both upright. He strained up mere inches before his muscles gave out, and he fell back with a pained grunt. They were stuck. Open targets. Another bolt hissed through the air. Nakai gasped as it brushed past the prince's head. Too close.

Oh, please Mother, no.

She yelled, "Hang on, Dante!" and aimed at the guard who'd picked up the fallen crossbow. Her arrow took him in the chest piercing the golden armor. He wouldn't be getting back up. She spared a glance at the two hanging from the rope.

Her sister's ankle was sliding out of Prince Dante's grasp. The rope spun slowly around, and the prince looked ill. Blood spilled from his rope-bitten arm, down over his face and shoulder. Nakai dropped her bow, willing it back into the glyph. She called her wings as her soul-wield vanished into the ether. The quiver of arrows was pushed to the middle of her back as white wings unfurled, stretching into the sky. The power of her dyre form usually thrilled her, but all she could think about was getting to Ashliene before she fell. Nakai climbed over the railing and dropped into the air. One great flap of her wings jerked her back up, controlling her descent. The seconds it took were torture. The prince moaned in agony as he held on to Ashe.

Nakai tucked a wing and swooped close enough to grab her sister out of the air. "I've got her." Relief made her giddy enough to ignore the pain in her wings as Ashliene's weight tore at her weakened body. Prince Dante wouldn't let go. They were all going to fall if he didn't.

"I've got her," she pleaded.

His eyes blearily traced up Ashliene to look into Nakai's face. "Oh," he wheezed. He let go. Finger-shaped bruises were already forming on Ashe's tender skin.

Nakai tucked her wings and rolled in the air before flapping hard and gliding away from the fight and clear over the wall. Landing hard, feet first, Nakai stumbled forward a step and fell to her knees. "Ashliene," she cried.

Please be alright, be alright. Please. Mother bless, please. Nakai turned her sister's limp body looking for a wound from the crossbow bolt. A line of blood stained the side of Ashe's filthy shirt. Nakai yanked it up. It was only a gash, but the sudden pain, added to the weeks of fear and starvation, must have been enough to make her pass out. Nakai wished she had thought to bring bandages.

The clangs of the fight stopped in the courtyard. Scooping Ashliene into her arms, Nakai walked over to the gate and peeked around the wall to see if it was safe. Alexion was yanking the crossbow bolt out of the protective leather of Prince Dante's jerkin. The bolt had lodged in the hardened leather. There would only be a bruise beneath. Thank the blessed Mother. She had thought the bolt would kill Ashe. It had nearly killed the prince instead.

Nakai tugged one-handed at the loose chain hanging around the iron bars. "Come on. We need to get out of the city before anyone else shows up!" She waited impatiently as the one twin prodded at the prince's misaligned shoulder.

"Should we put it back in?" She heard Derrick ask before he got his hand smacked away by Dante.

Raiven peered at it and shook his head. "I think Keer might have a better idea of how to do it properly from all those books he reads."

Prince Dante stepped away. "Let's go. Now is not the time to nurse minor wounds. I'm fine."

Alexion helped her unwrap the chain from the gate and pulled it open so they could get through. Nakai led them into the nearest alley and into the darkness. Every shadow seemed to leap out at them as they passed. She was sure they would run into patrol guards and be locked in the tower again. Then, if Kobrona was still in the city, he would sacrifice the twins and Dante's chevalier in front of them. Their deaths would likely power an enslavement spell to be placed on herself, the prince, and even Ashe. Kobrona would not risk losing them a second time. He seemed to need them alive for some reason.

By the time she led them to the edge of the city proper, Nakai half expected the entire army to have them surrounded.

Nothing happened. The city slept on.

Her arms strained under the weight of Ashe. Surprisingly, Derrick, the mouthy one, stepped forward when they paused in an alleyway. "Let me carry her for a while. You've been injured again. It would be better to rest now to heal faster. If you push too far it will take much longer to heal. Or you won't heal at all."

Nakai wanted badly to say no and cling forever to her baby sister. The constant screaming ache in her shoulders made her say otherwise. "Be careful. There's a gash in her side from the crossbow bolt. I wasn't able to bandage it."

The young thief nodded and took the cradled weight off her. Ashliene slumped against his chest. Nakai was ashamed at the relief the assistance brought her. "Thank you." She pushed a wealth of gratitude into her voice, meaning thanks for everything from the entire night.

"Let keep moving," Raiven said. "They will find the guards we killed soon and raise the alarm. It would be best to be well away from here by then."

Stepping out of the alley, Nakai led the way back toward the forest, once more leaving her home in the coils of Kobrona's grasp; however, this time she brought her sister, the only family she was able to save.

Chapter Fifteen

As soon as Derrick lifted the little girl away, the princess cradled her arm to her chest, almost a mirror to Dante. They were both crippled. His fingers tingled. Nerve damage was never a good sign, and with no healers to help, it might not heal properly. Dante buried his trepidation and followed as Princess Nakai took point again to lead them out of Hanehishou.

It was strangely calm and quiet as they crept through the foggy night, as if they hadn't just killed five soldiers and stolen a princess. The fog alternately muffled and echoed their footsteps, making it sound as though there were a dozen of them. The moonlight only enhanced the eerie effect, casting rippling shadows that stalked their path.

Nakai stopped.

"What is it?" Alex asked, hands reaching for his hilt.

"Soldiers, I think." Her shoulders hunched. "I'm sorry. The taint of death magic is muddling everything. I can barely hear Hanehishou. It was stronger after Mother was bound, but now…. The Heart is trying to help, but it's confusing."

Dante actively pushed magic into his eyes to see and immediately understood what she meant. The magic he saw on the cobblestones oozed like clotting blood. Feeling the city's Heart had to be so much worse.

She turned into an alley so narrow he had to turn sideways to keep from banging his shoulders on the walls.

"Anyone else feel hunted?" Derrick asked.

Raiven huffed an agreement, the encompassing fog swallowed the noise. Dante palmed a throwing blade. It gave him a sense of competence that he didn't otherwise feel. His senses screamed as the alley spewed them into the open.

They huddled together as Princess Nakai turned her head in circles, listening. "This fog is ridiculous," she muttered. Squaring her shoulders, she walked into the mist.

"Halt!" The command cut through the fog.

"Curse it all," Derrick spat and cradled the little girl tighter. His breath turned foul with a litany of filth heaped on all things scaled and slithery.

"This way!" the princess yelled. They ran.

A sharp whistle pierced the air. A call for backup. The rhythmic stomp of marching boots answered. The whistle blew again. Too close.

"Curfew is in effect. Halt." Yellow flickers of flame flared in front of them, and the pack skidded to a stop. More whistles blasted the air with threats.

"There's more, coming up on the left. We're surrounded," Alex said. He stood with his back to Dante's wounded shoulder, covering his weakness. Raiven had Derrick and Princess Nakai tucked behind him, shielding the girls between them. Boots marched closer. The fog burned as torches spread out around them.

Princess Nakai's bowstring groaned with tension as she readied an arrow. They could not win this fight, but they would go down fighting.

"Dante?" Derrick clutched little Ashe.

"If you see an opening, take it," Dante ordered. "Get her out. Princess Nakai, can you fly at all?"

"No." Her fearful answer was sharp and said with a certainty that sank his meager hopes. Gleaming spears jabbed out of the fog like rows of fangs closing in. "I'm sorry."

Raiven snorted. "We weighed the possibilities."

"But—" she started.

"No. We knew. We chose." Alexion refused her protests.

Soldiers followed the spear tips out of the fog, a wall of spiked armor between them and escape. One hissed around curved fangs. "Does Prince Kobrona still want examples made?"

"The order stands."

Dante raised his fistful of throwing knives.

A wild yell interrupted, "Not today!" breaking the standoff. Wings beat like war drums in the sky.

"Rebels! Draw bows!" The soldier snapped out the orders too late. Arrows hailed down, punching through golden armor.

Their savior, the rebel, called out again. "Draw, release." He gave commands with the ease of a general and a fresh cloud of arrows answered.

Now was their chance. "Let's go," Dante urged.

"What? No!" Princess Nakai scanned the fog-obscured skies as the volley of arrows cut down more soldiers. "They're my people. And, that man—"

"Is giving us the opportunity to save your sister." Raiven grabbed her elbow and shoved her into a sprint.

Dante's boots slipped on cobblestones. Alex grabbed the back of his shirt as Dante flailed for balance, hauling him up. "Shift, Dante. You are slowing us down."

He was right. The others hovered at the corner waiting.

"Go," Dante barked. Magic surged, and he fell forward to land on his paws. Agony ate at his dislocated shoulder. Dante tucked his front leg against his chest. Forcing his other legs to move, he ran to keep up.

"Milady! This way. I can lead you around the soldiers." The rebel leader swooped over them on large gray wings.

"Who are you?" Nakai asked. Whistles blasted behind them, and she received no answer as they fled. "We need to go north."

The rebel leading them turned east. "We can't go straight out. They'll follow too easily. My people will distract them."

Only the frightened gold eyes peering over Derrick's shoulder stopped Dante from cursing his decision to enter the city. If they had kept this little girl out of Kobrona's coils, then it was well done. If not, he'd failed the whole of his people tonight.

The rebel led them deftly through the tangled streets and alleys. Whistles still blew, but none too close. Finally, the city's buildings spread out into the hills. They were almost there.

Breaking free of the twisted, confusing streets was a relief.

The shadows in the fog moved.

Three dyre-shifted serpents, each with a sinuous riot of muscle, rushed them, radiating lethal strength. Dante knew in the depths of his soul that even his uninjured dyre form would have been outclassed in this fight. Ink-black hoods flared with menace, and long coils cut off their escape.

"Our prince wants an example made of you rebels," the soldier hissed.

Dante crowded against Alexion's legs as the half-shifted serpents herded them together.

"Get away from them." The rebel held a great bow pulled taut, arrow unwavering on its target.

"Do all of your people use bows?" Derrick asked under his breath.

Princess Nakai's hands were white-knuckled, but she answered. "We are creatures of the air."

"So, that's a yes."

Three nagas, the serpent's half-shift form, looped around them, tails intertwining into a fence of solid muscle.

Dante had never before appreciated the serpents' purely physical strength in their dyre form.

Alexion stood over him protectively, brandishing his swords like bared fangs. "Don't shift, sire. Stay low."

The rebel threw his head back and shrieked a war cry that echoed across the city. Stringing arrows as fast as they could fly, the rebel let loose. His barbed war arrows skipped off the nagas's armored scales.

Well, that wasn't promising. Holding his wounded leg to his chest, Dante felt remarkably small and worthless. Little Ashliene heaved great gasps of terror into Derrick's neck.

The flared cowls of the nagas bobbed and weaved a deadly dance. Neither the rebel's nor Nakai's arrows were having any significant effect. All the nagas had to do was keep them corralled like sheep until more soldiers arrived and they be lost; mission failed.

Dante's mind whirled, desperate for a solution, but they hadn't come prepared for this level of battle. It was supposed to be a quick in-and-out retrieval of the princess. Now, he had gotten them all captured.

The rebel dug one of his arrows into the flesh of his arm. Blood welled up. Runes flared to life along the shaft. The man was prepared for war at the deepest level; to take the time to etch the tiny runes into the head and shaft of the arrow, absolute dedication. Each arrow would have taken hours to engrave. The bow groaned with strain.

"When the way opens, go," the mysterious rebel said.

He released.

The enhanced arrow flew with deadly accuracy. Literally. Piercing through the armored scales, the arrow was an instant kill. The massive coils of the dead naga writhed in its death throes, tangling the others into a knotted mass. The nagas hissed curses as they struggled to free themselves from the corpse.

"Go!" the rebel yelled. "I will cover you, milady. Go!"

Princess Nakai hesitated. Alexion wrapped a strong arm around her waist and hoisted her off her feet, dragging her over the lifeless coils. Dante leapt after them. His injured paw took the force of the landing, and the bones ground wrongly in the joint. He couldn't even howl, the overwhelming pain froze in his throat. Derrick grabbed huge handfuls of his fur and threw him forward. He was getting tired of being manhandled today; however, it worked. Dante used the momentum and tucked his paw high, running awkwardly.

"We can't leave him!" Princess Nakai protested.

Alexion kept a hand planted between her shoulders and kept her running. "He is covering us. Once we are clear, he can fly."

The fog swallowed the sounds of the fight. Trees welcomed the fleeing group into their cover.

At the top of a hill, Nakai planted her feet, forcing them all to stop. Looking back, she rubbed the heel of her hand against her heart.

"What is it?" Raiven asked.

"I don't know. I feel as though I am leaving something behind."

Dante leaned against her. "We will get it back. We will get it all back." Somehow. He thought he knew how she felt. The loss of feeling Ookamimori's Pulse beneath his paws was keen.

Weary triumph warmed Dante. His pack was out of danger, and the little princess safe. No one was badly injured, except himself, and that was acceptable whether his chevaliers agreed or not. Princess Nakai would recover once the strained muscles healed.

Hobbling through the forest on three legs was hard. Dante half-shifted as soon as the threat of pursuit was gone. His arm throbbed—swollen, hot, and tingly. A small price to pay for the success of their mission.

Scouting ahead, Raiven tracked the other half of their pack. They didn't stop to rest until Ashliene stirred and woke up. Nakai jumped off Alexion's back, shifting midair to run to her sister.

Dante tried not to collapse to the ground in a whimpering heap, instead finding a tree and plopping in a v of roots. He tucked his hand between his knees to hide the trembling. He would not slow them down for a scratch that barely bled anymore. Never mind the clotted blood winding around his arm like a black brand, or the bruise on his ribs that throbbed too, reminding him it existed, as though he had forgotten. Dante pressed his other hand against the impact site. There was a divot in the leather of his jerkin from the crossbow. He sucked in a deep breath, filling his lungs. It hurt, but there was no explosion of pain. Nothing broken.

He didn't get away with hiding his injuries.

Raiven cornered him while Alexion helped the princesses. He grabbed Dante's forearm and forestalled any complaints. "We need to clean it at least. Derrick, give me your shirt. We can make a sling so his arm isn't flopping around." Pulling out a semi-clean rag, Raiven dabbed carefully around the long rope burn, lifting off the dried blood flakes.

"That's quite a bruise on your hand," he said when he reached

Dante's palm. "How'd you manage that?" Raiven prodded the dark skin with a finger.

Dante yelped. "Stop poking it!" The bruise didn't hurt compared to the rest of his arm, but it still hurt. "I'm not sure. I was paying more attention to not dropping the girl."

He really wasn't sure. The night had been busy. The odd zap from the collar came to mind, but that wouldn't have caused a bruise.

Dante put up with the tending until Raiven tried to twist his arm to get to the other side. "Ow. Let go already. Dislocated shoulder here." Dante tried to pull his arm free, making it throb in protest.

"Fine, stop whining. I'll put it up in a sling. Don't come moaning to me if it gets infected." Raiven folded the shirt Derrick handed him, tying it around Dante's neck. Maneuvering it gently, Raiven guided the arm into the makeshift sling, careful of Dante's sharp claws.

Gritting his teeth, Dante kept his complaints to a minimum. It hurt worse than the time he'd broken his wrist falling from the rooftops. He focused on the sisters' reunion to ignore the pain. He couldn't quite hear Nakai's soft whisperings.

Ashe appeared to just listen and nod. She clutched her big sister's shirt tightly in both hands as if afraid she'd wake up in the tower again, alone. Ashliene's fine-boned features were a near mirror to Nakai's. Both bore their royal bloodline with delicate grace, silvery beauty, and feathers in their hairline. Ashliene's downy feathers were just visible under her short, wavy hair. Nakai combed her fingers through her sister's hair, stopping to pick out a knot before working her way back up and combing through it again. Ashliene snuggled close, burying her face into Nakai's shoulder.

Dante looked away, his throat tightening and eyes stinging. This was worth any pain he endured. The watery, golden eyes peeking at him over Nakai's shoulder made the warm, fuzzy feeling grow.

"There," Raiven said, settling back to rest on his butt. "That should hold it until one of the others can look at it.

"We need to keep moving."

It was easier to run with the sling, painful instead of agonizing. Dante cradled his arm to keep it from bouncing and jarring with every step.

It felt strange to stay in his dyre form for so long. He rarely had a use for it. Before the princess showed up, he hadn't taken dyre for a couple of years. The last time had been to clock a burly bodyguard in a house he had been snooping in for signs of treason. He had not found any proof, but the guard took exception to his presence, as he should. A fast transformation to dyre form and a heavy punch to the nose had laid the guard out before he could defend himself properly, or identify Dante.

Dyre form also illustrated a gap in his training. The difference in height and shape was disorienting. In his journey carrying the princess, he had been half-fevered and concentrating on putting one foot in front of the other. Now, branches he thought he could run under with inches to spare, smacked him in the face. He overstepped, his stride longer than normal and jarring. He wished he had at least gone for a run in his half-shift every so often. His claws dug into the earth, catching occasionally and making him stumble. The unfamiliarity of his own body wearied him.

Dante opened his mouth to call for a stop, pride be damned, when a break in the trees revealed the mountains soaring into the sky and the narrow pass between. The majestic peaks completely dwarfed the foothills. Clouds buried the tops in white fluff.

"We should be able to catch up to the others soon. They only have a few hours' head start and we've been making good time," Alexion said, not mentioning the known fact that Lady Petria would have demanded a rest from the climb.

Derrick was not so kind. "The lady probably begged for several stops, so we will likely catch them over the next hill."

Dante sighed. "Derrick, brother, I love you, you know I do; however, the lady is my aunt and a royal, so, true though it may be, shut up." He would not allow anyone to disparage his family, even another member of it. This journey was changing his aunt too, unearthing the old strength that grief had buried. He was going to shield and support that strength, nurture it until it grew roots in her soul.

Raiven backed him up, nipping Derrick's ear in a physical reprimand.

The twins loped a steady escort around them, the walking wounded. Weighed down by Ashliene, Alexion used his dyre form to cradle her safely. The little girl was still bound by the death magic and could not shift to her owlet form.

Dante wondered how much of her easy compliance was trust versus sheer exhaustion. If he had been through the same torture, he would not be nearly as calm, but Ashe accepted being carried around like a fragile doll. Princess Nakai gamely clung to Raiven's harness. She seemed to swing from ecstatic relief, pain, and concern for her sister.

Chapter Sixteen

They climbed three more hills before the trail warmed.

"I see them," Dante said, pointing with his good arm. The missing six members of his pack stood silhouetted on the peak of the next hill.

"Race you there!" Derrick yipped and flat out ran for the far hill.

"Well, that's not fair," Alexion complained. Princess Ashliene clutched at Alexion as though she expected him to burst into flight too.

Raiven snorted a laugh. "That's Derrick."

Nakai ruffled her white feathers irritably. "I do hope you aren't going to act as immature. If you are, let me off now. I will walk since I cannot fly." Dante saw her talons raking through Raiven's fur with threat.

"Don't worry, I won't." Raiven huffed with amusement. "You can stop jabbing me now."

The urge to run and beat Derrick thrummed through Dante's veins, but his throbbing shoulder kept him from doing it. Alexion's loping pace quickened, his normal eagerness to play and compete curbed by the little girl he carried.

The ground was stonier here, and fewer trees dotted the hills. Dante saw Derrick reaching the others at the top of the foothill. In the minutes, it took for them to traverse the valley and start uphill, the morning dew fell, beading on their fur and the scraggly bushes around them.

When they caught up, Mysti was the first to rush to him and examine his wounds. "You got careless, didn't you!"

"No," Dante said, cutting off the incoming lecture. "I was careful not to drop a little girl onto stone from three stories up."

Mysti closed her mouth. Whatever scolding she'd been about to unleash stayed caged behind her teeth. She looked over at Alexion, who stood to the side, patiently waiting for Ashliene to get off. Princess Nakai didn't give her a chance, rushing to scoop the skinny ten-year-old into her arms, clutching her close once more.

"Oh." Mysti breathed, momentarily silenced by the sight of Ashliene.

Keer peered at his shoulder. "Is it dislocated?"

Dante stepped sideways when Keer reached to prod the misshapen joint. "Yes! It is dislocated. Why do you all need to poke it? It bloody hurts!"

Keer grimaced apologetically. "Sorry. Is that all of your wounds?"

"My arm is torn up a bit. Nothing major."

Keer frowned. "I am not certain I can set this, Dante." His fingers hovered over his shoulder, fluttering with the need to touch. "If I do this wrong, I could permanently damage your shoulder to an extent that even a healer won't be able to correct it. There are tendons, nerves, muscles in there, never mind if I break the joint bones." He was flustered, a rare sight. Keer held an extensive amount of random knowledge in his rat's nest of a brain that normally kept him analytical and precise.

Lady Petria glided over. "Let me see. I was an apprentice healer before I met your uncle."

Dante looked into her clear eyes, startled at the new information about his aunt. "Really?"

She pinned him in place with a once-familiar sharp glance, pressing gentle fingers against the protruding tissues of his shoulder. "Nothing feels broken. Resume your full human form. It will make putting it back in easier." Obedient to the strong, certain woman he had nearly forgotten existed, Dante shifted and the world shrank in a blur of magic. Her long fingers made quick work of the knot holding his makeshift sling together.

"You, Stipes, brace him from behind, and you"—she waved impatiently at Keer—"hold his good arm and push against his chest here."

The two men did as directed. Dante found himself walled in as they immobilized most of him. Lady Petria took his arm, and, without even pretending to count down, yanked, and twisted his arm. A sickening grind and pop accompanied the intense pain of bone scraping bone while sliding back into its proper place.

He couldn't stop the yelp of pain tearing from his throat. Blinking tears away, Dante leaned into his friends, grateful for the firm support. After a moment, the pain settled into a dull throb. Dante straightened from his slump onto Stipes's shoulder.

"I'm fine," Dante rasped. "Thank you, Lady Aunt. I didn't know you were a healer."

Sorrow creased Lady Petria's normally porcelain-smooth features, and Dante immediately regretted speaking of the past. It was a sure way to send her into hysterics.

"It was my childhood dream to be the best healer in all the lands, and then your uncle came in one day with a broken nose and walked out with my heart." She smiled. "He never returned it to me."

Before he could press for more fascinating history, Lady Petria steered him to sit on a cold rock. Dante winced under her brisk administrations as she examined the thick scab that wound three times around his forearm following the path the rope had cut into his flesh. Tilting his head back, he watched the clouds drifting overhead.

"It doesn't need stitches at least. One of you, bring me a canteen of water, and give up whatever bottle of brew you have." No one moved for a guilty second. "Don't give me that! I'm quite sure at least a couple of you have something in your bags. It is the best thing we have to clean this wound. Our prince does not need to catch another fever, especially so soon after the last." She spoke with the whiplash tone only a mother could, and everyone scurried.

Dante wasn't surprised to see both Raphael and Leigha moving to dig in their packs. Raphael produced a flask and Leigh a large canteen.

"Brandy." Raphael displayed his engraved flask like a smooth merchant trying to sell his wares.

"Whiskey." Leigha shook her canteen for emphasis.

"Brandy first," Lady Petria said. Her nose wrinkled in distaste. Dante knew the only liquor she drank was wine. His aunt took Raphael's flask and shoved it into his hand. "Drink."

Dante obeyed with a dark suspicion of what she intended. It was going to hurt more than resetting his shoulder had. The liquor slid down his throat with an expensively smooth burn.

Lady Petria accepted the whiskey from Leigha and unscrewed the cap. "Deep breath."

With a last pull from the brandy, the world swayed as the potent liquor hit his stomach. Dante sucked in a deep breath and held out his arm. Seeing her raise the canteen, Dante grit his teeth in preparation. Pure fire poured over his arm. A scream clogged his throat. Keer caught his hand, holding it tight to keep him from jerking away from the cleansing liquid.

As the burning eased, Lady Petra picked up the canteen of water and drenched a cloth. She scrubbed around the rope wound, removing the crusted blood and dirt.

"We should rest here," Stipes said. "We are well out of their scouting range, and it has been a long night already."

Raphael frowned in disagreement with his cousin, but Mysti nodded. "I agree. We could all use a break."

Ashliene watched all of them from Nakai's lap. Her lower lip trembled.

Korren, bless his ever-happy soul, wandered over and plopped in the dirt beside her. "Hello! My name is Korren. What is yours? Dante rescued you, right? Was it awesome? I bet it was. We've been running forever. The bad people were in my house, and Dante took us away to be safe. Now you can be safe too! We are going to our cousin's house over the mountains. The bad guys don't like the cold. Is Princess Nakai your sister? That means you are a princess too, right? I'm a prince. Isn't it boring to be a royal kid? We always have to study instead of playing outside. Dante sneaks me out sometimes though."

The six-year-old was irrepressible. Dante smiled as his cousin chattered endlessly. Lady's Petria's scrubbing got just a little firmer as Korren ratted him out, oblivious to his mother's sharp ears.

The added punishing sting was worth it when Ashliene giggled quietly. Her lips stopped trembling, and she sat up a little.

Jothan swaggered over. "You talk too much, pipsqueak." He crouched and ruffled Korren's blond hair. "Hiya, princess. I'm Jothan. I wanted to come and rescue you, but they wouldn't let me. I could've done it, though, cause I'm a thief."

"Gonna have to beat that out of him," Derrick muttered. "Can't go around announcing our profession to the whole damn world."

Amused wrinkles scrunched around Lady Petria's eyes. The rough touch she was using on Dante lightened, much to his relief.

As the camp slowly settled into place, his chevaliers slipped out in hunting formation. They would bring back fresh food. Dante hoped they hurried. His stomach roiled, nauseous with hunger. Nuts and berries only buffered a wolf's hunger for so long.

Lady Petria moved on from his wounds and traced a rune on Nakai's skin to reduce the strain on the muscles strained from her desperate flight carrying Ashe to the ground.

"Thank you, Lady Petria." Nakai said. A tight furl around her eyes relaxed as magic eased the pain.

Dante rested. Under Lady Petria's threatening glare, he didn't dare move. He watched as the Owlderah princesses curled together for lack of anything better to do.

Would the girl ever be able to shift again with the death magic binding her in human skin? What if…?

"Princess Nakai," he called softly. When her eyes swung to him, he asked, "That thing with the rune on the door, your blood erased the death magic, right? And your magic broke through the magic on your chains when you escaped. Would that work on the runes binding your sister?"

The hope blooming across her face was stunningly beautiful.

Nakai closed her eyes and ran her hands over Ashliene's bare arms. "I can feel it there, so perhaps?" She didn't hesitate to pull out her knife and dragged the sharp blade across her forearm to open a shallow cut.

"What are you doing, young lady?" Lady Petria shrieked.

Dante held up a hand. "Just wait, Aunt Petria. She's trying to wash away the death magic with her own blood. It's worked before. She stopped me from getting caught by a trapped door."

Nakai dipped her fingers in the blood that welled up and smeared it over Ashe's skin. "Shh. It's all right." Nakai closed her eyes. Using his magic to see, Dante saw her magic sweep through Ashe's arm, following the brush of her hand. It was as though she was wiping soot from Ashliene's arm. The death magic dissipated under Nakai's cleansing.

"There," Nakai said. "Try shifting for me?" she coaxed.

Ashe stifled her sniffle, and magic rose from within her, blurring her body. Dante knew it would work even before the magic calmed, revealing a fluffy white owlet.

"Oh, thank the Mother." Nakai scooped up her sister, cradling the tiny owl close.

"What just happened?" Lady Petria asked.

"Ashe is free of the death magic," Dante said.

"How?" Raiven asked. The thieves had sat up and paid attention when Lady Petria shrieked.

"Bloodline trait surfacing maybe?" Keer said. "It happens sometimes in the royal families. Like Dante being able to see magic. The traits come and go, skipping generations and then surfacing to the Mother's whim."

Lady Petria frowned but pushed magic into Nakai's fine cut. The bleeding stopped, and it scabbed over. Nakai had been careful. It was barely more than a scratch. Hardly worth the healing, except that they were fleeing for their lives and infection was a dangerous possibility out here in the wilds.

His chevaliers soon returned with meat, and Leigha produced a bunch of wild mushrooms. This far from the city, they risked starting a small fire.

Keer explained the small, but truly major, victory. Ashe stayed as an owlet, occasionally stretching her wings gleefully, until the food was ready. She shifted to human form to eat with a smile that lingered.

"Are these safe?" Derrick asked, poking at the spongy fungus.

"Yes. I've eaten them before. They are much harder to find at home, even though it is warmer there. They grow all over here though," Leigha said. Her brow twitched.

"She's right," Nakai agreed softly. "I've eaten them many times. They are the cook's favorite at this time of year. He likes to make a rabbit and mushroom soup. It is good."

When his chevaliers returned with meat, they had a small feast.

Korren wouldn't touch the fungi. Dante snickered as Lady Petria held one in front of his disgustedly pursed lips. "Mother," he whined. "I don't like mushrooms. They are icky." Korren turned his head away just in time to avoid the mushroom swooping into his complaining mouth. The fungus smeared his cheek. "Eww!" The six-year-old scrubbed at the mushroom juice on his face. "I'm full! I'm full!"

Jothan inspected his mushroom as though he could tell what it tasted like by visually consuming it.

"Right," Lady Petria sighed in disbelief. "And in five minutes you will be telling me you are hungry again. Eat the meat at least. That's all you are getting."

"Mushroomy-things are nasty." It was Korren's only defense.

Dante grinned and took a big bite out of his mushroom cap. He hadn't liked them much as a pup either.

"I like them," Ashliene said. She squeaked when all eyes turned to her, and she burrowed back into the shelter of Nakai's embrace.

Korren and Jothan silently dared one another. Dante saw the exact second the decision was made, that no girl was going to out eat them. Beating Korren to the draw, Jothan stuffed the whole mushroom in his mouth. His cheeks bulged. Korren's advance was more tentative. He nibbled at the edge, nose wrinkled in absolute disgust before it even reached his tongue.

Lady Petria nodded, satisfied with the minimal try, but Korren didn't stop there. Breaking off a bigger chunk, he bravely ate it. Then, he opened his mouth and stuck out his tongue proving that it was swallowed.

A strange green color tinged Jothan's face. Dante hoped the teenager wasn't going to hurl. The boy looked around frantically, but by now, everyone was watching the challenge. Derrick outright sniggered at him. There was only one way for Jothan to keep any dignity in front of the princess. He scrunched his face and chewed. Leigha scooted out of puking range when Jothan's scrawny shoulders lurched.

Dante laid his half-eaten mushroom aside. He couldn't eat and watch this at the same time.

The boy's pride kept him at it, despite the gross erping sounds coming out of his throat. Jothan clamped a hand over his mouth. Even Derrick stopped sniggering and watched with bemused disgust. Entranced silence reigned as the whole pack watched the battle between boy and food. Frozen in horror, Raphael held a piece of meat poised in front of his mouth.

Jothan breathed in through his nose. He swallowed. A lump slid visibly down his throat. Coughing, he scrambled for a canteen, gulping water. The clapping started with Leigha and grew around the fire as Lady Petria joined the applause. The princesses giggled together. Nakai whispered something into her sister's ear.

Ashliene said, "See mushrooms are good, right?"

Jothan paled.

Derrick pulled another stick of the fungi from the fire. "Here, want another one?"

Jothan gagged.

The laughter was good. For a moment, they could celebrate a victory and forget the darkness left behind, and to come.

Growling stomach sated, Dante shifted to ward off the night's chill with thick fur. Keer sat nearby, absently gnawing on a stick of venison while peering at a pile of leather in his lap. Dante hobbled over, suspecting he knew what the leather cloth protected. He drew closer. "Only you would bring a bloody heavy tome on a flight for your life."

"This book is priceless," Keer defended with a glare. Dante huffed a laugh at his best friend and wagged his tail. "I'm serious, Dante. There are only five original copies of these." Keer reverently stroked the embossed pages. "And it's my favorite." His ears pinkened. "Father would've too, you know he would."

Dante lay down so his back pressed against Keer's thigh. "That's the book, Myths and Tales of the Mother's Guardians, right? The one your father always read to us." He hoped it was. He had fond memories of that book. The two of them had spent hours after bedtime, whispering about the fantastic tales.

Keer ducked his head. "Yes."

"Read something?" Dante craned his head around in time to catch Keer's startled green eyes. "What? I liked them too." The Guardian Myths had been an oft chosen book.

"Alright," Keer agreed, flipping through the fancifully drawn pages. His pupils blew open, large and black, leaving only the barest ring of green in his irises. Sharper teeth and orbital ears accompanied the partial shift. There was just enough light for Keer's enhanced sight to read the handscribed story.

Dante plopped his head back down on his paws. Alexion dragged Mysti over like a child would his mother, and pulled her down to sit between his legs. "I want to hear too!" Mysti rolled her eyes but didn't fight out of his embrace. Little Korren didn't hesitate to crawl up to Dante and flop across his back so he could see the pages in Keer's lap.

As Keer started to read aloud, the other conversations quieted and they scooted closer so they could listen to the tales of ancient guardians and their glorious deeds. Keer's gentle voice guided them all into sleep. Dante felt Korren go completely limp over his back and, after about ten rustles of the pages turning, his own eyelids began to droop.

Sharp tingles in his paw woke him from a dark dream of fiery shadows chasing him. The urge to get up and flee welled in his chest. Dante wiggled out from beneath the dogpile. He shifted to massage his palm. It didn't really help, the pins-and-needles still hurt. The black bruise spread across his palm and halfway over his wrist now. It wasn't numb at the moment, just painful. Dante frowned, kneading the muscles in his hand around the rope wound.

"Prince Dante?" The older princess's whisper only just reached his ears from where she lay at the roots of a wide tree trunk. "Are you alright?"

"Yes, just a cramp I think." The lie fell out of his lips easily. He refused to add to the worries of his pack for just a bruise. Dante stood up and tiptoed out of the sleeping bodies. Once free from the sprawled puppy pile of his pack, he stretched. His spine cracked obscenely all the way up. "Ow," he moaned.

Princess Nakai giggled.

Dante sighed as some of the pressure relaxed in his neck. "What has you awake at this hour, princess? We can't be too far away from dawn." Indeed, he could see a light purple blooming just over the trees to the east. Soon, it would blend into pink and light blue as the sun claimed its throne from the moon. Birds already sang to greet the day.

"Restlessness, bad dreams. When I close my eyes, I see Ashe in that damned tower in chains, starving, and alone. Did you notice how thin she is? Her bones dig into me when I hug her." Nakai's voice wavered on a sob. "I can feel every single one of her ribs. She is so light, like a single feather of her wings instead of a little girl. Ashe has always been a slender child. Over a fortnight of little food has whittled her down to a shadow."

To keep from shredding his skin to stop the itching, Dante tucked his hand under his belt. He focused his attention on the princess, trying to ignore the sensation.

He reached for words of comfort. "Ashliene is safe now. We will give her the best of the food to help her get better." Dante floundered for more to offer. "The Lupinics are an honorable and welcoming family, despite their general seclusion, or, maybe, because of it. They will make us all welcome."

He could offer distraction if nothing else. "I met their wise woman once. She is a Far-dreamer. In tune with the Mother. She can heal the tears in your sister's soul." He hoped, anyway.

Pinecones crunched under her fingers. "I would not have thought to go to them," she said. "I had planned to flee to the Eagalia. They are a fierce warrior family we often do trade with. The guards said they were marching to Ookamimori next." She ducked her head. "I was relieved. Your city was in the opposite direction. My escape route was clear."

Dante felt sick. What if she hadn't warned them? Would he be enslaved to magic by now? Korren? Lady Petria? Would the blood of his chevaliers stain Ookamimori's streets?

"Ashe begged me to warn you. Even as I left her there in chains, she begged me. Said it was up to me to make sure he didn't hurt anyone else." Her laughed sounded forced. "She said that if I didn't I was a scared little chickadee. So, I had to warn you, for her. You saved her when I almost didn't save you. I can never repay that."

Dante's tongue stuck to the roof of his mouth. "It was the right thing to do." That had come out awfully self-righteous and falsely noble. "We do not leave our own behind when there is something we can do otherwise." Saying this left a bitter taste in his mouth. Wasn't that exactly what he had done to his people, left them behind?

"Ashliene isn't one of your own though," Princess Nakai pointed out. "You risked your people for one little girl."

"A girl we owe our lives and freedom to."

"You didn't know that!" She crushed the pinecone in her fist.

"It doesn't matter. We, I, owe both of you. My aunt and my heir are safe because she asked, and you did. Despite the fact it was the last damn place you wanted to go."

He cast a look over his still sleeping pack. Guilt churned and roiled in his stomach. His closest family was here, safe with him. What of those they had left behind? "We each owe the other an unpayable debt and feel like failures in our hearts."

"Thank you. For this alone, you have earned the Owlderah Family's alliance. Our families have had few dealing with one another in the past beyond the establishment of the borders, but perhaps we can pursue a closer relationship?"

The princess's words were completely sincere and innocent, but with Derrick's dubious influence on his teenage years, his mind immediately went into the gutter. "Ah, ahm" he coughed, trying madly to scramble a proper response between his divided feelings of displaced guilt and the abrupt ideas of a 'closer relationship' with a rather beautiful young woman. He was male, after all. Lucky Mysti wasn't awake to see him stumble and splutter. She'd know his train of thought and smack him upside the head. As a typical teenager, he had gotten smacked a lot by his First Chevalier.

"I am glad we were able to save your sister from Kobrona and would certainly welcome an alliance with your family." All this was true and didn't drag his brain deeper into the gutter. Thanks ever so much, Derrick. He fully blamed his brother figure for the corruption.

"We should attempt more sleep. It is still a long journey to my cousin's family. The mountain pass is a couple of days away at least."

The princess nodded and lay down to curl around the frail form of her sister. "Sleep well."
Dante called his fur, lying near enough that he could guard the two owls, he plopped his tail over his nose and closed his eyes. He didn't think sleep would claim him, but this way his dream wouldn't disturb the pack.

A sharp pain in his ear woke him with a lurch, fangs snapping at air. Alexion jumped away with a cackling bark. Lunging, Dante bowled his chevalier over in a tangle of limbs. Bared fangs hovered at Alexion's throat. A growl rolled out of his chest like angry thunder.

"Sorry, I am sorry!" Alexion yelped.

Dante snorted in doubt. Rolling his eyes, he stepped over Alexion, purposely stamping a heavy paw into his chevalier's unprotected stomach.

"Ow," Alexion squeaked.

"Serves you right," Mysti said when her partner looked at her, pleading for sympathy. Sniggers surrounded Alexion as the others looked on in amusement. Korren leaned against Jothan's legs as the boys laughed together.

"Dude, even I leave him alone when he is sleeping," Derrick derided. "He always gets pissy if you wake him up."

Alexion gave Derrick an odd look, and Dante realized that the two halves of his very separate lives were still not used to sharing. Shaking it off, Alexion grinned toothily. "That doesn't make it any less fun. You did hear our prince yelp like a puppy?" Derrick's answering smirk sent shivers up Dante's spine. Those two paired up in mischief would be the death of him, or themselves after he got through murdering them.

Dante waved Mysti away when she stepped up to mother his wounds. "It is fine, Mysti. There isn't anything else that can be done with it right now." The tingles had started again when he'd pinned Alexion. Grinding his teeth, Dante ignored it.

The pack didn't linger long. Thoughts of serpents slithering through the shadows behind them spurred them onward.

Chapter Seventeen

Little Ashliene's cheeks flushed with roses of fever. She wheezed. A painful sound. The moist, heavy air from the approaching thunderstorm made breathing hard for all of them. Lightning shattered through the gathering clouds in the distance.

"We should hole up," Raiven said, watching the storm. "She's sick." He nodded toward Ashe, who shivered with chills. "And that seems to be coming our way." He pointed to the sky.

"He's right," Raphael said.

The pack moved toward a sheltering circle of spruce trees. Dante held the prickly branches aside for ladies. Inside, the glen was shadows and dappled sunlight. The clouds hadn't smothered the light completely.

"Do we have time to stop?" Leigha asked.

Dante knew she was thinking of making a clean getaway, just as Calume had trained them to. You didn't stop and wait for marks to catch up after you picked their pockets clean. That just got you thrown in jail. It was too early to stop in the day.

Raphael glared at her. "There has been no sign of pursuit. We can stop and let the princess rest."

Raiven placed himself between Leigha and Raphael. "Leigha is right. We have been moving too slowly. We got away last night, but the more we stop, the more time they have to catch us."

Derrick crossed his arms in the background, ready and waiting to back up his twin. Dante ignored the posturing. His pack had to work some things out for themselves.

Leigha socked Raiven in the shoulder. "I can defend my own conversations, thank you. Bunch of male chauvinists," she muttered. She shoved Raiven out of the way and finished her point. "If they have our trail and we stop for more than a few hours, they will catch us. The whole detour will have been worthless. Worse so, because they will add the rest of us to their collection."

Spinning on her heel, effectively shutting the door on the conversation, Leigha asked, "Lady Petria, how necessary is this stop for her? And how long do you need to help her before we can move on?"

"We need to bring this fever down, or she will not survive the journey over the mountains."

"So, the need outweighs the risk. That's all I wanted to know. What can we do to help?"

Ashliene moaned as Nakai fluttered around her, anxiously coaxing her into drinking sips of water.

Lady Petria stood up, brushing pine needles from her knees. "It is settled then. Someone start a fire. The others can look for elderberries, willow bark, or mint leaves. Raspberries would help as well. It would make a tea to help the fever. Did Dante and Princess Nakai finished their potion regime? Those would be an excellent boost for her."

"The potions were gone a couple days ago. I haven't seen any willows around recently. They don't appear to grow in this region," Keer said, "but berries might grow in the valleys where it is moister and less rocky." He flicked his fingers, indicating the surrounding pines and rocky crags jutting out of the soil.

Dante rolled his eyes and nudged his bookworm brother in the ribs with a pointy elbow. "Is there anything you don't have stuffed in that pack-rat brain of yours?"

"Nope." Green eyes sparkled. "I know something about everything."

"That's what I thought." Dante smirked. "Right, we'll split up. Raphael, Stipes, you stay here and keep guard. The rest of us can pair up and see what we can find. Keer and I will go into the valley to the north." The plan sounded good anyway.

Keer disagreed. "Who says I want to go with you? I'm going with Raiven. You can go with Derrick." Keer moved to claim the quieter twin by grabbing his sleeve. "Raiven and I will go east; the sun should reach the valley there for a good part of the day, better for fruits and flowers." Raiven shrugged and didn't protest.

Derrick huffed. "Ditched by my own twin." He sneered and stuck his nose in the air. "Fine, be that way. Milord Dante, north, you decreed. Then, let us be off."

"Why, yes, my loyal friend. North, it shall be." Dante stooped in a low bow, gesturing for Derrick to lead the way.

Lady Petria stood, slender hands planted on her hips, "If you are going, get. The girl is not getting any better while you stand there gawping about." She fluffed her dirty skirts and turned back to her patient.

Shame flushed Dante's cheeks for abandoning his people and then playing foolishly when they were supposed to be gathering herbs to help.

"My Lady Aunt is right. Let's go and see what we can find. Mysti, Alexion, which way are you going?" Dante asked, attempting to keep his voice firm and unbroken.

Mysti eyed him narrowly, as she often did before deciding to smack him for something or other. "I believe we will try southward," she said, finally seeming to decide he was safe from her hand. Alexion shifted in a blur of magic and stretched his front paws out, belly fur brushing the ground and red tail wagging in the air.

Leigha pulled an empty pouch from her travel pack. "I guess that leaves west for me."

"You don't have anyone to cover you." Raphael frowned.

"Oh, shove the chivalry. I will be fine. Promise to scream my lungs out if I run into trouble I can't handle alone." Leigha's smile was all fangs.

Raphael opened his mouth to argue. Dante could see it written all over his face. She didn't give him the chance. Leigha ran, shifting in a smooth leap and bounding into the surrounding forest.

"Ah, that's all right. You might as well drop it. Better men than you have tried to tame that one. It ain't gonna happen." Derrick dared to pat Raphael on the shoulder.

Twisting his shoulder violently, Raphael snarled.

"Ooh, touchy!" Derrick laughed and darted away. "Dante! Come on, we have berries to hunt. Let's see how fast they can run away from us mighty wolves."

Rolling his eyes, Dante looked at Raphael. "It's fine, Raphael. He is right about Leigha too, actually. She is her own woman. Been hurt too many times not to be. She's strong. If we're being followed, they will have to see her first, then catch her, and then hold her. None of which are easy tasks."

"Dante, come on," Derrick yapped.

Dante called his inner magic and half-shifted, dyre-form paws stepping heavily into the loamy earth. His arm twinged at the change and surge of energy.

Derrick darted around him on all four feet. The red tips of his dyed fur gleamed against the black of his coat. "You're as slow as a turtle!" he yipped.

Even now, he was slowing down his pack. Worthless. He forced a grin. Dante swiped at Derrick, slapping him in the ribs with a heavy paw.

They raced across the pine-carpeted forest floor, the thuds of their paws muffled by the cushioning needles. The sinking sunlight was quickly lost to the shadows of the looming mountains as they descended into the valley. Pine boughs laden with clusters of seed cones enveloped the two, creating a presence of stillness that the soft chirping of sparrows and chickadees only added to.

Focusing his senses through the overbearing pine trees, he heard the burble of flowing water.

"Would that mint stuff grow near water?" Derrick yipped.

"I think so. Never really had a reason to look for it before," Dante said. "You know, being a prince and all."

"A prince of thieves!" Derrick sprang from a rotten log. The wet wood collapsed beneath his weight with a squelchy crunch. Avoiding the mess, Dante eyed the log crawling with red insects frantically carrying white eggs from the splintered ruin. He'd been bitten by those before. The bites had burned for three days. "At least we can tell what it is by the smell."

The stream, when they found it, filled from a waterfall spilling out of a jagged crevice. Green moss clumped over the surface of the rocky hill like veins. Nothing remotely minty looking grew along the shore.

Dante stepped into the clear, shallow water, intending to wade downstream since there was no upstream. Plunking a paw in, he immediately jerked it out. "It's bloody cold!"

Derrick sniggered from a safe distance, well out of Dante's reach.

"I thought the river at home was cold. This might as well freeze so it looks like it feels, and be done with it." Dante shook his paw vigorously, trying to warm the numb pads.

Derrick lapped the water with a long, pink tongue. He came up coughing. "I think my tongue is going to fall off."

"I told you it was cold." Dante shifted to human form, closing his eyes as the world shrank a few inches. "Did you bring your canteen?"

In answer, Derrick's form blurred and twisted. Kneeling on the damp bank, Derrick pulled the strap of his canteen over his head. He shook it, the water sloshing inside weakly. "I was getting a bit low anyway."

While filling his own, Dante glanced around. "I don't see any mint."

Derrick's pale, yellow eyes flashed over the banks looking for the precious green leaf. "Nope. Nothing"

"Downstream then," Dante said, watching the icy rain of the waterfall pouring out of a cleft in the jagged rock face. Veins of vivid green moss clung to the cracked wrinkles of the damp cliff face.

"No upstream to be had," Derrick pointed out.

They started out again, following a well-worn animal trail. Fingerlike raccoon prints pressed into the moist dirt, layering over hoppy rabbit and scratchy squirrel.

"Looks like a lot of traffic. I'm going to see if I can track something down." Derrick vanished into the brush, leaving Dante to resent the unsaid implication that he couldn't; though, honestly, it was the truth. His arm ached.

Dante stayed by the water looking for the tea plant. He stomped down the bank. He knew he would be little help in his current state, but it still irked. Out of Derrick's brotherly sight, Dante allowed his shoulders to slump for the first time since leaving Ookamimori. He hurt. He was tired. An ache persisted in his back from sleeping on lumpy dirt every night. He couldn't decide if it would be more satisfying to crawl under his blankets at home and stay there hiding or throw a screaming tantrum like a two-year-old. He did neither, of course.

He took a deep breath, struggling, searching for some kind of center. The ever-present Pulse of the Heart of Ookamimori wasn't there. It didn't thrum under his feet in perfect time to his own heartbeat. It was gone, out of reach because he had walked away. No wonder the Mother hadn't seen fit to give him an elemental companion. He was not worthy of the honor, his bloodline. Lord Kiba was right.

The pain in his hand spiked, tingling like a static shock. Dante hissed. Unfurling his swollen fingers, Dante studied the bruise. It had spread. The flesh around it was gray instead of purple, and it was numb to the touch. The tingling did not abate or worsen at the prodding, as if it were a separate thing.

On a whim, Dante plunged his hand into the frigid stream. Within a minute, he couldn't feel anything below his elbow. Dante clenched his hand into a fist. Only the sight of his bluish fingers curling told him they moved. Tingles still ran up his arm. Sharper than ever.

"Shit," Dante cussed. Water that he couldn't feel ran off his hand. This wasn't part of the rope injury. This was something different. Something magical.

The unlocking of a collar and a negligent zap came to mind. It wasn't a wound. It was a curse. But what was the purpose of the spell, besides the sheer irritation caused by the accursed enemy? Unless it had failed? Did he not get the full effect?

The gauze wrapped around his palm and forearm felt soggy and loose. It sagged around his wrist in dripping coils of fabric. Peeling it off like dead skin, he had the distinct impression he would see exposed muscle and sinew beneath it. Violently colored flesh was revealed—bruised, cursed, but whole. The gray spot had spread further over his palm and around the base of his thumb.

Dante balled up the soggy gauze, intending to throw it away when a thought stayed his hand. If he returned to the pack without it, Keer and his aunt would fuss. Little Ashliene needed their fervent care, far more than he did. The dead spot, he couldn't think of it in any other way, the dead spot would worry them. The pack had more than enough to deal with already.

He wrung out the gauze. Starting below his bicep, he wound it around and round, wincing when it snagged on his scabs. Knotting the damp fabric around his palm took a shameful amount of time.

How much time had he wasted? He didn't have any mint to show for his absence. The green, pungent leaf should be his only focus. Tromping further downstream gained him nothing. More time wasted.

Derrick gave him something better to do. From somewhere in the depths of the trees he yelled. "Hey, Dante, come here and help me. I found raspberries. Did you bring a good size pouch? There's a treasure trove of them. Even gimpy, you can pick berries."

Dante cocked his ears to get a feel from where Derrick yelled. "I'll be there in a minute." With a last lingering glance at the water's edge for minty greens, he strode into the woods to meet his friend. Derrick hadn't stretched the truth. Raspberries clustered together in a thick prickly patch in a clearing. The dying light of the sun touched the center of it, giving the berries a soft glow.

Derrick stood waist-deep in the bushes, steadily filling a pouch with the treats. "See, I told you! There's loads of them." The edges of his mouth looked bloody with the raspberry juice. "They're kinda small but really sweet."

"I'm surprised the birds left us any," Dante said. He aimed for the browner, mature bushes where most of the fruit would be. Derrick was chest-deep in the brambles. Dante wanted no part of that prickly hug. He pulled handfuls of the delicious berries from around the protective spines. Resisting the urge to eat them for three whole handfuls, he broke down and crammed the next tart handful into his mouth. The sweet berry juices flooded his mouth, and tiny seeds crunched in his molars. Soon his hands were stained crimson. The pouch filled quickly and berries rolled out and bounced on the ground as he reached for more. "Mine's full."

"Mine too." Derrick pushed his way out of the fruity briars. "We've been gone a long time."

"We should go back. They'll worry, and we have a long way to go." Derrick carefully buckled the pouch shut. The runes inscribed on it would protect the food and allow it to change with the shift. "Maybe one of the others found the mint your Lady Aunt wanted. Think we can snag a rabbit? Enough tracks around here."

"We should try. I'm not sure how much food we'll be able to catch once we get over the mountains. Our arctic cousins are hardy and know their frozen lands well, but, their home is in the center of the ice. We have to travel in deep."

Derrick nodded. "Should we head back and see what we can find?"

Closing the leather flap on his pouch, Dante agreed. "Come on." He shifted to all four feet. The one thing dyre form wasn't great for, was hunting small game. Even hobbling on three legs was better. "I'll flush them out. You catch them."

"I like it!" Derrick yipped and slunk into the woods with a silent lope.

Not so quietly, Dante hopped through the trees, not even attempting to hide his awkward stalking. Enough scent trails coated the area to know stirring up a rabbit should be easy. Derrick was the hunter tonight. Dante the bait.

Gingerly, Dante pressed his front paw to the ground. Pain immediately twisted up his leg. The thick scab from the rope burn twisted and pulled. Whining, he pulled the limb against his chest. That hadn't been his best idea. He loped forward as best he could and kept up a pretty good pace. Instead of returning upstream, Dante aimed almost straight uphill. His pack waited at the top, and perhaps a rabbit or two in between.

Scenting the cooling night air, Dante could smell fresh prey. Rabbits. Now, to stir one up for Derrick. Lowering his head, he sniffed the air to pick a direction. The musk of the wild hares drifted stronger to the right. He twitched his ears forward to silently tell Derrick, who was lurking somewhere in the shadows, that he'd found something.

Hobbling into the bushes as fast as he could, Dante flushed them out. A warning drum thundered on the ground. Leaves rustled and bushes exploded. Three brown blurs shot away in every direction. Dante lunged futilely, his ivory fangs snapping at tail fur.

Death screamed. Derrick had succeeded.

Dante limped out of the clearing. Derrick trotted out of the gloom with a large rabbit hanging, broken, in his jaws. His friend's tail wagged in triumph. Dante's mood lightened at the sight. Little Ashliene would have a broth and fruity tea, at least, to help her regain her strength.

She would need it all.

The land beyond the mountains was brutal. His father had taken him to meet his snow-bound cousins once before. The journey had been well provided for with a sledded caravan and an escort group meeting them at the pass to guide them around the dangers hidden beneath the snowfields. As young as he'd been, he had stayed well-burrowed beneath a mound of blankets snuggled into the nest with Keer, with only his nose to tell him of the chill outside. They bore no such protection for the little ones with them now. Jothan was older and streetwise enough to know when to suck it up, but Korren and Ashliene would have a much harder time of it.

Mysti and Alexion handed over their found elderberries in the warm light of a low fire. Lady Petria's blue eyes assessed Dante and Derrick as they approached. She nodded with stern approval at the sight of the rabbit. Shifting, Dante pulled his overflowing pouch of raspberries over his head. The smooth leather strap hung heavily in his hand. "We found lots of these. There was a clearing of them."

Laying down the rabbit, Derrick joined them around the fire with his own pouch of the sweet, tart berries. "I'll clean the rabbit for cooking." He pulled a gleaming knife from his boot.

Mysti stood up. "We'll get a pot of water warming. I think we might have a small bag of dried vegetables in a bag, and we have some of the mushrooms left. They will make a good addition to the soup."

A horrible cough interrupted them. Ashliene wheezed, only to cough again until she gagged for air. Nakai curled around her sister, radiating comfort. "Shh. It's all right. Breathe, Ashe, just breathe." The plea was almost a sob.

Renewed urgency rushed them through the meal's preparations.

When Raiven and Keer arrived, water bubbled furiously with the rehydrated vegetables and diced rabbit meat. Fresh mushrooms swirled around the liquid with bits of carrots and onions. Raiven held up a fragrant bunch of mint. The spear-like green leaves glowed in the warm firelight.

"Good," Lady Petria said. "Put them here with the raspberries. We will steep them once the stew is done."

Keer settled by the fireside, pulling his own pouch over his head. "We found a small group of hazelnut bushes. There were not many good ones left, but we found a few."

Dante leaned against a pine and closed his eyes, uncaring of the sticky and smelly sap he was sure oozed into his shirt from the contact. Trying to center himself into the magic of his bloodline, Dante started when a small weight landed against his thigh. Opening his eyes, he found a tousled head resting on his lap. "Korren?" He stroked his little cousin's hair gently, knowing the action always soothed the pup.

"Can we go home soon, Dante?" Korren whispered. "I'm tired of the woods. I want a cookie and that hot sweet drink Cook makes."

His heart quailed at Korren's tired whine. "We have to wait, Korren. There is a bad man there right now—the same one we saved Princess

Ashliene from—and we have to tell the other families that he is trying to hurt people."

Korren wrapped a small hand around Dante's calf and snuggled deeper. "Then can we go home?"

"Soon, pup, soon." Dante caught his aunt's worried frown in his direction. He couldn't believe how much his aunt had changed over the days in the woods. Had he been asked before, he'd have said she would have screamed and bawled like a two-year-old or would have fainted and needed to be carried the whole way. Instead, he'd discovered she was a healer and very few complaints came from her lips. The hysteria and terrors were gone like they had never existed. A blessing from the Mother.

Korren fell asleep, drooling on Dante's thigh. He was glad the leather of his pants had been treated to be water-resistant. Dante finished cleaning the berries and set the bowl to the side. He was effectively pinned in place until Korren woke up.

He slumped back, daring to close his eyes for a minute.

With his mind, he reached for Ookamimori. He needed to feel the Heart. Just for a minute. To know that everything was all right. It was outside the strength of his magic alone. He reached for the ley line. The wild magic singed as he soaked it in. It was dangerous to wield the magic without runes to channel and control it. But, he wasn't using it directly; he coasted over the magic and floated his conscience toward home.

The ley line followed the river to the Heart where it pooled beneath Ookamimori before flowing toward the Mother. Dante's soul drifted with the current of magic.

As soon as he felt the Pulse, he knew something was wrong. Horribly wrong. The magic of his lands felt cold and oily. He reached the Heart and horror suffused his very core. Death and decay swirled in a miasma around the Heart, the pool of magic was stagnant. Corrupted. Kobrona had killed his family, his people. Sacrificed them to fuel his conquest. Dante's soul wept. He had abandoned his home to suffer alone. He'd thought to save them, but Kobrona had slaughtered them anyway. Why? What purpose was there to this wanton bloodshed? The Heart echoed their dying screams. As though the city was his body, Dante felt his people's blood in the streets, clotting the grout of the cobblestones like dirt ground into the creases of his skin, the places they'd died like black bruises across his flesh.

The Heart's magic, tainted by their deaths, oozed into his magic like venom in his veins. Dante crawled to lie beside the Heart, but it lashed out, driving him away. He was helpless against its semi-sentient power. The Heart contained centuries of magic pooling beneath the city, his own was no match. His strength waned, the distance too great to maintain the connection. Dante withdrew, awareness returning to his body.

Grieving, he clamped a clammy palm over his mouth to stop the keen of pain. Dozens of his people slain. His birthright irrevocably stained in his absence. Dante shivered, wanting to run to the stream and scrub until he felt clean again, until he was utterly numb against this pain. His soul cried out at the taint, the deaths upon his people—people he had sworn to protect. His family. He had failed them. He'd thought to protect them with his absence, but he'd left them to face Kobrona's fury alone.

Dante stared, unseeing, into the campfire. Korren slept on, oblivious. The Heart of his land was injured; the unnatural deaths poisoned it. Touching his birthright had engraved the knowledge of the slaughter in his heart. He knew the exact number of deaths. Thirteen were killed in Kobrona's search for him. Dozens more in defense of Ookamimori, their city, their home. His stomach churned. Not all of them had been range or patrol wolves. Commoners too. Men, women, and children had fought for their lives. Kobrona had spared none.

Bile burned the back of his throat. Dante suddenly realized what Princess Nakai had felt leading them through her captured city, feeling the blood spilt beneath her feet. The strength it must have taken to walk across it without screaming or vomiting from the pain of it; even here, from this distance, it was agonizing to feel it. He shivered. How could he have left them to face that alone?

Korren mumbled sleepily against his thigh.

Even withdrawn from the touch of Ookamimori's magic, the death magic's stain corroded his soul, leaving an ache physically untouchable. Dante huddled on the damp ground, struggling to bring the tremors under control.

Mysti walked around the fire, bringing him food. "Here, eat something before you fall asleep."

He tried to force a smile and hoped he'd scrubbed the salty lines from his cheeks. Accepting the cup, he hissed as the hot soup sloshed on his fingers.

"What's wrong?" Mysti asked, staring at him with worried brown eyes.

Damn. His First could read him like a fresh scent trail laid by a lame deer.

"Prince Kobrona has reached Ookamimori." He didn't elaborate. Didn't list the number of his family who had died. She did not need to share that burden. He would carry it alone.

"No," she breathed. Whimpered. "So soon. Why? Why is he doing this?"

Dante stared into his soup, wishing he was drinking it at home in his selfish little world. "I could feel their pain, Mysti. Ookamimori showed me. I heard their screams." He never could hide anything emotional from her. "Lord Kobrona has cast death magic in Ookamimori."

Mysti breathed out in horror as the implications hit her. "But, why?" she asked, broken. "Oh, Mother's blessings, protect them." Mysti sighed and dropped to her knees beside him. She wrapped her warm arms around his shoulders and pulled his head to her breast, kissing his hair.

Dante choked back fresh sobs at the tender embrace. Turning the fierce pain into anger, he clenched his fist until his fingernails bit into his flesh. "I swear he will answer for this atrocity."

Somehow, even with Nakai's warning and the proof of it through assassins and her sister chained, starving, in the tower, the reality of Kobrona's threat had seemed distant. Now, feeling death magic shadowing the Heart, it was all too horrifyingly real. He had left his people to face a monster on his behalf. He pulled away from Mysti. "I'm fine. Let's not worry the others. It won't help."

"But—"

Dante cut her off. "They have enough to worry about right now. When we get to the Lupinic, we can tell them. Then, at least, they will feel safe and only have one thing to stress over." Dante brought the bowl to his lips and sipped the warm broth. It was tasteless in his cotton-dry mouth.

She sat back on her heels, wiping her eyes. "They need to know. Deserve to know," Mysti whispered. Her furious temper dulled with grief.

"I know. But what good does it do to know now rather than later?" Dante didn't want to see the pain in their faces. He could already see it mirrored in Princess Nakai's. He needed time to process his own before he supported theirs. He was their prince. Their leader. Their strength, and he would break under their pain on top of his own right now.

Mysti's sadness fractured the little composure he clung to. Any more added, and he knew he would shatter with it. "Just give me, them, some time, Mysti. Please."

Her watering brown eyes studied him intently. "I won't say anything, but they need to know soon. It is their home too. They have the right to know, and it is your duty to tell them."

The mantle of his shoulders cracked under that weight. He nodded and looked away, unable to bear the tears sparkling in his First's eyes. She leaned over and pressed another kiss to his temple before walking back to the fireside. Alexion sensed something and pulled her into his lap, whispering in her ear. She shook her head and burrowed deeper into her partner's embrace. Dante was glad she had someone to comfort her. Knowledge hurt.

Aunt Petria came over to wake Korren. "Let me have him. He needs to eat something before we leave." She draped Korren's small arm over her shoulder, wrapped her own arm under Korren's legs, and pulled him upright. He mumbled unintelligibly into her neck. Dante planted a hand on Korren's butt to hold him steady as she stood up. "Thank you, Dante." He looked up in askance as she propped Korren on her hip. "For trying to protect us. For protecting Korren. He's all I have left of my husband. All I have left of my heart." All Dante could do was nod. His throat knotted in his mouth. If he tried to talk, he was sure he would choke.

Lady Petria carried her son away. Dante watched her settle down and coax Korren awake. The herbal tea brewed while everyone ate the rabbit soup.

Keer was the one to bring him a cup. "Hey, everything all right?"

"No. But I don't want to talk about it." Dante accepted the tea in the metal travel mug.

"All right," Keer said. Dante loved his brother all the more for it. The lack of pressure, even though Keer desperately wanted to know. He always wanted to know everything. Especially if he thought he could help; however, he waited until you were ready to tell. Keer settled cross-legged beside him, sipping at his own tea.

Crickets chirped in tune with the crackling of the fire. Finishing his tea down to the leafy dregs, Dante nestled the cup next to his pack so it wouldn't be forgotten in the morning. Sitting in silence, he watched the flames flicker and burn, reminding him of the scars discoloring his side. The horror from that day bore nothing compared to the sick feelings in his heart now. He only prayed that Ookamimori could be cleansed.

A cry jolted him out of a nightmare into disarray.

"We have to leave." Nakai shook her sister awake. "Now," she snapped, when the pack stared at her in dumb confusion.

Jothan and Derrick hadn't even stirred at the commotion.

"Please." An angry sob. "I can feel them coming. Like slimy little shadows on my lands. We have to go."

That got them moving. Raiven kicked Derrick, and Leigha roused Jothan, nipping his ear when he didn't stir fast enough.

Raphael asked, "How far away?"

The princess's face blanked as she focused inward. When she returned, she said, "A few hours at most."

Dante fumbled with the buckles on his pack when the tingles resurged. He snuck a peek under the bandage. The gray-black bruise crept over his wrist now.

Keer stared at him.

Dante tried not to look like a guilty child. "What? It itches."

In dyre form, Stipes picked up Korren, cradling the boy to his sturdy chest. Alexion did the same for Ashe. The last of the packs were secured. Holding his arm out, Raphael let Princess Nakai grab on with razor-sharp talons. She mantled her wings, and he threw her into the air, giving her the height and velocity to take flight.

She winged away, leading them toward the distant mountain pass. The pack streamed in a line behind her, the two dyre wolves keeping pace in the middle of the group. They stopped only once for a brief pause at a small pool fed by water seeping through the cracked granite containing it. The princess occasionally perched on one of their harnesses to rest before returning to the air.

The mountain valleys gradually disappeared, and the hills grew larger until merging into one. The gray mountain was studded with pines, and flecks of blue crystals sparkled in the dark stone. Deeper into the mountain range, tiny elemental cribbits scurried sideways over the ground, gathering blue pebbles into mounded nests and hissing as the pack passed too close, clacking their pincers.

Nakai swooped low to land ahead and waited for them to catch up. "We have reached the borders of my lands. I cannot feel our pursuers anymore. They were closer the last time I sensed them. They are pursuing faster than we are running. I don't understand how. Serpents should not be capable of holding speed for long distances."

Keer cocked his head, ears tipping forward in question. "You said the serpents oozed death magic, right? Maybe spells give them their strength. With the right runes and enough power, you can do anything with magic."

Everyone exchanged horrified glances.

"If that is the case, will the Kobrona even stop to rest?" Raiven's point stretched into fearful silence.

Dante broke it. "I do not believe they can follow us beyond the pass. It will be too cold for them, no matter the magic they're using."

"Then, we cannot stop," Raphael said. "It is you and Korren being hunted. We will keep you from them no matter the cost."

His chevaliers nodded their agreement with Raphael, and his thieves agreed as well. Dante wanted to puke. He didn't want them to protect him no matter the cost. "We will all make it," he swore. "But we must run."

And they did.

Chapter Eighteen

The pads of his paws stung, scraped raw from running over rough stone for hours. They were all staggering from the brutal pace.

The split peaks that formed the mountain pass loomed near—and insurmountable. For every foothill they cleared, another lay before them.

Dante gasped. Pain throbbed between his eyes, and the world blurred. It was hard to breathe, like he couldn't suck enough air into his lungs.

"Is there no air up here?" Mysti asked, wheezing. Her ears drooped.

"Not much," Nakai answered. She sounded better than the pack. "The higher you go, the thinner it gets."

She would know, Dante supposed, since she could fly.

"We can't keep this up," Mysti said. "We need to find a place and make a stand, or they are going to catch us when we have nothing left to fight with." Protective fire kindled in the depths of her brown eyes. "The pass is another day's climb at the speed we are moving. I don't think we can physically make it in the condition we are in." His First Chevalier didn't look any better than he felt.

Raphael turned back to catch the last of the conversation. "I concur." His normally well-groomed fur was dirty and limp. "If they are to catch us, let them catch us rested and ready to fight honorably. Right now, we are weak and moving too slowly to stay ahead or hold strong in battle. We cannot run anymore."

Fear and relief warred in his chest. Dante wanted this to be over. He would give almost anything to be dealing with grumpy old nobles who felt they knew how to run his kingdom better than he did. The serpent soldiers tracking them represented only a small fraction of the trials facing him and the families; however, it would give them some breathing space, time to reach a sanctuary where his aunt and cousin would be safe until the council ruled to stop Lord Kobrona's madness. He only hoped his runners made it in time to warn the other families of the threat against their royals. Even the strongest armies would fall if the heads were cut off first.

They all jumped when Alexion yelled from higher up the mountainside. "Hey! You guys coming?" Quickly, they climbed the rocky slope to catch up.

Nakai flew low overhead. "A huge waterfall is ahead. I think it flows from the pass. That is what we've been hearing all this time. It is maybe another hour on foot."

With renewed determination, they climbed. Dante plucked the extra pack off Alexion's back when he caught up, slinging it over his shoulder next to his pack. As a dyre, he was stronger and there was nothing wrong with his back. Carrying two packs wouldn't hurt him.

A rumble in the distance grew louder as they climbed. Starting as a low hum, the noise became a deafening roar.

When Dante raised his head again to look for the mountain, he realized he was on it. The rocks leveled out and it was at their feet: a sheer drop into a watery ravine. The speeding river rushed down the distance between the twin peaks, cutting a clear path into the rocks. Halfway down the mountains, the river reached the cliffs, pouring over the drop with a resounding roar. The waters hit the bottom of the ravine in a silvery froth under the moonlight. The wide river a gleaming ribbon in the blackness.

Dante stared down the cliffs in dizzy awe. "This must be the mouth of the Crystalline River."

Keer nodded. "Yes, according to the maps, it feeds the whole of the Northern Circle. The tributaries branch over the lands to the Mother's circle in the center."

"Sire, over here," Mysti called.

Turning from the edge, Dante rubbed his eyes to refocus them. Mysti stood next to a human Nakai on wide, sloping steps carved into the stone. Blue veins of crystal sparkled in the light in the dark stone of the stairs.

"I bet the Elkians carved them to get their caravans through. The steps are shallow enough they can pull them up with barely a pause." Keer knelt, brushing a fine-boned hand over the worn surface. "This dip in the center of each step would keep the wheels from rolling backward or too fast if they are coming back down. We came at the pass from an angle. That's why we couldn't see any of this." He gestured at the steps continuing down the mountainside and disappearing into the trees. "There is probably even a road or at least a trail through the forest."

Dante dropped both packs on the ground with a thump, dust puffed out in a cloud. "We can rest here for a while."

"At least we won't roll down the mountain," Derrick quipped from where he sprawled over a step.

Raiven sat on the step above his twin, wrapping his tail around his paws, the red-dyed tip of it appearing as black as the rest of his fur in the night. "It's defensible."

Lady Petria didn't shift or speak, only curled at the bottom of the stone stairs and nuzzled Korren into her side when Stipes set the sleeping cub down. She was asleep in moments. Jothan did the same, curling his head on Leigha's lap. He had glommed onto the female thief as a big sister figure quickly. As the newest member of the thieves guild, Dante doubted the boy had had much time to make close companions with anyone before they'd left. Leigha didn't seem to mind, though.

Princess Nakai tried to coax Ashe into drinking the broth, but she took only a few meager beakfuls before turning away. The owlet's eyes wept from the fever, and she bobbled in Nakai's arms. Pale hair shrouded the princess's face as she slumped.

They needed rest—real rest—but they weren't getting it. Not with hunters on their trail.

Dante pushed his dyre shape into human and plopped down, leaning against the pile of travel packs with a pained sigh. His feet throbbed, and he was certain his spine had twisted into unnatural shapes, if his back had anything to say about it. Pulling the canteen out of the side pocket of the pack he leaned on, Dante unscrewed the metal cap and sucked down lukewarm water. With the mountain having so many small streams and trickles of water from the rocks, refilling the canteens was not a worry.

"I will stand guard first," Raphael said. "We won't risk them sneaking up on us while we sleep."

Stipes stood solidly behind his cousin and partner and nodded. Raphael summoned his soul-bound rapier and sheathed it at his side where it would be ready for a quick draw. Stipes did the same with his staff. The runes on the two weapons flared brightly as they came at their wielder's call, magic pulling the weapons into material existence.

"Don't hover over me, Stipes. Go over there or something. I don't need you looming over me all night," Raphael snapped. The family feud was never forgotten even when set aside for duty to their prince. Peaceably, Stipes did as he was asked, though Dante caught the sorrow flashing over his Fourth's face. Stipes didn't hold to the feud, one of the few in their split family.

A cold breeze brushed over his skin. Shivering, Dante shifted. His fur would protect him from the cold. Keer joined him as usual. They had shared a puppy pile as cubs, and the warmth was familiar. Stipes stood nearby, towering in his dyre form as he gazed down the mountain looking for shadows within shadows.

Fire burnt through his dreams, compelling him to run as it licked and snarled at his heels until it cornered him whichever way he turned.

His shoulder jostled, and he jumped out of sleep catching a fearful cry behind his clenched teeth.

Keer leaned over him, his face pinched with worry. "Hey there, you awake now?" Keer whispered, his hand warm in Dante's fur. Dante snuffled and Keer relaxed. "Need to talk about it?" Dante glared his refusal. "Fine. Don't talk. How long have you been having nightmares again?" Keer prodded. Dante turned his head away. It wasn't like they'd ever gone away; he'd just grown better at hiding them. "Stubborn," Keer reprimanded but lay back down to sleep, accepting Dante's silence. The weight of his brother against his side was warm and comforting. Dante was not sure he'd be able to sleep again despite his weariness, but he kept still, letting Keer sleep.

Mysti and Alexion were silent guards alert in the darkness. Mysti's shield lay at her feet ready for her to scoop up. He heard Raphael snoring on the other side of the pile. Stipes, with his bulky shape, lay on the step above Lady Petria and Korren.

Red stained the horizon when Dante crept up to sit beside Alexion who offered him an irrepressibly cheerful smile. "All quiet, sire. I guess they had to stop and rest after all."

Dante rubbed absently at his tingling palm. "I hope so." He tried to suck in deep breaths to combat the headache caused by the thin air. Sleep hadn't helped much. "Quite the view." From up here, the whole of Hanehishou and Ookamimori sprawled before them, stretching farther than they could see.

The river twined around the foothills and through the forest. Dante tilted his face to meet the warmth of the sun. Sunshine seeped into his bones, giving him the strength to enforce the command he'd decided upon during the night. He clung to that strength, waiting while the others woke and gathered around.

He didn't look at them, sure in his decision, but knowing that they were going to interrupt. "We should split up." He tossed the words out like stones into a lake and waited for the ripples. His pack shouted over each other in a wave of dissent. It took time for them to realize that he was ignoring their protests.

"We will split up." Dante cut away any mirage of choice. He called on every inch of his bloodline for the command. Looking to his Lady Aunt, he shut out his chevaliers and his thieves. This was for her—her and Korren—her son, his heir. "Raphael and Stipes, you will take Lady Petria and Korren ahead to the pass. Jothan, too. He is too young for what is to come." He saw understanding put steel in his aunt's eyes, and nodded.

"Princess Nakai." Still ignoring his pack, he turned to the princess. "You and your sister will be welcomed by the Lupinic family. They will give you sanctuary."

His family would be safe, even if he had to give his last breath to make it so. Raphael and Stipes would be good chevaliers for Korren. His heir would need their guidance. He had been seriously considering offering one of them the chance to be his cousin's Second Chevalier when he came of age. It was tradition to pass down a chevalier to be the heir's Second, a supportive guide for both the heir and the First. Raphael and Stipes would be happier working separately, but he'd intended to give them the choice as to who would take the position. Now, Korren would need both of them to rule if Dante died today. Alexion and Mysti would not be separated—life partners came as a pair.

"I want to go ahead. I want Korren safe." Lady Petria nuzzled her son closer and stayed curled protectively around him. "I would like Raphael to accompany me, along with your other friends." The way she said 'other friends' implied her distaste of the thieves' company.

"Princess Nakai."

Princess Nakai's chin tilted, golden eyes narrowed. "I will stand and fight beside you. It is as much my duty as yours." Dante knew that look. She would not be swayed. "I will help ensure that my sister will not be captured again."

With her determination behind his, he dared to face his furious chevaliers.

Raphael's face was a mask of hard, noble distain. "I will not leave your side, sire. You cannot ask that of me."

Dante grasped his wrist behind his back, digging his nails into the flesh until blood oozed between his fingers. "You will."

Dark circles under his Second's eyes made the piercing gray colder. Raphael stood at attention, spine as straight as his sword.

"You will because I am not giving you the luxury of choice." Dante locked everything down. Nothing could show. He was hurting one of the people closest to his heart, but this was the best way.

He deliberately twisted Raphael's sense of duty. "Would you deny me the protection of my heir, of Korren?" The words coated his tongue in ash. Knowing what he was doing and sealing the deal, even as he saw something akin to hatred in Raphael's glare. He wanted—needed—Raphael at his side, his strength and friendship, his big brother. Korren needed him more. If this failed, Korren was the last of the Canidea bloodline.

"I am making you Korren's First."

All of the protests from his chevaliers died from sheer horror.

"He is yours to guide and shield. Stipes, of course, is your Second." To protect his family, Dante sacrificed two vital chunks of his heart. What choice did he have? He had no one else to give to Korren, and right now, Korren was everything.

"No."

Dante's heart stuttered.

Raphael no longer looked him defiantly in the eyes but at the space over his shoulder. "I refuse Stipes as my Second, though I accept my duty," he almost spat the word. "I refuse a Second until such time as I choose a worthy partner."

Stipes paled, and Mysti curled a hand under his elbow in support as he swayed.

Blood scalded Dante's skin as it ran freely down his fingers from his palm.

He had shredded his pack. The binding runes on his wrist burned under the strain of shaken loyalties. It hurt and stayed Dante from enforcing the command on Stipes. Mother bless, this was all so wrong. The giving of a chevalier was supposed to be a choice, an honor, and years away. Not like this, forced and angry.

He saw the magic binding him to Raphael splinter. The bond whittled down to a weak strand, but it had to be done—for Korren. He had to keep him safe, and he trusted Raphael to do that.

"So be it. You will be First. The Second will be chosen at your discretion, or when Korren is of an age to choose for himself," Dante said.

Raphael bowed, betrayal screaming from every pore. "I accept my appointment to First and will endeavor to uphold my duties to the best of my capabilities."

Something inside Dante's chest relaxed, even as something else twisted and snapped. In one single command, he had lost a Second, a friend, and a brother.

It had to be done. It had to be. It had to be. But, not like this. He'd never wanted to cast Raphael aside, no matter how much he pushed him to stand up straighter and be polite. Raphael was a brother of his heart. He'd wanted to give him the choice to stay or go, but that choice had been stolen from them by necessity and desperation.

Dante knew if he looked at the tattoos on his wrist that one of the four would be dulled, though not quite dead. The actual bond didn't transfer so simply. There was ceremony, ink, and magic, but Dante trusted Raphael to uphold his spoken word. He might never forgive Dante for passing him to Korren, but Korren would need his knowledge and experience.

"Keer, Lady Petria will need your help with the children since Stipes is remaining with me." If he could, he would send them all through the pass and hold the line alone. He wanted them safe.

"Raiven, Leigha, Derrick, I cannot ask you to stay, nor order you to go." He didn't have the strength left to give.

The thieves clustered, murmuring while leaving the rest of them to suffer in stilted silence. Dante turned to stare over the forest, where somewhere their pursuers approached. What else could he do but keep them safe, no matter the cost to himself?

"Dante, I will go with your aunt," Leigha announced. A nasty smile twisted her lips. "If they catch up to us, I will have a few nasty surprises waiting for them." The unsaid, if you fail and die, stirred them into a frantic movement as they prepared to divide their forces.

His First stepped in to shepherd his pack into moving. Dante stayed where he was, listening to the hushed, worried tones passing back and forth. If he moved, he would crumble and it would all have been for naught. He was weak. Sending his family away, broken, was killing him.

Stipes approached his cousin and partner, laying a hand on his shoulder. "I will take care of him. You know I will."

Raphael turned on him, snarling. "You will protect him with your life. If he dies and you do not, I will finish you."

Frozen, Dante watched out of the corner of his eye as yet another part of his pack fractured under the strain he'd added to it.

Stipes flinched. Then, his broad shoulders straightened as he towered over Raphael. "I am a Grayus too, no matter how much you want to deny my bloodlines, and I will not fail him." The sun turned Stipes's blond hair a spiky gold, and Raphael's fell like golden silk down his back while their matching gray eyes clashed in a test of strength and spirit.

Raphael nodded. "See that you do the Grayus name honor." It was the first time Dante had heard Raphael acknowledge that Stipes was a Grayus.

Keer nudged him. Dante started at the touch and turned away from his Second and Fourth Chevaliers. "I don't think I should go," Keer said.

Fear spiked his chest. Keer was well trained, but he didn't like to fight and only joined him on his adventures in the city because Dante dragged him out. He didn't want the bookworm to stay and fight. "Raphael is going to need help." Dante tried.

"Jothan is old enough to do something useful. Ashliene isn't a heavy burden in any form right now. He can carry her if Raphael and Leigha need their hands free. I am of more use here. It is better to match them in numbers. Splitting up so much just gives them the advantage of beating us in stages. Raphael is strong enough to guide and protect them until we catch up," Keer stated. Dante crossed his arms and bowed his head, letting Keer's ranting plea wash over him, drowning him in words. He tried to physically hold the cracks in his soul together. How had he failed so utterly? It was no wonder the Mother wouldn't bless his right to rule. He couldn't save them. The serpents would slaughter them, and his pack, his family, begged to stand beside him while their throats were slit.

"I am staying." Keer frowned, daring Dante to tell him otherwise.

Dante knew the look well. He could order Keer to leave, risking damage to their lifelong brotherhood. Was his safety worth that, even when he knew Keer's points were stronger ones than his? Truthfully, he didn't have the strength to shatter another friendship.

"Keep him with you, sire. You are already sending me away. You need the fighters," Raphael said. "Keer is capable."

Dante's heart panged. He had lost some undefinable thing with his Second. He didn't know if he could earn it back once the nightmare was over. If it would ever be over. "Very well. Stay." He couldn't bring himself to be gracious about it.

The sun's warmth couldn't touch him. He was cold inside. His family, divided safely for so long, was more segregated brought together. And now he was pushing them apart even more, breaking pieces once whole.

His arm ached and tingled strangely, while his hand felt swollen, stiff, and slow to respond. A peek under the bandage brought no comfort. The gray flesh crawled halfway up his forearm. Could he even wield his katana in this state? He forced his fingers to curl into a fist. Weak. Fighting with his right hand was a handicap, but better than this numb tingling malady in his left. It was good that Alexion constantly challenged them to train with either hand.

Giving his frightened thoughts a shake before they paralyzed him, Dante plastered confidence across his face. He turned to join his pack for farewells. He had missed some discussion between his thieves.

Jothan looked mutinous. "I can help too! I want to fight!"

"Not happening. You are going with them and me," Leigha said as she pulled a black pouch out of her pack.

Derrick saw it and sidestepped. "Why did you bring that thing, and why are you getting it out?" He dramatically hid behind Raiven, keeping his twin between him and Leigha.

Leigha rolled her eyes. "It is perfectly safe. They're highly refined. More... impactful."

Dante eyed the ominous pouch with apprehension. "Is that what I think it is?" His boots scuffed on stone as he edged away.

"Hmm, probably." Leigha smirked, hefting the pouch. "Don't worry I haven't put on the fuses yet." She pulled out a painted clay ball about the size of an apple. Leigha tossed it in her scarred hands.

"Don't drop it!" Derrick yelped.

Leigha laughed. "Stop being a puppy. I told you I've refined it. It won't go off unless it is lit. It took some practice, of course. Got this burn from the last batch before I figured it out," she said, picking at a shiny starburst patch of skin on her forearm with blunt fingernails.

"What are they for besides big bangs?" Keer asked, moving closer to take one of the clay balls. He held it up and studied it. "What are the components?"

Dante stayed in the background, shaking his head at Keer's insatiable need for knowledge, no matter the personal risk. He'd seen Leigha making those before and intended to keep his distance. Almost losing his face the first time he got too close had taught him well.

"It explodes with a flame and it burns, plus there's the shrapnel from the clay. I fill it with bits of this and that. It works," Leigha said, dodging which ingredients she used. That was her secret—and a closely guarded one.

She pulled out a strange bundle of metal and fiber. Picking one out, she held it up to see. A fibrous string with a tiny iron ball dangling on the end threaded into a narrow metal tube. "See this?" Twisting the string around her finger and pinching the tube firmly, she yanked the string with the ball through the metal. Bright sparks flared out the end. "There's a flint inside. You can tie a line to it and set up tripwires." Holding up the clay ball in her hand, Leigha picked a plug of wet, uncured clay and pushed the metal tube snugly into the hole. "Or you can just light the string and throw it. Getting the timing right is tricky. You don't want the clay to break before it ignites. Most of the force comes from it being contained. If it breaks first, it's just a light show."

She pulled more out of the pouch and primed the explosives with the string-filled tubes. "My personal favorite is to tie a string about an arm's length to it and launch it at them." Her grin was more than a little malicious and Dante was glad she counted them as friends. "Since I'm off with the puppies, I suggest you stick with the tripwires. Less chance of blowing yourselves up and defeating the whole purpose. I can't believe you are taking all of the interesting things for yourself." A thin breeze ruffled her cropped hair. Dante winced at her glare. Nobody seemed to appreciate his decision, except his Lady Aunt.

"I can set them, Leigha," Raiven said, shoving his cowering brother and stepping up. "I've watched you do it enough."

She huffed, exasperated, while handing him the pouch of explosives. "I do wish you'd stop stalking people from the rafters."

"Why ever would I want to do that? No one ever looks up. I learn the most interesting things up there." Raiven took the pouch and offered his free hand to Leigha, pulling her onto her feet.

Dirt puffed around Leigha's fingers as she brushed her butt clean. Jothan handed Leigha her pack; his own smaller one slung over his shoulder. His knit hat was pulled tightly down over his ears, making his naturally spiky bangs bunch out straight like straw sticks.

"Are we ready?" Raphael barked. His face was as smooth as a glass mask, and his arms crossed to form a leather-coated shield protecting his core.

Korren whined in his mother's arms. She stood tall in dyre form, holding her son close. The fierce protective spark of a mother had flamed and revived the strong woman his uncle had loved.

Nakai cuddled Ashliene, whispering to her before handing the pale owlet to Raphael to carry to safety. Dante wished the crown princess would go too.

Leigha marched up the stone steps without a backward glance, Jothan staying close on her heels. He looked back every few steps. Lady Petria followed, and Raphael closed the gap quickly, his back ramrod straight. A wound gaped Dante's chest, but he couldn't bring himself to be truly sorry. He wanted them safely away more.

"We should set the tripwires." Raiven turned downhill, looking for likely paths the soldiers might use. He strung the first across the Elkian-carved pathway. That sealed off the cliff approach. Anything else from that direction would be climbing a sheer drop above a raging river. The rest watched him carefully to know where the traps were set and to hope the clay balls didn't explode in Raiven's face. Derrick chewed absently on a knuckle waiting for his twin to finish. Setting the flint-filled pins with the pull fuses first, Raiven picked his spots in the lower gaps between boulders until the flat area they stood in was half-surrounded with explosives. Hefting the last one, Raiven looked around for one final spot.

"On the steps," Mysti said. "Just in case."

Dante's heart quailed. A final, uncertain measure for if they failed.

Raiven's lips thinned, and he climbed up several steps, laying the last tripwire where scrubby grass jutting out of the cracks hid the line.

Now, as they chose their positions, all they could do was wait for their pursuers turned prey.

Chapter Nineteen

A bit-off curse and a tumble of pebbles alerted Dante, bringing him out of a numb haze. He lifted his head.

Raiven sat straighter on his perch in the scraggly tree. He gestured with expressive fingers that four soldiers approached the steps and another ten came from the rougher mountainside they'd climbed.

The princess sat high on the steps, beyond the last tripwire. A long, black bow lay across her knees. At Raiven's alert, she knelt on one knee, nocking an arrow, waiting for a target to appear.

Stipes stood in front of Dante like a rock wall. He planted his soul-wield on the stone. The metal staff tolled a knell.

The four shifters marched into sight, making no effort at silence. Their gold-embossed armor clanked and rattled, an attempted distraction while the others circled in from the side. They hadn't accounted for Raiven's sight range from the tree. Dante's pack stood ready to face both attacks.

Dante balanced on the balls of his feet. He had to consciously force his numb fingers to close around the sheath of his sword. With his good hand, he readied throwing knives, waiting for a target. The solder's armor did not leave many openings. How had they run for days wearing heavy plate armor? They should have died from sheer exhaustion.

Two of the first four soldiers carried crossbows at the ready. They fired. Bolts hissed through the air. Mysti spun into practiced motion. Taking one bolt on her shield with a dull thump, she reached out with her sword and cleaved the second in half. She sneered and beat her sword hilt on her shield once, daring the soldiers. "You have to do better than that!"

Dante tried to soak in her strength and conviction and use it as his own.

The other serpent shifters charged as the bowman reloaded. Spears led them in. One stumbled.

Dante fancied he heard the flint strike before the trap exploded. Shrapnel shredded everything except the boulders. The soldiers didn't stand a chance, even with their armor. It wasn't designed against Leigha's toys. Bile rose in Dante's throat. He vowed to never venture into Leigha's workroom again, no matter how much Derrick dared him. That was not a clean way to die.

Something whizzed past his ear. Dante ducked in delayed reaction. If the arrow had been meant for him, he would be dead. Another soldier crumpled from atop a boulder.

Tossing a look over his shoulder, Dante saw the princess nock another arrow. Her eyes fixed on a target, and the arrow flew. He whipped around, following the flight and a soldier fell under her onslaught.

He had no time to count the other strikes. The next tripwire triggered. The explosion blew an unfortunate soldier over the cliff side with a scream that echoed into the ravine. The soldier following him moaned, shrapnel studding his face grotesquely. As he turned to face a soldier leaping at him, Dante glimpsed a clay shard jutting out from the soldier's eye. Something oozed around it. Evil runes blazed across his face.

Dante flicked his hand. Throwing knives sprouted in a throat, felling a soldier rushing Alexion.

A spear lashed at his head. Dante deflected it with the metal sheath of his soul-wield. His katana sang a war cry as he unsheathed it and pressed in close, inside the range of the spear. Black scales lined the jawline of the soldier. The soldier hissed and his neck thinned and flattened. He spat.

Dante rolled away as venom hit the air where his face had been. "Watch out. They spit!" he yelled. Blocking the spear again, he lunged to the side. He kicked high. The soldier's head snapped back with an audible crack of spinal joints. Following up, Dante swung his sheath into the soldier's helmet. The soldier staggered, almost fell. Evil runes blazed around the soldier's wrists and throat like strings on a marionette.

So, they were enhanced by death magic. The blood of Princess Nakai's people inked their skin, fueling, enhancing, and apparently making them immune to head injuries.

A tripwire blew, shaking Dante's focus. An armored fist rammed his ribs.

"Sire, down!" Stipes yelled.

Dante dropped, a trained reflex. An iron rod jabbed over his head with crunching force into the soldier's breastplate. Dante kicked the Kobrona solder's feet from under him while he still clutched at his chest where Stipes's had hit him. Dante slashed the soldier's throat. Gurgling his last breath, the soldier hit the ground.

Dante looked for another target.

Raiven dropped out of the tree, tightening a garrote around Derrick's fourth attacker, leaving his twin free to fend off the other three. Dante rushed to help. He sank his katana through the back of a serpent shifter and up into its chest. The blade screeched against the metal of the dead soldier's armor as he yanked it back out. Keer appeared, parried another sword aimed at Derrick's back, and was gone again.

A furious scream and blurring magic rushed him from his blind side. Dante dodged, and a war hammer slammed into the dirt where he'd stood. The spiked hammer whipped back up inhumanly fast. Hundreds of runes, painted in blood, covered the soldier's face and arms. Dante caught a jarring hammer blow on his sheath. His arm went truly numb to the shoulder. The sheath fell from his limp hand. Dante fell in order to dodge the next swing. Only years of practice kept him from stabbing himself with his own sword.

He threw himself sideways on the stone. The hammer narrowly missed him. Chips of flying stone bit at his exposed skin.

On his back, Dante desperately flung out a full set of knives with his numb arm. Two of his weakly-thrown blades sank into the solder's knee, and the soldier staggered. Wounds to the knees like that would have a normal shifter crawling in the dirt. Dante rolled to his feet, not willing to die like a helpless, overturned turtle. The soldier didn't even limp as he stepped forward and flung his hammer at Dante's head. Dante crouched under the blow and tried to kick out the soldier's feet. It felt like he'd kicked a boulder. His foot throbbed.

Lunging forward beneath the backswing of the hammer, Dante pulled the length of his katana from the serpent's wounded knee up and over his hip. Dante felt his katana grate over the bone. Blood poured from the deep slice, drenching the soldier's breeches and puddling on the ground. The guard hissed. Venom arched through the air again. He limped after Dante.

Dante jumped to the side and stepped in behind the swing of the hammer. His katana plunged through the shoulder strap of the soldier's armor and down through the muscle.

Armor hanging askew, the soldier grunted in pain. He plowed his bleeding shoulder into Dante's gut. Dante couldn't breathe. He coughed, and stumbled, trying to get his feet back under him where they belonged. Bile crawled up his throat, and he spat the bitter fluid. Pain was an iron band around his chest.

The serpent soldier dragged his hammer, the heavy metal sparking against the stone. Dante clutched his stomach and drew a weak breath. The hammer rose over the soldier's head, and Dante tried to dodge the coming blow. He was too slow. The deadly hammer dropped. It was going to kill him. Dante knew this.

Iron rang on iron. Dante stared at a straining back. Stipes stood in front of him, his staff in both hands, blocking the hammer from its descent.

Sagging to his knees, Dante choked out a breath. "Death magic. Makes him stronger."

"I can take him," Stipes said. The soldier laughed, the sound a chuckling hiss. Stipes twisted to the side and whipped his staff back at the serpent's face. The serpent leaned back. The blow missed.

Stipes spun, bringing the other end of his staff around with the full force of his body's momentum. Cheekbone crunched. The soldier roared. The evil runes glowed stronger through the fresh coating of blood. Stipes didn't let up. He swung the iron staff around like it weighed nothing and smashed the soldier's arm. Armor crumpled. The bone inside cracked and splintered. The soldier's arm gruesomely folded where there was no joint to fold. The serpent shifter left his hammer where it lay and pulled a dagger from a hip sheath. Stipes swung at the back of the soldier's head. Dante saw the impact in the soldier's face, his eyes bulging and blood pouring from his nose as the back of his head caved inward.

"Thank you," Dante gasped out.

"Of course, sire," Stipes said. Dante turned to see who needed help. Alexion was kicking a soldier off Mysti's back as she reversed the hold on her sword and gutted the soldier. Raiven and Derrick stood back-to-back with nothing around them except corpses. He looked for the others.

"Sire!" His chevalier enveloped him in a hard embrace, throwing them to the ground.

The world spun and exploded.

A shrill tone rang in his ears. Dust clogged his mouth. Weight like a boulder crushed his chest. Had the mountain fallen? A rockfall?

The weight lifted off him, and hands lifted him up and pushed him to lean forward into his knees. His ribs ached from the scrunch, but air flowed in and out easier.

"Breathe, Dante. Can you hear me"

Keer's voice rattled around his ears, a confusing echo of sound. When he made sense of it, Dante nodded. It seemed to be enough of an answer.

"Thank the Mother you're all right."

His mouth tasted like dirt and black powder. "What—" His voice broke, and he doubled over from a coughing fit. Breathing seemed an issue today. He tried to find his voice again. "What happened?"

"We missed a wounded soldier. He crawled into one of the traps. You and Stipes were caught in the blast radius." Dante felt Keer gesturing, and he blinked at the ground between his knees. His ears rang.

"Stipes shielded you."

That was nice. Maybe Raphael would give Stipes some slack now. Stipes was strong, capable, and kind. It was a stupid family feud anyway.

"It looks bad, sire," Keer said. "Worse than it is, I hope, but he took the brunt of the shrapnel."

Dante wished the ringing in his ears would stop. Then, maybe he could actually figure out what was happening. Keer's voice was shaky and wrong. He just couldn't think.

Forcing his head to roll on his knees, Dante saw the rest of his pack clustering over Stipes. Keer's words finally penetrated the thrumming in his skull. Stipes had taken the shrapnel for him, covering his body with his own. He couldn't see much, but the blood spreading on the ground told him more then he wanted to know.

Alexion moved out of the way. Dante wished he hadn't. Stipes lay on his side, back toward him. Dante gagged. Moaning a wounded gurgle, Dante buried his face into his knees. His chevalier's back looked like a mosaic, studded with shrapnel and painted in blood.

"Everyone else?" he asked when he could speak without vomiting.

Keer's hand stayed steady on his back. "Nothing more than a few scrapes and bruises." A note of forlorn triumph twisted Keer's voice. "We did it. We are safe."

That thought took a little while to settle into his fuzzy thoughts. They were safe; everyone was alive. As long as Stipes lived.

"Here, drink. It will help." Keer pressed a canteen to his lips. Dante swished the first gritty mouthful around and spat it by his boots. He tried to grab the canteen to hold it himself, but his numb arm hung at his side. His other hand trembled so badly he dropped the water into Keer's waiting grasp.

"Sorry," Dante rasped, "I'm so sorry."

"None of this is your fault," Keer said. "Your arm?" Keer set the canteen down, clinking metal on the stone.

"Guy hit like an avalanche. I blocked instead of parrying." Dante looked at his arm. He willed it to move, and it flexed and twitched weakly. "Can't feel it really. Not even the weird tingling." He hadn't meant to say that.

"What do you mean?" Keer grabbed his arm and rolled up the sleeve. Dante grunted in protest. "What is this?" Keer growled at the dark gray smear growing over his skin. "Sire, how long has it been like this?" Dante winced at Keer's formality; he was pissed.

With her sharp, sisterly senses, Mysti heard him from where she knelt in Stipes's blood. "What's wrong? I thought you said he wasn't seriously injured?"

Keer stretched the limb into the air so she could see, shaking it somewhat for emphasis.

Dante whined as his shoulder throbbed.

"It started at Hanehishou, didn't it? It's wrong, Dante, dead. Can you even move your fingers?"

He cringed. He'd known they wouldn't like it when they found out, but there had been no point in them knowing.

Mysti came over, leaving Stipes in her concern for him.

"No!" Dante barked. "Help Stipes. I'm fine." Pulling his arm out of Keer's grasp, he cradled it to his chest. "There is nothing you could have done then, and there is nothing you can do for it now. So, blessed leave it."

Blood-covered boots stomped over and a hand swatted his head. Black warred with color as his vision swam. She'd barely tapped him, but, Mother bless, that hurt. Dante planted his hand on the ground and curled into his knees with a keen of pain.

Keer lit into her for him. "Why did you do that? He just woke from being knocked out and you smack him on the head! What were you thinking? I don't care how idiotic he is: don't mess with head wounds! He's stupid, that's nothing new. Save the beating for later."

Their shouts reverberated in his head. "If he wasn't being a dense, bloody ninny, I wouldn't have hit him!" Mysti snapped, but her feet shuffled guiltily, the sound like a whetstone on his nerves.

A warm presence pressed against his back. "Enough! You are making things worse." Derrick knelt behind him.

Gentle fingers probed the back of Dante's skull, and he hissed when Derrick probed a swollen bump. "Good-sized egg here, sire." Derrick's fingers combed through his hair looking for more wounds. "No bleeding at least. Just a goose egg."

Alexion yelled for their attention. "Mysti, Keer, help please!"

"Mysti, I need you to press here after I pull this shrapnel out. It will help stop the bleeding. Lady Petria would have a better idea of what to do, but we have to do what we can before we catch up to them," Raiven said, redirecting Mysti's wrathful attention back to Stipes's mutilated back.

"But, Dante?" Mysti asked, concern finally escaping the fear-filled anger.

"I've got him. Go," Derrick ordered.

Mysti walked away, but Dante didn't watch her leave.

Fleshy squelches as the shrapnel was pulled out of Stipes skin told a blood-inked story. Dante cringed into his knees. Stipes was hurt because of him.

Feather-light footsteps whispered across the stone. "Here are the rest of the canteens."

"Thank you, Princess Nakai. We'll need the water to wash his wounds. I am sure you are weary, but would you be able to catch up to Raphael and Lady Petria?" Keer asked. "I would think they are at the peak of the pass or just over with the few hours start they've had. If they could wait there for us? I fear we will need Lady Petria's healing skills. Most of Stipes's wounds are minor, but with so many of them...."

"Certainly." Her sister was with the other half of his pack, and Dante was sure she was glad to go. "Is there anything else I can do to help before I leave?"

"No. There is not much we can do either. We will be along as soon as we can." Keer spoke from farther away, moving downhill, Dante guessed, without raising his throbbing head. He didn't have the will to fight the pull of sleep.

"Very well. We will wait for you. Take care." Princess Nakai flew away with a swoosh of her wings.

Nausea roiled in his stomach as the earth seemed to roll beneath him. Dante unwrapped a hand from around his knees and braced it on the earth trying to stop the rocky surface from swaying. A steady throbbing pulsed in his skull.

"Hey, you all right?" Derrick asked. He placed a hand on Dante's shoulder. The heat from the touch traveled through Dante's body.

Dante shivered. "Hmm?"

"Dante?" Derrick shook him gently. "Hey, don't turn into a helpless princess now."

"Lemme sleeep," Dante slurred.

"No, I don't think so. Keer, get your ass back here!" Derrick yelled.

Despite Dante's best efforts to push away the mental fog, darkness wavered at the edges of his sight, and he swayed.

"Dante. Snap out of it. No sleeping for you. Keer!" Derrick slapped Dante across the cheek then pulled him close to his chest. Dante felt the sting, but only distantly, as if it happened to someone else. "Hey. Wake your lazy butt up."

Dante blinked and saw Keer, but his edges were fuzzy. Something wet and cool wiped over his forehead. A wet rag. It cleared his head somewhat. "Lean him forward. Let's check that bump on his head again. It might be worse than we thought." Derrick pushed him, and Dante slumped into Keer's shoulder. Pain flared as they jostled his head, and Dante moaned. "Sorry, just let me look."

Keer's long fingers threaded through his hair, searching and probing, and he hit the sore spot.

Growling, Dante tried to pull away. "Stop it."

Keer held the dripping rag to the swollen lump. Soothing cold broke through the pain. Dante flinched against Keer's shoulder when he pressed too hard. "Sorry," Keer muttered.

"Dizzy."

Keer lifted the rag. "I know. Just do not puke on me."

"Mmm," Dante moaned, wishing Keer hadn't reminded him of his convulsing stomach. The inner muscles of his gut flopped around. He wrapped an arm over his stomach in a sorry attempt to settle it.

"Will you be able to walk? Stipes needs Lady Petria's help as soon as we can reach her," Derrick asked. At the thought of trying to stand up and climb the mountain, Dante couldn't control it anymore. Leaning over to the side, he barely made it clear of his friends and puked. Little but water and bile spewed out.

"I'll take that as a firm no," Derrick said, supporting Dante as he righted. "It will be hard to carry them both."

Dante took the rag Keer held out and wiped his mouth. He threw the soiled rag toward the rocks where it landed with a splat. He tried to ignore the violent tremor in his hands and focused on Stipes instead; Stipes needed for him to be strong. "Help me up."

"Dante, are you certain?"

He wobbled to his knees and collapsed. Keer and Derrick caught him under the elbows and lifted him to his feet. Dante swayed, willing his stomach to settle. They let go, and his knees buckled. Easing him back down, they talked over his head.

"What's wrong with him?" Derrick asked.

"I can do it, just let me up."

They ignored him.

"Not certain. I didn't think the lump on his head was that good. Hold on." Keer's hands tilted Dante's head to the side. "Dante, do your ears hurt?"

"Hmph." Dante tried to struggle up, but his strength failed. "There's a bell in my head."

"I think it's his ears."

Derrick agreed. "That makes sense. I've done this to someone before, now that you mention it. I clapped my hands over someone's ears once, and they dropped like I'd hit them with a rock."

Keer had a strange, calculating look on his face. "This might not do much, if it even works." He didn't explain himself.

"What?" Derrick asked as Keer pushed Dante into his arms.

Dante watched with slit eyes as Keer unsheathed a gleaming sharp knife. "Don't worry, sire, this is not revenge for stupidly kept secrets." Keer drew a bloody line on his own forearm and grimaced. "This is as basic as magic gets; however, it should take the edge off your concussion."

Dante felt like a manhandled doll as Keer gripped his arm and turned it over, pushing his sleeve up over the elbow. Dipping his finger into the well of blood, Keer used it as a quill to sketch a rune on Dante's skin. The sticky slickness of the blood clotting on his skin crept on Dante's nerves, and he tried to pull away.

Clamping a hand over the rune, Keer ordered, "Hold still."

Subsiding, Dante shivered as heat bloomed across his skin where Keer held him. Even through Keer's hand, Dante could see the rune glowing. The greenish light of Keer's magic seeped into his skin and spread slowly into his veins. Fresh purple bruises turned to the days-old yellow. The deep scab twisting around his arm lightened to a healthy pink. The warmth of Keer's magic stopped where his flesh had turned gray from the curse. His forearm and hand remained numb and tingly.

Keer growled and pushed more magic into the rune. Dante's blurry vision cleared, and the ringing in his ears lessened. The cursed flesh remained numb.

The flow of magic dimmed, and Keer slumped with a wheeze. Derrick caught him before he fell into the puddle of vomited water.

"Better?" Keer asked.

"Yes, what was that?" Dante asked, "Are you alright?"

"I am fine. Just a little tired now." Keer brushed Derrick's hand away. "That was a basic healing rune I read about in a book." He grabbed Dante's head and twisted it until he could see the lump.

"Hey!" Dante grumbled. "I'm not a doll."

Keer released him enough to prod at the diminished bump. "That worked a lot better than I believed it would." He completely ignored Dante's complaints and inspected the other wounds. "Well, this rope bite is healing, but this huge bruise you neglected to inform us about hasn't changed. I wish I had my books."

Ced Dante shook Keer off and sat up. "Enough already, I'm fine now. Will that work for Stipes? It should help him too, right?"

Scrambling to his feet, Keer covered the short distance to where the others still worked on Stipes's back. Dante and Derrick stayed where they were, watching Keer explain. Alexion held up his dagger, prepared to use his own blood for the rune.

Mysti stopped them. "We should get the rest of the shrapnel out first. It will heal around it and get worse if we don't. My cousin had something like that once. The healers had to cut it open again because it got infected."

Dante was grateful that enough people swarmed over Stipes that he couldn't see the shredded flesh. The sight was already burned into his memory. It took them long, agonizing minutes to finish pulling the clay shards free.

Alexion cut his arm and carefully drew the rune under Keer's direction. Dante hated waiting. Hated feeling useless. There was nothing he could do to help.

"Well?" Dante demanded when no one cleared the way for him to see the results. Mysti propped up a drooping Alexion while Raiven leaned in to inspect Stipes's wounds.

With a fresh wet rag, Raiven wiped away the blood. "The wounds look days old. They might reopen if we aren't careful, though," he said with an almost reverent tone. "I've never seen someone without healer training do anything like this."

"I think it is a basic, and archaic, brute force method. A healer would have done more with cleaner results and half the energy expense," Keer said.

Stipes stirred, moaning feebly, "Prince Dante." The steadfast chevalier pushed up on his elbow with a pained grunt.

Mysti pushed him back down. "Easy, our prince is fine. You protected him well. Rest. You got torn up pretty bad."

Stipes resisted, trying to sit up.

Dante struggled to his feet. Derrick pulled him up with a hand under his elbow, guiding him to the cluster of people around Stipes. Dante tugged free of Derrick's support and dropped down beside his wounded chevalier. Groaning, Stipes made to sit up again. "Stand down!" Dante ordered. "You did your duty. Now let us do ours." At last, Stipes obeyed and settled back with a stifled gasp of pain.

He continued to soothe his chevalier. "We are safe for now. They can't catch up to us again without crossing the ice lands."

"We will need a way to carry him," Keer said, as Stipes slid back into unconsciousness.

Raiven stood up, followed closely by his twin. "We can do that. Calume taught us a few things." Derrick smirked in agreement, moving in tandem with his twin.

"Calume?" Mysti asked. She brushed messy, sweat-flattened bangs out of her face.

The two thieves ghosted into the surrounding mountainside leaving Dante to answer.

Dante grimaced. He was starting to wish he had left them all at home. This subject kept biting him in the ass. "Calume is the guild leader of the thieves. He's the one who found me in the streets. That's how I came to know them. He is a wise man."

Mysti glared at him, her weariness making her spitfire temper all the shorter. "He's a bloody thief—with a huge bounty on his head. My sister has been scouring the city for years for him. Any of this ringing a bell?"

"He has never been caught or proven guilty of anything." Dante grinned a little proudly. He had been trained by the best.

Mysti snarled her indignation. "You are the prince! Ruler of our people. Of course, he has never been caught—you've been protecting him!"

Were they really doing this now? Had he shaken his pack's loyalty so thoroughly?

"I've not! He has not done any evil to force my hand. They are the eyes and ears of every family. They see things even my range-wolves do not. I have protected my city and nobles from horrendous feuds and captured murderers with the help of Calume's guild," Dante defended his mentor. "That rogue that cut out his kill's tongues to eat? He would have gotten away with many more slaughters without their dangerously-gained information. You sound as judgmental as Raphael all of the sudden. I thought we'd passed this. They are a part of me as much as you are. Get used to it."

Mysti looked taken-aback. Guilt and anger whirled in his gut. He had not intended to snap like that. His judgments felt so precarious and she questioned him too, making him question himself and his decisions all the more.

His head throbbed. Dante bowed over Stipes and prayed to the Mother for guidance and strength. The ringing in his ears was all he could hear.

Saving him from more argument and self-doubt, Raiven and Derrick came back, dragging a pole cut from a young pine tree. Sticky sap oozed from the branch where they had hacked the sharp points off. Pulling two ropes out of the packs, Raiven handed one to Derrick, knotting his in half with a loop on each end.

Derrick folded his rope over Raiven's and tied the ends to the pole. "Are we ready to move?" Derrick finished tying the knots with a sharp jerk.

"I am. Stipes is not going to get any better lying there. My Lady Aunt can help him. If you are ready, we should leave."

Alexion huffed. "Agreed." He tugged his weapons harness around so it sat balanced on his shoulders. "I'm ready. Mysti?" His partner was already shrugging into her pack. "Right then. What's the plan?"

The twin thieves picked up the ropes threading their arms into the loops. The pole swung at the back of their knees leaving the sticky pitch on their pants. As he got ready, Raiven started dropping orders. "Alexion, Keer, can you two get him up for us. Mysti, slide the pole underneath him." The two shifted into the stronger dyre form.

Coming to stand behind Stipes's head, the twins crouched so the pole rested on the ground. Alexion straddled Stipes, getting his arms under Stipes's shoulders and heaving the larger man upward. Keer pushed from the back and they got Stipes sitting upright. Raiven and Derrick waddled forward as Mysti pushed the pole farther under Stipes. The ropes crossed beneath Stipes's back.

"Get him higher," Mysti said.

With a strained grunt, Alexion heaved again. Keer got hold of Stipes's belt and lifted. Together, they got the unconscious man mostly off the ground. Mysti positioned the pole under his thighs and the twins knelt to get ahold of the pine pole. Dante felt utterly useless as the halves of his pack worked together to get Stipes travel ready.

"Steady him," Derrick said. In a chorus of grunts, they lifted Stipes. He slumped in the makeshift sling.

"Should we tie him in?" Alexion asked. He kept a supporting hand on Stipes's chest.

Mysti eyed the setup. "It's not like he's awake to hold on."

"True," Raiven agreed, standing braced against Stipes's weight on the pole in his hands. "If we stumble going up those steps..." Alexion dug out another rope. Mysti took an end of it, and the two secured Stipes's limp body.

Keer scooped up his pack along with his own. Alexion carried the one other bag left behind, the other supplies having been sent on with Raphael.

Opening his mouth, Dante made to protest—despite the weakness plaguing him—but Keer glared at him. He shut up without making a sound. He truly didn't have the strength to carry a loaded pack and climb the stairs. Pointless to argue.

The twin dyre wolves synchronized their steps and began the arduous climb. Even with the extra strength provided by the wolf, they struggled under Stipes's unconscious weight. Dante wobbled upward several steps behind his chevaliers who stayed on Raiven and Derrick's heels.

Keer kept an eye on him in their stead. "How are you holding up with everything?"

"I'm fine," Dante growled attempting to fend off the probing questions. Keer was good at prodding out his more uncomfortable feelings. Never mind that he still felt quite ill and dizzy, despite the healing. Dante had the feeling that Keer's rune was more like a bandage than stitches.

"Uh-huh, and that's why you are cowering way back here."

Hunching his shoulders, Dante said, "Fine, I'm tired. Exhausted. Happy now?"

"No." Keer bumped his shoulder with a fist. "I'm not. I am far away from my home and my books. I haven't had a decent night's sleep in weeks and some snakes just tried to kill me. My friends are all politely fighting amongst themselves because they don't appreciate the other's professions, and my best friend is keeping weird, secret injuries from me so I won't know when he might need help."

Guilt welled in his heart, making it ache almost physically. Dante stared at the silvery trace of the river in the shadowed canyon, refusing to look at Keer. He wrapped his arms around his ribs, trying to hold himself together physically, mentally, and emotionally. His world was coming apart, and even this victory couldn't put it back together.

Keer continued, "And if I am feeling all that horribly, I can't imagine what my brother must be feeling when he has to leave the kingdom he rules, and people he loves, to flee the serpents hunting him; is wounded; and believes he is failing everyone."

Dante glanced at Keer; his insight was spot-on. He didn't know why he was surprised that Keer cut to the heart of his turmoil. He had earned his place as his right-hand honestly.

"It's all right, you know," Keer said. "I get it. You are trying to protect us from more hardship. It is your duty as prince to provide and protect." Keer stopped him with a hand on his arm. "You do that all you need to. Just remember we are your pack and we are here, standing at your back. You are not in this alone. We aren't helpless puppies." He shook Dante with the grip on his sleeve. "Are you listening to me?" Dante nodded, still staring into the abyss of shadow broken only by the glimmering waters. "Good." Keer punctuated his words with a sharp elbow. "That's for not telling me you were hurt. I will be looking at that again later."

Dante forced a wry smirk, glad to know that at least one of his relationships remained whole.

Chapter Twenty

They climbed the mountain steps side-by-side and caught up to the others. The roar of the waterfall grew so loud they couldn't hear except to shout, so any more conversation was drowned out. The cold bit deeper with every step.

A shadow moved over the frost-edged steps. Tilting his head back, Dante's eyes met those like warm gold. Princess Nakai flew past in a low circle. The breeze from her wings ruffled his hair. She had found the others and returned to check on them.

Firelight flickered on the mountainside above. The others had made a camp. Dante exhaled, and a visible puff of air escaped his mouth; it was so much colder here. The mere idea of the waiting campfire chased away the chill for a moment, until he realized that a few minutes of flight for Nakai meant an hour's worth of climbing for them.

Cradling his arm, Dante hunched his shoulders to cover his cold ears and trudged on. He wheezed in and out, a counterpoint to the throbbing in his temples. It felt as though the whole of the mountain sat on him. He stopped. Bending over, he braced against his knees.

A violent shiver shook him to the bones. If it was this cold here—he shivered again—how cold was it on the other side? Vague memories of powdered, crusty snow and spit globs freezing before it hit the ground came to mind. Were they prepared? Dante tried to remember what had been packed before they left. Thinking made his head hurt more.

Keer caught him under the elbow. "Come on. You can rest when we get to the top."

Raphael and Leigha came down to help them when they drew level with the top of the waterfall cascading out the gaping mouth of the mountain. "What can we do?" Leigha asked, before Raphael could start barking the furious questions Dante could see building up in him like a thundercloud.

"Carry one of the packs, please. Thank you Leigha." Keer passed one to the thief. "Raphael, catch our prince before he passes out from sheer stubbornness."

Raphael didn't need to be told twice. He stormed over to Dante's side and pulled his good arm over his shoulders. "You are a bloody idiot! I knew I shouldn't have left you behind."

Dante struggled to focus on his glowering chevalier. "'Ello, Raphael. It's nice to see you again."

Keer caught Raphael's worried look. "We tried to heal them as best we could, but they need Lady Petria. He smacked his head rather hard. His lucidity is fading as the cold and exertion get to him," Keer said. "It is not good, but if Stipes's hadn't shielded him from the blast, Dante would have taken it to the face. It would have killed him."

A tremor in Keer's voice hooked Dante out of his haze, and he patted his brother's shoulder. "M'fine, Keer."

"Of course, sire." Annoyance sparked with the worry in Keer's green eyes. The fog dimmed Dante's reasoning as to why. "I pray to the Mother that Lady Petria has enough strength to heal them both."

Raphael climbed, hoisting Dante along with him. "The sooner we get there, the sooner she can start."

Dante drifted. Suspended on Raphael's rigid height, he forced his feet to move in time with his second's jarring strides. Not a word broke their silence as Raphael hauled him up the mountain.

Lady Petria stood waiting, fingers twisted in her skirts as the group entered the small circle of warmth cast by the fire. "Put them down there."

She pointed at the two heaps of blankets piled close to the fire. Jothan huddled on the other side of the warmth with a blanket wrapped around himself and over his head like a cloak. Dante blinked. A pair of brilliantly golden eyes peered out from a gap in the draping fabric. Since Nakai stood beside his Lady Aunt, Dante surmised that little Ashliene was sharing Jothan's warmth.

Raphael deposited him semi-smoothly on a bedroll and he sat there, numbly watching the others bustling around Stipes. Leigha dropped the pack and hurried to pick out the knots holding Stipes upright in the sling while the twins held him steady.

"We should try to lay him on his side if we can," Mysti said. Dirt and blood streaked her face. "Most of the wounds are on his back."

Alex and Raphael pulled Stipes forward into their arms as the twins knelt on a knee to lower him down. Dante felt like he should be helping somehow. His head hurt again, pulsing with a dull throb that made his eyes water. The bells in his ears rang loudly.

"Sire, lay down before you fall over," Mysti said.

The last thing he saw was his aunt peering at the wounds shredding Stipes's back.

Chapter Twenty-one

Nakai

Even as she rushed to obey Lady Petria's orders, Nakai cast a glance at the blanketed figure of the youngest thief. Two sleepy, golden eyes peered through the gap in the fabric. A black, snuffling nose poked out into the air for a moment while she watched, and it quickly retreated into the warmth of the trio's shared body heat. The children were safe.

"Go sit out of the way!" Lady Petria ordered. The clustered pack broke apart but kept their eyes on their fallen man. "Bring me the water off the fire," she told Nakai, who hurried to obey. Healers outranked everyone when it came to matters of health. Wrapping her hand in a spare shirt, Nakai lifted the steaming pot from the fire. Heat threatened her skin, even through the fabric. "Set it there." Lady Petria peeled back the blood-caked shirt plastered to the chevalier's back.

Nakai hissed in sympathy. Small nicks and gouges, red and angry, pockmarked the skin from the hair at the base of his neck to his hipbones. Fresh blood from broken scabs stained the damp rag Lady Petria used to re-clean the wounds. "Chevalier Raphael, hand me a knife, and stoke up that fire while you are just standing around. Leigha, please check on my nephew. Wake him up. I do not want him sleeping with a head wound. I will be with him in a few minutes." Lady Petria pricked her finger on the knife Raphael handed her. "Hold him upright on his side."

Nakai took a firm hold of Stipes's muscled shoulder and kept him balanced so the worst of his injuries faced Lady Petria. "Can you do much?"

Lady Petria nodded while chaining basic runes in her own blood down Stipes's back. "These are mostly shallow wounds, thanks to Keer's emergency rune. This will heal them—though, not without scarring. I am not trained enough to do more. When I was in training, I prepped patients for the healer rather than doing the actual healing."

Nakai sent Lady Petria a questioning glance as Leigha settled beside Prince Dante, poking him in the face and snickering when he swatted at the annoyance.

"I've known about Dante's odd choice of friends for years. His uncle, my husband, spent more time down in the city with the smithy guild than in my bed; always came to me smelling of molten iron and smoke. A Canidea prince needs to spend time with his people, and every one of them favors a guild of their choosing. It's more an expected tradition than the great secret they think it is. His father spent a lot of time with his range-wolves in the woods. However, Dante's grandfather had friends among the thieves too. I believe that is part of why the Thief Lord took Dante in so readily. I have known where he was running off to since the month he joined the guild. It has been good for him, strengthening.

"He was becoming a man, and his father was finally starting to see him. Then the greater fire elemental came, and it rampaged with the fury of an inferno. The king died protecting Dante." Her fingers continued to paint precise lines over the torn skin as she talked. "It almost killed him too, burning him beyond what magic could fix entirely. Unfortunately, I was already lost within myself. I have not been there for him, as family should be. I am the closest thing he has to a mother, and I abandoned him to grow up alone, doing nothing except making his life more difficult. I made unreasonable demands and slapped his face when he accomplished all that I asked. He grew up while I was lost inside myself." Lady Petria sighed and scrubbed her face with a sleeve. "You are all so young. Too young to have seen a war such as this."

Lady Petria grew quiet, pausing to focus her magic through the finished chain of runes. Nakai watched, awestruck by the purity of the act, the beauty of the self-sacrifice that a healer put forth. She couldn't see the magic flowing into the chevalier, but she could feel it. It was gentle and clean, soothing over the wounds until nothing except fleshy bumps and dimples of fresh scars remained.

"You would have made a good healer," Nakai whispered, not wanting to break the Lady's concentration, but needing to say something rather than sit there being useless.

Lady Petria sat back on her heels and wiped her bloody hand with a rag. "I do not understand this strange conflict Kobrona is stirring up. The serpent family is primarily artisans. The last I heard of the young prince, he was exploring ruins, looking for the old statues to unearth and restore. This hunt for power?" She shook her head. "I met him once, at a Communion long before Korren was born. Dante was just a pup. They are about the same age. The Crown Prince Kobrona was a bright, inquisitive child. Always asking intelligent questions, and he was sweet, wanting to meet everyone and know everything. This war. I do not understand it. I don't understand why. He cannot hope to control that much land even with the royals captured. The families and the Mother will not stand for it."

Lady Petria stood, her split skirts falling to her ankles. Moving around the knot of worried chevaliers, she perched down beside Prince Dante. Leigha scooted out of the way to give her room. Nakai followed, bringing more hot water. It was all she could offer in aid at the moment, and she owed this family more than she could ever repay. Bringing water to wash their wounds was not beneath her.

"It's good to see your eyes open, Dante." Placing gentle fingers under his chin, Lady Petria tilted Dante's head until she peered into his eyes. "Definitely a concussion, love."

"Could you make the bells stop?" he mumbled.

Nakai watched almost enviously as Lady Petria pet his hair back. She missed her mother. There were some things only a mother's touch could soothe.

Lady Petria smiled. "We will get you fixed up." Prince Dante nuzzled into her hand. Feeling like an intruder, Nakai looked away, giving them a moment. She held her breath to stop the trembling of her nerves. Staring at her hands, Nakai clenched them until her knuckles turned white, willing the grief to fade. A breakdown right now was not allowed. She had to stay strong for Ashe.

When her emotions were stable again, she looked up to find the woman thief watching. "You're not bad for a royal," Leigha observed dryly.

Nakai frowned. "Your Dante is a royal as well, you know," she said, not sure what the woman was getting at.

Leigha waved her comment away. "Of course, he is, but we started on him early. Most of the nobles are soft, helpless. You are soft, but not helpless. You would still be in that tower or dead in the forest if you were." Leigha moved to the side, giving Lady Petria room to work. "The Kobrona are artisans yes; however, they have made close combat an art form. A dance. And, they know it well. That speaks also for your strength." Nakai sat stunned at the thief's insight into something she had not even realized. "You would have done as well as Dante in our guild."

"Thank you." Years of etiquette training forced the polite response through her confusion.

Leigha nodded, and they both turned back to Dante.

Lady Petria pressed her hands to the chain of runes drawn over Dante's cheek and down his shoulder. "I'm not sure if it will heal this black mark. I've never seen anything like it." She released her magic.

Nakai closed her eyes to feel the magic coursing through the prince's blood, healing the bruises and rope wound. Her brow furrowed. The Lady's magic slowed and struggled upon reaching the bruise. Opening her eyes didn't change the outcome. She could not see the magic fighting to heal, only feel it. The darkness staining his arm was not receding; the twisting rope wound healed slightly, the scab tightening almost into new skin. Something inside made her want to reach out and help the magic, to give it an extra push.

On impulse, she laid a hand on Dante's arm. The gray staining his skin felt clammy, dead. Lady Petria's healing was going to fail. This death was a curse that would spread deep into his flesh and throughout his body. It would suck him dry. She felt Lady's Petria's magic fluttering weakly at the edges of the curses, but the death magic consumed the spark.

With an instinct she could not refuse, Nakai sliced her finger and, ignoring Leigha's gasp, drew a line of blood over the deadened flesh from his bicep to the tip of his ring finger. She willed her magic to surge into Dante, a dual attack on the curse. Her magic burned a channel through the death magic, and Lady Petria's healing flooded into it.

It felt as though her magic turned on the sun under his skin, searing at the dying flesh, burning out the curse. Only when they'd cauterized the decay did Nakai pull her hand away. Sweat slid down her temples.

"What was that?" Leigha demanded. "What did you do?" How couldn't they have felt that? A force like the sun under her fingers, and they sat oblivious around the campfire?

"Whatever you did, you foolish girl," Lady Petria said, "did what I could not. You burned out that death magic, but don't you ever interfere with a healing again. You could have killed him. A body can only handle so much magic in a controlled balance. There was nothing controlled about what you did."

Nakai stared at her hands, Lady Petria's scolding a mere backdrop to her befuddled wonder. She should feel exhausted after wielding something like lightning, but energy thrummed through her veins. "I'm sorry. I don't know what happened. I just…knew."

She needed to move. To fly.

"I'll be back." Before anyone could protest, she was running, leaping right over the cliff's edge. She tucked her wings and rolled. She soared.

Light filled her skin until she felt as though she was luminescent. The power carried her far and high until, at last, the static settled and she could think again.

What had she done? Was this an awakening bloodline trait?

She knew without the slightest doubt that the death magic was gone from the prince, that he was all right, healed. But, what in the Mother's blessed name, had she done?

The light, dull and quiescent now, would blind her should she reach for it from where it hummed under her breastbone.

Air caught Nakai's wings, lifting her from the heavy earth. The frightening cares of the day fell away as she let the currents take her where they willed with naught but a beat of her wings.

Flight, as always, soothed her. The Mother's gentle magic drifted around her as soft as the clouds, always present for her children.

Looping in a high circle over the crystal-veined mountain, Nakai watched for more of the animal signs she'd seen on their climb up the steps. Her feathers sliced through air in a silent hunt. The wolves were likely as hungry as she was. If she could track the goats, she could, in some part, recompense the wolves for the grief she had brought upon them.

A cluster of dirty white amidst the gray of the rocks caught her eyes. The herd of goats was farther away than she hoped. Not too far, however. Twisting her head around looking over her shoulder, she could just see the glow of the campfire dotting the mountainside. Close enough. Landing high on the rocks above the herd, Nakai shifted, calling her soul-wield to hand. The black bow came with a greeting hum of magic. Golden runes glowed along its length, heated from use before cooling to copper engravings twisting around the bow. She pulled a broad-headed hunting arrow from her quiver. In the skirmish earlier today, she had wished for the barbed war arrows her Owlderah warriors carried routinely, especially after watching the enhanced soldiers yank her simple broadheads from their flesh without so much as a whimper. The warhead would have caused far more damage on the way out than on the way in.

The well-oiled string groaned not at all, as she drew it back until the white-fletched arrow lined up with her ear. Archery gloves protected her hand from the pressure of the taut string. A goat kid limped behind the rest of the herd as they made impressive leaps of daring over the steep boulders. One leg dangled unnaturally, tucked high against the goat's stomach, kept out of the way. A weakness. The beast was doomed to forever trail behind or die.

She released.

The arrow flew with a quick, silent death. The goat fell to its knees with a final bleat bubbling from its throat. The rest of the herd took immediate flight. Warning bleats echoed the danger. Nakai ignored them, having done what she needed. Jumping down the boulders, Nakai let her soul-wield fade into the containing magic. She pulled a large hunting knife from her boot, knelt beside the animal, and finished the job. Blood pooled across the stone as the last few beats of the goat's heart pushed it through the severed artery. She bent to clean out the guts with ruthless efficiency. Slicing through the taut skin over the stomach, more blood spilled out, steaming over the cold stone.

Cleanly cutting out the heart and liver, Nakai set them on another rock, saving the highest valued organs for feeding the wounded in the pack. The organ meat would make a broth full of nutrition.

A pampered, spoiled princess she was not. Her people were hunters, one and all. As Crown Princess, she was among the best. A hunt alone never happened; her chevaliers escorted her hunts from a distance. As an owl, she hunted in a different manner than the wolves—by sight and hearing instead of scent. It was how she had seen the faint trail marks across the mountain high above them.

Gutted and empty, except for the heart and liver, the small goat was light enough for her to hoist into the air if she took dyre form. Nakai bound the four hooves together with her belt. With a surge of magic, Nakai tested the strength of her wings, stretching them to their fullest. She felt not a twinge as she flexed her flight muscles.

With a hop and a beat of her wings, she was in the air. Circling the rock, she caught the hooves in her talons. A warm draft pushed under her wings, and she drifted on the buoyant air.

Now that the humming under her skin had calmed, she was ashamed. She'd done something strange and dangerous by interfering with the prince's healing and then ran away like a scolded child. Never mind that she might've saved his life. Her behavior was reprehensible. His protective wolf pack had every right to be incensed.

Her warm breath puffed thin clouds in the cold air. Minnow-like air sylphings swarmed around her, punching holes through her breaths before they faded. Nakai laughed as one airy sylphing overshot its target cloud. It crashed into her cheek and dissipated, only to reform inches away with a breezy giggle.

The orange spot of light grew ever closer as Nakai angled her wings to glide toward it. As she approached the camp, the curious sylphings left her cloudy breath in favor of investigating the column of smoke from the fire. The sylphings drew the smoke into strange and beautiful swirls before dashing them through with gleefully childish destruction. Leaving the little sylphings to their play, Nakai tried to pick a clean stone to lay the goat as she landed amidst the wolf pack. Raphael came to her rescue and caught the bound hooves from her talons as she drew near.

Well, they hadn't attacked her on sight. She would have deserved it. She hadn't even channeled the magic she had used with runes. Nakai landed as the pack dealt with the food.

"Alexion, let's get a spit made!" he ordered. Alexion scrambled to obey. Raiven and Derrick got up to help too, each with small hatchets in hand. Dry scrub added to the fire quickly brought the flames to cooking heat. The three axe-wielding men brought down three scrubby trees and made fast work of chopping off the limbs to make two forks and a pole. Raphael stood with stoic impatience, trying to hold the carcass off the ground and away from his clothes while they rigged the spit holding the pole to the forks with leather strips.

Nothing was said beyond the necessary requests as they worked to get the food prepared. Nakai kept waiting for something, anything, to be said. All she got were sideways glances. Nerves twisted in her stomach as the food cooked. She didn't know how to explain what had happened when they asked.

"That smells good!" Alexion said.

A strange rumble rolled through the camp. Lady Petria's cheeks bloomed a pretty rose. Before she could turn completely red, Mysti's stomach growled even louder in unison with Jothan's. Nakai could not hold back a nervous giggle as they laughed at the hungry sounds of empty stomachs.

When she could gasp out a breath, Mysti snickered. "What? Food is good!"

"It's ready too," Derrick said. He grabbed a stick of meat off the fire and sank his strong teeth into the freshly cooked meat. "Hot! Hot, hot, hot, hot!" Derrick yelped around the food.

"Idiot." Raiven rolled his eyes at his twin's stupidity.

Nakai heeded Derrick's example and blew on her meat before taking a nibble. She hissed air in around it to cool it more. The goat meat was gamey and a little stringy compared to what she was used too, but it was rich and filling. Ashliene curled into her lap, and Raphael passed over a bowl of broth and stewed meat. In between bites of her own, Nakai spoon-fed her sister, making sure the bites were small enough.

Ashliene sneezed.

"Eww." Nakai wiped her snot-slimed arm on her shirt.

Ashliene giggled. "Sorry, Nakai." Her laughter quickly turned into a raspy cough. Nakai patted her bony back gently, cringing at the feel of protruding vertebrae. She held a canteen to Ashe's lips.

"Shh. I've got you." Ashliene's coughs turned into quiet sobs, and

Nakai tucked Ashliene's wet face into her shoulder.

"I want mamma," Ashliene said. Nakai rocked her, eyes dry even as her little sister's tears soaked her neck. She had done all the crying she had any right to. She had to be strong now. Never mind that her father was murdered and her mother enslaved to an insane royal. She had gotten her Chevaliers murdered, failed her sister, and lost her people. She was at her weakest, yet she needed to be at her strongest.

Alexion draped a cloak over her shoulders and tucked the edges around Ashliene. Nakai smiled at him and hummed to Ashe the lullaby their mother had sung to them before the nursemaids took over the raising of them. The wolf pack retreated to the other side of the fire, allowing them some personal space to grieve and comfort. Nakai hummed the same tune endlessly, swaying back and forth. Slowly, the sobbing quieted into silent tears and heaving breaths. Nakai rested her chin on top of Ashliene's soft hair. When the heaving breath turned to chilled shivers, Nakai coaxed Ashliene up. She smeared tears off Ashe's cheeks with her thumbs.

"Here, drink a little more." Nakai held the canteen steady while Ashliene drank. Water ran down her chin in little trails. Nakai wiped her sister's wet chin with a sleeve. "There, all better. Now, can you change for me? You will stay much warmer," Nakai promised.

Even her soft, silver curls drooped. Ashliene nodded. Magic took over, shrinking her into the little ball of fluff. Nakai drew Ashliene close, tucking her into the cloak's warm folds with a smile. Still wheezing from the illness and the bout of heavy crying, Ashliene fluffed her feathers and closed her eyes.

None of the pack looked directly at her, but eyes flickered toward her and away. It was time, apparently, and it was for her to explain. Not that she could.

"I don't know what I did exactly," she announced. "It was instinct. If I hadn't done it, I believe the dead parts would have kept spreading."

If she thought about it from their side, Nakai was surprised there weren't swords hovering at her throat. One did not potentially threaten a royal's life in front of their chevaliers without consequence.

"I know, Princess Nakai. That's why I'm not angrier. It was still a very risky action, interfering with a healing," Lady Petria said.

"Do you have any idea what actually happened?" Keer asked. He looked poised to take notes with a quill, even though his hands were empty.

"Not really. It was like holding lightning."

Keer gnawed on his lips. "Maybe it is part of the Mother's Test? Or an awakening bloodline trait?"

Grief drowned her. Yes, it could be exactly that. Her mother was enslaved by death magic; therefore, dead to the Mother. As heir, she was ascending the throne and accepting the trials that came with it. The Mother's Test could certainly be a part of this. If the crown was moving to her, bloodline traits would awaken as well.

Looking around, Nakai saw that the wolves had bedded down for the night already. Only Alexion sat up with his back to the fire, watching their surroundings. She buried the spike of fear at the thought that they might not be safe, even after the battle earlier. Kobrona could have sent more than one group of soldiers after them. How were they to know? Out here in the wilderness, the land did not speak so clearly. They were far from the Heart of Hanehishou.

Nakai huddled into a miserable ball around her sister. Hunched in on herself, the unwillingness to sleep kept Nakai from changing to warmer feathers. Sleep was horrifying. Shadow images of her beautiful mother covered in bloody runes and sitting, enslaved by her king's slaughter, complacently at Kobrona's feet. Kobrona had murdered her father to chain her royal mother to his side. When she closed her eyes, the serpent lord's crimson eyes burned coldly at anyone who earned his easy displeasure. Blood-splattered cobblestones soaked in the lifeblood of her chevaliers stained her subconscious. The ghosts of her beloved protectors haunted her, and now her own hands were stained with the blood of the serpents they had killed today.

She shivered, even in the fire's circle of warmth. The memories were hard to deal with in the daylight. Night terrors woke her. Screams choked in her throat.

Ashliene chirred and blinked.

Nakai buried her fears and stroked her sister's feathers. "It will be all right now. Everything is going to get better. We have friends now, and a plan. The families will unite against Lord Kobrona. Not even he can fight them all. The council will rescue Mother. Everyone will be safe soon." She projected a trained confidence into her voice. How, she didn't know, but she'd fake it until she dropped.

Nakai forced the discouragement down before it reached her face.

Kobrona had some unknown strength beyond the death magic. One man could not do this through their own energies. Death magic drained even as it empowered. Moreover, he held at least seven royals captive, including her mother and those from the Elkian Family. The council would have to consider their safety in the skirmish. The Elkians, in particular, were the entirety of the family bloodlines. If they died, it would leave the family of deer in disarray until the Mother blessed a new royal line, which could take years to surface.

Ashliene chirred again, pushing her head against Nakai's arm. Nakai smiled bitterly as Ashliene settled back into sleep. Through all of this, it was her little sister doing the comforting. Nakai wondered how her sister was stronger than she. With a final nuzzle, Ashliene settled back to sleep.

Nakai wished it were that easy to forget her cares.

The wolf pack lay sprawled in a large puppy pile. The chevaliers lay carefully over and around Stipes, who had yet to awaken and did not have the advantage of his fur to keep him warm, so they shared theirs.

Nakai tucked the cloak tighter around Ashliene and stared into the flames. Sleep finally tugged at her harder than she could ignore, and she lay down and curled around Ashliene. On the verge of unconsciousness, Nakai called the change, and the cloak enveloped them both in its warmth as Nakai tucked Ashliene under her wing.

Chapter Twenty-two

With a weary sigh of inevitable acceptance, Dante tucked his nose tighter under his tail in a vain attempt to block out the morning light. He peeked through the shield of his fur, waiting for the sun to stab his brain. Nothing came except for a dull ache in his bones. His thoughts were muzzy. Frost tipped his fur until the sunbeams grew warm enough to melt it away. Mysti watched him from where she rested her head on Alexion's back. With the chill eating at his bones, Dante wished he had stayed nearer the pack. When the first nightmare had struck, induced by the fierce crackling of the fire and the memories associated with it, he had moved to the edge of its warmth in the hope of escaping its influence and to save disturbing the others.

He had held himself at the halfway point between dozing and true sleep after the third nightmare. He hated it. Hated that he couldn't sleep because of the sound of flames burning hungrily, as was its nature. When he closed his eyes, flame flickered and whispered dreadful things. The snap and crackle of the fire crooned a threat, a warning. Dante feared the sound.

Dante stepped out of the fire's circle. The crackling flames still scratched his nerves, but that originated more from his brain, whispering fearful, dark things. He shifted, glad for the duller hearing of his human form. Absently, Dante tore at the burn scars on his hip, his chipped fingernails leaving aching welts.

A firm hand stopped his scratching. "Dante." Mysti had left her warm spot snuggled with Alexion. "Everything all right?" She held his arm captive and secure, brown eyes searching his.

"Of course," he answered shortly, knowing she would know the truth of it, but not wishing to discuss his shortcomings.

"How is your head? It took a nasty bump yesterday." Mysti let his deflection slide with a purse of her lips.

Reflexively, Dante ran a hand through his hair feeling for goose eggs. A residual ache spread under his prodding fingers. "Just a little bruised. I can see straight now."

"Good," Mysti said.

Dante eyed her sideways, muscles twitching in anticipation.

She raised a hand, smacking the back of his head.

He'd ducked a split-second too late. "Ow!" He rubbed the sting out of his scalp.

Mysti wagged a scolding finger in his face. "That's for not telling us about your injury. It was stupid and irresponsible. What if it had interfered with your ability to fight? Huh? Then we would have had to protect your pathetic sorry ass instead of our own." She radiated fury. Her crossed arms were a promise of the pain to come next time they were in a training bout. She wouldn't forget his transgression.

Guilt ripped through his gut. That was exactly what had happened, and Stipes had paid the price. "It was my choice, and it is done. You know now. There's nothing more to it."

Mysti actually growled, a visceral sound issued from deep in her throat. "I want you to promise not to do it again. Not to hide something so stupid." Her voice softened. "My Prince, my Alpha, mine to protect and defend. How am I to do so when I do not have all the knowledge? If I don't know that there is a weakness in that defense." Mysti laid a hand on his face, a loving sisterly touch. "Please, Dante, promise me. I'm supposed to take care of you. I need to know how."

He could not resist the tender tone of his strong, temperamental First. She rarely pulled it out, generally willing to let her rage beat her worries out, showing her love in a multitude of bruises. "I will try." The promise came reluctantly, dragging out of his throat. He hated relying on his people, however deeply they were sworn to his protection.

"Well!" Mysti said. "Now that that's out of the way! What's wrong? I can tell something is bothering you. More than the lack of real sleep."

Scuffing his feet, Dante pushed his shaggy hair out of his face. It was longer than he liked. "I don't think we should tarry here. I know our pursuers are gone and everyone is tired and need rest, but I feel exposed out here." Dante stared over the valley. The nightmare and fire were making him jumpy. Logically, he knew this, but the instinct to flee the flames thrummed through his veins. The red scars over his flesh itched at the reminder of burnt pain.

Mysti frowned. "This is the first real chance we've had to rest. We've been running for a fortnight. Princess Ashliene is still ill. Everyone else is exhausted and near collapse, including you," she said, with a pointed look. "If we keep pushing too hard, and refuse our chance to stop, more of us will be sick. Stipes certainly is not in any condition to travel. He has yet to awaken. Despite Lady Petria's and Princess Nakai's healing, recovery takes time."

The fire crackled and snapped as a log fell into the coals. Dante flinched. The whispering in his ears taunted him. He wanted to run far and run fast. "One more night then," he acquiesced, hiding his unease. He had no logical reason to make the pack move on. His nerves screaming at him were not enough. They deserved a good rest and more. Mysti smiled in obvious relief that he wasn't fighting her on it, but Dante was unable to smile back at her. He left her standing there, bewildered by his surly attitude. He felt bad for it, making him sulkier still.

He went to the cliff's edge, hoping that the distance from camp and the roar of the river would drown out the fire's ominous sparks. Was it only his phobia speaking?

The widespread spray from the waterfalls watered the green moss covered the rocks. Clear ice crystals sparkled like fragile jewels on the tips and edges of the fuzzy plants. Dante crouched to feel the frozen gems. The chill kissed his fingers, turning to small drips of water as his body heat melted the ice. It was soothing.

Leaning over the cliff's edge, Dante craned his head to peer at the cave mouth where the frothy river water rushed out in a torrent. A thin ledge, carpeted thickly in the damp moss, led to it. A glance over his shoulder checked that Mysti wasn't hovering. She had returned to the fire and was busy adding wood to it while the few others awake trimmed the last of the meat off the goat corpse to roast over the hot flame.

Allowing the curiosity and need to move to get the better of him, Dante stepped over the edge, making sure his foot planted firmly on the narrow stone. The blanket of moss squished under his boot, leaving dark footprints in the tiny plants to mark his passage. As sure-footed as he was running on the edges of rooftops, Dante moved easily down the ledge. He brushed a hand along the rock wall with his fingertips.

Ice-crusted water puddled on the stone and moss as he drew even with the first tier of the falls. Water voilently spilled out of the gaping cave mouth. The mountain was like a spewing giant. By the time, he reached the entrance, Dante was treading through an inch of water spread over the floor, despite the actual river being several feet over and lower. His pants stuck to his legs from the spitting spray.

Darkness swallowed him as he splashed into the cave. The light from outside only pierced the murk for a few yards.

Pausing a moment to let his eyes adjust and pushing magic into his eyes, Dante found a blue glow illuminating the shadows. Blue veins of crystal bled through the dark stone, glowing with the innate, wild magic flowing through them. The vein-like crystals and the river were all Dante's right eye picked up in the darkness. His left eye registered only blackness.

It threw him off-balance to be half-blind without the Heart feeding him magic to see by. His right usually caught the ghost images of the magic left behind by the life stream. To be totally blind…. Dante felt his eyes itch and strain to see within the depths of the cave, but the only light source was behind him, leaving him completely reliant on his magic sight.

He waded deeper into the cave. The river seemed calmer here, spreading its fury across the stone floor, before channeling out of the throat of the cave. Magic glistened in the rippling water as he stepped through the shallows. He walked with trepidation, but anything was better than being surrounded by his sundered family and listening to flames crackle and laugh.

Dante wanted the excitement of exploration, the thrill of the hunt, for new sights to distract him. A frision of fear chilled his blood. It didn't stop Dante from walking deeper into the cavern. The river's roar quieted and softened, strangely echoed by the stony walls. The ceiling, seen dimly by the veins of magic, shot up abruptly. Tilting his head back, he strained his eyes, seeing only blackness hanging above. Thick veins of crystal ran up the wall and disappeared into the shadowed heights. Dante took in the heavy feel of the mountain pressing around him, a suffocating weight. The air stirred. Something moved beyond his sight. The tremors of it moved through the stone beneath his feet.

Extending his sense onto that single point of reverberation, Dante called on his wolf to sharpen his focus. The immensity of the creature in the depths stole his strength. He should have stayed at camp. A greater elemental. It had to be. It felt bigger than the dryad queen's presence. He'd felt a strength like this only once before: it had irrevocably changed his life and taken his father's.

Dante retreated a single step, and the immensity fell upon him. The attention absolute. Judging. As though the whole mountain was deciding whether to crush him or not.

Insignificant.

Its judgment was passed. The weight of its attention lifted. The miasma of its elemental magic drifted away.

He didn't run. He didn't scurry away like a frightened mouse. He wanted to. Mother bless it. He wanted to flee. Dante forced his pace to remain steady and even. He didn't turn his back on the darkness. One foot behind the other, he crept backward.

The sound of stone grinding on stone made his teeth ache. It had to be an earth elemental. The sound faded as the creature moved deeper into the caves.

Dante edged backward until he was certain the elemental was not going to return—and then he ran. He fell to his knees and soaked his elbows, before scrabbling back to his feet. He didn't stop sprinting until the outside ledge narrowed. Sunlight burnt his eyes, leaving spots on his vision. Clinging to the stonewall, Dante stopped, heaving for breath. Pushing the wolf back down to soften his senses, Dante glanced over his shoulder and saw nothing but water emerging from the cave mouth.

The blinding sunlight forced him to stop and think without the animalistic fear. The elemental was gone. Only a fleeting taste of its magic as a threat. A greater elemental. He'd prayed almost daily to the Mother to never meet one again. The burn scars wrapped around his hip and thigh itched, a lifelong reminder of the first he'd met.

Clambering back onto the clifftop, Dante saw his pack busying themselves with food, having not noticed his absence. Unwilling to join in, or be at all cheerful, Dante plunked down on the cliff edge, staring at the cave mouth. He hated the unnerving itchiness between his shoulder blades.

Should he tell the pack? What, that a greater elemental dwelled within the mountain? It wasn't going to eat them. It was an earth elemental. It probably fed off the crystals the mountains were named for. Unlikely that it would emerge from its home to climb the cliff and sit on them. He sure as hell wasn't going to let anyone go in there, though. They were safer outside.

Shuddering, Dante rested his head on a knee. Exhaustion brought irrationality.

They were safe. The pack could rest.

He clung to that mantra.

Sinking into meditation, Dante cast his innate magic into the earth, looking for a ley line to tap into to enhance his spiritual magic. Briefly, he thought of calling one of the others to anchor him but discarded the thought in favor of being alone. Anchoring brought someone into personal magic contact that he did not feel like experiencing at that moment. He'd done this in practice, he could do it again. The distance was the only difference.

The ley line flowed directly beneath the river, mirroring every twist and tributary. Carefully, he dropped into the untamed magic. He risked a glance upstream where he would sense the elemental. Nothing remained of its presence but a ghostly trail of magic leading deeper into the depths.

Satisfied with the pack's current safety, Dante swung around, allowing the magic to tow his ethereal-self downstream. His magic drew on the ley and stretched out in a thin cord. Death magic tainted the battle site where the dead serpents bled into the ground. He drifted around it. Nakai's city, Hanehishou, bled a murky cloud into the magic that he felt, even at a distance.

The ley branch carried him through the forest where tiny veins of it fed the age-old trees. The dryads' grove held a pure, clean pool of magic. The dryad queen floated alongside him for a stretch. Her alien curiosity brushed against him. She lost interest and turned back, gathering one of her straying children as she left. Dante hadn't known the elementals could reach the ley, but it made sense seeing how the creatures were born of magic.

The ley drew him westward, deeper into his lands. The crossing of the borders came with immediate wash of welcoming. Ookamimori still bled; Dante sobbed. Death stained his city nearly to the core. It was sick to the deepest level. His home felt diminished. Reaching the Heart, Dante touched it mournfully. Darkness clouded the surface. Ookamimori pulsed in recognition of his touch. It no longer had the strength to push him away. Dim gray and angry red stained the living green of the Heart. The poison of it sucked at him, pulling him toward the maelstrom of dark energy attacking the city. Fury lanced through him. This city was his home, the people within under his protection. He had thought to leave them in some safety by removing his presence, and perhaps he had lessened the danger, but this was heartbreaking.

Gathering his magic and all of the ley line's wild power he could channel, Dante poured it into the Heart, burning away the darkness staining it, pushing the death magic back. Ookamimori crooned at him, brightening around him as the magic cleared. His people's emotions lightened, their connection to the Heart pure again. He could not clear all of the death from his city's magic but he could protect it for a while. Dante pulled in a dangerous amount of the ley line—the pure magic scorched painfully, burning his channels, and still he called on more. Shaping the power, Dante melded it into a shimmering shield around the Heart. Layer upon layer, he built the shield, the tainted magic swirling around him, until his ethereal self shook and flickered from the strain. The line of magic leading back to his physical self was a mere thread.

Unable to attach to the Heart, the poison was caught in the flow of the ley line running downstream toward the Mother Tree where the leys intercepted. Dante scowled. That was bad as well. Was this Kobrona's grand plan? To taint the cities' Hearts and the ley lines feeding the Mother? But why? What purpose would that serve? Dante wanted to weep at the thought, but the Mother was strong. It would take far more than Kobrona's horrible evilness killing his city to harm her. Dante had no more strength to give; it would take more magic than he could wield in a lifetime to dam the tainted ley line from reaching the Mother.

Adding one last layer to the shield, Dante withdrew reluctantly. The upstream journey back was easier as his body called to his soul. Surfacing in his body and opening his eyes was a dizzying rush of sensation. Dante swayed forward on the cliff's edge. A hand clamped on his shoulder, steadying him.

"Easy there." Keer crouched beside him holding him upright. "What was that? Is your head still bothering you? You almost fell over the cliff, Dante."

Dante shook his head, leaning back into the support. "I went home," he rasped.

Keer sat back on his heels. "Oh."

"Yeah," Dante sniffed and scrubbed at his face, wiping away the salty tracks. When had he started crying? Morose silence descended on them until Dante exploded. "My people need me. He is killing them. My city is poisoned."

"Your people need you alive. If you were still at home, you would be dead or a slave to Death magic right now. Where would they be then? With no hope, no Alpha? You said the city is weak. Too weak to survive the choosing of a new royal family for sure. You are doing the best you can, and we will save them." Keer nudged his shoulder. "Now come on before the others decide I am planning to push you over the edge. There is food. That makes everything look better." Dante let Keer tug him away from the canyon's edge. "We will find out how to stop him. We need more information about what his soldiers were talking about. If he is mentally ill, perhaps there is something that can help him. Honestly, that would make a lot more sense than a grab for power. The Hearts don't succumb that easily. There cannot be one family, one king."

Dante nodded to placate him. Remembering the acidic poison of the death magic flowing toward the Mother Tree's roots Dante shuddered in disgust. If Ookamimori was that stained, what about Hanehishou, where one royal was already enslaved? He kept his thoughts to himself as they approached the camp.

Lady Petria handed him a cup of tea. Dante ignored her pursed lips and furrowed brows and moved away from the press of bodies huddling around the fire. Sitting still did not suit his mood. He felt more restless now than before. Dante raised the tea, and the hot liquid sloshed over his hand. He'd felt that. It wasn't numb anymore. His hand functioned again. When had that happened?

"Princess Nakai did it. She used her own magic somehow and killed whatever dark magic was spreading through you."

Another thing he owed the princess for; the list was growing. He already owed her more than he could ever repay.

Dante drank his tea.

He was freezing and dizzy. War drums pounded in his skull. It felt like he had a concussion again, and he did not remember hitting his head on anything. Thinking about it, everything hurt. An overworked ache ran through his muscles as though he'd just done ten rounds in the training ring with all his chevaliers at once. The ley lines were not to be channeled by raw force. Runes directed, controlled, and contained the magic. He'd risked his channels in shielding the Heart. He wished he'd thought of it the first time.

Keer held out a stick of goat meat as Dante paced. Dante snatched it quickly, trying to hide the tremors. Taking a bite of the smoked meat, Dante found that he was voraciously hungry. It took him only moments to gnaw off the meat and toss the stick into the bushes. The food eased the exhaustion.

He continued to pace. He needed to do more. He couldn't save his people while sitting around on the mountain.

Everyone was finally up and huddled around the fire, weary and in no shape to continue. Dante felt the last hopeful thoughts of chivvying them onward slip away. Not that he felt like he could handle a mountain climb now, though if he thought they'd leave he would damn well give it his best shot.

"Hey! Stipes is awake!" Korren crowed as only a six-year-old can. He bounced on his toes, obviously wanting to pounce on the chevalier for a well-deserved hug, but he restrained himself, knowing Stipes was still hurt.

Raphael reached Stipes's side first, helping his cousin sit up. "Good to see you awake."

"Where are we?" Stipes asked. His voice sounded like it was full of gravel. "Are we safe here?"

"Hush now and drink this." Lady Petria knelt beside Stipes, holding out a cup of water. Tipping it to his lips, she helped Stipes drink the clear mountain water.

"We are further up the mountain. We're free from pursuit for now. Everyone is safe." Raphael resolved Stipes's questions.

Dante nodded when Raphael met his eyes. Stipes was Raphael's family, and it seemed Raphael had finally realized that.

With his feet aching and legs trembling from sheer over-exhaustion, Dante climbed up the steps to a cluster of boulders where he could sit and keep watch. Dante sat on the cold stone, feet braced on the neighboring boulder. He had never seen so many random boulders in his life. The huge stones littered the mountainside. Being so hectic the last few days, he hadn't noticed how they clustered around. The mountain was as much a maze as the planted hedges surrounding his home. It was serenely melancholic.

Finishing their breakfast, the pack got up and started bustling around with a sense of purpose, refilling the cooking pots with fresh water. Dante watched the activity but did not feel the need to go and investigate. Soon, his brooding spot on the boulder was invaded by the other males who slunk toward him with sullen frowns.

Jothan reached him first and flopped on the ground between the boulders with a huff. "We've been banned from the fire while the girls have a bath." The word bath slurred from his lips in a disgusted sneer only a male street kid could pull off. "Why do they think it's so necessary now? I mean, it's freakin' cold! Who needs to be clean?"

Dante scooted over so Keer and Derrick could pile in beside him. Korren plopped into his lap and curled up in his arms. Dante winced as a pointy elbow jabbed into his ribs.

The women took turns shielding each other from the snooping eyes of the males by forming a bodily wall while each had a turn scrubbing down with the fire-heated water. Dante could only just hear them murmuring to one another.

"What I wouldn't give to be able to wash my hair!" Lady Petria whined. "But, it is too cold. I think it would freeze off my head."

Dante watched out of the corner of his eye, not dumb enough to be caught looking directly at them. His aunt had just finished her turn and was brushing out said white-blond hair as she took up the position of point guard, peering sternly in their direction. Dante quickly turned away. He was not going to stir up that bunch of trouble. The brush in her hand was capable of being wielded with deadly force upon one's rear. It had been many years since he'd felt its bite and he was not going to incite it.

Everyone exiled to the rock behaved themselves with courteous manners until Alexion noticed that it was Mysti's turn at the bath water. Before Dante could grab his collar, he was off their rock of safety and darting around the edge of the camp using the boulders and scrubby bushes as cover.

"Oh boy, we are so in trouble now," Dante groaned and buried his face in Korren's hair.

"Doomed," Raphael muttered.

"We could run?" Derrick suggested.

Raphael slumped farther between the rocks. "There's nowhere far enough to run," he mourned, breaking his aristocratic arrogance in the manly, shared fear of angry women.

Jothan hopped up, nearly bouncing in anticipation. "I bet I could catch him! I'm real fast!"

Stipes reached up, grabbed Jothan's shirt, and yanked him back down. "You do not want to get caught with him, and he is getting caught." They all nodded. Alexion was dead. They would attend to his funeral rites and scatter the ashes of his corpse into the wind. He'd gone to his execution willingly.

Angry shrieks pierced the mountain. Jothan's eyes widened and he tucked in behind Raiven.

"Mama sounds mad," Korren whimpered from within Dante's arms. Lady Petria scolded Alexion loudly. Dante risked a glance over his shoulder. Lady Petria gripped Alexion's ear between her fingers, twisting the tender flesh and making him bend to keep it from tearing.

"Ow, ow, ow!" Alexion yelped.

Dante winced in sympathy and turned away quickly when the furious females glanced at the rock where they cowered. Better not to be caught looking, even from here. Alex would be taking his punishment alone. This was not an instance where male unity came together. The women were already on a roll. Protests of pain echoed in the valley.

Raphael rolled his eyes. "Idiot."

Dante snickered. His reserved, prudish chevalier wouldn't dream of peeking in on a woman's bath, even if she was his mate. He likely wouldn't kiss more than his lady's hand until their wedding night. Suddenly, thoughts of shiny, silver hair filled his mind's eye. He wondered about the petite princess and what she might look like bare. Heat suffused his cheeks.

Raiven eyed him suspiciously. "Stop it right now or you are going to get your ear pulled off too."

Dante spluttered, turning redder. "I ain't doin' nothing!"

Derrick snorted in derision. "Yeah, right. When you start with the street slang, you're getting yourself into trouble for sure."

Heat burned clear down his neck. "I'm not doing anything!"

"No, but you are thinking it, and as riled up as they are, our ladies will slaughter you if they catch it," Raiven said.

Dante groaned and gave up. "This is why I never court anyone, ever. I have you lot to deal with."

Lady Petria marched Alexion back to the rock. They cowered from her fierce glare. "Keep a better chokehold on your pets, Dante," his aunt ordered. She marched back to the fire.

Raphael cuffed Alexion over the head as soon as the danger cleared. "Idiot."

"But it was Mysti!" Alexion protested. "I'm allowed to see her. She's mine! I see her all time."

"Dude, it's girl time." Derrick said. "You don't mess with that. It's suicide."

His thieves had a healthy sense of self preservation. Alexion slumped against the rock with a huff at the lack of supportrt.

It was another hour before the women finished hoarding the heat of the fire. By then, Dante was wearied enough of the chill to flop close to the flames and ignore its crackling whispers, whatever he imagined they said.

Chapter Twenty-three

The morning was fleeting, and they weren't on the move until the sun was high. The steps led steeply over the river's cavern mouth, cutting between the mountain's jagged peaks. Korren bounded ahead with all the enthusiasm of a well-rested child. The day's rest had undeniably helped the pack. Purple smudges faded from around their eyes.

Raphael walked close beside Stipes, ready to lend a supportive shoulder. His attitude toward his cousin seemed to have softened since the battle and Stipes's injuries. Alexion hovered behind, though not close enough to intrude on the moment of peace between cousins but near enough to catch Stipes if he tripped on the steps.

The stairs leveled to a rough-hewn pathway. Light snow dusted every surface and heaped into small drifts against the boulders. Thick, gray clouds smothered them like wet blankets. Damp oozed into the layers of their fur. The air smelled like rain, but sharper. A snow storm was coming.

Dante prayed that the storm waited. There was no shelter on this side of the mountain.

There was no true descent when they crossed the mountain. Endless white spread out before them, the ice plains in all their glorious splendor.

"How do we know where to go," Dante asked before he could stop the words from tumbling out. Dante wanted to kick himself. Let's just prove how inept he was as a leader.

Keer spoke up before he could berate his inaptitude for long. "We can use the stars when the sky clears."

Dante only vaguely remembered Keer's father pointing this out on the journey when they were children. Of course, Keer's nest of a brain would squirrel this tidbit away, only to pull it out again when it was most needed. This was why his pack brother was his closest advisor.

"Best trek on then, yes?" Leigha strode forward first with strong steps. Jothan followed, traipsing in her footprints. Derrick followed close behind with Raiven at his back, the thieves sticking close together against the protective chevaliers who chose to shield their injured pack member. Dante stepped into the middle to divide them from each other. Once again bridging the two halves of his life.

Snow came above their knees as their paws broke through the crust of the snow. Ice built up beneath his claws and clumped his fur. Dante winced as he fell through again.

"We need to go single file," Mysti said. "Take turns leading the way, breaking the trail." There were no protests as they fell in line. Leigha switched leads with Derrick, who plowed forward in dyre form, breaking through the thick crusts with his heavier weight. Night fell quickly. The mountains cast dark shadows as the sun sank.

"How are we going to make camp? There is no shelter, no fuel for a fire. It's all buried under snow," Raphael brought up a valid question.

"There is dry grass beneath the snow. We can light a fire with that for a bit," Keer piped up with more bits of random information.

"I'm cold. I want to stop soon, and Korren is freezing," Lady Petria whined, a touch of her old hysteria returning in her weariness.

Dante agreed with her, though. Little Ashliene was quivering on his back, and he was cold.

It was a miserable night. They hunkered down in a hole dug through the snow to find grass to burn. A fire smoldered slowly in the center of the dry patch. A scrubby bush kept the small flames fed. The snow-covered plains made strange creaks and rustles. Even the wind sounded different without the trees to break it up. The moon gleamed in the sky, and the snow reflected the light upward, making it nearly as bright as day.

A blue spider crawled up the cliff of snow they'd created by digging their hole. Its sharp legs climbed with sleek strength. Only a small spark of magic glowed from within it. It was a real spider. Flesh and blood, not born of elements and magic. Dante marveled at the creature and its vibrant color. Spiders at home were a drab black or brown.

Nature was strange and beautiful in all its forms.

The next day's journey brought them out of the shadow of the mountain and well into the snow-covered plains. The wind was calmer, so the cold was not as bitter.

The unease that had plagued him for days peaked. Dante glanced over his shoulder, scanning the surrounding snow for the hundredth time.

"Something still bothering you?" Keer asked, right at his tail as they walked at the back of the single-file line.

"It never stopped," Dante admitted. His skin crawled as though something stared at his back. The seared scars on his thigh tightened and cramped from the cold. "Something feels wrong and it's growing stronger." Why couldn't it all just be over? He wanted to reach the Lupinic lands and have the Lupinic King tell him what to do and how to fix all of this.

Alexion yelled from the front of the line. "Hold up. There's something moving ahead of us."

Oh, Mother bless it all, now what?

Curious, the pack grouped up, trampling the snow into a circle while they watched the blot on the horizon grow larger and separate into multiple figures.

"This is wrong," Dante said, stepping backward into his aunt, forcing her into the center of the pack with Korren.

The creatures prowled closer, surrounding them. "It is as though they are made of ice," Keer said, his curiosity taking over his caution as he stepped toward the icy elementals. One of the elementals growled. Keer stopped. Dante took advantage of his hesitation to shoulder his friend into the circle away from the five cat-like ice elementals. The cats were huge, easily two or three times their size.

"How the hell do you kill something made of ice?" Derrick asked, his back pressed against Raiven's shoulder.

"Form up. We are going to need weapons for this. Not fangs," Mysti ordered. Immediately, the chevaliers obeyed their training, taking dyre form and calling their soul-wields.

Dante found himself shoved into the center of the circle next to the princess and his aunt. Acting quickly, he squirmed out of the circle and called his dyre strength to the surface. Nakai shifted, her wings unfurling. She held her bow at the ready, the string already taut and quivering. They would fight alongside his chevaliers.

The elemental cats yowled, a nightmarish shriek piercing in its pitch. Dante winced, wanting to stuff his fingers in his ears.

Lady Petria pushed Korren at Jothan. "Protect him with your life!"

Already standing with Ashliene at his side, Jothan nodded, his pale lips pressed together in determination.

Summoning her soul-wield, Lady Petria made a striking sight. Her naginata's curved blade gleaming fiercely at the end of the metal spear. Bracing her legs and brandishing the weapon, Lady Petria took a protective stance in front of the children.

Dante put her at his back, turning to face the biggest cat. It snarled. Even in his dyre form, the cat towered over him. Touching the tattoo on his palm, Dante summoned his katana.

Huge claws dug deep furrows in the ground. The cat swiped out, missing Derrick as he leapt back. Dante dashed into the swipe, running ahead of the claws, slicing his sword where an animal's jugular was. The metal of his sword squealed, dragging harmlessly over the ice and leaving a faint white scratch in its wake.

"Mother bless!" Dante ducked and rolled under the cat's angry slash. The deadly claws slashed through his hair as he hit the ground between its paws. Raiven grabbed Dante's heel, hauling him back into the protective circle.

"My sword didn't touch it!"

"Mine either!" Alexion yelled back.

A pained yowl.

"Their eyes are vulnerable!" The princess sent out arrows as fast as she strung them.

Dante sheathed his sword, pulling out his throwing knives. Raiven and Derrick moved to do the same. A blade whistled past Dante's head, sinking into the cat's glowering eyeball with a squelch of eye juices.

"Ha! Take that beast!" Jothan hollered over its pained wails.

"Nice one, kid," Derrick praised.

Dante let his knife fly true, blinding the cat entirely.

An explosion behind him made him risk a look over his shoulder. Leigha cheered, dancing on the spot and waving a fist in the air. "Yeah, ya'd better run." One of the smaller cats retreated. Purple blood splattered the snow.

"Down!"

Dante's collar dug into his throat as he was yanked backward. Air whooshed over him in the wake of the cat's lightning-fast strike. "Thanks," he said. His lungs burned from the frozen air.

Scrambling to his feet, Dante threw himself into Derrick's knees as the elemental reared up. It batted out with both paws, claws unsheathed spread wide. They fell together with a thump. Flinging up his metal sheath, Dante parried and turned the cat to the side. Raiven stabbed at the remaining eye. He missed.

A wild yell told Dante that the others had their own problems still.

Another cherry bomb exploded, followed by another. Leigha was well prepared to make lots of noise. It failed to scare off the remaining four elementals. Damn. One of the creatures would have been enough. Five might prove too much for his pack.

"Leigha, how many of those do you have?" Alexion asked.

"Not enough!" Leigha pulled the fuse on another explosive and tossed it at the feet of her attacker. Dante slashed at the cat, driving it back. Derrick stabbed at the remaining eye. His blade scrapped over its icy face, slicing across the eyeball. The thin ice covering the surface of the eye shattered and something like slush poured out.

The elemental screamed.

Thrashing around, the cat clawed out blindly, twisting and turning in a frenzy. Dante ducked as a heavy tail, and in turn, a clawed paw, swept out wildly. He lunged beneath the cat, trying to get at its head.

"Hey!" Derrick yelled, getting it to pause in its panic.

Holding his sword tight in both hands and discarding the sheath, Dante thrust with all his strength. The gleam of his sword disappeared into the elemental's skull through its eye socket. It reared back too late. The blade scraped inside the skull bone. The katana jerked out of his hands as the cat reared up nearly three times taller than Dante. Dante fell on his butt and scrambled sideways as the cat teetered on its hind legs. Its body went limp, falling to the ground with a heavy thump as it died.

"Here." Derrick held out a hand to haul Dante back to his feet.

"Move!" Lady Petria shrieked

They whirled to find another cat bearing down on them, Mysti and Raphael behind it. On instinct, Dante reached for his sword at his back only to come up empty, and he remembered: it protruded from the eye socket of the dead cat.

"Shit!" He focused his will and magic into one purpose. The rune on his palm flared to life, and metal sang in his hands as his soul-wield answered his summons. Flinging up both the blade and sheath, Dante deflected the cat's sideswipe as it loped by, circling around to charge back at Mysti.

Mysti dodged, slipped, and fell to a knee. Raphael stood over her, whipping his rapier at the cat's face to keep it away from her. Dante rushed to help while Raiven and Derrick ran to help Leigha fend off the other two.

Dante sliced at the cat's rear hamstrings, succeeding only in gaining its attention. With the cat's focus on Dante, Raphael was able to help Mysti up. Blood blanketed her side from four ugly gashes on her ribcage. White bone contrasted with the red life streaming out around it. Dante blanched. His First was gravely wounded.

Pained yells came from behind him. Dante hated that he couldn't look, couldn't see who else in his pack was wounded. The cat hissed and fangs snapped inches from his face. Dante caught the teeth on his sword. The force of the blow sent him to his knees. The sharp taste of copper filled his mouth, and Dante realized he'd bitten his tongue. He spat a glob of blood out. Dante's arms strained to hold back the hissing elemental.

"A little help here!" Dante yelled as his knees slipped in the snow and he slid backward.

Alexion appeared behind him, his legs planted firmly at Dante's back. His knees dug into Dante's shoulder blades, stopping his slide. Alexion panted. His twin swords dripped with purple blood. Roaring, the chevalier thrust both of his swords forward in an arc around Dante's head. The bloodstained swords pierced both eyes of the cat with a sickening, gloopy squelch.

The cat dropped, and Dante crumpled under its onerous weight.

"Dante!" Alexion grabbed at him.

"I'm all right, but my leg is pinned under its head." The way his legs were twisted painfully beneath the cat, Dante could not get the leverage to squirm out. Tossing his swords down, Alexion pushed at the elemental's head trying to move it off Dante.

"Wait!" Dante cried. When Alexion shoved the head, the cat's fangs dug into Dante's knee. Blood trickled down his leg, almost burning hot in comparison to where the snow had chilled his skin.

"We have to get you out of there," Alexion said.

Dante braced his hand in the snow to ease the strain on his back from the awkward position. "Try pulling me instead. I think that will keep my leg from twisting the wrong way."

"Right." Alexion crouched behind him, looping his arms under Dante's shoulders and locking his fingers around his chest. Dante braced his hands on the elemental's muzzle. Sounds of a losing battle waging behind them made Dante's heart beat anxiously.

"Let's go. They need us." A whining whimper enforced that sense of urgency. That had been Leigha in pain.

Alexion braced, wiggling his feet deep into the powdery snow until he hit dirt. In one violent heave, Alexion threw himself backward, pulling Dante with him until they both sprawled, together and free. Dante rolled off Alexion, reaching for his sword in the same motion. His leg crumpled, and Dante fell to his side. He hissed in agony.

"Sire!" Alexion scrambled up and reached to steady him.

Dante batted Alexion's hand away and tried again a little more cautiously. "It's just sorer than I thought, that's all." He ignored the fresh trickle of blood running down his leg. "Come on." Scooping up his sword, Dante broke into a sprint. There was no time to allow any weakness. His pack was in danger of dying around him.

Two of the elementals remained.

Running to help, Dante saw that Leigha lay lifelessly in the snow while Stipes swung his heavy weapon at the creature one-handedly, staggering from old and new injuries. His arm hung useless at his side. Blood covered it so thickly that Dante couldn't even see the wounds.

Even as he ran to aid his chevalier, the cat proved the stronger and faster. It reached around Stipes's weakened defenses and slammed a massive paw into his chest. Dante thought he heard the crack of rib bones. Broken bones or not, his chevalier flew through the air and didn't move after he landed.

"No!" Dante roared. The single syllable ripped out of his throat, leaving it stinging and raw.

Before he could reach the remnants of his pack, young Jothan ran out in front of Lady Petria. The teen flung knives with stunning accuracy and quantity. The cat's face bristled with metal. The elemental was completely blind, but that didn't stop it from biting the boy's shoulder and shaking him like a rag doll. Jothan screamed, an agonized sound that fueled Dante's fury.

Dante came in swinging. His sword scraped over the ice fangs piercing Jothan's shoulder. The cat swiped. Dante leapt back to keep his intestines where they belonged. Growling, Dante stepped around, coming in again, trying to get at the cat's eyes.

A rapid glance showed everyone, except for Lady Petria, fighting with the other elemental or on the ground. No one was coming to help.

Shaking Jothan one last time, the cat flung the boy into the air. Horrified, Dante followed the movement. He dropped his sword to snatch Jothan out of the air. He staggered under the teen's weight.

Jothan lay limp in his arms. Dante couldn't bring himself to check for Jothan's breath; there was nothing he could do except move on. He had to keep fighting. Laying the young thief beside Leigha, Dante summoned his soul-wield back to his hand.

"Dante, watch out!" Raphael yelled.

Dante spun around to see another elemental crouched and ready to spring. It was the one that had ran. Mother bless it all. It had come back.

Looking around wildly in the hope of escape or help, Dante found only blood staining the once white snow: pink, crimson, and black where it saturated the most. His pack bled. Even as he watched, Raiven fell beneath a cat, joining his twin.

Helpless fury overwhelmed him. He froze, until the cat leapt into the air, spurring him into reaction. Dante ran to meet it. What less could he do? There was nowhere to run. Too many of his beloved pack lay still. The others likely to join them in minutes. Focusing all the magic he could gather, Dante swung his sword to meet the pouncing cat. Ice and metal clashed together. Hope bloomed in his chest as he felt his sword dig into its unnatural skin, but the feeling died. The tip of his sword finished the stroke, and all that was left on the elemental was a deep gouge, not even bleeding the strange purple blood. He had put everything he had into the blow, and it wasn't enough to do more than scratch it.

He had no more time or will to react as the cat spun back. It swiped out with a vicious anger. The horrendous claws ripped down his back.

Dante screamed as the cat flayed him. Darkness edged his vision. A faltering drum beat in his ears; it was the only sound he could hear. The world tilted. The cat stood undefeated above him. As his sight dimmed, fire bloomed in the air.

Chapter Twenty-four

Everything hurt. Dante stirred, and he tried to roll over. Nothing moved at his command. He was anchored to the bed by his own dead limbs. The minor act took too much of his strength, and he subsided back onto his stomach as firm hands rested on his shoulders. An unfamiliar voice crooned at him to stay calm. Warm magic pooled over the skin of his back, the heat of it calmed him back to sleep.

The next time he woke, his eyes responded to his commands, slitting open. Dozens of beeswax candles cast a warm, homey light and added their warmth to the room.

Nothing quite hurt, but a low ache thrummed in his bones. After several minutes of trying to gather his muddled thoughts, Dante found the strength to sit up. He ignored the silent flames surrounding him. He would rather be cold and have the crystal light, than look at flame all the time. A heavy fur trapped heat around him. Goosebumps popped over his skin as he pushed the fur away. Heat burned his ears. He was nearly starkers. Pulling the blanket of white fur around his shoulders, Dante slowly got to his feet, swaying.

The pack!

Where were the others?

Dante stumbled across the room, tripping over the lush fur rugs. He had to find them.

In the hall, crystals glowed a soft blue, lighting the way. The air was noticeably cooler without the numerous candles radiating warmth. Thick tapestries draped over the walls featured the Lupinic family crest. Somehow, they'd made it. Muffled voices drew him down the hall and to the right. Three doors further down and he could make out what they said.

"I'm going back now. I wanted to see how you were doing. Knowing him, he's going to wake up and hare off to do something stupid." That was Keer. Something unnamed inside, eased at the knowledge that at least one of his people survived the battle.

Swaying again, Dante paused and braced a hand on the wall until the dizziness passed. He felt like a wrung-out dishrag.

Keer backed out of a doorway and into the hall. Dante's friend slumped on the edge of the doorframe as he leaned back in. "Stay out of trouble, and keep your mitts off things that aren't yours."

A smile twitched his lips at Keer's bossy commands. From the type of orders, Dante presumed that his thieves resided in that room. Please let it be all of them.

Blood-soaked snow saturated his memories. So much blood. Using the wall for support, Dante walked closer clutching the fur with his free hand to keep it from falling off his shoulders. He had to see them. Check they were all still breathing.

"I will be back later. The others are down and across the hall with the princesses and Lady Petria. I will let you know when I find out anything new from the healers," Keer said.

That last statement twisted Dante's stomach. Someone was still with the healers. He didn't know how long he'd been out, but the Lupinic surely had many healers to go around, meaning it was taking a particularly long time to heal whatever grievous wounds they worked on. Mysti's injury had maybe been that severe. Her ribcage had been stripped of skin. Stipes had been struck while still weak and healing from the last battle. Was it him?

Just as he opened his mouth to question Keer, the man turned and started. "Dante! You are awake—finally! And running around first thing, of course. How are you feeling?" Keer didn't give him time to answer. "Well, since you are here, come and sit down. The healers will want to talk to you when they are available."

It was the perfect opening. "Who is it? Who are they still healing?" Dante asked. Keer didn't answer right away, instead looping an arm around him and supporting him the rest of the way into the room.

"Dante!" A pale Derrick cheered from his spot on the bed, albeit quietly as Raiven slept tucked up against his side in a tight ball, a cloak draped over his face to block out the light.

"Here, sit down. You probably shouldn't run around much for a while. Healing really takes it out of you." Keer steered him into a chair beside the bed where Leigha and Jothan lay curled together. Leigha smiled in welcome over Jothan's head. Keer pulled an extra blanket from the foot of the bed and tucked it around him.

Worry gripped his heart like icy fingers. "That bad, huh? Who is it?"

Keer's face paled. Sighing, Keer sank down on the edge of Leigha's bed. "Raphael and Alexion are still with the healers. I think they each have three of them. They've been in with them for a long time. Stipes is staying with Lady Petria, Korren, and the princesses. Mysti is still resting. The healers finished with her a couple hours ago." Keer scrubbed his face with both hands, impatiently pushing aside his long bangs.

His heart plummeted. Three healers were a lot for one person. Easier on the magic, but a lot, meaning it was dangerous or impossible for one healer to expend enough magic. Dante clutched the fur tighter around his shoulders, trying to ward off the fearful chill. "What are their injuries?"

Keer shuddered. "Raphael was mauled. Nearly eviscerated."

Reflexively, Dante wrapped an arm around his stomach as though to hold in his innards. "If the Lupinic hadn't arrived when they did, he would be dead. As would we all. The cats utterly overwhelmed us."

"How did they happen to come in time to help? How did they beat them?"

"Magic. They used runes and crystals to create a fire glyph. They knew to come because they have a seer." Keer quirked a wan smile. "She is a fascinating woman from a long line of Far-dreamers. There are two of them, actually. The one I spoke to is the younger."

Something in Keer's eyes had Dante eying him suspiciously. "You like her!" Amusement sparked through his weary grief.

Pink spread through Keer's cheeks. "I just think she is an interesting woman."

They shared a snicker at Keer's embarrassment before lapsing into miserable silence. Dante was vaguely able to remember his father coming here to talk to the Far-dreamer. That had been the main reason for their journey. He'd been too young to understand or care about the reason. He did remember a strange lady of grandmotherly age looking like a dried, shriveled apple.

"Alexion?" Dante dared ask, dreading the answer.

"Bitten and thrown around. Like that one," Keer tilted his head at the sleeping Jothan. "Only worse."

He wondered how it could have been worse. He'd seen Jothan tossed around by his shoulder before he'd passed out.

Keer answered that thought all too soon. "Alexion couldn't feel anything in his legs."

Dante slouched in the chair, shock making him lose all coordination. One of his chevaliers nearly dead, the other crippled. How had it come to this?

"That's enough of that, boy!" a crinkly voice ordered from the doorway. They all jumped, and Dante looked up. An old, wrinkly crone waggled a knobby finger. Her face was like a shriveled apple. "You have done all that you can, boy. Now, what's important is that you do all that you are able. That is the best anyone can do."

"How did you...?" Dante asked.

"Know? Boy, I am a seer, and you are as easy to read as a book. I don't even need my far-sight to read you."

Dante refrained from pointing out the woman couldn't physically see anything at all. Her eyes were completely covered in blue-white clouds. She waggled her crooked finger at him again. "Silly, silly boy," she crooned. He cringed like a chastised child. She hobbled into the room, hunched over a knotted, twisty cane studded with crystals. Planting her wrinkled self in the middle of the room, she rested her gnarled hands on the hilt of her cane. "Now, boy"—that name was really starting to grate on his over-wrought nerves—"pay attention. You coming here was the best choice I saw you able to make. There was a great deal more blood and misery lying in your other options.

"I have many things to tell you, boy. Many things. Not so many today, although you must know that some of your pack will be staying with us until the council convenes. You will continue your journey of growth without them."

Dante opened his mouth to protest that he would not be leaving any of his pack behind, even with his cousins—and why would they be going anywhere else? Then his teeth clacked together as a few implications became clear: he would be leaving someone behind because they could not travel anymore. As ice clutched his heart again, Dante only prayed—Mother willing—that they all still breathed as they remained. Alexion or Raphael? Both? And their partners? Would he have to break them up? Now that Stipes and Raphael were talking as a family for the first time in years? Mysti and Alex were life-bound. Separation would be torture.

The old seer cleared her throat. "We will discuss it more later, but it is not Kobrona causing this darkness. He is lost. Part of your journey will be to find him."

"Mother, you are wearing out the prince and adding weight to weary shoulders. Give them time to rest and heal as much as they are able. Bring the hammer to a heated blade too soon, and it will shatter." A tall, slender woman stood framed by the doorway. With a gentle smile and fine cheekbones, she was beautiful and striking. And she was blind too. Red cloth bound her eyes, holding the hundreds of thin braids that cascaded to her ankles out of her face.

This was Keer's seer.

Dante could see his pack brother's fascination. She turned to address Dante. "The healers are done with your people. They've done all they can for them. Now it is up to their own strength to recover fully. I believe the healers will be looking for you shortly, to check you over now that you are awake and can answer any questions they have about your wellbeing. Mother and I will leave you to rest now. We will talk more tomorrow." The young seer inclined her head gracefully before turning and stealing her mother's cane at the same time as catching her arm and tucking it into her own. "Come, Mother, we have work of our own to do."

They were all left staring after the Far-dreamers, having not gotten a word in edgewise and being left with more questions than they'd started with.

A portly man bustled into the room before the women could have disappeared out of the hall. "Ah, there you are Prince Canidea. A change of rooms, eh? How are you feeling? You were quite banged up. Those helcat elementals are nasty creatures."

What was it with healers and onslaughts of questions?

The healer babbled on, poking and prodding at various places that ached as soon as the healer touched them. Dante hadn't realized how many bruises he bore. The healers had left the minor wounds, conserving their energy for serious injuries. "Have you eaten?"

"No." He didn't care about food. "I haven't been up long. How is everyone else doing? Do you know anything about Alexion and Raphael?"

The reason for the healer's babbling became clear as he sobered and seemed reluctant to answer.

"Well?" Dante prodded snappishly.

"Raphael, the blond one, yes?" The healer paused for confirmation and continued. "He is weak but will make a full recovery with a few new scars to show off for the ladies."

The idea of Raphael showing off for the ladies was laughable, but he couldn't crack a smile over it.

"Alexion. He will recover as well yes?" Dante's tone dared the healer to tell him otherwise.

The man sagged. "Not completely, I'm afraid. He is alive and has some feeling and control in his legs; however, he is weak. Any excessive exertion will set back his healing. He is going to need several concentrated sessions to regain full mobility. If he is willing to work for it."

Swaying in his chair, Dante reeled with the revelation. Derrick pulled the still-sleeping Raiven a little closer to his side. Keer leaned over, dropping a hand on Dante's shoulder. "Alexion will be fine. He won't let this stop him."

Dante forced himself to nod. "Alexion's spirit will not be so easily broken." He was certain of the truth of the words, but he didn't know whether his own inner strength could withstand these unending trials. Alexion was nearly crippled because of him. "We will make sure of it." Dante forced his aching body to straighten, and he glared at the healer for daring to imply that Alexion wasn't strong enough.

The healer didn't bat an eye, grinning toothily instead. "Good, good. A pack is always stronger than the lone wolf."

Suppressing a sneer, Dante leaned back and pulled the furs around his shoulders, covering the bruises the healer had so delighted in prodding with his pudgy fingers. Keer's green eyes narrowed at the healer, seemingly just as insulted that he thought they would cast aside a member of their pack because he was wounded.

The healer continued, seemingly oblivious to the tension that even Derrick was casting in his direction. "You should eat." He reached over and tapped a crystal hanging on the wall. The stone brightened to a soft glow. "There, you all will have something from the kitchens in a few minutes. Now, how are the rest of you feeling? Any serious pains remaining?" As he glanced around, everyone shook their heads. "Very good. Let me check the wound on this one before I leave you to rest. As close as it is to his eyes, I want to make sure we healed the scar tissue well enough. I don't have a lot of energy left, but I will give it a little more."

Bewildered, Dante peered closer at the man and saw the beads of sweat on his brow and the fine tremors of exhaustion, but that didn't explain why he was addressing Derrick.

"I can check him while he's asleep. You don't need to wake him," the healer whispered.

Derrick was solemn and he nodded, sitting up a little. Hating all the pain this journey was causing, Dante watched as Derrick tugged the concealing hood away from Raiven's face. When the healer reached down to touch Raiven, a hand clamped around his wrist, halting him with iron force. Holding the healer captive, Raiven looked around with sleep-dulled eyes.

"It's all right, Raiven. He just wants to look for a moment, then you can go back to sleep," Derrick soothed, pulling Raiven's hand off the healer's wrist.

Raiven let the man go and with the hand out of the way, Dante got his first clear look at Raiven. He felt sick. He wasn't sure how much more of this he could take. Seeing his people so terribly wounded around him, helpless to stop it. Three angry lines destroyed the twin's identical symmetry. One of claw lines scrapped terrifyingly close to Raiven's right eye, clearly the reason the healer was so concerned.

"I can do a little more for it now, if you will let me." The healer again reached out, slowly this time, so that Raiven could see his approach. Laying his fingers gently on Raiven's brow, the healer closed his eyes, and Dante watched the golden glow of his magic pool under his fingers, spreading over the ravaged skin. The magic faded, taking with it a little of the inflamed redness.

Dante scrubbed his palms over his face, suppressing tears. His pack was grievously wounded in some form. All because of him. If he'd stayed and faced Kobrona, perhaps it would have been only himself who was hurt. Inwardly, he knew that thought was foolish, but he would have willingly sacrificed anything to spare his pack this pain.

The healer tucked his trembling fingers into his long sleeves. "You should all rest while you wait for food to be brought. You too, Prince Dante. Up onto the bed with you. It won't hurt you any to sleep next to your pack mates."

Keer seemed to readily agree to the idea, propelling Dante up and out of the chair and down onto the bed beside Raiven. Not having the strength to fight, tired inside and out, he curled into a ball. Dante tucked his back against Raiven's knees, sandwiching the thief between him and Derrick. As the healer nodded and left, Keer settled across the foot of Leigha's bed.

Pulling up the fur to block out the light and, conveniently enough, the sight of his bruised and battered family, Dante tucked his head in and closed his eyes against the threatening tears. He had failed them all. A heavy arm dropped around his shoulders as Raiven moved closer to his warmth.

"Stop it. It's not your fault," Raiven muttered, his voice was heavy with sleep. Dante relaxed somewhat at his brother's reassurances. At least they didn't seem to think it was his fault, even if it was.

He hid in the warm darkness until shuffling and clanking sounds announced the arrival of food. Derrick's hushed voice instructed someone to set the food on a side table. Taking another moment to gather his strength, Dante waited until the shuffling of shoes and skirts left the room and sat up, careful to keep from jarring Raiven awake. The meal arrayed on the table was a simple fare of a light broth, fresh bread, and white cheese.

Dante filled a bowl and buttered some bread, adding a slice of cheese before carefully handing it to Derrick, who was the only one still awake. Keer had slumped over Leigha's legs, and she curled around Jothan with her face buried in the kid's hair.

Dante mirrored Derrick's position on the bed, cradling the bowl to his chest and leaning back against the wall to dip his bread into the soup. The crusty slice soaked up the juice, and he stuffed it in his mouth, glad it was only Derrick to see him. Mysti, Raphael, or Keer would smack him for eating with a distinct lack of decorum. He was too hungry to care.

After shoving three more cheese-filled slices of bread down his throat with the soup, Dante thought about curling up and sleeping for about three hundred years until this was all over; however, a need larger than sleep hovered over his head. He gathered the fur around his shoulders again and padded out of the room with a wave to Derrick, who nodded. He stayed silent, obviously planning to stay up to keep watch over the sleeping members of their pack.

A few doors down the chilly hall he found the rest of his pack. They were split up on each side of the hallway. Sticking his head inside the left, Dante found Stipes on watch.

Stipes sat tall in a chair between Lady Petria's bed and Raphael's. He looked up when Dante came in, relaxing quickly with a welcoming, relieved smile. "Sire, you are all right. I mean, I knew you would be, but it is good to see you up and about."

Dante edged into the room. "How are they?"

"Your aunt and Korren are just tired. Lady Petria was fierce in her defense of the children. She held one of the helcats off by herself until the Lupinic arrived." Dante cast a surprised glance at his aunt. She was proving to be made of sterner stuff than he would ever have dreamed. Before he could ask, Stipes continued, "Raphael just came back from the healers. He was pretty torn up. I got off easy compared."

Disbelief colored his emotions. "You didn't get off easy, Stipes. You nearly died covering me in that explosion. And you didn't get off free in the last battle either."

Stipes shrugged. "It was still better than him."

Wincing, Dante gave up. "Make sure you get some rest too. We are among friends here." Giving a last glance at his sleeping family, Dante grimaced at how pale and drawn Raphael looked, lacking any sign of his usual haughty attitude, making him seem so much smaller.

Across the hall, Princess Nakai sat up against the headboard doing the same as Derrick and Stipes, keeping watch over their wounded. Relief filled Dante at finding the last of his pack safe, despite having been told they were fine. He'd needed to see them.

"Prince Dante, you are well?" the princess whispered so not to wake the small girl sprawled in her lap.

"Well enough. I am glad to see that you and Ashliene escaped any serious harm?" He drew it out as a question, unsure how they had truly fared in the battle.

"Yes. Lady Petria held her own, protecting my sister as well as her son."

Slumped over the other bed containing Alexion, Mysti groaned and raised her head. Her eyes widened, and she sat up so fast the chair tilted and she had to grab the bed to keep from falling out of it. "Sire, you should not be running around. Alone too!"

Dante cocked his head. "We are safe here, Mysti. I am perfectly capable of walking a few feet down the hall to check on my people." Always with the overprotectiveness. She looked tired, Dante realized. Memories of torn flesh, blood, and white rib bones had him paling. "I'm actually fine, Mysti. I promise. The healer just poked and prodded all my bruises a few mintutse ago. I'm fine. Alexion?" he asked, even knowing everything the healer had told him. He wanted to know that his First was not going to fall apart in front of him, or at all.

Mysti's eyes glittered, and she wrung her fingers together. "It is going to be a long time until he's all right, I think. The healers said they could only do so much for him. They plan on more healing sessions, but it was a bad injury." She hugged herself, obviously afraid to touch her partner for fear of hurting him further. "Dante, he couldn't feel his legs."

Dante leaned down and pulled her into a tight embrace, trying to will courage back into his fiercest protector. Sobs shook her compact frame. Alarmed, Dante almost pulled back. Mysti was not supposed to cry. Ever. Alexion would know what to do. He always knew how to balance out his life-mate. Only, Alexion lay unconscious, flat on his back and supported by pillows on all sides to keep him from flopping around and twisting his fragile spine. Mysti gasped for breath, trying to swallow her keening wails. Kneeling on the floor, Dante cupped her head, turning her into his shoulder and wrapping her as tightly in his arms as he could. It was an awkward position, and he was sure Mysti would be feeling the pain of it in a few minutes; however, he could do nothing except hold her through the agony of her breaking heart.

Her sobs slowed and breath came deeper. "I can't leave him, sire. Not like this. He needs me."

"Leave? I said nothing of leaving him," Dante said, confused.

Princess Nakai cleared up the confusion, handing over a damp cloth for Mysti. "The old Far-dreamer was here. She said we had another journey and that I have a lot of learning to do before I can do my part. She says our light is so weak as to gutter out, but the journey will either stoke it to burn like the sun or snuff it. I have no idea what she's talking about."

Right. The bossy, ancient Seer. She'd certainly made her rounds. Putting his hands on her shoulders, he made Mysti sit up and look at him. Her eyes were red and puffy. She was not a neat crier. "I will not make you leave him behind, Mysti. I don't know what this journey will be, but Alexion will not be left alone. We will not abandon him."

"Alright," she whispered. Wiping her face with the wet cloth, Mysti composed herself much to his relief. Mysti's tears were Alexion's forte.

A thought occurred to him, and he turned to the princess. "What if our journey had something to do with how you were able to burn out that curse on my hand?"

"Oh," Nakai breathed. "But, what is there to learn about that? I don't really know what I did. I assumed it was a bloodline trait." Nakai looked at her open hands in wonder. "I don't know how that would even help right now. It's not like I can just walk up to Prince Kobrona and touch him and will him to stop killing people."

Dante raked his fingers through his hair, unable to cope with anything else on his shoulders. He already felt so heavy he could sink into the floor. "I suppose that is the point of the journey then? To learn what we can do."

He stood up and his knees cracked in a jolt of pain. "I'm going back to the other room. If you are all right here?" They nodded. "I think we should rest as much as we can. The crone's daughter can only hold her back for so long. I think she was ready to shove us out the door today."

He rested a hand on Mysti's back. "We won't leave him alone. Even if some of us have to go, he won't stay here alone."

Mysti smiled weakly and curled up in her chair sideways, laying her head back down on Alexion's bed. Nakai fussed with retucking the blanket around her little sister.

He left them to follow his own advice, cursing the cold hallway floor on his bare feet for the third time. Sleeping alone in the room he'd woken in didn't appeal to him. It was too soon to be parted from his pack.

Derrick was dozing when he entered, and his eyelids opened to slits to see who it was before shutting them again. Dante shifted and leapt up next to Raiven. This time, he curled into a tight ball and tucked in his tail, leaving room for all three of them to lie fully down in the puppy-like pile.

It was with firm determination that he closed his eyes. Now that he had seen all the members of his pack, furred and feathered, he could rest. They were safe. The nightmares could come, and journeys would be discussed and planned.

For now, he was going to sleep. Life outside this brief moment of hard-won respite could wait until the 'morrow.

C. H. Knyght lives in Minnesota next door to her family with her critters: two dogs, a cat, and a horse. Her library takes up most of her home with eleven bookshelves and counting. (She dreads ever moving for this reason.) When she's not writing, she's drawing. Magic is what you choose to create of it.

Connect Online
www.twitter.com/chknyght
www.chknyght.com
www.facebook.com/chknyght